DISCO
TH

THE FRANKLINS—A banking dynasty of towering stature among Louisiana's oldest aristocrats . . . now its last son has inherited all the family's ruthless ambitions and wealth. And dares to gamble his heritage for the promise that awaits him in the state senate.

THE FARLEYS—A business empire built by new money and new blood, its members fought a life-and-death battle with the Franklins. And they had an ex-street fighter who knew the back alleys as well as the bedrooms of New Orleans on their side . . .

AND TALIA—Bound to both families, the one woman who could destroy them all, the beautiful woman whose talent and perseverance shone as brilliantly as the diamonds that adorned her. Only she could shift the ultimate prize in New Orleans from hard cash to soft whispers and the warmth of an embrace. Wife to one family, but loving another . . . could anyone resist the temptation of Talia?

&

"A tender love story . . . Orwig's strong character development adds dimension to her absorbing plot."
—***Publishers Weekly* on *Sweet Desire***

Also by Sara Orwig

TIDES OF PASSION
SWEET DESIRE
SAN ANTONIO

Family Fortunes

SARA ORWIG

WARNER BOOKS

A Warner Communications Company

WARNER BOOKS EDITION

Cover photograph by Nancy Brown

Warner Books, Inc.
666 Fifth Avenue
New York, N.Y. 10103

 A Warner Communications Company

Printed in the United States of America

First Printing: March, 1989

10 9 8 7 6 5 4 3 2 1

This book is dedicated to Jeanne Tiedge.

Author's Note: I would like to thank the following people: B. Howe, M. Cole, M. E. Lee, G. Orr, G. Dawes, W. Kendall, L. Hall, T. Orwig, J. Wilkes, K. Roberts, and Maureen Walters.

Prologue

A high board fence enclosed the palm-shaded patio and pool of a New Orleans mansion. Aqua water reflected the white thunderclouds above and the steady drone of cicadas was the only sound as a woman got up from a yellow chaise longue. Her shoulder-length golden hair caught glints of sunlight as she removed her dark glasses and placed them at the edge of the pool. In leggy strides she walked to the end of the diving board and stood poised above the inviting water.

Three hundred yards away on the roof of a vacant neighboring house, a man shifted and blinked before peering through a telescopic lens. He lined up the cross hairs so that they centered on the scrap of black swimsuit partially covering the diver's full breasts. Exhaling with a grunt, he surveyed her long slender body with its narrow waist and model legs.

Damn shame, he thought. Beautiful women weren't meant to be destroyed except in bed where sweet destruction was only temporary. Her body was too sleekly perfect, too healthy to be torn by a .30/06 slug. He knew exactly what size hole the bullet would blast through tawny tissue, arteries, muscles, and bone upon impact. The shot would knock her off her feet. He could imagine the acrid odor of cordite and blood.

She turned her face to the sun, her toes curling over the end of the board while he aimed directly at her heart. He raised the lens to search her features, appraising her face for the first time without the dark glasses. She had prominent cheekbones, a long, slender nose, and thick, brown lashes that were downcast as she studied the pool. Her face was as breathtaking as her body. He was sure that wherever she went, heads would turn in admiration.

There was something vaguely familiar about her. Had he met her before? He knew he hadn't been to bed with her. He was too discriminating to have possessed an army of women, and those he had known intimately, he wouldn't forget. But a nagging familiarity remained. Women who acquired power and wealth often changed in appearance as a result of health spas, designer clothes, and talented hairdressers. Perhaps she had dyed her hair?

The image of her body on a cold slab in the morgue brought a sour taste to his mouth. How could any man hate her enough to destroy her? Her crime had to be more than mild dishonesty.

While he speculated she dived, slicing into the sparkling water and then surfacing, blinking away the moisture in her eyes before swimming across the oval pool in long, even strokes. She lifted herself onto the concrete apron, pulled on the ever-present glasses, and swung her long, shapely legs out of the water. Standing, she tugged the brief bit of black nylon and spandex down over her tanned bottom. He focused on the clench of firm cheeks as she walked and he noticed that the black suit was cut high enough to reveal her slender thighs and protruding hip bones.

With the stillness of a stalking cat, a tactic he had learned in 'Nam and honed in his civilian contracts, he watched her stretch on the chaise and pull off her bikini top. He sucked in his breath, and for a moment he yielded to fantasies until the beginnings of an erection brought him back to reality. He lowered the Garand, a World War II and Korean eight-shot, clip-loading rifle that he found satisfactory. It was available at surplus, which made it less traceable, and the rounds were economical for practice; there was no need to spend a dollar unnecessarily.

The muscles in his calves remained as still as the corded biceps in his tanned arms. He made one last lingering assessment that caused creases in his wide brow. What had she done to generate such hate that it blinded the man to her beauty? Perhaps it wasn't a man who wanted her dead, but a woman. An intermediary had hired him so his identity and that of the person putting out the contract were kept secret.

Suddenly the man lowered the rifle to his thigh. In the past he had always known what the person had done and had only taken contracts if he knew he was destroying somebody the law wouldn't deal with, a person who willfully hurt innocent victims. When Emil Prague's fireworks factory blew to pieces, killing many despite the reports from safety inspectors outlining the factory's improper storage facilities, he didn't feel sorry for the owner. Prague spent over one hundred thousand dollars fighting his way through the courts. His lawyers won, but the son of one of the victims put out a contract on Prague's life. His second contract was for a man who had raped and mutilated a young girl. She survived, but was permanently institutionalized. Despite testimony about her flawless character, the jury turned the man free because he was prominent in the community and because his father had hired the best of lawyers. He received a seven-year probationary sentence.

Yet with this contract he had reversed his modus operandi. The money was too good to ask a lot of questions. Until now he had wanted his female victim anonymous, because it bothered him more to contemplate killing a woman than a man. He liked women. They were soft and gentle and marvelous. He didn't want her to haunt his dreams. But now doubts assailed him; he wanted to know more about her. He suspected that the only wickedness about her was her body. He imagined people could kill for it, or perhaps because of it.

He adjusted the rifle and focused again. With only a quarter-of-an-inch squeeze of his finger she would no longer be a problem to someone. This was the moment he had been waiting for. She was home alone—no gardeners on Saturday afternoons. He had seen the maid leave over two hours ago so the house was empty. He had access to the roof of a vacant home nearby that was for sale with the Kettering Real Estate Company.

Propping his arm on the warm parapet, the man watched her, his curiosity growing like a weed in the summer sun. For a moment he mentally stripped away the triangle of black between her legs and his mouth became dry. He could squeeze the trigger and be in his blue rental Ford in twenty-three seconds and at the New Orleans International Airport in twenty-eight minutes. The plane ticket was in his pocket. No one would find the body for hours. He gazed through the sight at her bare right breast with a small brown mole beneath the nipple. His tongue ran across his lip as he thought about the touch and taste of that nipple. His hand was steady, his finger firm on the trigger, the sight making a black cross over a rosy nipple.

But he lowered the gun. He had been given four months to fulfill the contract; there was plenty of time left him. A wealthy man, he could easily meet the right people, learn their pasts, and judge this victim for himself. She deserved as much.

Four months. He surveyed the sparkling white graveled roof where he stood. This house might not be vacant in another four months. But there would be other places, other ways. Finding the right moment had never been a problem. Unless he was convinced otherwise, he decided that she was too beautiful to destroy.

He raised the gun. She opened her wide eyes. It might not take four months to find out if she should be eliminated. It might take only days.

1

The tall spires of St. Louis Cathedral thrust upward toward an azure sky while on the wide steps pigeons strutted, their muted coos heralding the morning before chatting tourists and strolling musicians drowned out the birds. In front of the cathedral gardeners tended purple azaleas and pink camellias in Jackson Square where long ago the flag of Bourbon Spain had been replaced by the tricolor of the Republic of France to be followed only twenty days later by the flag of the United States. In this square, General Jackson rode victorious after battling the British in 1815.

Always fascinated when her family drove into the French Quarter, thirteen-year-old Talia Mignon Wade sat close to the open window of their maroon Mercury. Below straight blond hair cut short with bangs, her green eyes studied her surroundings while she leaned forward to catch the cool morning breeze. When she was in the Quarter, she loved to look at the houses that set flush with the sidewalks, called "banquettes" in New Orleans, the balconies with their cast-iron grillwork, particularly one apartment balcony where a slender, golden collie sometimes sunned itself. It was her family's

5

monthly Sunday morning excursion when her father drove to the Café du Monde to get hot beignets and tangy orange juice before they went to church. Interrupting her daydreams, her fourteen-year-old sister Rebecca gave her a sharp nudge then turned away quickly. The second time, Talia said, "Stop that, Rebecca!"

"Stop what?" Rebecca asked with feigned innocence. "I haven't done anything!"

"Girls," their mother Kate said without turning around.

Rebecca gave Talia a sly smile. "Mom, Talia has a necklace and I don't."

Kate turned her head. "You should have worn one of yours, Rebecca."

"I don't have one like that. You gave it to Talia, but I didn't get one."

"It was my birthday," Talia said, staring out the window, trying to ignore Rebecca, knowing the result of Rebecca's wheedling would be a new necklace exactly like her own.

"I want one like that!"

"I'm sure Talia will let you wear hers," Kate said softly.

"No, she wouldn't when I asked," Rebecca said, finally stirring Kate to turn and stare at Talia.

"The first time you asked was this morning after I was already wearing it!" Talia said.

"Talia, you should share," Kate admonished gently and turned her back again while Rebecca gave Talia a smug smile.

"Can I wear it tomorrow?"

Talia was tempted to refuse Rebecca, but her sister would only talk Kate into making Talia share, so Talia nodded, relieved to have quiet once again descend. Judging from her friends' parents, she thought her own were indulgent, particularly her father, but no matter what they did, Rebecca never seemed satisfied. Full of restless energy, she always wanted something she didn't have. Talia stared at the balcony on the Pontalba Apartments until her father returned to the car with a crisp white sack of beignets.

His hands were full and Talia leaned out through the open window to take the plastic cups of juice and pass them out, carefully handing the first to her mother.

"Kate, here," Darcy Wade said, settling behind the wheel while Kate took the sack of hot beignets.

"Careful, girls," Kate said in her soft voice. As she leaned close over the back seat, the scent of tea rose perfume carried to Talia. Kate's curly black hair matched Rebecca's, so different from Talia's pale, straight hair. Rebecca also shared her mother's delicate features with a slightly upturned nose.

"Everyone settled?" Darcy Wade asked after a moment.

Talia nodded while she bit into the hot, square French doughnut carefully, trying to avoid dropping sugar on her starched green Sunday dress. She searched again for the collie but instead she saw a young man. To Talia's thirteen years, he looked grown. His faded jeans were tattered and his curly brown hair was in a tangle over his startling blue eyes. He lounged against the apartment building, idly watching people.

The car started, and she glanced again at the empty balcony, then down into a level blue-eyed gaze.

Watching the maroon Mercury drive away, Michael Stanton shifted his shoulder against the warm red-brick wall of the apartment that was built in 1849. At this early hour only half a dozen customers were seated in the open-air Café du Monde. He hadn't found the ones for which he was searching, but within the next five minutes he spotted them, a likely looking couple, a Nikon dangling around the husband's neck, the wife's diamonds catching rays of sunlight as she looked at a map in her hand and then pointed to the street sign.

They appeared to be successful, well-fed tourists. At eighteen, if he had to, he could write a dossier on them: middle-class, middle-American, from Iowa or Oklahoma or Illinois or Nebraska. He could not detect an accent, so that placed them in the upper Midwest. Mike stepped into their path, altering his expression to an appropriate degree of sadness.

"Sir, my Mom's ill, and my Dad didn't come home last night. I can't get Mom's pills, and she's groaning and my little brother's crying. Can you please spare fifty cents?"

"Oh, William," the woman whispered.

"How old are you, son?"

"Eighteen. I'm a senior this year. I work at night, but my pay is all gone for Mom's medicine."

"What kind of work?" the man asked, frowning.

Once Mike had gotten so bored with the game, he had answered, "I'm a pimp," and promptly lost any donation. "I carry out groceries at the A & P, but I need a little extra with Dad not showing. . . ."

While he talked he made a discovery that drove boredom away. The woman's white leather handbag, bulging with objects, was open, and a thick wad of bills was visible. Mike moved closer to her, keeping his attention on the man as he dug in his pocket, and handed Mike a dollar bill.

"Here, son. You keep your job at the store. Work hard. That's always a salvation."

"Yes, sir," Mike said, trying to sound humble. "Thank you, sir! Thanks a lot!"

"Will that get your mother's pills?"

"Yes, sir! It'll help. With what I've saved, I needed another fifty cents."

"Maybe he'll know, William, where the shop is that has the antique guns."

"Antique guns?" Mike repeated. "You must want a shop on Royal." He moved closer to her, pointing to show them directions. "You go straight down here past the square, turn right on St. Peter . . ." His fingers closed on the sheaf of bills in her purse while they both stared in the direction he was telling them to go. As he watched the man, who was the most threatening, Mike withdrew the bills and jammed them into his pocket. He began to move away.

"The shop won't be open this morning, though. It's Sunday."

They grinned at each other. "We forgot the day! We were in such a hurry to get down here for beignets."

"If you want to learn where everything is, take a buggy ride first," Mike suggested. He waved his hand toward the waiting line of horse-drawn carriages along Decatur at the end of the square. "The drivers will tell you about the Quarter, and then you'll know what you'd like to see," Mike said, moving away. They nodded while he walked backward. "Thank you, sir. Thank you both," he said with sincerity. They smiled at him.

Forcing each step to be leisurely, he left, holding his breath while he braced for her scream. Half a dozen more steps. His skin tingled. His fingers closed on a latch and an iron gate swung open. He stepped into a narrow courtyard, glancing back down Decatur Street. The husband was talking to the driver of a carriage, and the woman was looking at the cathedral.

Mike closed the iron gate and ran over flagstones damp from the morning dew. He opened another gate and walked down a cobblestoned alleyway, moving with sureness between buildings faded by time, their weathered shutters and iron trim adding to their appeal. The Quarter was his home, and he knew it the way a cat knows its own territory, the dangers, the areas he could prowl. He stepped out between two buildings and someone blocked his path.

One glance at Leech, with his long pigtail of black hair and his heavy beard, his dark eyes glittering, and Mike turned to race back down the alley the way he had come. Suddenly he stopped in his tracks.

Stepping from a doorway, Big John faced him, arms folded over his massive chest, his booted feet spread apart. A tremor of hatred and frustration shook Mike. He couldn't get past Big John. He saw Leech coming toward him. A switchblade snapped in Leech's hand, its thin silver blade shining, and Leech's grin widened to a smirk of satisfaction.

"We saw the money. Gimme it, kid."

"What money?" Mike asked, flicking open the blade to his own knife, gauging his chances as they both closed in on him. He had to fight them, and in spite of the knife, Leech was the smaller and more vulnerable.

Mike lunged forward, hearing the click of metal against metal as Leech's knife sliced across his. Then came burning pain when the blade slashed Mike's arm. He retaliated, feeling his knife bite into Leech's flesh, seeing the crimson line that followed its path.

Big John hit him from behind and he fell, pain exploding in his head. He scrambled to get to his feet, but Big John's foot came down with enough pressure on his windpipe to force him to lie still.

"One step and you're gone," Big John said, increasing the pressure enough that Mike lay still and stared up at them.

Leech glared at him. "Little shithead, I ought to skin you. Gimme the green."

Mike tightened his fist around the knife. Leech kicked him in the ribs, and Mike gasped with pain. Big John's foot came down hard enough to cut off his breath.

"The dough!" Leech demanded.

Mike could see only blackness. Anger and frustration tore through him. "I don't have any money!" he rasped.

Leech leaned down, swinging the knife, slashing Mike's face from his temple to his jaw. "Money, asshole, or it's your eye next!"

Searing pain followed the blade. Feeling warm blood on his face, Mike pulled out the roll of bills and threw them at Leech. The instant Big John's foot was gone, Mike jumped to his feet.

They hit him at the same time, his knife flying from his hand, but Big John was more powerful and he easily grabbed him and pinned Mike's arms behind him.

"Now, you little asshole, you listen up!" Leech snarled while he gathered up the bills. "You're gonna bring me money like this every day. You bring me—" He paused to count, and Mike felt sick at his stomach to see the money in Leech's grimy fingers. That was his money! Those were dollars he had risked his neck to steal. Eighty-three dollars! A fortune. Gone as swiftly as it had come. Blood ran in his eye, and his face burned with pain.

Leech's black eyes glittered, his foul breath reeked of whiskey and tobacco. "Bring me five dollars every morning. Down at the end of the market. You understand?"

Mike wanted to spit on him, but he knew he wouldn't gain anything except a worse beating. He nodded. "Yeah, I understand," he whispered, hating Leech and Big John, rage making spots appear before his eyes.

"Don't ever fail," Leech said, leaning closer, holding the tip of his knife against Mike's neck, letting the point prick his flesh. Mike sucked in his breath, but he wouldn't cry out.

Leech laughed, a guttural chuckle that made Mike's skin crawl. How he hated the man! He wanted to knot his fingers around Leech's long, dirty neck and squeeze until there wasn't breath left.

"You have a brother, little Claude. You want Claude protected, eh?"

"You dirty bastard!"

Leech hit Mike hard enough to make him feel faint. He blinked, trying to focus on his captors.

"Shut up! Five dollars every morning. Starting tomorrow. Understand?"

"Yeah."

"You ever miss a day, you know what will happen?"

They glared at each other, and Mike tensed; he knew a blow was coming before Leech doubled his fist and hit him in the stomach. Pain enveloped him like a bursting flame, but he didn't cry out. When Big John released him, Mike dropped to his knees, retching and shaking with rage.

"That's what you'll get, punk, and Claude will get worse. Much worse," came the raspy voice. "If you don't show, little Claude pays instead. Five dollars every morning. Half-past seven."

Then they were gone. Mike rested his hands on his knees, while he cursed in a slow, monotonous voice. He looked down the empty alley. "I'll get you for this, Leech," he whispered.

Hurting all over, he picked up his knife and yanked off his shirt. He held it to his face as he started home. Home. His thin nostrils flared with distaste. His ailing mother and missing father. Like hell. Whatever man she had picked up last night would still be with her. But she might have gone home with one instead. He couldn't remember ever seeing his father. He varied the stories he gave tourists when he begged for money. Sometimes it was ailing father and pregnant mother, sometimes ailing mother and ailing father, sometimes aged grandparents and no parents.

He swore again, thinking about his life, yet he couldn't hate his mother. She did what she could; he understood. His younger brother Brett had pushed drugs, stolen cars, and finally been killed in a high speed chase with the cops. Claude was the baby of the family at eleven years old. Mike would get the five dollars each day to protect Claude. He, Brett, and Claude had each had a different father, but none of them had ever seen his father. Brett had been stocky, thick in the shoulders, auburn-haired. Claude was dark and swarthy with straight black hair and black eyes.

Getting five dollars a day was an impossible task. Mike had worked at odd jobs almost as long as they had lived in the small apartment on the fringe of the Quarter: grocery sacker, errand boy, dishwasher, anything to earn a few dollars. But earning money from small jobs was slow. And his mother often needed what he earned. Evangeline Renée Tate Stanton. An elegant name for a whore.

When the men started appearing, years ago, Mike had gone into a rage one night. Vangie had lashed right back, slapping him, an act that had shocked them both out of their anger. She crumpled up, crying, sinking down at the wooden kitchen table, her head on her folded arms. "It's the only way we can survive! Can't you see, Michael? I have to depend on men. I don't have any skills."

"You can answer a phone; sell things, work at the grocery. Aw, shit, don't cry," he had added through clenched teeth, hating his inability to solve her problems. "Things will get better, Vangie," he said, calling her by the nickname all three boys used. He couldn't remember ever calling her anything else. "When I get older, I'll have better jobs and I can help."

"I can't spell," she said, wiping away her tears. "I can barely read. That's why I want you to go to school."

School. She always talked about school—as if books could put money in his pockets! He could dimly remember their life on the bayou before they had come to the Quarter, He had spent long, lazy hours fishing with his grandfather. Granny Tate had taught him to read. Her books had been an odd and worn assortment, but he had learned and he had liked to read as much as he liked to fish. Then his mother had taken the three boys and moved to the Quarter, and later his grandparents had been killed in a storm. He didn't think of them often anymore, but on pretty spring days he skipped school, sometimes taking Claude in a pirogue back on a bayou where they could catch bream, crawfish, and bass.

Touching his cheek lightly with his fingers near the cut, he remembered the problems at hand. He kicked a rock and swore, unaware of the quiet Sunday morning because of his seething emotions. Someday he would have money!

When he washed at home, he stared at the cut and wondered if it would make a difference with girls.

Through the next few days he managed to steal the money or talk his mother out of enough for Leech, but he couldn't do that indefinitely. When Mike went to school, he sat there turning his dilemma over and over in his mind.

He usually liked school. He was curious about everything, and couldn't resist the stories in his English texts. Math was easy, and he could work problems swiftly if his interest held. Even Felicity with her flashing black eyes and the smiles she gave him during trig class couldn't shake his worries. When she began smiling and slipping him notes, it meant she wanted him to walk her home. In the past that knowledge had stirred such erotic pictures in his mind that nothing else mattered. But not now. Claude was in danger if Mike didn't do what Leech wanted.

Mike ran his fingers along his cheek, conscious of the healing cut. Evidently it hadn't ruined his looks enough to bother Felicity, so maybe it wouldn't bother other girls.

Mike stared at the live oak near the building. Its trunk was over a foot thick and had initials cut into it. Survival. He was damn well going to survive in spite of Leech and Big John, and someday he was going to have enough money so that he would be able to do the things he wanted.

Leech was scum. Mike drew circles on the paper while those around him studied the angles of an isosceles triangle. He could easily get rid of a body in a bayou. It was the murder he couldn't figure out. Could he kill Leech? When he thought of the five dollars for the rest of his life, he decided he could do most anything to Leech. Could he do it and avoid getting caught? "Aye, there's the rub," he thought, the line from an English assignment echoing in his mind.

It would take time and care, but once Leech was gone, he would be free. Big John was all muscle, but no wits. He couldn't extort five cents if Leech wasn't there. The bell rang; Felicity turned to pick up her books, bending over from the waist to reveal her long, bare legs, giving him a glimpse of her ass and pink panties. She smiled at Mike, waiting expectantly. He slammed his notebook shut and moved up the aisle to walk beside her, the problem of Leech momentarily forgotten.

It wasn't forgotten for long, however, because three weeks later, Mike couldn't pay. He missed two days in a row; his mother hadn't come home for four days. Frustrated and angry, he warned Claude to stay home.

That night when Mike returned from the A & P he found Claude frying a hamburger. The tiny kitchen was filled with a tempting smell and gray smoke.

"I'll put one more on—" Claude stopped abruptly to study Mike. "You've been in a fight."

"It's nothing. I'll throw on another burger for me."

"Who hit you? You have a black eye."

"It was someone at school."

"It was Leech, wasn't it?" Claude asked.

"Nah!" Mike answered, wondering why he couldn't ever successfully lie to Claude. Claude was tiny for his age, slender and short, but his mind was quick. He was intelligent, always making top grades in school although he spent very few hours studying at home. Mike couldn't figure it, and he had long ago given up asking Vangie who Claude's father was. He believed her when she always replied she simply didn't know. Whoever he had been, he must have had some sense.

Claude gave up questioning Mike and got out more hamburger meat, his slender dark hands forming a patty swiftly.

"A few more days, kid, and I'll have money for Leech."

"Sure, Mike."

"In the meantime, don't open the door to anyone. And get word to me the moment Vangie gets back. She'll have money with her." He punched his brother's shoulder in a playful thump and worked to help him, moving around the tiny kitchen that was little more than a closet with a rusty gas stove and a refrigerator that rattled and squeaked, yet couldn't freeze water enough to make ice cubes.

"We'll eat and watch John Wayne," Claude said happily. "There's a John Wayne movie that starts at eight."

"And how many times have you seen it?" Mike asked dryly.

"Only three."

"Three! Don't you ever get tired of John Wayne?"

"Now look," Claude said, doing a fair imitation of the actor, "you think I'll get tired of John Wayne? Like hell I will, for Chrissakes!"

"You better leave off the last if you want to sound like him!"·

After the burgers were eaten, Mike left the apartment. He descended the narrow flight of wooden stairs that had been worn smooth through the years. Leech had given him an ultimatum this morning, but those few brief blows had merely been warnings. Claude would be next. Mike clenched his fists and swore as he sauntered toward the honky-tonk strip on Bourbon Street. He knew he might pick up enough money here to pay Leech.

Neon lights made the street as bright as day, softening the effect of peeling paint, and giving a warm patina to old buildings behind the fancy cast-iron grillwork. Music wafted from bars: ragtime, rock, and country-western. While horse-drawn buggies inched their way down narrow streets with a steady clop of hooves, tourists roamed in and out of bars and hotels.

A mime performed in silence; a tap dancer snapped his fingers, his fast patter of jive matching his steps, while half a block down the street Jimmy tried to coax the crowd inside to watch nude dancing. Next door there were men in drag. Prostitutes worked the street. Thank God his mother was a cut above that! he thought. Her johns were fairly well heeled and she didn't have to stay on the street.

Without hesitation Mike stepped into a bar and ordered a beer, his only one in weeks because he hadn't been able to afford anything extra. He turned to watch a dart game, knowing that Sammy would win and fleece the tourists, keeping a percentage of the profits for himself, turning the rest over to the owner of the bar. Mike wouldn't play Sammy for money unless it was under a quarter. Although there were scams on the street, Sammy was truly talented in darts. Tiring of watching, he wandered back on the street, nodding a greeting to Teddy, watching her walk past, her short, tight skirt swishing with each step. While he loathed his mother's occupation, he accepted sex as something as natural as breathing.

His first experience with a girl had been after school when he was thirteen and he had walked Deborah home. She was a year older than he was, and she had invited him inside the one room where she lived with her mother and two younger sisters. He'd been there after school before and knew she would let him kiss her and fondle her small, firm breasts. This time she didn't push him away or tell him to stop when he peeled away her flimsy bikini panties. Her hands guided him, her hips had raised to meet him, and he had come swiftly, too soon because she clung to him, moving her thin hips in a frenzy. The next time he'd tried to take more time, to explore the intricacies of the female body. Deborah had moved away from the Quarter when the school year ended, and he never saw her again.

By half-past nine he had begged seven dollars and eighty-three cents from tourists. It was enough to pay Leech something tomorrow morning. He would get another beating for having only part of the money, but it would protect Claude.

Two dancers and a trumpet player were drawing a crowd in the center of the block. A few yards away a couple emerged from a bar. Mike gave the man a cursory glance, barely noticing his elegant black suit and conservative tie. He stared at the woman who looked shorter than five feet tall with white-gold hair and perfect skin; her dark eyes were large, mysterious. Mike sucked in his breath as his gaze raked her red silk dress that clung and nipped in around her tiny waist. She couldn't be wearing a bra because her breasts swung with each step, her nipples faintly outlined in the material.

The man took her arm and Mike followed them until they entered The Court of Two Sisters, disappearing through the entrance into the courtyard. Mike felt as dazed as if he had looked into a blinding light. He found an empty doorway and leaned against the jamb, staring at the restaurant across the street, fantasizing about the woman.

It was a little over an hour when the couple reappeared; Mike followed them in and out of bars, to Preservation Hall where he lolled outside, listening to the Dixieland jazz, spinning erotic mental pictures of the woman whom he named

"Blondie" in his mind. Later in the evening he spotted the glittering diamond and gold band on her finger and had to laugh at himself, because of the rush of disappointment he suffered. Married or single, she was as attainable to him as a star in the sky. He clenched his fists, momentarily aware of the limitations he faced, determined to rise to a better level of living.

The next time they drifted from one bar to the other, the man's step wasn't quite as steady; her laughter was louder and more frequent. Mike followed them until four in the morning when they strolled down Bourbon.

He wandered along behind them, barely hearing the music that he had grown as accustomed to as the presence of the wide Mississippi River. After three more blocks the lights and music faded. The doorways were dark, the street was still, and the only sound was the couple's footsteps. Mike guessed they were headed for one of the elegant hotels on the fringe of the Quarter. They were pigeons, flying right into a trap to get caught and plucked. A few years earlier such a stroll would have been safe, but not now.

Mike jammed his hand into his pocket, slipping on brass knuckles. Trouble was coming, and for a moment he started to turn back to the lights and people on Bourbon, but as he stared at the blonde's stunning figure, he was drawn to follow her.

"Dumb ass," he muttered, glaring at the man who by any definition would be called handsome with thick black hair and broad shoulders, a cleft in his chin, and deep blue eyes.

Mike kept to the shadows when they crossed the street, walking under the circle of yellow light. Her tinkling peal of laughter mixed with the deep rumble of the man's voice.

Mike's gaze searched the block with its multitude of recessed doorways and openings onto narrow courtyards. He gave them another block, but they only made it halfway when a shadow separated from an inky archway. A man wielding a knife confronted the couple; then a shorter man stepped out behind them.

Mike froze in a doorway, hoping the man had enough sense to toss over his money quickly. Instead, he began to argue with the two while pulling the woman closer. Mike shook his head, debating whether to intervene or mind his own business. The damn fool was going to get cut, but it was Blondie who concerned him. He knew it was ridiculous, but he couldn't bear to think of her being hurt.

With a sigh he moved closer, trying to keep out of sight in the shadows, staying on his toes, his sneakers enabling him to step silently. As he listened to demands for money and protests from the man, who was growing belligerent, he sized up the situation.

"Hand over the wallet and the foxy lady—"

"Here's the money!" the man snapped, reaching into his hip pocket. "You can have it, but leave her alone!"

They were closing in on the man. Hugging the building, Mike edged forward. They were ten yards away. Then five. They were busy worrying about their victims and too occupied watching the woman to notice him.

Mike plunged out of the doorway. The shorter thief started to turn when Mike, putting all his weight behind the blow, hit him across his skull. He went down in a slump.

In the split second when Mike appeared, the man burst into action, lashing out with his foot to kick the thief who was holding the knife.

Then both thieves were up and running. Blondie stuck out her foot, tripped one, and he fell. The billfold went tumbling from his hand, sliding across the concrete and dropping off the curb. As the crook jumped to his feet the man hit him again. He slammed against the building, then ran with Mike chasing both thieves until they raced around a corner and vaulted a wall. Mike stopped, returning to the couple.

"You should take a cab," Mike said, looking at them speculatively.

"Thanks a million," the man replied and thrust forward his hand. "Ben Holloway. This is my wife, Simone."

"Mike Stanton," Mike replied and shook hands firmly with Ben while he smiled at Simone.

"Yes, thank you," she said, returning his smile, and he felt as if the brief confrontation had been worth the risk.

"Here," the man held out some bills.

"No, thanks," Mike said, not believing his own ears, but he didn't want to take the money in front of her.

"C'mon, I insist."

"I can't," he said, fighting strangely opposing reactions, something new in his life.

"Nonsense! Here, I insist you take this. Get yourself something. We should've taken a cab."

"Aw, gee, that's nice," Mike replied, succumbing to his natural instincts with relief.

"Do you work, Mike?"

"At the A & P."

"You ever want a job, come see me." Ben Holloway dug in his billfold and held out a card. "Here. I mean it about the job."

"Jeez, thanks, mister," Mike said, staring at Simone. She smiled at him, and he was dazzled. "You live here?"

"Yeah. We're meeting friends back at one of the hotels. Next time we'll take a cab."

"Thanks," Mike repeated without knowing what he was saying.

"We're the ones who owe you thanks."

They walked away and disappeared around a corner. Mike jammed the card into his jeans pocket, looked at the bills with amazement.

"Holy shit!" he whispered, momentarily stunned, unable to believe his eyes as he stared at the smiling likeness of Benjamin Franklin. Two fifty-dollar bills! One hundred dollars! It was a fortune!

Surveying his surroundings, he stepped back into a doorway and cautiously put the bills in his shoe. He'd learned his lesson with Leech and Big John.

He stood watching the street for another twenty minutes, thinking constantly of the two fifties stuffed in his shoe. When he didn't see any movement except a stray cat, he headed back toward Toulouse Street and home. Exultant, he now had enough to pay Leech! He had to find a way to be rid of the miserable creep. He could shoot Leech, weight the body, and drop it into a bayou, but every time the temptation came, along came reluctance, because Mike could imagine getting caught and being locked away in a prison filled with men like Leech.

At the apartment, Claude was asleep, curled in the chair,

the black and white television set playing on the only channel they could pick up.

Mike stood a moment over his younger brother, deciding to leave Claude alone. He could tell him about the money in the morning. His brother's thin face looked even younger in sleep, his black hair falling over his eyes, his long lashes dark shadows on his gaunt cheeks. Mike went to the narrow bedroom where both boys shared the sagging iron bed. He turned the bills and the card in his hands:

BEN HOLLOWAY, SOUTHERN MARKET, INC.

Mike remembered Simone down to the smallest detail. And he was certain Simone and Ben Holloway had been around; they hadn't always lived a sheltered life, because when they'd had a chance, they had reacted quickly. He remembered how she had tripped the thief, and then Ben Holloway had slugged the guy. Beneath the glamor, little Simone was tough.

With a creak of bedsprings, Mike stretched out on the bare mattress and folded his hands behind his head, closing his eyes and giving himself up to fantasies about Simone. He imagined peeling the red silk dress off her, touching her fantastic body—her high, swinging breasts that jiggled provocatively with every step she took. If he went to work for Ben Holloway, he might see her again.

Exhausted and happy, he was asleep in minutes. Early the next morning with the money in his pocket, he paced restlessly back and forth by the last stall at the market. Where was Leech?

The early morning air was cool; the sun hadn't climbed above treetops yet and the market wasn't in full swing. A few vendors moved around in their stalls; workmen unloaded a truck with bushel baskets of brown potatoes while Mike watched. He had the money—what had happened to Leech?

The sun splashed golden rays across the long roof of the market when he went home. He meandered along the streets, watching for a sign of Leech or Big John. There was no one to ask; everyone avoided Leech and Big John as much as possible. Leech was like a draconian monster that had crawled out from under a rock. There couldn't have been a mother.

The closer Mike got to home, the more his spirits lifted,

his thoughts shifting abruptly to Felicity. He opened the door to the narrow flight of stairs and heard a shrill cry.

2

Puzzled, Mike frowned until he heard another cry. Then he ran, taking the steps two at a time. The cries were coming from his apartment at the head of the stairs. With one hard kick the lock yielded, and he burst into the room.

Big John was holding Claude's arms behind his back. A trickle of blood ran down Claude's chin from his swollen lips, a crimson slash cut across his cheek, and he struggled as Leech hit him in the stomach.

Blind rage exploded in Mike. He heard Claude screaming above a roaring in his ears as he struck Leech. Leech fell back, and Mike was at him, hammering his fists against him wildly, striking him with all his might.

Without warning a hard object crashed against Mike's skull. A burst of white-hot pain was followed by oblivion.

When he opened his eyes, he stared at the dusty, bare wooden floor until memory returned and he sat up, looking around.

"Mike—" Claude came into the room with a wet cloth in his hand. Mike took the cloth, wiped the blood off his neck and head, wincing when he touched a tender spot. He glanced up at Claude, whose face was abnormally pale with high spots of color in his cheeks. He had a cut from his ear to his nose, another long cut on his hand, a split lip, and bruises that were beginning to show in spite of his dark skin.

"I'm okay!" Claude stated, lifting his chin. One dark eye was swollen shut, and he squinted at Mike.

Mike's rage returned like a surging tide. "The sonofa-bitch!" he cursed but immediately lowered his head in pain.

He was more concerned about Claude. "Want to go to a doctor?"

"No, please, Mike." Claude gave a negative shake of his head, his eyes filled with worry. "Don't go after him."

"I'm sorry, Claude," Mike said, reaching into his pocket where he had placed the money. His pocket was empty. He jammed his hand into his other pockets.

"They took your money." Claude looked away, and his voice wavered. "They made me tell them where you had money hidden."

"How the hell did they know?"

"I think they guessed. I'm sorry, Mike. I had to tell."

Mike put his arm around his brother, and Claude stood there, head hanging down while he tried to hold back tears. Abruptly Mike strode toward the door until Claude blocked his way.

"Where are you going?"

"Out. I'll be back soon."

"You're going after Leech and you'll get hurt! I know you. You always get even if someone hurts one of us. Don't—"

"Move out of my way, Claude. You can't hold me here, and I'm late for work."

"You told me you don't work until four."

"I'm filling in for Tom Martin."

"I know you're going after Leech."

"So if I am? You can't let people run over you in life. If I let him get away with this, he'll do something worse. I'm going to get him for this, and you can't stop me."

"You always want revenge," Claude said in a whisper. "You're strong, and you're strong deep down inside. You wouldn't have told them about the money. But even if you're strong, you can get hurt."

"There are some things worse than getting hurt." They stared at each other. "C'mon, Claude. I'll get a new lock and fix the door. I don't think they'll be back today."

Claude nodded, his eyes filled with doubt and fear as he stepped out of the way. Mike went down the stairs, his thoughts swirling in his mind. He would have to catch Leech without Big John, because that was the only way he could fight him and win. He wanted to slit Leech's throat whenever he remembered the earlier scene in his apartment.

He finally found Leech and Big John near the market on Decatur and he hung back, trailing them. They disappeared into a building and after three hours, Mike gave up and went home. However, his rage didn't cool with the passage of time.

Before dusk one Thursday evening, Mike spotted Leech all alone with Big John nowhere in sight. Mike stayed half a block behind Leech as he followed him along the fringes of the Quarter on a circuitous route that didn't seem to have any particular destination. Mike doggedly trailed after Leech, waiting for a chance to jump him. Leech disappeared, and Mike hurried after him down a narrow alley bordered by shuttered buildings built in a time of duels and balls, silent sentinels to past trysts and violence.

The stones were slippery from the afternoon rain, the area deserted; a steamy scent of moisture still hung in the air along with the muted sounds of music from Bourbon. Mike moved cautiously, closing the distance, looking at Leech's lanky figure, his long braid of hair, and sloping shoulders. Leech's black leather vest swung with each step; his T-shirt had holes in the sleeves. He wasn't formidable looking, but Mike knew his appearance was deceiving. He closed the gap between them until Leech heard him and turned.

"What the hell?"

"You damned sonofabitch!" Mike yelled with rage. He attacked Leech, and they both went down.

Mike's fury goaded him to destroy the man who had hurt Claude. He slammed his fists against Leech's jaw, oblivious of the blows he received in return, unable to forget the sight of Leech hitting Claude and the knife slashes on Claude's face that would leave permanent scars.

Knocking each other into trash cans that tipped over with a clatter, the combatants fell on the wet stones to slug out their anger. Scrambling to his feet, Leech staggered and slammed back against a wall, breaking a drain pipe from a building. It fell with a clang while Mike shoved his knee into Leech's groin, then tagged him with a left hook as he was falling over.

His control gone, Mike dropped on him, raining blow after

blow. "No more five dollars! And don't ever come near my brother! Do you understand?"

Leech tried to break free, and Mike banged his head on uneven senna stones which were now red with blood. "Do you understand?" he yelled.

"Asshole," Leech rasped.

Mike hit him until Leech was unconscious. He pressed his fingers closed around Leech's throat, squeezing the carotid arteries.

"Damn you!" he snapped, releasing Leech. Gasping for breath he backed off, watching Leech's chest rise and fall in ragged breathing. He could kill Leech so easily now. Mike stared at Leech for long moments. He reached down and wrapped his fingers around Leech's throat. "I'm through paying, you understand?"

One dark eye squinted at him and Mike tightened his fingers. "Next time I'll slit your throat, so help me God!"

His hands dropped away from Leech's throat. Every breath hurt, and Mike held his side as he lurched to his feet, staggering against the wall. He couldn't think or see straight. He fell, then got to his feet and stumbled down the alley. Becoming aware of pain in a hundred different places, he breathed heavily through swollen lips and puffy eyes as he made his way home.

The next morning between classes Mike called Ben Holloway to ask for an appointment.

"The office is closed Friday. I'm taking a long weekend. Just come by the house anytime and I'll talk to you." Ben Holloway's deep voice sounded brisk over the phone.

"Thanks, Mr. Holloway. I'll be there!" Mike said, replacing the receiver and praying Ben Holloway had sincerely meant what he had said. Friday morning Mike skipped school, hitched a ride, and then walked to Ben Holloway's home in a suburban area. As he walked, he noticed that the blocks became longer, the houses were set back farther, and the yards were more landscaped. Purple wisteria graced a white gazebo, and the sweet scent of honeysuckle filled the air. While Mike followed a curving gravel drive between a double row of tall crape myrtles, he stared at the elegant Louisiana Classic mansion with its hip roof and plastered Tuscan columns—he counted twelve across the façade and along the east side. Rooms opened onto the encircling first- and second-floor galleries, the doorways flanked by green shutters, the mansion surrounded by beds of flowers. What would it be like to have money? To live in a house with room after room? To go to sleep without wondering how to scrape together enough to get by the next day?

His gaze returned to the mansion. Somewhere in one of those bedrooms Simone slept; somewhere in one of the bathrooms, she bathed. He felt a sense of excitement and anticipation. Occasionally he wondered about Ben Holloway and how he had become wealthy. Mike walked up wide steps and crossed the gallery, turning to stare in awe at the large crystal-and-brass hanging lamp over his head. He wanted a house like this someday, and he wanted to feel at home in it, not as awestruck as he was now.

He rang the bell, listened to the melodic chimes and faced a uniformed servant.

"Yes, sir?"

Mike held out the card. "I'm Mike Stanton. Mr. Holloway told me to come see him," Mike said, and hoped the uncertainty he felt wasn't revealed in his voice.

The butler looked Mike over and nodded. "If you'll please wait," he said and closed the door.

In minutes he was back. "This way, sir."

Relieved to pass the first hurdle, Mike stepped inside a cool hall where a ceiling fan turned. Scents of lemon polish, freshly cut roses, and floor wax mingled together. The bare cypress floor had a mirrored shine; the elegant Sheraton-style tables, a regence armoire, and oil paintings on the wall silently proclaimed the tasteful wealth of the owner. The hall was more elegant than the lobbies of some of the fancy hotels around the Quarter. He glanced at the wide staircase sweeping up to the second floor, and his heart seemed to slam against his ribs.

Simone stood at the top dressed in red shorts and a sleeveless top. As she descended the stairs, she gave him a haughty, disdainful look for a second, but then her features softened.

"Mike Stanton isn't it?" she said with a smile that made him forget the house.

"Mrs. Holloway, how are you?" he asked warmly, his nervousness evaporating.

"I'm fine. Call me Simone. You've come to see Ben."

Mike was aware of the butler waiting, aware of her enticing perfume and her dark eyes that held a mysterious, beckoning gleam in their depths.

"Yeah."

"He's swimming. Thanks, Dalton, I'll show Mike the way."

"Yes, ma'am," the butler replied and faded out of sight. Mike caught a whiff of flowers again. Her white-gold hair was pushed back with a red silk band.

"You can't imagine how grateful we are to you for rescuing us that night."

"It was nothing," he replied, wishing he could think of something witty to say. The top of her head didn't come to his shoulder. "You have an accent," he said studying her, something he could continue to do forever, her skin reminding him of a soft peach.

"I'm French."

"No kidding! French!" he exclaimed, and she became more mysterious and desirable to him.

"I met Ben in Paris," she said as they passed through a spacious room decorated with white Danish furniture that Mike barely noticed. The south end of the room was glass doors; beyond them were the patio and a rectangular pool surrounded by exotic tropical plants. As they stepped outside, Ben swam to the edge of the pool.

"Look who's here!" she called to him.

"I know. Dalton told me," Ben said, coming up out of the water and picking up a towel to wrap it around his waist. He offered his hand. "Glad to see you. Come sit down."

Mike felt as if he had died and gone to paradise. The day was muggy, he had walked miles; the pool looked like a dream, and the Holloways were treating him with all the courtesy possible. Simone was smiling at him, waiting for him to sit beside her.

A maid appeared with a tray of iced drinks, and Mike sank down on a navy webbed chair. Simone took a glass of iced tea off the tray, crossed her shapely legs, and Mike had to fight the urge to stare.

"How've you been?" Ben Holloway asked.

"Fine," Mike replied, glancing at Simone. "This is some home!"

"Thanks," Ben replied. "Simone and I enjoy it. Is school out today?"

Suddenly uneasy, Mike shifted. He hadn't expected Ben to give a thought to school. "Naw. I didn't think it would hurt to miss," he said. "I'll be there for afternoon classes."

"You should've come on Saturday," Ben said.

"Yeah." Silence lengthened until Mike blurted, "Mr. Holloway, you said to come see you if I need a job."

"Sure, Mike. What can you do?"

Mike's face grew warm as he mulled over how to answer. His experience was nil. Grocery sacker, delivery boy, beggar, pickpocket . . .

Simone stood up. "While you two discuss business, if you'll excuse me, I'll swim. It was nice to see you again, Mike."

"Thanks, Simone," he said, wondering if his embarrassment showed. He stood when she did and in his haste, he knocked over his glass of tea.

"Aw, Jesus!" he said, feeling clumsy as he yanked up the glass and tried to catch the ice cubes.

"Just leave it alone. Hannah will bring you another drink," Simone said, picking up a towel to blot up the spilled tea.

Mike burned with embarrassment and didn't want to face either one of them. He shouldn't have come; nothing was going right. What had made him think a man like Ben Holloway could use his services?

"I'm sorry," he mumbled.

The maid reappeared with another glass of tea. She wiped off the table and took the empty glass away.

"Don't worry about the tea," Simone said gently and winked at him.

He was awed. The wink would be in his memory forever.

"What kind of jobs have you held?" Ben asked as if nothing had happened.

"I've sacked groceries, delivered papers, run errands . . ." Mike replied.

Simone stepped out of her shorts, yanked off the tank top and walked toward the deep end of the sparkling pool. Mike was paralysed. She wore two tiny strips of electric blue cloth, and he had never viewed such a perfect female body. She was a marvel, the suit barely hiding anything from her enticing, jiggling bottom to her full, upthrusting breasts. She jumped into the deep end with a spray of water and vanished from sight.

"How old are you?"

"Eighteen," he said bemused. Simone surfaced, wiping the water away from her face, her wide, dark eyes focusing on him before she began to swim in short choppy strokes.

"I need someone to work in the yard. Would you like to do that on Saturdays and after school, full-time during the summer?"

"Yeah, sure!" Mike replied eagerly.

"I have a gardener, Stanley, who comes daily in summer, three times a week in winter. He cares for the pool and the yard. He has a helper most of the year and has had two men working until recently. I'll tell him you'll be here tomorrow. Be here at eight o'clock in the morning."

"Yes, sir! Thanks. I appreciate the job," Mike said, trying to avoid watching Simone but failing. She swam across the deep end of the pool.

"Don't you want to know what you'll get paid?" Ben asked dryly.

"What? Oh, yeah, sure."

"Fifty cents an hour above minimum wage to start."

"Jeez! That's great!" Mike said with enthusiasm. His other jobs had started at minimum wage or less. "Thanks, Mr. Holloway," he said, wondering how much older Holloway was than his wife, estimating a good twenty years. Simone had to be closer to Mike's age than her husband's. She looked about twenty-four or twenty-five.

"You'll have to work or out you go," Ben said pleasantly, but the coolness in his blue eyes confirmed what he was saying.

"You bet! I'll work my butt off for you."

"You don't have to do that. Just whatever Stanley wants."

"Yes, sir."

There was a moment of silence while Ben Holloway drank the last of his tea. Mike watched Simone until he realized Ben Holloway was waiting for him to go. He stood up, carefully avoiding his half-full glass of tea. "Thank you, sir."

"Sure. See you here tomorrow. Report to the kitchen door, and Hannah will tell you where to find Stanley."

"Yes, sir. Thanks."

"You can go out the gate and you won't have to go through the house," Ben said standing up and peeling away the towel. For a moment Mike noticed his new employer had a lean body and powerful muscles. There was no fat on him in spite of the luxury surrounding him. Once again Mike remembered Ben's quick reflexes when confronting the thieves. He wondered once more about Ben's background.

"Thanks again," Mike said, and turned to wave at Simone as he left.

She waved back and as he watched, Ben made a long dive into the pool. Mike prayed she swam every day, all day long. Yard work. He hadn't mowed a lawn or pulled a weed in his life. He glanced at the rows of blooming flowers by the gate. "See you little buggers tomorrow," he said to the flowers and let himself out of the black iron gate. As it clanked shut, he glanced between the bars at the pool. "See you too, honey," he said softly.

"What's that?" a male voice snapped, and Mike spun around to face a tall, freckled man in overalls and a straw hat.

"I said I'll see you too, if it's sunny. I start work tomorrow for the Holloways. I'm Mike Stanton," he added, offering his hand.

"Yeah, I'm Stanley," the man said, giving Mike a crushing shake. "Be here at eight sharp. Go around the east side of the garage and you'll find me."

"Yes, sir!"

"Ever tended flowers before?"

"Not too many, but I'm willing to learn!" Mike said, putting eagerness into his voice, his gaze going over the Porsche and Lincoln parked on the drive.

"Yeah."

Mike started down the drive.

"Sonny, watch out for the dogs," Stanley called.

"Sure," Mike answered, bemused over Simone, astonished that he had a job so easily.

He sauntered down the drive, whistling a tune. Tomorrow and tomorrow and tomorrow—Simone in the pool, Simone in the yard, Simone sunning on the patio. He would breathe air that was sweet and clean, and he could explore a house he hungered to know. Spinning images of Ben Holloway asking him to join them for dinner and of Simone inviting him to swim, Mike sauntered past mansions that fired his imagination with chimeras of grandeur. He thought about pulling off the scraps of Simone's bikini to reveal a blue tiny triangle that barely covered fleshy globes that were smooth and golden. When he began to get an erection, he dismissed his fantasies. He was sure that everything in his life was taking a turn for the better. He was on the road to success now!

Leech was off his back so there were no more five-dollar payments, no more constant worrying, no more fear for Claude. He should have killed Leech, but he just couldn't deliberately squeeze the last breath of life out of the bastard! He hadn't seen or heard of him since the fight.

No more Darrel Haywood nagging at him at the A & P and causing him trouble! He had a new, exciting job—one that held endless possibilities. He laughed and pulled a wisp of Spanish moss down out of his pathway, ducking his head as he passed under a low branch of an oak. Everything was better, much better.

Twenty-eight hours later the same walk home was twice as long, but until he was paid, he didn't want to spend a cent on the streetcar that would save him part of the trip. He was exhausted from the yard work and he hadn't glimpsed Simone once the whole day. The yappy little dogs were almost as big a pest as Darrell Haywood, but he thought tomorrow would be better. A week later, he wondered if he had lost his mind. Every muscle ached from carrying bags of fertilizer, rocks, and from digging up trees. He planted trees. He was a damned tree mover! He hadn't known it would take the muscles of Samson to make minimum wage plus fifty cents an hour and grow petunias!

Added to that was the long walk to and from the Quarter. His old job at the A & P was beginning to look better to him. Nevertheless he ran part of the way and walked the rest to the Holloway's mansion after school. But he could only walk all the way home and at a far slower pace unless he was lucky enough to hitch a ride. After a few weeks he walked *and* jogged on the return. Gradually his muscles stopped aching, and he began to fill out. And to his delight, Simone did come out to swim while he was tending pots of hibiscus around the pool. She was as easy to talk to as any of the girls at school, but she was one thousand times better looking!

Ben Holloway had it all—and Mike's determination to rise in life compounded. He wanted a home like Holloway's and all the other trappings money could buy: the Porsche, the phones, the clothes. Mike began to apply himself diligently at school and found it didn't take too big an effort. He paid close attention to everything Stanley told him, learning the names of trees and flowers, working harder than he had ever worked in his life. Like a sponge, he absorbed everything around him, trying to learn. And the more he talked to Simone, the more she became a friend. At night he would remember and indulge in fantasies in which Simone did all sorts of wonderfully erotic things to him. When school was out, he worked full-time Monday through Friday.

One July afternoon he came home to find Vangie frying burgers. Smoke filled the tiny apartment that had shrunk in size when he had to compare it daily with the Holloway mansion; threadbare spots in the furniture became noticeable to him. Dressed in a yellow halter and yellow shorts, she had her brown hair tied up behind her head. Even so, she looked hot and sweat beaded her brow.

"Hi. Smells good. I think I can eat four," he said, opening the refrigerator and bending down to see what he could find inside. He took out a bottle of milk, uncapped it, and drank it all.

"You get two. You're getting real muscles," she remarked, eyeing him. "Where's Claude?"

"I don't know."

"I guess he's with Bobby. I'm going out after dinner."

"I hope where it's air-conditioned."

"Oh, God, yes! Wash your hands and slice an onion."

"Sure."

They ate watching the evening news on television, then he cleaned up the few dishes while she dressed.

"Claude ought to be home by now."

"Yeah, but you know Claude. He could be reading a book somewhere and lose all track of time. Zip me up." As she crossed the room, he realized his mother was still a good-looking woman with a slender, shapely figure and thick brown hair. She stopped and waved her hand. "Whoo, you need a shower!"

"That's no news," he answered, pulling up the zipper to her flowered dress.

Someone knocked on the door, and she motioned to Mike. "You go bathe, and I'll go to the door. No need your causing the guy to faint."

"I'm going," he said without rancor. She never bothered him too much or too long. When he emerged from the shower with a towel tied around his middle, she was gone. Claude wasn't home, and the first glimmer of worry struck him. He glanced outside at the dusky sky. Soon it would be dark and it was a rule that Claude was to be home by dark. It was an order that Claude faithfully kept as he did the other rules in his life.

Dressed in jeans and a T-shirt, Mike roamed the streets until long after dark. When he returned home, the empty apartment gave him a cold stab of fear. Fighting a growing panic, Mike returned to Bourbon Street, searching until he found someone who had seen Claude talking to Leech near the Old Absinthe House.

Mike went straight to the police, striding into the lighted building. He knew some cops; more of them had known Brett. They went to work as soon as they had taken the scanty information he could provide. He told them about his fight with Leech.

Detective Clayton clasped him on the shoulder, his black

eyes full of concern. "Mike, don't try to wring anything out of Leech if you find him. Call us. Let us handle it."

Unable to promise anything, Mike glared at him.

"You don't want to go to prison. We'll work hard, but I want your word that you'll leave Leech to us. If you want our cooperation, you give us some."

"Yeah, okay," he said, wondering if he could keep the promise if he found Leech. "I'll try."

"Don't try, dammit. Keep your hands off him!"

With cold panic gnawing at him, Mike left the station, searching the bars and hotel lobbies, the joints and shops that stayed open, trying to get some clue about Claude. Music and noise was shrouded by a haze of pain while fear became an execrable monster.

At seven in the morning as sunshine dispelled a mist that filled the Quarter, Mike found a pay phone and called Stanley to tell him that he wouldn't be reporting to work because Claude was missing. Stanley offered sympathy, and Mike returned to prowling the streets, using what little money he had to try to bribe people into talking about Leech's whereabouts.

That evening a policeman on a motorcycle spotted Mike. Turning in a circle, the cop pulled alongside the curb where Mike waited.

Mike took one look at his grim face and wanted to scream with hurt and rage. "He's dead, isn't he?"

The policeman nodded. "I'm sorry, son. A fisherman found a body back in a bayou. It's a hell of a remote place, but the description fits. We need you to identify the body."

"Then you don't know you've found Claude," Mike whispered, clutching at the faint hope.

"No, we don't until someone identifies the corpse. Your mother isn't home."

"I'll go," Mike said woodenly. His mother hadn't been home since dinner last night—yesterday evening seemed like years in his past. He climbed on the back of the cycle and they left. Wind battered his face as he stared ahead. Seldom in his life had he prayed, having little belief, but he prayed now that the body wasn't Claude's. Memories flashed through his mind of his brother—playing a practical joke on him, playing ball on the street.

"Please, God," he whispered, knowing the wind would catch his words, and the cop couldn't hear him.

They stopped at the station where he changed to a squad car. They took Highway 90 southwest into St. Charles Parish, then dropped south along the flat bayous where he had been born. Sedge and palmetto in opaque green water crowded the narrow roadway. Like silent observers, tall cypress and tupelo lined the road, their dark shapes swept by headlights. Yesterday morning at this same time, everything had been all right.

They turned on a shell road, one that would be under water whenever there was a heavy rain. A muskrat picked its way, scurrying out of sight at the roar of the squad car.

The thought flashed in Mike's mind that whoever had brought a body out here probably thought the chances of its being discovered were zero. But Cajun fishermen hunted out the secluded crannies where the fishing was good. The squad car bounced through small puddles and turned a bend.

Up ahead the path was blocked by police cars, and Mike felt sick. The cars appeared incongruous in the swamp with the glare of their lights playing over dark water. Praying silently, Mike stepped out of the car with the eerie red light of the police car shining on him. Never in his life had he dreaded a moment as much as this one. He saw the ambulance with its flashing lights; the back door was open.

Detective Clayton separated himself from a cluster of policemen and came towards him. He clamped his hand on Mike's shoulder. "Sorry, Mike. And I'm sorry you have to do this, but we need an official identification."

"You think it's Claude?" Mike could barely hear his own words over a strange buzzing in his head. His fists knotted at his sides.

Clayton nodded. "I think so, son. Would you rather wait until we find your mother?"

"No," Mike replied stonily, jamming his hands into his pockets.

They walked around a car, and he saw the small sheet-draped body. Detective Clayton knelt down and pulled back the sheet.

Mike wanted to be dead too. He spun around, turning his back, the moment carved into his mind and soul and heart.

"Sweet Jesus, it's him," he said while hot tears coursed down his cheeks. He slammed his fist against the trunk of a police car, unaware of the pain that shot up his arm. "Dammit!"

"C'mon, Mike. You're not needed here."

"I want to ride with Claude." He hurt all over, wondering if he would survive the moment.

"C'mon, son," Clayton urged and took his arm, "I'll help you make the arrangements."

Mike jerked away, kneeling beside Claude to touch the body that felt solid, yet was colorless, lifeless. Hands lifted Mike up and led him away while he cried quietly.

In the car on the way back to town he got a grip on his emotions and sat staring out of the car, the surroundings as dark as his feelings. For the next twenty-four hours Mike felt as if he was in a daze. The parish handled the burial, and Claude was laid to rest in a plain pine box. Holding his mother's arm while she wept, Mike stood in stony silence beside the grave, determined he would get enough money someday to get the right kind of stone as a marker for the grave.

Then it was over, and the next day Vangie vanished with one of her men friends. Mike couldn't go back to work; he couldn't eat and he didn't want to talk to anyone. He spent three days in a silent rage, prowling through the Quarter hunting Leech to no avail. One morning while he sat in the empty apartment staring into space, he heard a knock. His first thought was that it might be Leech and Big John, and he clenched his fists, ready for a fight.

He opened the door and faced Simone. Her tailored navy silk blouse and slacks gave her a more somber appearance and her luminous dark eyes were filled with sympathy. "I'm sorry, Mike."

"Thank you for coming," he said woodenly, and she frowned. "Is your mother here? Stanley said you live with your mother."

"No, she's not here."

There was another long silence. "Can I come inside?"

"Oh, damn, Simone, I'm sorry. Come in." He stepped back, and she entered the narrow room with overstuffed second-hand furniture, a yellow chintz chair, a mahogany rocker with one arm missing.

Trailing a scent of perfume, she perched on the armchair while he sat on the gray-and-yellow striped sofa.

"Will your mother be home soon?"

"I don't know," he said, thinking Simone looked ridiculous in his home. It was like finding an orchid in a weed patch.

"Mike, can I help with anything?"

"No, but thanks. Thanks a lot for coming," he said, feeling awkward.

"When did you last eat?"

He blinked at her. The thought of food had hardly crossed his mind. "I don't know."

"Well, then it's time you do," she said and to his horror, she stood up and looked around.

"Jeez, Simone, my kitchen is a mess. You don't need to do anything."

"Don't be ridiculous! I can help."

"I can't eat," he snapped. "So forget it!"

She walked up and hugged him, and he wrapped his arms around her. "Some hurts are so bad," she said softly.

He didn't answer but he stood stiffly until she leaned back to look up at him. Her skin was perfection, her lashes dark and thick. "Have you taken care of his clothing and things? Would you like me to help you?"

"Naw, thanks," he answered numbly, not caring what happened.

"C'mon. We'll get it done," she said, taking his hand. They worked, bundling up Claude's meager belongings, and if she noticed the house was different from hers, or if she minded the shabby disorder in the room he had shared with Claude, she didn't show it. Each item of clothing brought memories, and Mike's chest was tight with pain. When they finished, she led him to the couch. "You sit right here while I fix you something to eat."

"I can't eat anything!"

She sat down beside him, her dark eyes wide and full of sympathy. "*Chéri*, you have to pick up your life and go on."

"Yeah, but not today."

She stroked his arm. "You look as if you've lost weight. You should eat."

"I will when I get hungry," he said, turning to look down at her. She was pressed to his side, her fingers moving back and forth on his forearm, her scent sweet and heady while her wide dark eyes seemed to pull him closer.

"Aw, damn," he said, turning to crush her to him. She felt warm, comforting. He held her, burying his face against her neck while she stroked his back. Suddenly the emotions damned up in him burst, and he cried against her shoulder. How much time passed, he never knew, but eventually he became aware of her as a woman. Her legs were pressed against his; her full breasts were crushed against his chest. She smelled wonderful. It was Simone in his arms, Simone who held him.

He turned his head to kiss her cheek. Her dark velvet eyes widened, and he wanted her desperately. His erection came swiftly, but when he slid his hand over her knee, she caught his wrist and gave a gentle shake of her head. "*Non, chéri.* I love Ben with all my heart . . . You and I were caught up in a moment that was a pull on emotions, both yours and mine. My little brother died when he was young, and I can imagine some of your hurt."

Trying to control his emotions, he sat in silence, assessing her designer blouse and slacks, the solid gold jewelry, thinking she was the most beautiful woman on earth.

"Someday perhaps, you'll comfort me in a moment of need. Now I'll fix you something to eat, and then I must go."

"I can feed myself."

Her dark eyes sparkled. "I insist." She poked his stomach with her forefinger. "You will blow away with the next big wind."

He grinned, and then realized it was the first he had smiled in days and it felt good.

They ate sandwiches on stale bread in his narrow living room and exchanged stories, and even more than when they had talked at her poolside, she was delightful company. She wasn't too sophisticated for him, nor did she seem bored by him.

"How'd you meet Ben?" he asked, curious about anything that concerned her.

"He was in Paris on business. He had a French client who wanted to exchange property there for property here."

"And? Did you have a job?"

She nodded her head. "I was a typist in my uncle's office."

Remembering how curious he had been when he had met her and how quickly she had acted with Ben at the robbery, he couldn't help but probe more deeply into her background.

"What kind of family did you have?"

Her dark eyes slid away, staring beyond him at the cracked wall. "My father worked in an auto factory and my mother was a secretary. She—"

"Bull," he said, watching her.

Her startled gaze met his, a flash of alarm appearing in her wide eyes.

"Your mother wasn't a secretary, Simone."

She looked away.

"Where'd you come from?"

"Lyon."

"And your father worked where?"

"An auto factory."

She was lying, and he didn't know how he knew, but he did. At the same time, he was sorry he had asked, because his questions had alarmed her, and the last thing he wanted to do was hurt her. He leaned across the scarred table. "Sorry I asked. You don't have to answer to me. It's none of my damn business."

"You're very discerning," she said, studying him while her frown disappeared. "Someday, Mike, you'll make some woman happy. And you'll probably break many hearts along the way. I was a prostitute when Ben met me." She waved her hand. "I had a family much like yours and I tried to care for my younger brother, but I couldn't, just as you couldn't protect Claude. My father did work in an auto factory once before he drank himself to death. Now how did you guess?"

"The night we met—when you tripped the thief, I wondered then about your background. Most women aren't accustomed to violence. Especially wealthy, sheltered women. They don't react like a cat ready to fight."

"I'm relieved! I thought maybe something more significant had slipped." She laughed and put her hand over her heart. "I've been so careful for Ben's sake." She laughed again. "Darling Mike! Don't frown. Ben knows about my past."

"I shouldn't have pried," he said, jolted by her admission.

"At first I was terrified the truth would be discovered and ruin Ben. Gradually I decided I was safe—and now look! You guessed the truth! But no one knows except Ben and now you. I trust you both."

"Don't worry that I guessed." Feeling inordinately pleased that he had her trust, he leaned back in his chair and folded his arms across his chest. "How does it feel to be wealthy?"

"Just exactly like you think it would feel. Maybe better to someone who comes from the gutter. How else did you know? It wasn't just that one thing, was it?"

"That was enough. A hunch." He would never tell her that her easy friendship with him added to his suspicions.

They spent the next two hours talking, and he felt as if he were with someone his own age. He was startled to learn she was thirty-two years old; she looked ten years younger, and in spite of her solemn declaration about her love for Ben, Mike wove erotic fantasies about her that he hoped would come true. With his arm draped across her shoulders he walked to the door where he turned her to face him.

"I owe you something for today," he said, looking into her black eyes.

"You needed someone, and I was here," she answered. "You're old beyond your eighteen years, Mike."

He shrugged, studying her mouth, wanting to kiss her.

She stood on tiptoe and kissed his cheek. "You will make some woman very happy," she whispered with a faint trace of her French accent. "But we'll always be friends, eh?"

"Always. If you ever need—" He laughed. "Hell, you'll never need anything with Ben."

"No, I won't need anything," she replied. "That's part of why I love him so much, but I wanted to come visit you today to let you know I'm your friend."

Something constricted around his heart with the way she made the statement, and he knew Simone was a friend in the fullest sense of the word.

"You're special, *chéri*, and I'm sorry about Claude," she said softly, and then she left.

He stood watching her until the dark green Porsche raced around the corner out of sight. He closed the door and looked at the sagging sofa, remembering holding Simone, convinced she was the most beautiful, wonderful woman in the world.

Soon thereafter Mike bought his first car: a six-year-old Chevrolet, four-door, vinyl upholstery, with forty thousand miles. It was cheap, but there would be no more walking to the Holloways'. One sunny morning a week later when he was only blocks from Ben's house, he noticed a police car behind him. In seconds as Ben's house loomed in sight, a red light flashed, and Mike pulled to the curb. Two cops climbed out, walking up to him.

"Is this your car?"

"Yes, sir."

"May I see your vehicle registration."

Mike leaned across the seat and opened the glove compartment and stared at the empty space in dismay. "My registration slip should be here," he said dumbly.

"Will you step out of the car. You're under arrest for possession of a stolen vehicle."

For the next few minutes, Mike was in a daze, answering questions automatically, stunned over the absence of his registration, the charges, the possibility he had bought a hot car. He glanced to his right to see Ben striding toward them, his brows arched in curiosity. Beneath the shade of an oak Ben paused to talk to one of the officers while Mike continued to answer questions, telling the officer where he purchased the car and details of the exchange.

After a brief consultation with a policeman, Ben motioned

to Mike. "I told them I wanted to talk to you a moment. Step over here."

Mike followed him a few feet down the walk. He stared at the police car, hearing the voice come over the car radio, as Ben faced him. "That's a stolen car you're driving."

"I bought it. I didn't steal it."

Seeing the anger and disbelief in Ben's eyes, Mike raised his jaw. "Just because I'm poor doesn't mean I steal!"

"The evidence is sitting ten yards away. Who sold it to you?"

"A man in a bar," Mike answered, realizing how flimsy his answer sounded. "I didn't steal it."

"Do you have a record?"

"No," Mike snapped, biting off the word. "I got caught once stealing apples when I was eight, but they didn't book me," he said with cynicism. His mind began to function, racing over what had happened and how it had happened. A cold premonition of disaster rose like fog coming in off the Gulf.

"I've been set up," he whispered, more to himself than anyone else. He glanced over his shoulder to see the cops waiting. Mike drew a deep breath. He felt trapped and only one person would be interested in going to so much trouble to have him removed—Leech. Mike wanted to slam his fist into the car as anger welled up in him; he fought to keep his voice normal.

"I bought this car from a man in a bar on Bourbon. I paid cash for it and it was legal," Mike told Ben defiantly. "Someone stole my registration." He could see the contempt and disbelief in Ben's face, augmenting his own frustration.

"The police are waiting," Ben said with unconcealed disgust. "I asked for a minute to talk to you," he said, stepping away.

Haunted by his background, Mike stood in silent anger. He was poor and he had needed a car, so Ben and some of the men accepted his guilt without question. It rankled that Ben had asked if he had a record, simply assuming it was a possibility. He caught up with Ben, who was striding back to his driveway.

"Ben, do you want me to collect my pay now?" He faced Ben squarely and saw the searching look in the older man's eyes.

"You can get your pay later."

"Yeah, sure thing, Ben!" he snapped, striding angrily back to the police.

Ben stared at the kid, seeing the defiance and burning anger in his demeanor. He thought Mike was lying, but if he was, he was putting on a damned good act. It occurred to Ben that he might have been too hasty in condemning Mike simply because it seemed likely that he had stolen the car. He was a tough, impecunious street kid, and Ben wouldn't put car theft past him, yet he had worked diligently for him for months. It was the deadly burning rage of innocence, not guilt, that showed in Mike's blue eyes and rang in his voice. Mike could get help from the the Indigent Defender Board, but Ben thought about how Mike had come to his rescue that night in the Quarter. He headed into the house to call his lawyer.

At the parish jail seated in a plain room at a scarred table, Mike stared at the slight, trim man facing him. Gerald Norwich Stein, attorney-at-law. Mike didn't care if Ben thought he was innocent or guilty at this moment. All he could feel was an overwhelming sense of relief, because his chances of being cleared had just jumped a hundredfold as far as he was concerned.

Looking as if he weighed less than one hundred pounds dripping wet, Gerald Stein, Ben's attorney, was not an awesome or inspiring figure, but when Mike looked into the lawyer's intense black eyes, he felt reassured.

"Now tell me everything that happened. Everything you remember," Stein said in a raspy voice.

"Sure," Mike said, relating the few facts while Jerry Stein made unreadable squiggles on a pad of paper.

"Go over it again," Jerry said when he was through. "This depredator—Leech, you call him—tell me about him, and go through the night of the sale."

"I've been thinking about it ever since they brought me in. I think it was Leech who stole the registration. He saw the car the first night I brought it home. He may have set me up to buy it. I hang out in that bar.''

"Why would he go to all that bother and risk?"

"Because he knows I'll kill him if I get my hands on him." In a few terse sentences, Mike told him about Claude. "If Leech can put me away for any time at all, it would help him. Then I might not ever come back. I'd be willing to stake everything that he did it. How long will I have to stay in jail?'' Mike asked while Jerry wrote.

"You'll leave with me shortly."

"I will? *Tonight*?"

"Yes," came an impassive answer.

"Then, man, why don't we leave now?'' Mike loathed the jail more than anywhere he had been in his life. The realization that he could get out but wasn't out, was intolerable.

"We might as well talk here. You think Leech murdered Claude?"

"Yes."

"If you could find substantial evidence, it would help eliminate a spot of trouble in your life."

"It sure as hell would," Mike said dryly, thinking no one had ever referred to Leech as a spot of trouble.

"Tell me about that night again."

Mike started over until he got to the moment of paying the money. He looked up. "Diego was there."

"Excuse me."

"Diego. I don't know if he has another name," Mike said, his heart beginning to thud with an undercurrent of excitement. "I started to pay the man and looked up and saw Diego leaning against a lamppost watching me. He'd been in the bar and he'll steal anything that isn't nailed down. Diego is a petty thief, a pimp, a pusher. I told him to beat it, I was buying a car. We exchanged words. He asked, 'That going to be yours?' I told him yes. He wouldn't go, so I counted out the cash in front of him."

"Sorry. You could bring in fifty witnesses, but no one will believe them," Jerry said, seeing the flare of hope in Mike's eyes. A witness wouldn't ever forget Mike Stanton. He had the bluest eyes fringed with thick brown lashes that Jerry had ever seen. That combined with the scar down the left side of his face made him distinctive. And until a few moments ago, Mike's eyes had burned with anger that was as fiery as Jerry had ever seen.

"That's just it," Mike persisted, leaning closer across the table. "I think Diego is an undercover street cop."

"Sorry, Mike," Jerry said gently, knowing the kid was grabbing at every straw in the wind. "You'd never recognize the real McCoy."

"Diego does all the things I told you, pretty thievery, pimping. I live on the street. You get used to seeing people, watching what they do. And you develop a sense for things. Diego gets around. He was in the bar, close enough to hear when the guy was talking about the car. Then when the money exchanges hands—there he was leaning against the lamppost. I had a friend who was a stoolie. I know how he operated. It's just a hunch, but it's one I've had for a long time about Diego."

"Don't get your hopes up," Jerry said, looking down at his notes. "Clayton. Is that the name of the cop who's your friend?"

"Yes."

"I'll talk to them about bond for you, and then we'll be on our way."

"Mr. Stein, thanks a lot. I'll get my bill paid. It may take me a while, but I'll do it."

"You won't have to. Ben Holloway is paying the bill. I'd say you're a lucky person, Mike."

"If I beat this, it'll give Leech a shock."

Jerry Stein didn't doubt him for a second.

Late that night Mike wandered down the darkened blocks of Toulouse toward the river, the lights of Bourbon behind him. He was on foot, minus his car, which had been impounded as stolen property. Somewhere in the Quarter was his nemesis. He walked in long strides, yet with the quietness of a cat. Since Vangie had the apartment locked because she was entertaining a man, Mike didn't have anywhere to go for the night, so he hunted around for Diego. Jerry Stein had little comment on Diego, and Mike knew Jerry had dismissed his suggestions as useless.

He moved through the crowd in a smoky bar, his eyes scanning everyone, searching for Diego, who seemed to have vanished. Mike stepped back outside, and halfway down the block he spotted a sleek black Lincoln cruising toward him. It whipped over to his side of the street and the door opened.

"Mike, get in," Jerry Stein said, closing the door behind him.

"Charges against you have been dropped. The D.A. said it was insufficient evidence, but that was the official statement. I talked to your friend, Detective Clayton, and told him what you said about Diego. You were right and that's all we needed. He did see you buy the car." For the first time since Mike had met him, Jerry Stein smiled.

When Mike faced Ben in his office on Monday he felt a strong surge of gratitude. Dressed to leave town, Ben wore a charcoal suit with gold links flashing in his snowy cuffs, a conservative navy and gray tie with a perfect Windsor knot.

"I was a little rough on you the morning the cops came."

Mike shrugged, willing to forgive Ben anything. "It's understandable. I'm not one of the Brady Bunch, and I don't have two nickels to rub together. Thanks for paying the bills for Mr. Stein. I know it was Leech. I'm putting pressure on him."

"Don't get yourself killed. Leech has murdered once."

"Yeah. I'll be careful, but I'm going to nail him."

Ben's eyes narrowed. "Then get him with your brains and not your fists. You were smart enough to catch on to Diego. Jerry Stein said that's as rare as ice in an oven. Use your head. Your fists will only cause more trouble." Ben looked as if he were debating something, and Mike waited in silent curiosity.

"Look, I wasn't born to all this. I came from the wrong side of the tracks in Buquoi, a little town west of here. My old man lost a leg working for the railroad and never did do much after that. I had five older sisters who scattered God knows where. I was a poor kid and worked from the time I was nine years old. I got here by using my brains." While Ben talked, blue eyes faced him without a trace of surprise.

"I wondered about you."

Ben's brows arched. "I'll be damned!" Inwardly Ben laughed at himself. Only once or twice in his life had he admitted his past and he had debated whether to tell Mike. He should have saved himself the worry. "Simone told me you're sensitive. Jerry said you're alert."

"I guess I just notice things. And wonder about them,"
Mike added with a grin, pleased that Simone had paid him
the compliment.

"What was it that made you wonder? Very few people
know about my background."

"That night of the robbery. You acted fast like someone
accustomed to rough situations."

Ben grinned. "Yeah, but I should have known better
than to walk through that area so late at night. You become cushioned and accustomed to protection and you
forget."

"I don't think I'll ever forget," Mike said.

"Just use your head. You have one, and it's a lot better
than your fists." Ben glanced at his watch. "I have a plane
to catch."

"Sure. Thanks, Ben." Mike left the house, going outside
to dig a new bed, working vigorously, thankful to be away
from the stinking jail that had disgusted him, thankful to be
in the hot sunshine, to use his muscles and breathe fresh air,
thinking about what Ben had said. He paused, leaning on the
hoe, his gaze sweeping over the mansion. Ben had come from
poverty and now he had all this. *Use your head, not your
fists*, Mike thought.

For the next few weeks he thought about Ben's advice,
and then he knew what he wanted to do.

3

New Orleans
April 1972

Talia Wade shook her short blond hair away from her face
and licked the melting chocolate ice cream cone in her hand
as she walked beside Patsy Turner, her best friend from high

school. Together they sauntered from school down a broad, tree-shaded avenue in Metairie, a suburban area of New Orleans.

"Come over to my house," Patsy said, a sparkle in her dark eyes. "I want to show you something."

"My mother plays bridge today and this is Mandy's day off," Talia replied, thinking aloud. "I guess it's all right."

"Super!"

Talia strolled along in contentment. On her mother's bridge afternoons and when the maid had the day off, the Wade family would go to the country club for dinner, and Talia liked to eat out.

The girls went around the Turners' two-story colonial house to the back yard, walking down a brick lane between banks of pink azaleas. Spring in New Orleans was her favorite time of the year. A week ago she had turned eighteen; soon she would graduate, and she was eager for college. Thunder rumbled as a bank of gray clouds loomed over treetops to the south.

The Turners' green kitchen smelled of freshly baked cookies, and Patsy tossed down her books to rush to the counter. "Chocolate cookies! Let's get some pop, and then I want to show you something. I have a surprise!"

She poured fizzy soda pop over ice, and then they went upstairs to Patsy's blue bedroom.

"Look," Patsy said, pushing aside stuffed bears as she reached under her bed to produce a shoe box. "Mary Jane. Pot."

Shocked, Talia stared at the contents that looked like a handful of dead leaves from the yard. "I don't think we should. I don't even know how to smoke a cigarette," she said.

"Don't be silly. We can't go to college and not know anything about pot! It's bad enough to be a virgin."

"I have to go home in a little while. Suppose it makes me nutty or something?"

"We have hours before you have to go. C'mon, Talia. Let's try it!" Patsy urged while she got out a cardboard toilet paper roller and cut a hole in it.

"What are you doing?"

"Making a pipe. They told me how," she answered as she concentrated, punching tiny holes in a scrap of foil, then inserting it into the hole in the roller. She poured the marijuana into the foil carefully.

"Who told you how? Where'd you get this?"

"From Jason Bo Reems. He sells it under the stairs down by the cafeteria." She blew out a match, raising the roller. "Close up one end and then take a drag on the other, just like a pipe," she said, demonstrating what to do before passing it to Talia.

"It smells like burned toast," Talia remarked dubiously. "I don't know about this. I have to walk home."

"You can walk home. Don't be ridiculous! You just don't have any curiosity! You're such a fraidycat!"

"All right." With a last suspicious look at the makeshift pipe, Talia followed Patsy's example, coughing after the first drag.

"Try it again. I know it'll get better," Patsy said, taking the roller from Talia for another puff.

Two hours later, feeling much more like a woman of the world, Talia told Patsy she had to go home.

The last faint traces of euphoria from the pot were wearing away, replaced by hunger, and she quickened her step. The sky was dark with black clouds while a sudden gust of spring wind cut through the sultry heat like a knife. Wind whipped at her legs as she carried her books and hurried along. She went to the side of the garage where they kept a house key hidden. As the first big, cold drops of rain splattered on her face, making splotches on her blue cotton dress, she opened the garage door.

She stepped inside and almost missed the note until she noticed it lying on the floor in front of the door. Recognizing her father's handwriting, she picked up the paper, at first unable to comprehend what she read.

Talia:
Destroy this note after you read it. I want you to know, because you're the strong one in the family.

She paused, looking up in confusion. Through the open door to the adjoining room that was a workshop for her father, the tips of her father's shoes dangled in the air. She stiffened and dropped her books, crumpling the note in her hand as she moved closer, feeling a scream rising in her throat.

"Daddy? *Daddy*?"

4

Over two hours later, Talia locked the door to the bathroom and retched again, gagging as her stomach heaved. She wiped her face with a cold washcloth, staring at her image briefly, her bulbous red nose, red eyes, her hair a tangle, tears coming as if they would never stop.

With shaking fingers she dug in her pocket and withdrew the crumpled note to read it again. Pain and guilt engulfed her as she skimmed it.

Talia:
Destroy this note after you read it. I want you to know, because you're the strong one in the family. I took some money from the office. I hope all three of my girls understand I did this for you. I meant to put it back. There is ten thousand dollars I have hidden away. Keep it. You may need it desperately, and it won't begin to repay the amount I took. The ten thousand is in a coffee can buried under the north side of the apple tree. Be strong. Remember always that I love you.
All my love, Daddy.

The police, neighbors, and friends filled the house. Rebecca had arrived home from college twenty minutes ago and was sobbing in her room. The paramedics took away the body while the police continued their endless questions. Her mother's older brother, Beau, and his wife, Gloria, had arrived. Amidst all the turmoil, Talia cried quietly, feeling her world crumble around her, trying to cope with the painful knowledge that the father she loved would no longer be part of her life. She debated with herself over her father's note. Should she dutifully give it to the police? Should she return the ten thousand dollars because it wasn't her father's to give to his family?

For a brief time the police had reacted as if it might have been murder instead of suicide until a detective had contacted G. R. Baker, head of her father's firm, Dyer, Baker, and Gray, Engineering Consultants, Inc. According to the note, ten thousand dollars was only a small part—how much had he taken? One minute she decided she would return the money, the next she wanted to keep it. She washed her face, squared her shoulders, and went out to put her arm around her mother's thin shoulders while Kate cried.

The next day Talia selected the casket, made the arrangements for the service, and went with her mother to the bank. The following morning when the detectives returned, the family discovered the full extent of her father's malefaction. He had embezzled over four hundred thousand dollars from his company. Talia's head buzzed while her mother wept and the detectives waited with grim expressions. Four hundred thousand dollars was an incredible amount. Stunned, her gaze went over their elegant living room with its fine oil paintings and antiques, the expensive furniture, the fancy wallpaper. Her mother's dress had cost over one hundred dollars. They had taken wonderful vacations; they had done magical things, gone to the races at the Fair Grounds Track or Evangeline Downs, gone to Audubon Park, to the theater with her father. At least once a month he had surprised them all with gifts, beaming with happiness as they thanked and hugged him. But he had paid for it with four hundred thousand dollars of the company's money!

The quiet service was held and afterward a few friends came by the house, but the people who called were dwindling as the news spread of her father's perfidy. Each day brought new aftershocks of the disaster. On Talia's first day back at school, she was stunned by the change in her classmates, by their stares and whispers. Even Patsy wasn't as friendly. Talia ate lunch alone from then on and as she walked home, she felt the crushing weight of shame upon her. She straightened her shoulders, refusing to be beaten down by tragedy as her mother had been. If she had lost friends over her father's actions, then they weren't true friends anyway. Her step quickened, and she refused to dwell on the changes, but they confronted her at every turn. She learned their house was mortgaged, and they would have to move because they couldn't pay the huge monthly payments. It was put on the market and sold within the week. The maid, as well as the gardener, had to go.

Kate seemed unable to cope with the simplest task so Talia cooked meals. As she made patties and put hamburgers on to fry, Rebecca came into the room.

"I hate this!" Rebecca fumed, swinging her head, jiggling her thick jet-black curls. "Tomorrow I'm going back to college."

"We need to talk about that, Rebecca. About what we'll do. I don't think Mom can handle this alone."

Rebecca's dark eyes glared at her defiantly, her full red lips closed in a pout. "I'm finishing this semester."

"You have a month until it's out for the summer, so if possible, you should finish. I'll get a job now after school. You can get a job as soon as your term is over."

"Oh, Lord, I hate this! How could he do this to us!"

"Dad probably took every penny just for us," Talia said.

"You know they said he had lost tons of money betting on horses. He loved the races, and he loved to gamble."

Talia didn't argue because more recent evidence indicated that their father had indeed lost large sums at the track.

"Mom could get a job now, and we might be able to go on," Rebecca said petulantly.

"You know Mom has never worked in her life and doesn't have any skills. Get the lettuce."

"Our mother can't do anything. I don't know how she had us! She just lies up there in bed in her room in the dark like she wanted to die too. She might as well be dead!"

"Rebecca, hush! She'll hear you."

"I don't care if she does," Rebecca snapped, raising her voice. "I hate this, and we didn't do a thing to cause it! I'm going out. This house is like a tomb!" She crossed the room to the empty canister where they had put the last three hundred dollars from the bank. Instantly Talia stepped in front of the counter to block Rebecca's path.

"That money has to last us until you and I get jobs!"

"Get out of my way!"

"Girls. What's happening?" came Kate's soft voice from the doorway. Her eyes had dark circles, and she had lost so much weight that her clothes hung loosely on her thin frame. Talia knew that Kate would never be able to hold the simplest job. Kate's hands shook, and she laced her fingers tightly together.

"We're trying to plan what we can do."

"Plans?" Kate repeated vaguely. "It's so dark at night."

Talia drew a sharp breath while she tried to ignore the rolling of Rebecca's eyes and her arched brows.

"We don't have much money left," Talia said quietly, ignoring Kate's remark about the night.

"Can you get a job, Mom?" Rebecca asked abruptly.

Kate winced as if someone had struck her; she ran her hand across her brow. "A job?" she murmured, looking confused. "I don't know what I'll do. I haven't ever worked. If only Mama and Papa were still alive."

Something twisted inside of Talia. She ran her hand across Kate's shoulders. "We'll worry about it later. Right now, I'm getting dinner, and Rebecca is going to help," Talia said matter-of-factly. "Come sit down."

"Are you going to get a job, Mama?" Rebecca persisted.

"We'll talk about it later," Talia rejoined emphatically. "You can pour the water."

"I'm not going to help!" Rebecca snapped. "You two can decide what you want to do! I'm sick of scandal, sick of this house and everyone in it!" She turned and ran from the house, banging open the back door and leaving it open in her flight.

The phone rang and Talia's attention shifted. She answered to hear Beau's cheerful voice, and pictured her handsome uncle with his golden hair. His eyes were hazel, startling against the skin he kept tan year-round. At forty-two, he was a year older than her mother, and Talia prayed he wanted to help them, but as he talked, she realized that his offers of help were vague, merely polite gestures and nothing more. When Talia replaced the receiver, she knew the decisions for the family rested squarely on her shoulders.

Pouring a large glass of brandy, Kate drifted from the kitchen after dinner without seeming to give a thought to washing dishes or cleaning, and Talia was surprised again at how little her mother was able to cope with chores. Kate was more helpless now than she had been when their father had been alive. She seemed wrapped in a panic that made her unable to function, and nothing could shake her out of it.

They had to move soon, but Talia needed to know if ten thousand was actually buried beneath the apple tree. That night she waited until all was quiet before she slipped outside.

Blackness enveloped her; crickets chirped, and tonight their cheerful sounds grated on her nerves. She slipped to the garage, pausing a moment as she realized she had to walk into her father's workroom. Memories returned of the last time she was there when she had found his body. She stared at the inky darkness beyond the door and her skin prickled. Taking a deep breath, she moved forward, feeling chilled to the bone in spite of the pleasant night.

Her hand closed around the smooth handle of the shovel. Beside it was a small hand spade. Stealthily she crept back to the apple tree and began to dig, praying the hidden canister with the ten thousand dollars really did exist. It took half an hour before she heard a clink and knelt, using the hand spade. Reaching down, her fingers touched the curved, smooth metal side of a can and she finished her task, removing the coffee can and replacing the dirt. She left the can beneath the tree and carried the tools back to the garage, setting them inside the garage until morning, loath to go into the workroom again. She started back to pick up the coffee can and stopped, because she faced someone leaning against the back of the house only yards from the can.

5

"Rebecca! What are you doing out here? You scared me!"

"The important question is, what are you doing, Talia? What's in the can?"

Wariness came over Talia. She knew Rebecca well, and if Rebecca discovered there was ten thousand dollars, she would want the money for herself. Talia tried to force a lightness into her voice.

"Just old trinkets buried long ago. When we move, I want to take them with me."

Rebecca laughed. "Let's go inside and look at the old trinkets!" she exclaimed in cynical tones, turning toward the kitchen.

With a sinking feeling, Talia followed her inside. Rebecca had turned on the soft light over the stove and she was peeling away binding tape that held the lid of the can in place. With a swift movement, Talia yanked it from her hands.

"You can't have it!"

"Trinkets are that important?"

"Yes. This is mine."

"I don't believe you. You're hiding something. If you don't tell me your secret, I'll scream this house down."

"Do you know what that will do to Mom?"

"It'll be on your head."

Anger blazed in Talia, because Rebecca would carry out her threat. Always pampered by Kate, Rebecca had thrown tantrums to get what she wanted since she was a baby.

"It's money Dad left, and I'll use it for all three of us as I see best for the family."

"How much?" Rebecca's dark eyes glittered with eagerness.

"I don't know until I count it, but you'd take it without leaving a dime for Mom."

"You hate me, don't you, Talia?"

"No, I don't hate you. You're my sister. But I think you're spoiled and sometimes you won't take responsibility when you should."

"I don't want responsibility! You're scared I'll take the money from you. You want it all to yourself—don't try to kid me! You slipped out in the dead of night to dig it up and keep it hidden for yourself!"

"This is all we have to live on! I have to save it."

"Crap! I don't believe you." With a lunge Rebecca grabbed the can. Talia hung on. They hadn't physically fought since they were children, and seldom then, and Talia was swamped with revulsion over what was happening between them, yet she felt a desperate need to keep the money.

Rebecca wound her fist in Talia's hair and pulled. Talia yelped and released her hold on the can. It fell on the kitchen table with a clatter, the lid popping off and money spilling out in the dim light, waded hundred dollar bills, a final gift from their father. Rebecca pounced to grab a handful, her black eyes glittering. "All this money buried out there! Is there more?"

"No, there's not!"

"You have to divide it into thirds. One third for Mom, a third for you, and a third for me."

"I intend to save it for all of us. I don't know what an apartment will cost. Suppose Mom gets sick?"

"Suppose, suppose! Suppose the world explodes! You're too practical. I want my third. Give it to me or I'll tell Mom and she'll make you give me a share."

"Don't worry her! You know she's having trouble."

"Trouble! She's as balmy as winds over the Gulf, but I'll tell her if you don't share. I'll scream until she's a wreck and it'll be your fault!"

Talia shook with rage. "Damn you, Rebecca! You don't care if you hurt someone as long as you get your way."

"That's right, little sister. Let's count the money." Rebecca pullsed out a chair and sat down, smoothing out the bills. Reluctantly Talia joined her until they had three stacks of bills. Rebecca snatched up one and jammed it into her pocket.

"Daddy should have left more, but this helps."

"I don't know how you can be so cold."

"She's the spoiled and selfish one, not me! She can't think of anyone except herself. The same with Beau. They love only themselves and Dad pampered her. You'll have to admit that!"

"I think you're being hard on her. She's never been selfish with us," Talia said quietly.

"Can you imagine our mother holding down a job?"

Talia couldn't, but she wouldn't admit it. "She may surprise you."

"Yeah, and turtles can fly. I'll take this money, use it for an apartment, maybe get a job, but I'm not coming back here!"

"You always run away from what you don't like. You'll spend that money and then you won't be able to afford an apartment."

"I'll find someone who can!" Rebecca swung her head and went striding out of the house, leaving Talia staring after her. Rebecca had taken to leaving in the dead of night, and Talia couldn't imagine where she went or what she did. And she knew it would be useless to ask. She couldn't keep her from going, so she ignored her worries about Rebecca.

Exhilarated by the money, Rebecca raced her red Corvette, a graduation gift from her father. She would be damned if she would live with Talia and Kate! They weren't going to pull her down with them. A fun life was ready for the taking if she had the nerve to reach out for it. Her father had taken what he wanted; he'd just had the misfortune to get caught. She parked in front of a popular bar.

Music wafted into the night, and inside, her eyes narrowed as she peered through the dusky interior, a haze of smoke hanging like a low cloud, until she spotted a table of people she knew. She started toward them, then glanced at the bar to see two men watching her. Swinging her hips as she walked, she went to the bar, her gaze raking past the men studying her. She spotted two likely men, swiftly trying to decide which might be the wealthiest, and then she slid onto the empty barstool beside him. She bumped his shoulder and when he turned she apologized.

"I'm sorry, mister."

"No harm done," he said, smiling, his gaze giving her a swift appraisal.

Money or not, he was attractive and she smiled.

"I'll buy you a drink."

"Thanks, no need," she replied, leaning towards him. "I have some friends and I'm going to join them."

"It isn't every day I get bumped by a beautiful woman. Let me get you a drink. And then you can join your friends."

She twisted around, crossed her legs and smiled more broadly at him. "You talked me into it," she said in her sultriest voice, noticing the slim gold watch on his wrist.

"I'm Greg Verrette," he said, smoothing straight black hair away from his face.

"Rebecca Wade," she replied, gazing directly into his brown eyes. In thirty minutes she led him to the table of people she knew and everyone made room for them. In two hours she left with him, settling back against the cushions of his Honda, listening to the roar of the motor as they sped to Greg's apartment. As soon as he closed the door behind them, he reached for her. She had one brief glimpse of a nice apartment before she turned to wind her arms around his neck and raise her mouth for his kiss.

Saturday morning Talia went apartment hunting, and in the afternoon she tried to get a job. Terrified at how quickly their funds might dwindle, she was dismayed at the cost of apartments and realized she would have to search for something cheaper than those she had first viewed. The next weekend she found a small apartment. It was in a frightening part of town, yet Talia wondered if it was dangerous, or simply seemed so because of the secure neighborhood where she had grown up. She drove home, determined to tell Kate the news, bracing for the multitude of arguments she knew would come. Most of the furniture and household goods were sold at auction, and the first of May Talia and Kate

moved. For the first three days, Kate kept to her room
and wept unconsolably. Talia knew she was drinking too
much, going out and buying her own supply when Talia
was away.

Beau found Kate a job selling perfume, and Talia's hopes
soared, but the first day Kate wandered off and went to the
park, and within three days she lost the job. In the meantime
Talia had a part-time job as a clerk at Inbau Drug. Rebecca
called occasionally; she had her own apartment and a job
selling cosmetics in a department store.

Saturday after work, when Talia returned home, the apartment was empty. Alarmed, Talia called friends, then drove
past the closest liquor stores. When she did not find her mother
she called Beau, who said he would come right over. While
she waited the phone rang and she answered. A deep male
voice asked if Katherine Wade lived at this address.

Panicky, Talia clutched the receiver tightly. "I'm her
daughter."

"I think the lady is upstairs in my hotel, and I had an idea
her family might be searching for her. She looks like a nice
lady. She's a little tipsy."

"Thank you for calling!" Talia exclaimed, relief pouring
over her. "I'll get there as quickly as possible if you'll give
me the address." She heard knocking on the door as she
scribbled an address and thanked the man again, hurrying to
the door to find Beau.

"A man just called. She's in some hotel," Talia said,
showing him the paper. "He said she was tipsy."

"Jeez, that address is a stretch of highway with dumps and
bait places," he said hesitantly, and Talia experienced a
twinge of impatience. "Maybe you ought to call the cops."

"I'm not calling cops to get Mom. I'm going to get her.
Do you want to come along?"

"Sure, kid," he said, going downstairs to her car, which
was parked at the curb in front of his. As they reached the
car he held the door, his gaze raking over her boldly and she
felt a prickle of embarrassment mingled with disgust. Drawing a sharp breath she climbed into the car and waited until
he sat down beside her.

From what the man had said, Kate was drunk, and Beau's

help might be needed. Talia showed him the address. "Where is this?"

"South out on Highway 90 to the east. We'll take the Causeway."

Afraid of what she would find, she tried to concentrate on driving.

"Don't worry, kid. She'll be all right." Beau squeezed her shoulder. She concentrated on weaving through traffic as she reached a freeway and pressed the accelerator, whipping along the Lake Pontchartrain Causeway. The day was stormy with waters rolling, spindrift foaming, the twenty-four-mile-wide lake blending with gray sky in the distance. Waves crashed against the pilings, breaking and seething, eddying beneath the wide strips of paving while traffic rushed along only feet above it. The car sped along through traffic on the Interstate, leaving New Orleans and dropping down toward the coast. On the fringe of a town she slowed. Metal buildings, concrete block structures, and frame houses lined the highway, along with gaudy neon signs, litter, and bait shops.

The hotel was little more than a two-story house. The sign, Shady Rest Inn, hung at an angle, swinging and creaking in the wind. Talia was two steps ahead of Beau, striding to the front desk. She punched a silver bell, and a short, balding man appeared, a cigar clenched between his teeth, a stream of smoke trailing behind him.

"I'm Talia Wade. What room is my mother in?"

"That woman's hung one on, but I knew when I looked at her, she was a classy dame, that she didn't come from the gutter," he said, retrieving a long, silver key. He didn't hand it over, but closed it in his thick fist and leaned on the counter. "I figured you wouldn't want her to get hurt. That you'd want to know about her and come get her."

"Yes. Thank you. What room is she in?"

"I figured you'd be grateful to hear about your mother."

"Give us the key," Beau interjected while Talia realized the man wanted a reward. She reached into her purse and pulled out a couple of bills, sliding them over the counter.

"Thank you for calling."

"Room two-oh-eight," he said, dropping the key on the counter and closing his hand over the bills.

Talia picked up the key and headed for the stairs, climbing rapidly, barely aware of Beau at her side, wondering what she would find. The narrow corridor reeked of a mixture of smoke and mildew. She knocked on a splintered door.

"Yeah?" a masculine voice asked.

As she put the key in the lock, Beau reached forward to grab her hand. "Hey, wait, kid. Don't just walk in."

The door was yanked open. A man in jeans and a T-shirt, his brown hair tousled, stood there staring at them. "What you want?"

"I'm looking for a woman. Katherine Wade."

The man looked at Talia, then at Beau. He jerked his head. "She's here. And I'm going." He strode past them down the hall. Talia stepped inside, drawing a deep breath. Whiskey fumes assailed her. Three empty bottles lay on the floor. Kate was in bed, a sheet pulled over her, her bare shoulders revealed. For an instant Talia experienced a rising panic that Kate might not be alive, but then Talia saw the sheet rise and fall with Kate's deep breathing.

"Jesus!" Beau said behind her, his voice full of disgust.

Talia ignored him, and worry gripped her as she moved to the bed. "Mom, it's me, Talia."

Kate stared at her a moment. "Talia?"

"I'll dress her. You wait outside," she told Beau. He glanced past her at Kate, then left, closing the door behind him.

"Talia?" Kate sat up, the sheet falling to her waist while she rubbed her head. "Why are you here?" Kate pulled the sheet to her chin. "Where am I?"

Talia had to fight back tears. "I've come to take you home."

"Home? Where's Mama? I want her."

"She's not here," Talia said, fear growing over Kate's condition.

"Beau's here. Ask him where Mama is? Is she home?"

"No. We're going to our home, Mom. The apartment—"

"I want to go to Mama's!"

"Just a minute," Talia said and left the room, closing the door quietly to turn to Beau. "She wants to go home to her mother and dad."

"Aw, Jeez," Beau said, frowning. "We had an aunt who wound up in the loony bin. You're too young to know her—"

"I know who you're talking about. Aunt Martha. Don't call it a loony bin, Beau," Talia said. "Maybe you should talk to Mom."

"When she's dressed, tell me, and I'll help. I think I can reason with her." He placed his hand on Talia's arm. "I doubt if you know—her last year in high school, the folks took her to a shrink."

"Mom?" she asked, shocked.

"Yeah. Then she went to college and met your dad. Darcy could always keep her in a good frame of mind. The problems vanished, the folks loved him, she loved him, he pampered her like a baby."

"That he did," Talia agreed, adjusting to the new revelation. "They were so happy."

"He seemed to be what she needed in every way. The folks thought she was over her problems, that it had just been part of growing up. Darcy was an anchor for her, keeping her sheltered and happy. Sorry, kid. You may be in for a rough time."

Talia went back into the room. Kate was dressed, looking fragile and lovely. It was impossible to think how she had spent the past few hours.

"Mom, let's go home to our apartment."

"I want to go home to Mama!" She backed against the crooked dresser with its cracked mirror that distorted her image.

"We can't now. We have to go to our home. Beau's waiting."

"Beau?" She ran her hand across her brow again in a gesture that tore at Talia. "If Darcy were here, he would take care of us."

"Mom. Come with me. We'll be home soon." Glancing around the small room once more, at the iron bed, the bare floor, Talia knew the memory of that room would remain with her forever. "Here's Beau. He came with me."

"Come along, Kate. I'll take you two pretty ladies home," Beau said with false cheerfulness. Talia drove because it was easier to keep occupied than to simply sit and think. Once they were back at Beau's house, Kate shut herself into the bathroom and soaked in a hot tub of water.

Talia moved numbly, aware she had to get Kate to a doctor as soon as possible. She knew Kate despised their apartment, that it upset her not only to lose their beautiful home, but to live in such squalid surroundings. Talia made an appointment on Monday with Kate's doctor, but in the meantime, she decided to try again to get Rebecca to move in with them. If there were two incomes, they could afford a better place to live, and it might help Kate's unstable condition.

Seizing the fleeting hope, Talia went to see her sister, on Friday after work, knowing she could plead better in person than over the phone. It was the first time she had seen Rebecca's apartment, and she hadn't been invited, but she intended to persuade her sister. She paused a moment when she stepped out of the taxi. It was a huge complex of apartments, and Talia had envisioned something new and fairly economical, but this was many cuts above that. It was landscaped with pines and flowering shrubs, and it was built of wood and brick and glass. Each apartment looked attractive from the outside. She walked up a narrow strip of concrete through an iron gate and leaned against the wall to wait for Rebecca to come home. In fifteen minutes Rebecca's red Corvette whipped into sight, slowing for the adjoining garage. Rebecca saw Talia and stopped, climbing out.

"Hi. I wanted to see you."

"Why didn't you call?" Rebecca asked. "I have a date in thirty minutes."

"I won't be long, but I need to talk."

Rebecca hurried to unlock the door. The apartment was tasteful and lovely, and far nicer than Talia would have dreamed Rebecca could afford.

"This is beautiful!"

"You didn't expect me to manage so well, did you? I told you I don't ever want to be poor again! Never!" She closed the door and seemed to relax. "Want a drink?"

"No, thank you," Talia said, receiving another shock. "You have a drink after work?"

"Don't sound so disapproving. Sometimes I do, sometimes I don't," she said, dropping her purse on a chair.

"I wanted to see if you would live with us. With your salary and mine combined—"

"No!" Rebecca answered, looking amused. "No way! I'm not giving up my independence to take you and Mom under my roof!"

Talia's temper rose to hear Rebecca's instant rejection. "What does this cost you?"

"More than you can afford!"

"Then how can you afford it? I know you're not making much more than I am at your job."

"I may be making a—"

She broke off as a key turned in the lock, and a masculine voice called, "Hon, it's me!"

"I'm in here, Greg," Rebecca said with a smile. In that moment Talia knew how Rebecca could afford the comfortable apartment as well as why she refused to consider moving. A man appeared, slender, tall, handsome with straight black hair combed neatly above pale brown eyes.

"I saw the car in front. You have company," he said, looking at Talia with curiosity, then focusing on Rebecca. He crossed to her to kiss her on the mouth, draping his arm around her shoulders to pull her close. "Who's the beautiful lady?" he asked, pushing black hair away from his face.

"Meet my sister, Talia. This is my friend, Greg Verrette."

"I'm glad to meet you," Talia said, still in shock, because it hadn't occurred to her Rebecca would live with a man to maintain her lifestyle. And she had never heard Rebecca mention a man named Greg.

When Talia rose to go, both insisted on her joining them for dinner. At the thought of returning to Beau's with her mother, who probably was unwilling to come to the table, and Gloria, who would sulk through dinner, Talia capitulated and went out with them first for happy hour, then dinner, then bar hopping. It was fun. When Rebecca was in a good mood, she could be charming and the life of the party. Greg was equally so, and they introduced Talia to people only a few years older than she. She called to tell her mother that she would be late and why, and she was happy to hear Gloria was with her mother. But she suspected that if she hadn't called, she wouldn't have caused anyone concern.

One thing she remembered long after the evening was over was that a friend of Greg's, Alicia, a blond, blue-eyed woman who was a junior in college, was earning her way through school as a nanny. She leaned close to Talia, talking in a loud voice that was difficult to hear in the crowded, smoky bar.

"It's a wonderful job. I live there, they feed me, they're good to me, they take me on trips, and treat me like one of the family. I get to go everywhere the kiddies go, and the pay is fabulous! I can go to school and then come home and take care of the kids, yet I'm free on alternate Friday and Saturday nights! Just get a rich family. That's the secret! The richer, the better," Alicia had said.

Talia remembered her words and mulled them over. Such a position would leave Kate alone, so she dismissed the notion from her mind, but she was searching for some way to go on to college in the fall. An education was the only hope for a change in her life and she clung to it like a falling man clinging to a ledge.

As Talia climbed out of the car in front of Rebecca's apartment, her sister suddenly hugged her. "Don't be mad at me! Greg is divine!"

Talia laughed, unable to resist Rebecca after the past hours of more fun than she had had in months. "I'll agree with you about Greg! Be careful, Rebecca."

"You're the mother in our family, not Kate," Rebecca said, suddenly sober and moving away. Greg dropped his arm around Rebecca's shoulders and smiled in a vague manner, swaying slightly. " 'Night, little Sis."

"Good night, Greg. Thanks for the drinks and dinner."

"Sure, Sis. Anytime."

Talia climbed behind the wheel and glanced over to see Greg holding Rebecca while he kissed her. Then they went inside the apartment. As Talia drove home, she had never felt more alone in her life. Most of her friends were traveling in the summer or too busy to see her. She hadn't dated much in high school so there were no boyfriends. And more and more she worried about Kate. After the last visit, their family doctor had recommended taking Kate to a psychiatrist. Their appointment was for Monday.

His prognosis was shattering. Hospitalization was the only

hope. Talia's first reaction was refusal, then sorrow, but as she faced facts and discussed it with him, she began to see that she had little choice.

Kate's medical bills were increasing, and she realized Rebecca would not help. Rebecca had found her own solution, but Talia thought it was a bad one. She rubbed her neck, determined she would survive some way.

She told the doctor she wanted to think about committing Kate to a hospital. While she was trying to decide, continuing to work, and saving to enroll in a local college in the fall, Kate disappeared again. Talia phoned Beau, and together they searched and were on the verge of notifying the police when Kate called Talia to come get her out of a rundown bar. This time Talia knew what she had to do, and she began procedures to have Kate committed to Louisiana State Hospital. Kate went willingly, seeming to no longer care where she was or what happened, but Talia cried all the way back to the shabby apartment.

She shivered again as if a cold draft of winter air were blowing through the open window. Her gaze shifted to the stars and she remembered her father's note, ". . . *you are the strong one in the family.* . . ."

She didn't want to be the strong one! Kate's mental problems, Rebecca's decision to live with a man who was a little less than a stranger, plus the stigma of what her father had done had . . .

She ran her hand across her brow. Anger began to replace defeat. She would get out of this some way, and it wouldn't ever happen again. She had depended on her father, and he had not only failed, but had brought them all down. Beau, Kate, Rebecca—none of them was able to help the others. Talia sat up a little straighter. She had learned one lesson: She could not depend on others. She needed to be strong herself; she needed to earn an income great enough to care for herself and Kate.

Her determination to attend college in the fall was stronger than ever. One dark night two weeks later Talia parked her car at the curb and locked it before hurrying across the narrow sidewalk. Several men stood a block away in front of a bar, but she barely glanced their way. Steeling herself, she entered

the empty hallway. Inside the door a single low-watt bulb
burned, revealing the cracks in the walls and the litter of
cigarette butts and paper on the stairs. The top of the stairs
was in darkness. She frowned. She hated coming in late after
work when it was so dark. She rushed to her apartment. Talia
knew she couldn't continue to live alone in this neighborhood.
But how could she find someone reliable to share an apartment? There was no one at work. She remembered Greg's
friend who was a nanny. Talia had had a few babysitting jobs
during high school; being a nanny couldn't be that different,
and it would leave her free to take some college classes. She
would also have a decent place to live. She wished she had
asked Greg's friend more questions and decided to call Rebecca in the morning.

At half-past eight she called Rebecca who sounded sleepy
and cross.

"Rebecca, I want to call one of Greg's friends I met that
night."

"Oh, oh!" she exclaimed, sounding a little more awake.
"Which one, Jim—the cute blond? He's single."

"No. Her name was Alicia, and she works as a nanny."

"What do you want to call her for?"

"I want to find a job like that."

"A nanny to little brats? Ugh!"

"I have to find somewhere else to live. I'm alone, and this
is a bad neighborhood."

"Okay. I'll get her number from Greg."

"Rebecca, why don't you go by and see Mom sometime
soon?"

"I think that place would depress me. I might as well tell
you now. Greg's been transferred to Chicago and I'm going
with him."

"Are you getting married?"

Rebecca's high peal of laughter came. "No! I'm not the
marrying kind. I don't want to be tied down, but he's taking
good care of me and he's moving up in his company."

"What'll you do if Greg walks out?"

"I don't intend to find out, because I plan to walk first.
Talia, don't be so straight. I can introduce you to someone

and you won't have to worry about a place to live or a car or countless other little things. You're doing it the hard way."

"Will you just get Alicia's number for me?"

"Will do," Rebecca answered with a casual quickness that made Talia wonder if she would ever hear from her again.

"How soon are you moving?"

"Next Monday. I meant to tell you sooner."

"Go by and see Mom before you leave."

"I'll think about it," Rebecca said, her standard evasive answer that meant she wouldn't do it.

Saturday morning Talia answered the phone to hear a feminine voice announce she was Alicia Massarini.

When Talia told her what she wanted, Alicia said, "I'll recommend you to the Whites, my employers. They may know someone who's looking for a nanny."

"Don't call me at this number. I'm moving. Call me at work. Thank you, Alicia, more than I can tell you."

"Sure. Glad to do it. You ought to join us again for happy hour."

"Thanks," Talia said, knowing she didn't have money to spend on happy hours.

Monday afternoon at work Alicia called and gave her the name of a family, and Talia's spirits rose. The first phone interview was brief. Talia sent references, and Mrs. Millard Carlin Franklin, of the Franklin family of bankers, called again to set up an appointment for an interview.

A week later Talia stepped out of her car in front of the house, and faced the massive fluted Ionic columns that graced wide double galleries and brought memories of childhood that seemed far in her past now. She felt a trace of sorrow but she replaced it with hope that was tinged with fear. The enormous house and grounds were so far removed from her tiny, shabby apartment that she could only stare in awe of it all. To her right was a landscaped yard with a reflecting pool and fountain, water sparkling in the morning sunshine, banks of yellow chrysanthemums surrounding the far end. The house had twin wings, each with a tall chimney, arched windows with fan lights, and side lights by the carved oak door at the entrance. The physical trappings silently proclaimed security, and her fear yielded to determination to acquire such protection for herself.

Thankful she still had fashionable dresses to wear, she smoothed her navy linen skirt, knowing the white pique collar and red silk bow broke the severity of the plain lines of her dress. She punched a white button and heard melodic chimes. The door was opened by a uniformed maid.

"Yes'm?"

"I'm Miss Wade," Talia said, timidly, her heart fluttering with fear.

"Beg pardon, miss?" the maid asked, frowning.

Talia spoke up. "I'm Miss Wade. I have an appointment with Mrs. Franklin."

"Yes'm. Come this way, please. Mizz Franklin is expecting you."

Talia entered a wide hallway with a diamond-patterned marble floor and crystal chandeliers. A sweeping curved staircase disappeared into the upper floor. On a pedestal in the center of the hallway was a silver urn of tropical red anthurium. Oil paintings decorated the walls adding to the lavish splendor. As Talia walked into a spacious sitting room, she thought that no one could be unhappy in such a cheerful room. Sunlight shone through floor-to-ceiling glass doors that opened onto the gallery. The walls were papered in a muted yellow that was a pleasant backdrop for the yellow-and-white decor, all of it touched with a brilliant lustre by the bright sunshine. Talia's attention shifted from the impressive surroundings to the thin woman standing by the wide mantel. Flawlessly dressed in a pale green cotton dress that complemented the room's color, she was as elegant as her home. Her thick chestnut hair was pulled into a bun behind her head, which made her look older than Talia expected the mother of twin four-year-olds to look.

"How do you do, Miss Wade. I'm Mrs. Franklin. Please have a seat." Pauline Lecomte Franklin barely smiled, but her voice was the soft gentle drawl of a native. Her gaze assessed the slender young girl with a Dutch boy's bob. Trying to set her at ease, Pauline said, "You have good recommendations; I've talked to Cecelia Bertaut. And I see your mother was in United Daughters of the Confederacy.

You also have a good recommendation from your current employer.''

''Thank you,'' Talia said, relaxing a degree. Their polite conversation centered around the job and details about Talia's background. She twisted her hands nervously; her voice was breathless as she told Mrs. Franklin that her father had died this past year and as a result her mother had suffered a nervous collapse and was in a state hospital. Talia prayed Mrs. Franklin didn't know any details about her father's embezzlement or her mother's breakdown.

At some point in the interview, she felt she had lost the job. Warm and gracious, Mrs. Franklin had approved of Talia's background, yet her unfortunate present circumstances left a clear barrier between them, and Talia detected a condescending air in the conversation. Mrs. Franklin sat smiling and nodding while Talia answered the questions, but there were no positive statements, fewer questions, so when Mrs. Franklin said, ''What we'd like you to do, is live here,'' Talia was surprised. As if weights had been lifted, her spirits soared.

''Oh, thank you, Mrs. Franklin! That would be grand!''

''Good. I have the twins, and they're a handful. You see, we have two families. I have two older sons, Tyler and Sloane, who are young men. Then later we had the twins. The time to have children is when you're young. It's much simpler then.''

Talia barely heard the latter statement because she was adjusting her thinking to the earlier bit of information. Two grown young men in the family were more than she had expected, but it shouldn't make any difference. Leaning forward, Talia was determined to win a concession in spite of the fact that her heart was beating with fear that she might spoil the offer.

''Mrs. Franklin, one thing I'd like to work into my schedule, is college courses. Someone told me Huey Long once said, 'Everyone can go to L.S.U.' It doesn't have to be L.S.U., but I intend to get an education.''

''That's wise these days, Miss Wade, when you know you'll have to support yourself. Of course with our boys, degrees are imperative. We can work out a schedule so you can take courses, and you'll have certain Friday and Saturday nights off. Each Sunday I'll take the boys," she said, smiling, and Talia wondered how much time she spent with her children. They agreed Talia would start work on Monday, and Talia wanted to click her heels with joy.

"I'll introduce you to Bertha, our maid, and she'll show you around and get you familiar with things. On Monday, I'll introduce you to the boys, Travis and Jeff. Since it's summer, you'll have to spend more time with them than you will once school starts. As I said before, part of your job will be to drive them to their activities. Of course you'll use the family car. There'll be room for your car in the garage, and your room will be upstairs next to the boys'. We'll expect you to eat with us and in many ways to be like a member of the family. I think it'll work best for the boys that way."

"Yes, ma'am," Talia said, wondering if she would live up to expectations and if she could get along with the boys. She imagined two small copies of Pauline Franklin, polite and pleasant and yet aloof.

"If it's convenient for you, you might want to come Sunday afternoon."

"That would be fine," Talia said eagerly.

"Good. I'll show you your room because we may not be at home when you arrive. Bertha will be here until six o'clock, so if you can come around two or three, drive to the back and she'll let you in through the kitchen. That way you can get settled before Monday morning when you take charge of the boys. They have an organized schedule, so I think you'll find your work not too burdensome."

"I'm sure I'm going to love it here!"

Footsteps sounded in the marble hallway, and a handsome man thrust his head into the room, his eyes glancing with curiosity at Talia, then going to Pauline. "Am I interrupting?"

Pauline laughed. "You know full well you're interrupting! Come in and meet our new nanny for the boys."

"You poor soul! Did she warn you that you're taking charge of Attila the Second and Count Dracula, Jr.?"

"Sloane! For heaven's sake. You'll scare Miss Wade away before she meets her charges. Your brothers are very nice and well behaved, whereas their older siblings—'' Contrary to her gentle admonition, Pauline's voice was warm. "Miss Wade, this is my middle son, Sloane Franklin. Sloane, meet Miss Wade."

He was so handsome he was almost beautiful, with a graceful saunter to his slender, long legs as he crossed the room to take Talia's hand and shake it. His eyes were chocolate brown, as warm as Pauline's were reserved; his mauve and white cotton shirt with maroon cotton slacks were more extreme than most men's fashions, yet Sloane wore them with a casual naturalness.

"Welcome to our home," he said in a deep voice. "I hope you like it; I know we'll like you. The last nanny weighed five hundred pounds and couldn't keep sight of her charges."

While Talia laughed, Pauline contradicted him. "Sloane, she weighed no such thing as five hundred pounds! You're not helping here, so why don't you find something useful to do?"

He turned to wink at his mother and there was a quick exchange of smiles between them. "Of course. I know when I'm not wanted. I'm leaving to go back to work. And I'm eating dinner out tonight. I wanted to know if I may take your car. Mine's in the shop with a sudden attack of transmissionitis."

"I have bridge at Martha's this afternoon."

"Laura Flettrich will drive right past here. You can ride with her and I'll appreciate the favor forever, or until tomorrow, whichever comes first."

"Sloane, I really do need—"

"And I'll drive you to early church Sunday morning if Millard isn't going. It's important," he said in a coaxing tone.

"Very well. Will I see you tomorrow?"

"Probably," he said as he headed toward the door. He turned to walk backward, looking at Talia. "No kidding, welcome to the Franklins'. Just don't nap in the same room with the boys."

"Sloane!" Pauline laughed and turned to Talia. "Ignore him. He's only teasing. Do you have any questions?"

"Not right now," Talia answered, feeling fortunate and

slightly overwhelmed. "I appreciate this opportunity and I'll do my best."

"I'm sure you will. If you like, I'll have Bertha show you around now."

"Fine," Talia said, thinking it was the understatement of her life. She was so eager to move into the elegant house that she would have moved that day if given the chance.

Pauline pressed the button on an intercom: "Bertha, will you come here, please."

Talia relaxed as she toured the mansion with Bertha, learning it was built by a Franklin ancestor in 1841. The red brick had been fired on the Franklin plantation, Devonwick, near Loreauville, and hauled into New Orleans. On either side of the central portion were one-story wings, one of which included a ballroom. Impressed by its opulence, Talia viewed the double parlors with their antique rosewood furniture, the dining-room table that could accommodate twenty easily, the hand-carved wooden punkah overhead. Curiosity stirred when she glanced into the sitting room and bedroom designated as Mr. Ty's. A wall of shelves was filled with trophies.

"Mr. Ty must be quite an athlete."

"Yes'm. Mr. Ty always wins."

As they passed Sloane's room, she saw tennis trophies, but not as many as Ty's collection.

"Is Mr. Sloane as much of an athlete as his brother?"

"No, ma'am," Bertha added politely, looking as if her thoughts were far away. "But that boy is one sweet man."

The house had a decorator's professional touch with colors and wallpaper and carpets meticulously coordinated. Talia had always been comfortable in the homes of her friends that were similar to her own two-story four-bedroom house, but she was awed by the Franklin mansion, finally gazing with joy at the lovely pink and white room that was to be hers.

Sunday afternoon as she set her suitcases down in the room, she spun in circles with her arms flung wide. She was safe, she could pursue her college courses, and life was full of hope again. Sunlight poured through the wide south and east windows, through French doors that opened onto the upstairs gallery.

Uncertain about what to wear, she had decided on a white

cotton blouse and blue linen slacks. She had an idea that Pauline Franklin wouldn't approve of jeans. Talia's simple short hair style was never a problem to manage and she merely ran a comb through it.

She opened her suitcase when something smashed through the far south window, shattering bits of glass in the sparkling sunshine, demolishing the windowpane, and Talia flinched with surprise.

6

Talia picked up a football and stepped through the double glass doors onto the upstairs gallery. Four young men including Sloane were scattered on the lawn below. At a glance she knew which one had thrown the football through the window because when his gaze met hers, his scowl changed to a smile in an attempt at innocence.

"Miss Wade!" Sloane waved.

"A direct hit!" she said to the tall man with thick black hair.

He laughed and placed his fists on his hips. She threw the football in an underhanded toss, but to her dismay it sailed high in the air and crashed into an oak where it wedged in a high branch.

"Oh, no!" She clasped her hand to her mouth as an embarrassing blush flooded her cheeks. When they applauded and cheered, her discomfort grew.

"Come down and get the ball!" one of them urged her while the dark-haired man grasped a low tree limb and climbed up to retrieve the football. When he reached the ball, he was on her level close to the gallery. "Hi, Miss Wade. I'm Ty Franklin."

"I'm sorry I threw the ball into the tree."

"Fair enough. I tossed it through your window."

"It's your window, actually."

"Ty, are you coming down here?" one of his friends called.

"Yep." He winked at her and clambered down, dropping to the ground from the lowest branch, landing like a cat on his feet, and striding toward the house. "Go ahead. I better assess the damage."

With hoots and jeers and playful remarks, they tossed the ball between them and turned their backs on him as he disappeared into the house. Talia knew he was coming up to her room. She sensed that he was a dynamic man, and the thought of meeting him up close made her heart race. She heard his footsteps on the polished oak floor of the hall before the light rap on her door. She opened it and faced the most handsome man she had ever seen. His straight black hair was tousled in boyish disarray above his wide forehead. But it was his enigmatic black eyes that intrigued her the most. He looked directly into her eyes, and in that instant Talia felt that he could read her every thought.

"I'm the culprit who smashed your window and I came to help. As I said, I'm Ty Franklin."

"How do you do, Ty Franklin," she said, aware of the breathlessness in her voice. "I'm Talia Wade."

"Ty and Talia. Our names go together, don't you think?" he asked, leaning his hip against the door and moving a few inches closer to her. Overwhelmed, she backed up a step. He smiled in amusement. She had heard of charisma, and now she understood what it meant, because Ty Franklin had more than a fair share of it.

"I haven't met your brothers yet," she said. An oak leaf was caught in his hair and, surprising herself, she removed it. "I'm not good at throwing a ball."

"What are you good at?"

"Reading, taking care of small children, school work—rather dull things."

"Maybe you haven't tried enough things," he drawled in a tone that made her tingle inside.

"I'm sure I've led a very sheltered life compared to you," she said, amazed by their conversation. This was the home of her new employer and Pauline Franklin had looked far too conservative to approve of even a mild flirtation between her son and the hired help. Yet Talia couldn't help meeting the challenges Ty Franklin threw her way. She had seldom dated and had never flirted in this manner. A current of excitement churned within her.

"Maybe it's time we changed that," he stated, but the playfulness had left his voice and the seriousness in his dark eyes was commanding. "Shall we clean up the glass?"

"Glass?" She felt lost. What was he talking about? And then she remembered, but it was too late. He had noticed her momentary blank stare, heard her inane question, and a grin flashed across his face, revealing his white teeth. She told herself then that Ty Franklin was as dangerous as a stick of dynamite. If she didn't resist his charm, she might find herself without a job. She stepped back. "I forgot about the broken window," she admitted, and they both laughed.

Ty saw her blush for the second time. She was interesting, he thought. Her straight, short hair style wasn't particularly flattering, and her mouth was a little too wide, yet her eyes were as green as new spring leaves. They sparkled when she laughed. His gaze raked over her figure as she turned toward the broken window. She was willowy; he estimated her height about seven inches over five feet, yet her waist was tiny. Her breasts were high and full, straining against the simple white blouse she wore. He noticed the quality of her wristwatch, the linen slacks she wore, and his curiosity was heightened. Who was she and why was she taking this job?

"We need a broom, and I'm not too familiar with your home yet," she said.

The compelling urge to reach out and touch her surprised him. He seldom was attracted to someone so swiftly unless she was blatantly after him, and Talia looked as innocent as a daisy. He wondered how easy it would be to get her into his bed.

"I'll get the broom and a vacuum. Don't do anything until I get back. Most of all—don't disappear!"

She laughed and a dimple appeared in her right cheek, making her look even prettier.

In minutes he was back with a vacuum and broom and dustpan, insisting that since it was his fault she should just watch while he cleaned.

"Don't be ridiculous!" she exclaimed and knelt down to pick up bits of glass.

He caught her wrist and the simple touch was electric. He saw the quick intake of her breath, a softening in her expression, and his pulse quickened. She was sexually aware of the slightest touch and she responded instantly. His desire immediately increased a hundredfold.

"Please," she whispered, glancing at her wrist, and he released her, because now wasn't the time or place to pursue further possibilities.

"You needn't help me," he said, noticing her features again with closer scrutiny. Her skin was as smooth and flawless as a ripe peach. "It was a stupid thing I did. I don't usually throw footballs through windows."

"What do you usually do?" she asked.

"Try and seduce beautiful young women," he answered, expecting her reaction. Talia drew a sharp breath and tried to resume the original topic of conversation.

"I insist on helping clean the floor," she announced firmly.

"Do you always do exactly what you want to do?" he asked with a teasing glint in his eyes.

"No, not always, but I'm learning."

He grinned, intrigued by her. One moment she seemed poised, the next innocent and uncertain. As he worked, he glanced at the thin gold watch on his wrist. In a few minutes his parents and the twins would arrive home. Glancing at Talia's long legs, he decided that his mother had done a fine job hiring this nanny. He would have to be careful or she would fire her just as swiftly.

Suddenly he remembered his date with Stephanie for the evening, and he almost lost interest in Talia Wade. They finished picking up the last pieces of glass.

When he faced her, he touched her collar and watched her blush. "Come play football. It's touch. We don't tackle."

"I can't play. And no one else would want me."

"Of course, they would."

"No. Really, no!" she said.

"Okay," he answered casually, winked, and left. Maybe someday, he would take Miss Talia Wade to bed, but it wasn't wise, and if she was a good nanny there was no need to cause problems for the family. He strode out on the lawn and after a few questions and curious stares from his friends they were all playing football again and Ty forgot everything except the game.

Talia sat down near the gallery rail and watched. Ty was aggressive, determined, and sometimes too rough, causing howls of protest and shouted reminders from his friends that this was touch football and only a game. Ty's grin and flippant remarks always smoothed over whatever violations he had committed. None of them noticed her, and she leaned back in the chair. She could tell that Ty Franklin was a natural athlete with a lithe masculine grace in his movements and strength in his actions. He didn't stick to the rules; he was ruthlessly determined to win and was more adept at the game than the others.

She heard a car pull up in the driveway and within seconds two small boys were watching the game from the edge of the lawn. Talia studied the twins and realized that they were fraternal because one had straight black hair, the other wavy brown hair. She stood up and went downstairs to meet them, discovering that Travis was the one with straight black hair, blue eyes, and a shy manner while Jeff was the outgoing twin with a mischievous twinkle in his brown eyes.

In two weeks she had settled into a routine and she loved her charges. Sloane had turned into a friend; she seldom saw Tyler. She learned that he had finished college and gone to work at First Bayou National Bank for his dad. In addition to running sugar cane plantations in Louisiana and Brazil, Millard Franklin was president of the First Bayou National Bank of New Orleans. The granite and limestone bank with its broad front steps, four fluted columns, and high pediment with figures depicting the Battle of New Orleans had been built in the late 1800's in the business district. Inside the lobby, the ceiling was two stories high, with marble columns, and the tellers' windows were trimmed in brass. Talia could remember her father taking her to look at the enormous Christmas tree in First Bayou's lobby when she was a child.

Since Ty had his own apartment and an active social life, he was away from the Franklin home ninety percent of the time. As far as Millard Franklin was concerned, Talia was invisible. He was polite to her, but she suspected he had difficulty remembering her name and couldn't have told anyone whether her hair was blond, black, or red. Sloane had graduated with a degree in landscape architecture and had started his own business, a matter that Talia soon realized was a subject of contention between father and son.

Talia felt that she didn't fit in with either the family or the rest of the servants. As a nanny who shared family meals and occasional outings, she didn't belong with the servants, and Pauline Franklin had made that clear to all concerned. But she also wasn't a member of the family, and that was re-emphasized in subtle ways to Talia, and explained to guests. Seldom was she included in social functions; she was banished along with the twins to other parts of the house.

She learned something each day. Pauline was an excellent role model who quietly managed a large household and instructed Talia if she seemed at a loss on any matter concerning proper etiquette. Talia listened and absorbed everything she was told.

The Franklin beach house, a five bedroom two-story colonial in a small town along the Mississippi Gulf Coast was only a few hours' drive from New Orleans, and in warm weather the family traveled regularly between the two houses. The twins were fun, and more of Talia's time was spent with them than was required by her job. After classes started, she often studied when the four-year-old twins napped or while they were at nursery school, and that, coupled with a determination to succeed, earned her excellent grades. Changes in herself were so gradual that Talia was barely aware of them, yet Pauline noticed how quick Talia was to catch on to everything around her, how she was becoming more poised when meeting guests, and how helpful she was at parties and teas.

During a warm May afternoon Talia played with the twins

in the long oval shaped pool. They were hunting a penny that Talia had tossed in the deep end of the pool. Jeff and Travis immediately disappeared beneath the surface, but in a moment they both burst through the water, gasping for air and laughing, shaking their heads.

"Your turn, Tali," they cried in unison. With a deep breath she dived underwater. She couldn't spot the penny and surfaced to tell them, coming up beside the wall beneath the diving board. But the twins were now at the shallow end. With a gulp, she went under again, this time spotting the bright copper coin. She pushed to the bottom and retrieved it and was starting to surface when something cut through the water. She moved to one side to get out of its path, but was struck on the shoulder, and then became tangled in arms and legs.

A warm body pressed against hers, and firm hands held her as they both shot to the surface.

7

Ty Franklin's dark hair was plastered to his head and his expression was so full of concern that Talia smiled, hoping to reassure him that she was all right.

"I didn't know you were in the pool. I didn't see anyone!"

"I was under the water!"

"For how long? Ten minutes? I walked out, put my things down and paused on the diving board."

Laughing, she shook water away from her face. "I surfaced once under the diving board, and then I went down again." Her eyes sparkled, and he began to relax, anger at his own carelessness replacing his worry.

"Lord, I thought I'd killed someone. Are you hurt?"

"No!"

His worried annoyance evaporated as he gazed into her

green eyes. "I seem to be a klutz around you. I've never thrown a football through a window before or since the first day we met, and I've never jumped into a pool right on top of someone, believe it or not."

"I believe you, and I'm not hurt, so it's not important." Her voice softened. "And you don't have to hold me up. I can swim."

He was aware of the narrowness of her waist, the flare of her hips, and, most of all, the warmth of her body. He also knew that she was only nineteen years old, too young as far as he was concerned. He preferred older and more sophisticated women, but something happened when he was in Talia Wade's presence and he couldn't deny his attraction. Drops of water sparkled on her lashes; her eyes were the color of emeralds in sunlight. He lowered his gaze to where the black one-piece suit clung to her curves. He could make out the faint outline of her nipples beneath the Lycra spandex. Staring into her eyes, he moved his thumbs back and forth over her ribs, lightly brushing the underside of the soft swelling of her breasts.

"Mr. Franklin—"

"Oh, come on! That sounds like you're talking to my dad. I'm Ty. Let me hear you say it," he said, not caring what she said, just trying to draw her attention away from his hands. She seemed so slight where he held her that his fingers almost encircled her waist. He knew that right above his hands, she filled out her suit more provocatively than any other woman he knew.

"Say it," he demanded.

"Ty, take your hands away," she said, realizing they were in full view of the house. She glanced at the twins who were splashing in the shallow part of the pool, oblivious of Ty or her.

"Let's swim, then. A slow lap around the pool so we can talk."

"The twins need me."

"I'll handle the twins." He swam a few yards away. "Come on."

She took long, easy strokes, and he swam effortlessly beside her, his muscular arms slicing into the crystal water with precision. "Why did you accept this job?"

"I need to work, and I want a nice place to live. As it is, I have an interesting job and a fabulous place to live."

"What about your family?"

"I don't have anyone to live with here," she answered in a matter-of-fact tone. "My sister lives in Chicago. My father died last year and my mother had a nervous breakdown because of it. She's in an institution now."

"I'm sorry."

"Thanks. What about you? I understand you work at the bank with your father."

"That's right. Someone has to follow in the family footsteps, and Sloane is out."

"Why is Sloane out?"

"He hates banking, or any of its ilk."

"He works, just the same as you."

"Oh, yeah, puttering around flowers."

"He told me he has his own landscape architecture business, and since high school he's supplemented his income with modeling."

"Much to Dad's disappointment." They talked and swam in a circle around the pool, and she was thankful she could carry on a coherent conversation. But it was difficult. Ty Franklin wore brief black trunks that revealed a lithe, powerful body that was well muscled and tanned to the color of teak. She found it impossible to ignore the desire he ignited in her.

Once Jeff called to her, "Tali, watch me turn a flip."

As she watched his thin legs appear and his feet wiggle in the air while his head was hidden beneath the surface, Ty said, "They call you Tali. They like you."

"I like them. They're fun and good and intelligent."

"I hope you're that complimentary about me someday," he said with a straight face.

She wrinkled her nose at him. "No doubt about it. You're fun and intelligent and good."

"Good? That's a new one from a female!"

"Sure. When you broke the window, you cleaned up the

glass and you apologized for jumping into the pool earlier. That's pretty nice, I'd say.''

He groaned. "Good and nice! My ego just took a battering.''

"Good and nice are wonderful qualities! For heaven's sake, what do you want to be?''

"Dangerous and appealing," he said, pleased when she looked away quickly because he realized that he was exactly that to her. He wanted to hear her say it, but she quickened her stroke and swam ahead. He caught her and their feet touched in the shallow part of the pool. His chest was half out of water, as were her slender shoulders. "Why did you speed up? Scared?''

"Yes, a little,'' she admitted without looking him in the eye, but her gaze raked over his chest before she glanced away.

"Why?'' he persisted, wanting to hear her say the words.

"Because you're dangerous and appealing,'' she replied breathlessly, and he felt a rush of excitement. She wiggled free to swim away, and he caught up swiftly.

"This is a beautiful pool.''

"And you're changing the subject.''

"I'll go inside if *you* don't.''

"You can't go inside—your charges are out here.''

"I can leave them for a moment, especially if their older brother is here, or I can take them with me. I should go inside and study.''

"Okay, okay. What courses are you taking?'' he asked.

"Business. I want to be able to earn a living when I get out.''

"You'll get married and never use your degree.''

"I'll use it, I can promise you that.'' Amused by the force in her voice, he noticed that she swam with graceful ease.

"Tyler!''

He twisted in the water to see his mother standing at the side of the pool. "Yes?''

"May I see you a moment now? I want to talk to you.''

"Of course. I'll be right in.''

"I'll be in the solarium,'' she said as she turned and left.

He twisted to face Talia and saw the worry in her expression and the spots of color in her cheeks.

"Relax. You live here. You look as if she caught you with your hand in the cookie jar," he said with amusement. "You can swim with me and you can talk to me. You talk to Sloane."

"Sloane is like a good friend."

She looked as if she wanted to bite her tongue, and he felt a swift stab of excitement. "And what am I?"

"Your mother's waiting to see you," she said and disappeared beneath the surface. He couldn't resist. He dived, spotting her swimming away from him beneath the water. He caught her and held her while she struggled. Her body was warm, slippery, soft, and full of curves. When their legs brushed, his arousal was swift and strong. He released her, and they both resurfaced gasping for air.

"Ty! You'll get me fired."

"No, I won't," he said, his voice somber, surprised by his strong attraction to her. "But I'm going to get to know you, Tali."

"Your mother is waiting," she said in a quiet voice. He swam away, jumped up on the side of the pool, and stood, picking up his towel. As he reached the gate to the pool area, he glanced back over his shoulder. She was in the deep end, watching him, sinking beneath the surface the moment he glanced at her. She was sensual, and although nineteen was young, she didn't seem nineteen when he was with her. He toweled himself dry and stepped into the cabana to dress in white cotton slacks and sandals. As he strode toward the house, he yanked on a cotton shirt, wondering idly what his mother wanted. He had hardly talked to her all week. He had a date tonight with Janet and would have to dress soon, yet all he could think about was spending more time at home and getting to know Talia. He thought about her full, red lips, her wide mouth, and he speculated what it would be like to kiss her, to seduce her.

He entered the solarium, and his mother looked up from a book she was reading. "Ty, close the door, please."

Puzzled, he closed it, knowing from her tone of voice that something he had done had displeased her. Whatever it was, it wouldn't take long to fix. He knew how to appease his mother. Assured of the outcome, Ty sank down in a chair across from her, crossing his long legs.

"Yes, ma'am?"

"Ty, I noticed you swimming with Miss Wade."

He kept his laughter in check. "Mother, you didn't call me in here because I swam around the pool with our little nineteen-year-old nanny!"

"Well, she isn't in your class, Ty, and things can happen before you know it."

"What kind of things, Mother?" he asked, enjoying himself, although annoyed that he'd had to stop swimming to listen to such nonsense.

"Now, Tyler, you know what I'm talking about!"

He laughed. "Yes, I do. How many dates have I had this month?"

"I couldn't possibly keep track."

"And has one of them been with Nanny?"

"Please don't call her Nanny! It's Miss Wade."

"Now you're protecting her. A moment ago, you were ready to protect me from her."

"Don't be difficult. And don't become too familiar with her."

"I know, 'Familiarity breeds.' "

"Just be careful and don't get too close."

"Have you given Sloane this same lecture?"

"Sloane? Why, no! Should I?"

Suddenly Tyler had enough and stood up. "I'm grown, Mother. And don't fire little Miss Wade because I swam a couple of laps with her. I jumped into the pool and landed on top of her and we could have had a disaster. She wasn't hurt and she's a good sport, but I could hardly pull the child up from the bottom and tell her to go away from me."

"Oh, Tyler! That isn't like you."

"I didn't know she was in the pool. And I have a date in a couple of hours. Is that all?"

"Yes, but—"

"Then I'll run along. I'm going out with Janet. Now if you want something to worry about, think about us driving to Mississippi for dinner."

"Please be careful."

He strode out of the room, whistling a tune, taking the stairs two at a time, the scene with his mother already out of mind. He felt restless and full of energy. In his room he went out on the gallery. The twins still cavorted in the shallow part of the pool, and Talia floated in the water on her back. He could see the tantalizing curves of her body, and in his mind, he stripped away the black swimsuit. His body responded to his heated images. "Soon, I'm going to find out what you feel like," he said softly.

Sloane appeared and spoke to her, pausing at the edge of the pool, and Ty's eyes narrowed. He knew his brother as well as he knew himself. Their sexual appetites were as strong as their father's. Ty had long known about his father's infidelities as well as Sloane's sexual quirks. Ty could remember his first fumbling experience with a girl at fourteen. He knew that when Sloane described his first time with a female he had already been experimenting with males. Ty was often repelled by his brother's unconventional behavior. Sloane seemed to have no discrimination of any sort, in Ty's opinion. When Sloane left, Talia floated backward, facing the house, and she saw Ty watching her. She shifted, her feet trailing down in the water while she waved to him. He waved back. "I'm going to know what it's like to have you," he said to himself again.

Sunday was Talia's day off, and two weeks later when she returned to her room from church, she met Ty in the hall. He wore shorts, Nikes, and a T-shirt that revealed his powerful muscles. "We're playing touch football." He threw up his hands. "I promise, no football through the window!"

"I didn't accuse you of it!"

"Come join us."

The casual invitation hung in the air like a tempting tidbit to a dieter. She suspected his mother disapproved of the slightest social exchange between her eldest son and herself. "I've seen you play," she said. "You tackle."

"I won't tackle you," he said with a sparkle in his eyes that quickened her pulse. He was without question the most handsome man she had ever known. Sophisticated, intelligent, and fun, he was someone she could dream about. And that was all she could ever do about him.

He held her arm, and his casual touch was electric. "Come on. You can sit in the shade and watch if you don't want to play. I promise you, none of us will tackle you."

"I can just hear the others groan at the sight of a female wanting to join the game."

"*Au contraire*!" He winked. "Wear your red shorts. They'll welcome you with something akin to Christmas joy." He headed for the stairs without a backward glance as if the matter was settled while she stared at him. When had he seen her in her red shorts? She wondered.

She changed. Looking at them below her window, she noticed that Sloane was with them. He was as broad shouldered as Ty, just as muscular, and both men moved with agility and balance. Yet in some ways Sloane was lighter on his feet; he reminded Talia more of a dancer evading his partner than a football player.

As she sat on the sidelines and cheered them on, she enjoyed herself, relaxed in the knowledge that the senior Franklins had taken the twins to the Franklin beach house on the Mississippi coast for the afternoon.

She joined the game, and true to his word, Ty didn't tackle her as he did his friends. Even so, she realized he always played to win and always did his best. Last week when she had been in the pool racing with the twins she had allowed them to win. Ty had seen her and asked her why.

"They expect you to beat them, because you're grown. They'll respect you more if you win," he had told her.

Laughing, she had swum away. "That's ridiculous. They should win sometimes."

"Not with me, they won't," he said and jumped in calling to the twins. "I'll race all three of you. Jeff, you and Travis can start from the middle of the pool," he said, giving them an enormous head start, "Talia you start a yard behind them—"

She had wrinkled her nose at him. "Not on your sweet Nellie, I won't! I'll start where you do."

He grinned and motioned the twins to go ahead. When he yelled to start, Talia swam for all she was worth, but he beat her by yards, waiting and grinning at her as the boys caught up and pounced on him, laughing and trying to climb on his shoulders.

"See—they don't suffer from losing."

"While big brother does."

"Not often," he answered softly, dumping the boys in the water and leaning forward. "Some day, Tali—"

Whatever he had been about to say was interrupted as the boys pulled him under, and she swam away with her heart beating faster than before.

Remembrance faded as the touch football broke up and the guys left. She sat on the gallery with Sloane and Ty, drinking iced tea until Sloane said he had to leave for a dinner date.

"Let's go somewhere and get a hamburger," Ty asked casually when they were alone.

"I shouldn't."

"Why not? You don't do anything much except stay cooped up in the house. C'mon. It'll do you good."

She didn't argue and the evening was fun. They talked so much that they barely ate. When they drove home it was dusk and her pulse hummed with excitement. The garage door was open on the empty stall where the long Continental would park when the Franklins returned home.

At the back gate Ty caught her hand. The patio was dark except for the lights beneath the surface of the aqua swimming pool, which glowed like an iridescent jewel against black velvet. Crickets chirped, but otherwise it was quiet.

"Let's sit outside by the pool. It's cooler. How about a moonlight swim?"

"No. I can't."

"Why can't you?" he asked with amusement. He touched her collar, brushing her jaw with his knuckles.

"Ty, we have different lives. You're very charming, but you live in a whole different world than I do."

"A moonlight swim—what's complicated about that?"

Suddenly she was hot with embarrassment, realizing that he hadn't experienced the same excitement around her that she did around him. She was just a casual companion to him, a family employee. He might have asked Bertha to swim in the same casual way for all Talia knew. She was afraid that she had made somewhat of a fool of herself. "I'd better go in," she said. "Thanks for the hamburger."

He caught her arm and pulled her back to face him. "Are you scared of my mother?"

"No," she answered solemnly. Her eyes were now adjusted to the semidarkness and she could tell he was looking at her mouth.

"What are you afraid of, Tali?" he asked in a husky voice.

"You," she answered with frankness, knowing she was afraid of his charm, his sophistication, and her own vulnerability and inexperience. He dazzled her as if she were too close to a bright star.

Tilting her chin up, he drew her to him. Her gaze was riveted on his, and her fears evaporated as his arm slipped around her waist. Her pulse drummed in her ears.

Ty watched her. She was appealing, but not the type of woman who usually attracted him. She wasn't sophisticated. Sometimes he thought she was a virgin, yet sometimes he suspected she was sexually knowledgeable because there was a sensuality to her as sultry as the New Orleans air. He wanted to know what she was like in bed. He wanted to possess her, to touch and caress and kiss those high, firm breasts that drew his attention so much of the time. He wanted to caress her long, fabulous legs and feel them entwined with his.

"I've been looking forward to this all evening," he said in a raspy voice.

He bent his head; her eyes were wide and startled and as full of curiosity as he felt. His lips brushed hers, then settled there firmly and when she opened her mouth, his tongue thrust into it, tasting her sweetness, demanding that she yield. She returned his kiss with just as much passion, setting him aflame. Shaken, he raised his head to study her. Her lashes shadowed her cheeks as she slowly opened her eyes.

"I told you I was afraid of your charm," she said with her usual frankness. "We should—"

He lowered his head, settling his mouth on hers, his pulse hammering more fiercely than before. Her body melted against his, and his arm tightened around her slender waist while his erection came swiftly.

Her hips pressed against his, and in that moment as his cock was hard and hot and felt as if he might burst, he decided to seduce her if it took all summer. As she wound her fingers in his hair, he suspected it might not take longer than the next few hours.

His hands slipped beneath the knit shirt she wore, seeking the fullness of her soft breasts. His thumbs played over her nipples, and her gasp of pleasure was barely audible to him above the drumming of his pulse. He moved closer, their bare legs touching. In an agile movement, he caught her shirt and pulled it over her head, tossing it away.

"Ty—"

He lowered his head swiftly to cut off her protest as his arm banded tightly around her waist and he bent over her, forcing her to cling to him while he kissed her deeply. Her body became pliable, her hips thrust against his, and he shifted slightly, his hand roaming over her hip to her thigh, down to the silken flesh of her bare leg. His hand moved between her thighs and she gasped, twisting against him, her eyes opening when he touched her intimately.

He felt her back arch beneath his arm, saw the searing passion flare in her eyes before her lashes closed. He ached to possess her. He wanted to strip away their restrictive clothing, to look at her, to kiss and touch her and watch her respond to him. His fingers slipped beneath the lace to feel her bare, moist flesh and she moaned. Her body felt like a burning flame, supple and yielding to his touch. Her hands moved tentatively over him, exploring him cautiously at first.

When she touched his swollen cock, he groaned, moving her hands away, because his control was slipping. He flicked the catch on her lacy bra and pushed it away from her shoulders, stepping back swiftly to cup her breasts, fondling her while he watched her. She set him on fire with her immediate sensual response.

Her head tilted back, her eyes closed, and her hands traced his chest, tugging his shirt away. She opened her eyes languorously to study his bare chest. Then she gazed below his belt. While her cheeks turned pink, her desire was plain and strong.

"Look at me," he commanded, relishing the reaction he could ignite in her, wanting to see her desire for him.

She closed her eyes as he stroked her, and he spoke again, leaning closer. "Look at me, Talia."

Her thick lashes raised slowly, her eyes opened wide, displaying the passion she felt. She licked her lips when he cupped her breasts, desire nearly overwhelming her. Slowly, taunting her leisurely, he drew his thumbs over her throbbing nipples.

She moaned and tilted her head farther back.

"Open your eyes. I want to watch you," he commanded, his excitement mounting.

"I can't," she whispered, barely looking at him.

"Yes, you can," he cajoled, seeing her struggle to maintain her control, knowing she was losing her battle. Excited by her soft cry he leaned down to take a rosy nipple in his mouth, and he felt her fingers wind wildly in his hair.

He swore, yanking her to him almost violently, kissing her hard, wanting her and knowing he couldn't wait much longer. Her bare breasts were crushed against his chest. Their hearts pounded violently; their breathing became ragged. His hand slid over her back drawing her closer, holding her tightly, fastening on her buttocks and pulling her hard against him.

Talia was lost in a maelstrom of sensation and emotion; her senses stormed, desire raging like a prairie fire in a summer wind. It was too soon and too many risks threatened her; she didn't really know what Ty felt—was this lust or hunger for conquest?

She wanted him to continue to touch and kiss her, yet she was far too aware of the perils involved. This would not only complicate her life, but she could lose her job and jeopardize her future.

She gazed at him as he caressed her slowly. His touch was as experienced as that of a musician playing a violin. She should make Ty stop, yet she wanted him to continue forever.

He pushed her shorts down over her hips, letting them fall to her ankles.

She stepped out of them, knowing she would have to stop soon or not at all. As she watched him look at her, she burned with anticipation, yet she had to protest.

"Ty, not so fast. Oh, please, not so fast!" she gasped, trying to cling to reason, to tear her gaze from his riveting perusal. She caught up her clothes and moved away, knowing if she looked back at him, she would be lost. She went inside the house, stopping at the door to face him.

"I work for your family. This isn't right."

"It seems more right than anything I've ever wanted to do," he said solemnly, and her heart thudded.

"You can postpone things, but you can't stop what's inevitable," he added in a husky voice, coming closer, halting only yards away. "Someday you'll be mine, Talia. I want to touch you all over, to put my hands everywhere, to watch you respond to me—"

"Ty, don't say that to me! You know it's the same as touching me!" she urged breathlessly.

"The same?" came a sardonic reply. "Hardly. Let me show you—"

"No! Not yet. Good night, Ty," she said emphatically, wanting to run back and throw herself into his arms, yet knowing that it would be her downfall.

He studied her from head to toe. "You're a beautiful woman," he said.

"We'll talk tomorrow."

"Coward," he accused, but it was said gently. Both of them were regaining control, yet she knew the only way to maintain it was to get out of his company. She went upstairs and spent lonely hours in the darkness, remembering how badly she wanted him. She couldn't help wondering if tomorrow morning Ty would go back to work and then go out in the evening with the current woman in his life. Would he forget all about tonight? Could she?

8

Spring 1974

Mike sat back in his chair, hoping he looked and sounded relaxed as he discussed again the features of the apartment complex he had just showed H.T. Larkin. He couldn't tell anything from Larkin's lugubrious expression except that he was listening. Larkin's balding head nodded periodically, but his brown eyes were impassive. Mike wanted this sale with an intensity that surprised him. It wasn't a spectacular sale compared to some of Ben's, but it would be the largest Mike had made. The one-hundred-unit apartment house at fifteen thousand dollars per unit would be a million-and-a-half-dollar deal, yielding a commission that Mike refused to contemplate at this point.

He had worked months on this, and felt he had done all he could do.

"I think I can have a good investment in the apartments," Larkin finally said, and Mike fought back a grin.

"Yes, sir, I'd imagine you can."

"I'll meet their offer. You let me know when you can have the papers ready."

"Mr. Larkin, I have the papers ready now if you want to sign."

For a rare moment, H.T. Larkin laughed. "All ready for me to sign, huh?"

"Yes, sir," Mike said, smiling in return as he turned the contract and pushed the paper across his desk. His first thought was telling Simone. His second was telling Ben.

Fifteen minutes later, when he had shaken hands and seen H.T. Larkin to the front door, Mike returned to his office and yelled with pleasure as he picked up the check and contract and studied the figures. His first really big sale of commercial property! Mike clipped the check to the contract carefully, placed it in his briefcase, and left for the Holloway home.

At twenty-five, he thought of Ben as a father, but not for one second had he ever viewed Simone as a mother. True to her word, she was faithful to Ben, whom she adored. Simone and Ben were the best friends Mike had, and he hoped that one day he could have the same kind of marriage. He knew for certain that until he met a woman he could be as good friends with as he was with Simone, he wouldn't marry.

He remembered the morning seven years ago when he had been stopped by the police only yards from the Holloway mansion. That crisis had changed Ben's attitude toward Mike, and Mike had in turn changed his own view of the world. He had intended to murder Leech, but Ben's admonition to use his brains instead of his fists, coupled with the discovery that Ben had risen from a background of poverty convinced Mike that he must get an education. Ben's example gave him hope. In 1967 he enrolled in two night classes at New Orleans University and discovered they weren't much more difficult for him than high school. He saw Vangie less, yet she used the apartment more, kicking him out in the evenings when he wanted to study. Not one of his friends was taking college classes, and Mike never mentioned to anyone that he was. Vangie thought getting his college degree was a good idea, but beyond giving him her opinion, she didn't care what he did.

Occasionally when Mike worked late on Saturday afternoons, he was the only person at home with Ben. The servants had the afternoon off, Stanley quit at noon, and Simone had her hair done and was always gone for hours. He and Ben had gotten into the habit of sharing a beer on the patio or poolside. Mike found Ben easy to talk to, and a closer bond developed between them. And Mike discovered that Ben liked to fish, and on some Saturday afternoons the two would go back on bayous that Mike knew in the old pirogue Mike kept tied to a cypress. One afternoon as they fished Ben said, "I don't know why you ever left this for the city."

"Can't buy much living this way," Mike answered, trailing a line in the murky water.

"You wouldn't need to buy anything. Just build a little shack out here, fish, and enjoy life."

Mike grinned, thinking of Ben's mansion and pool and servants. "Yeah, Ben. Sure. This semester I'm taking general courses. Any recommendations about what I should major in?"

"What interests you?"

"Business."

"Get into finance or accounting."

The second semester Mike took Ben's advice. He enrolled in two three-hour night courses, Finance and Accounting 1.

Mardi Gras came with its excitement and Simone reveled in it. Her costume cost enough to pay his tuition for a year.

Then on one unseasonably hot Saturday afternoon in April when Mike and Ben were alone, they had a conversation that changed Mike's life forever.

It was a hot day and rain the night before had made the weather humid. Mike got two bottles of Corona out of the cabana and sank down on a chair beside the pool, stretching his long legs in front of him. He handed Ben a beer.

"Are you saving to buy another car?" Ben asked.

"Yeah, but it's slow."

Ben rubbed the back of his neck. "How many hours in college are you taking?"

"Six."

"At six a semester, it's going to take you a long time to finish."

"Yeah, but I will," Mike said.

"You've been with us quite a while, and we've been through a few things together."

"You mean *I've* been through a few things. The only crisis you and Simone had was that first time I met you."

Ben laughed. "The years have been good." His smile faded. "Simone can't have children."

Mike felt uncomfortable. He couldn't imagine why Ben

was imparting something so personal to him, and he drank his beer quickly while studying the smooth, clear water of the pool.

"Someday I want to retire and travel."

"Yeah? You're a little young to be thinking about that, aren't you?" Mike asked, his eyes raking over Ben's lean frame that looked as fit as Mike's. For the first time he realized Ben's hair had more gray streaks in it.

"I always think about the future."

"Not me. A day at a time. If I could have seen ahead, I think I might have slit my throat back there when I was five."

"It hasn't been that bad!"

"No, except Claude. That still hurts," Mike said with candor.

"Yeah, I know." After a pause Ben said, "I'm getting older; some friends have talked to me about going into politics. Simone and I have talked about traveling. I'd like to have someone bright to take over my business."

"Yep, I suppose you would."

"You're usually quicker on the uptake than this."

Mike turned his head, the drift of their conversation suddenly dawning on him. His jaw dropped. "I'm from nothing. I'm your gardener. Not even the main gardener," he said, wondering the moment the words were out if he had jumped to the wrong conclusion.

"You're bright and you're trying to get educated." Ben's voice deepened. "Plus you've become like a son to me."

Mike was astounded, and something deep inside him was touched. His throat felt tight and it was difficult to find the right words, but he made an attempt. "Thanks, Ben. I think of you as my father because I never knew mine. You've been good to me."

"Simone and I made it up the ladder. You will too. I know you want a degree in business, and I know your grades are excellent. Think you'd be interested in learning commercial real estate?"

Mike sat up straighter, his jaw snapping shut. "Yes, sir! I sure would!"

Ben smiled. "I thought you might," he said with satisfaction. "Let's make some plans."

"Yes, sir!" In the past every time Ben had made an offer, it had meant a better life for Mike, so he listened attentively.

"You need a decent home. Come live over the garage in the servants' quarters. Malcolm quit and it's empty, because none of the servants live here now. If you need a car, I'll help you get one and you can make payments.

"You start putting in more hours for me, errands, gardening, whatever you can do, and I'll pay you for it. If you can't make ends meet, come to me. I won't charge you rent. I'd like to groom you to take over my business. I'll pay your college costs."

"You're sure you want to do this?"

"Yes. I've given it a lot of thought and discussed it with Simone." Ben offered his hand.

Mike laughed, a surge of excitement hitting him like an electric current. He fought the urge to look at the mansion as he gripped Ben's hand in a vigorous shake. Ben was offering him a chance to climb out of the gutter and up to the top of the world, and he intended to take it and never look back.

"You bet! I'll try my best to do what you want. I'll work."

"I know you will," Ben said, remembering the kid who had promised to work his butt off and knocked over his drink that first afternoon. Mike had changed; in spite of being a street kid, he was bright enough to be all that Ben wanted if he tried. All his life Ben had followed his hunches and more often than not he had been right. As he shook hands with Mike he looked into sparkling blue eyes and he knew his offer to Mike would pay off.

"If anytime along the way, I change my mind, you'll know it," Ben said, and Mike heeded the warning and threat.

"That's fair enough. If I change my mind, I'll let you know."

"All right. First thing is to move here and tell the local lady love in your life you're moving out."

Mike's face flushed. "How'd you know I was living with someone?"

"You mention names now and then."

"Women give me a place to stay. Vangie keeps me locked out of the apartment half the time."

"Just move in here—alone."

"I will! Gladly!" Mike didn't have to give it a second's thought, because he wasn't seriously interested in any of the women he had ever dated. "I'll move in today."

"Good. There's a key on the table in the cabana for the apartment. You can drive our Ford temporarily. That key is there too. In the meantime, how about a few hours fishing on the bayou before you move?"

Only Vangie dampened his happy mood.

"I'm moving to the Holloways'. And I won't be back."

"We'll see," she said, her brow furrowing in a frown. "There was a man asking for you last night."

Mike paused while packing the few things he wanted. "Who?"

She shrugged her thin shoulders. "He said his name was Patty. He said you'd know. He has some information."

"God, why didn't you tell me!"

"I am telling you! What are you getting information about? You're not pushing, are you?"

"No. It's about Claude. I'm going to nail Leech for what he did, and he's going to pay."

She capped a bottle of fingernail polish. "Knowing you, you'll stick with it until you do. You're like a bulldog, you know? If someone does you wrong, too bad for them."

"After what Leech did, you want him to go free?"

"No, but I don't want you in Angola for murder."

"I won't be, I promise you. But Leech is going to pay."

"You always get revenge. Even when you were little, like the time when Grandpa whipped you and you hadn't done what he accused you of. You ran away from home at four years old."

"That wasn't revenge."

"If you knew how it worried him, you'd know it was revenge. He was so glad to find you, he didn't give you the whomping you deserved. And he wouldn't let me give you one, either. When you come back tomorrow—"

He turned to give her a look, and she bit off the words. "You'll be back."

"I'll send you money regularly," he said, closing a paper bag with all his possessions, "that's a promise, but I can't live here again."

"Aren't you getting to be Mr. Snooty! Why are you so pissed?"

"Vangie, you've had me locked out of here half the time since Claude's death. I've slept in alleys and studied in bars—"

"Go on. Go ahead and go. You've always wanted something better. Maybe you'll get it."

"Here," he said, pulling out five twenty-dollar bills and tossing them onto a table. "'Bye."

As he moved toward the door, she called to him.

"Thanks for the money," she said, scooping it up. He had expected her to ask him to stay. He left without looking back, striding down to the Ford Ben said he could use and driving away.

His grades were good in summer school, but it bothered him to take Ben's money, just as it had bothered him to let his girlfriends keep him. He kept busy every waking hour, taking off on Saturday nights and at odd times to prowl the Quarter. He was tracing back through time and he had come up with some leads he had taken to the police. He told them about Paul Joyner, a man who, according to rumors, was supposed to know what had happened to Claude. Mike was tempted to follow the lead himself, but he decided to leave it to the authorities. Lieutenant Clayton had been promoted to Captain, and Mike had given him the information.

When Mike left the parish police station, he headed down the street where he had parked in the only available space. Half a block from his car, his eyes narrowed; something was different from when he had parked the car. He quickly realized that the area was deserted. No cars, no people, even though he was a stone's throw from the station.

His skin tingled with a sense of danger that was instinct, but he had learned years ago to follow gut feelings about unseen threats. He slowed, studying the area, and then he noticed that the street light was out and it had been on when he had parked the car. He reached into his pocket for his switchblade, yanking it out and holding it open against his thigh. The possibility of going back to the station and getting a cop to escort him was dismissed as swiftly as it came. He was accustomed to fighting his own battles.

He moved into the street, walking past the line of parked cars. Because he wore sneakers, his steps were silent. He no longer felt a chill of apprehension, but he was tight with anger, ready for a fight, wondering if it were street punks or Leech who was waiting. Suddenly he bent down, dropping to his knees. He saw two pairs of feet behind his car.

He glanced over his shoulder. If it was Leech, there would be someone to close in from behind. Mingled with his anger was elation. He must be getting hotter on Leech's trail or he wouldn't have taken the risk of following him here. If Leech jumped him, Mike could fight back in self-defense. Eager for a fight, he tightened his grip on the knife. From behind a car, two guys burst out, lunging at him.

Mike swung his knife, slashing one across the belly. He rolled to the ground and got back up to face Leech.

"Get off my back, punk!" Leech snapped.

"I'll get you for Claude, but it won't be here on the street," Mike taunted, hoping to goad Leech into fighting. "You're going to burn, baby. Think of me when you're on death row. I've been after you a long time now, and I'm going to get you!"

Mike swung around and his knife clashed with Leech's as he circled to his left, moving closer to the car, trying to get his back protected. He heard a sound behind him and jumped, swinging his foot to kick someone coming up behind him. Big John and two others closed in. With a lunge Mike flung himself across the car hood, dropping like a cat on his feet to the other side. They came around the car after him and he lashed out with his knife, the silver flashing dully in the darkness, hitting solid flesh and bone. One of his assailants went down.

Something sliced across his arm in a stinging cut, then someone hit him from behind, jamming him full force into the car. He gasped while his head was jerked back by the hair.

Mike twisted, feeling his hair yanked out as he pulled them down with him. He kicked and heard a groan, a jar telescoping up his leg when his foot slammed into one of them. A boot stomped on his wrist, and the knife flew from his hand. When he rolled over he faced three of them. Leech held his knife as he plunged forward trying to slice into Mike's stomach. Mike wrenched away, kicking at Big John, landing a blow between his legs. Mike saw the glint of a knife to his right.

He flung away, but not fast enough and the blade sank in, slipping over his rib. Headlights bathed them, creating a grotesque moment when everyone froze; then his assailants fled. Tires squealed, and a patrol car rocked to a stop. There were yells, then a blur of sounds while hands lifted him up. Pain came in waves and he groaned.

"Hold him!" a cop snapped, and jammed a credit card against the wound. In seconds the card was changed for a compress, and then tires squealed and a siren wailed as Mike was rushed to the trauma unit at Charity Hospital.

While he was in the hospital, Ben and Simone and three girls from school visited him. Vangie never came by. Healthy and fit from all the yard work, Mike mended fast and was released soon. Five weeks later the only evidence was a two-inch scar along his right rib cage. He had given his report, agreeing to be a witness against the two assailants the cops had arrested.

One morning as Mike was digging in the flower bed near the street, an unmarked car slid to a stop and Captain Clayton climbed out. He leaned against the car with his elbows on the hood and smiled at Mike. "You're a hard worker."

"It pays."

"Ready for good news?"

"Yeah." Mike wiped the sweat off his brow, pushing away a tangle of brown curls.

"We got the break we wanted. The name of the man you gave us—Paul Joyner—he was involved with Leech the night they murdered Claude. He'll turn state's witness. We've got a warrant for Leech for Claude's murder. We're trying to pick him up."

"Thank God!" Mike closed his eyes. "And thank you."

"Don't thank us. You did most of the leg work."

"I'll testify if you need me."

"We'll try to put him so far away, he won't ever come out."

"Do better than that," Mike said. "Finish him off."

"Yeah. Don't work too hard."

"I feel like I could move a mountain now!" Mike said with a savage elation.

"Remind me not to ever cross you. I'm glad you left him to us."

"Don't make me regret that I did."

"We've got good witnesses. And we have the assault charge the night you were attacked, but that's secondary."

"Thanks for coming all the way out here to tell me."

"Yeah. I was going this way. Besides, you deserved to know." Clayton climbed into the car and drove away.

With intense satisfaction and a renewed sense of loss, Mike attended each day of the murder trial. It hurt to listen to the testimony, to know what had happened that night to Claude, but he had to see Leech on trial. Leech received the death penalty. As he turned to leave the courtroom, he glanced across the crowd into Mike's eyes. Rage burned in his gaze, and Mike glared back at him with clenched fists. Mike raised his arm in a swift, obscene gesture, whispering, "For Claude."

That summer after completing two courses in summer school, Mike signed on for a stint in Vietnam, something that sent Ben into a rare rage, but Mike wanted the government to pay for his college. He wanted more independence. Promising to come back to work after the service, he finally soothed Ben's anger.

Mike signed up for a four-year hitch, the USAF Pararescue unit. Jump school was at Fort Bragg, North Carolina. Jungle survival training was in Panama, sea survival was at Patrick Air Force Base, and one week of winter survival was in Alaska. Uncle Sam taught him to use an M-16, and he had scuba training, weapons training, hand-to-hand combat training. He went to three medic schools, eventually earning his red beret.

He was twenty and it was 1969; Richard Nixon was president, and in January there were over five hundred thousand U.S. troops in Vietnam. Mike was stationed at Camp Evans.

Flat, barren, dusty, and excavated in preparation for constructing the hospital base, Camp Evans was surrounded by the greenest country Mike had ever seen. Flying in a four-man-crew Dust-Off chopper—a Huey UH-1H with a big red cross on the side, he made an excellent target. He was wounded once while attempting to rescue a pilot whose F-4 Phantom had gone down in North Vietnam. They had maintained radio control with the injured pilot, and when Mike found him, he had put the pilot in the sling so the chopper could lift him out of danger. But before the chopper could return for Mike, he was jumped from behind and knifed high in the shoulder. He killed his attacker and started walking back across the DMZ. Medics weren't supposed to be armed, but Mike had worn a knife on his left shin and a .357 magnum on his right shin. To the satisfaction of the chopper crew, a grateful marine had given him an M-79 grenade launcher that he wore strapped on his back in case he went down behind enemy lines.

In April 1972 the United States resumed bombing North Vietnam. That fall Mike returned home, his four-year stint having ended. He enrolled in classes and lived again at Ben's, working for him part-time at Southern Market, Inc. Trying to forget the horrors of the past four years, Mike became obsessed with learning the business. With credits he had. earned in courses he had taken in the army, he finished college sooner than expected.

Now, almost two years later, in the spring of 1974, he had his own small apartment in a good section of town. He never went to his old home on the fringe of the Quarter, and he felt as cut off from his childhood as if he had been transformed into another person at age eighteen. His only tie was to send money regularly to Vangie. He had helped her move to a nice apartment, and she had a decent job as a receptionist in an office. She was dating a man she liked a lot, but Mike didn't see her often. Working for Ben full-time, Mike made steady progress, learning to call on investors, owners of shopping centers, bankers, and apartment owners, making contacts, seeking good investments. He had grown closer to Ben each year, finding in him the father he'd never had. When Ben had been elected as a state representative, he had turned more of the business over to Mike. Now that his term was nearly over he was gearing up to run for governor. Mike knew that he would be drawn into the campaign although he preferred to concentrate on the business. Ben had asked him to be his campaign manager and he couldn't refuse him. His thoughts shifted back to his sale, his first spectacular sale, and he wanted to celebrate.

He pressed the accelerator, and the car speeded up, passing the UNO campus as classes changed, and he remembered when he had been one of them, thankful he had his business degree, because he liked the challenge of work. He liked making money and was determined to have wealth and luxury. He glanced at the pretty coeds dressed in spring dresses and shorts, their long, shapely legs bared.

Across campus, Talia rushed toward her class, aware that she had only seconds before it began. She slipped into her seat and opened her book to the assignment, getting out her accounting notes. She sat in the front row, giving her full attention to the short, balding professor who spoke in a monotone. Her grades were top-notch; her time was spent between the twins and her studies. Occasionally she dated but no one sparked her interest as she hoped. She wouldn't acknowledge or admit to herself that one person did arouse her senses when she was in his presence because he was as available to her as the moon—and as remote. During the summer Tyler had spent hours at home with her, taking her out once or twice, but then a new woman, Becky Crane, appeared in his life and Talia had hardly seen him since. He had his own condo now and was executive vice president of the Commercial Lending Department.

When she returned to the Franklins' house to get ready for a date, Talia's pulse jumped when she noticed the forest green Jaguar parked in the drive. She knew Ty had recently dropped Becky for the beautiful and black-haired Victoria Simoneaux, whom he had known for years, but she was younger than he and currently a senior in college at Emory. With Victoria away at school, Ty had been home more often lately, but Talia didn't presume it was because of her. After that one torrid night last summer she had been careful not to be alone with Tyler. But she couldn't forget or stop the excitement she felt every time she was around him.

Talia knew that Pauline had watched them with hawklike attentiveness for a few weeks after she saw them in the pool, but as months passed and Ty continued dating socially acceptable women, Pauline seemed to relax and accept that Ty was friendly with Talia just as he was friendly with Bertha. Sloane's friendship with Talia was stronger and warmer and of a different nature. Talia felt at ease with Sloane, as if she were with an old friend. She now understood some of the relationship nuances in the family. Pauline spoiled her two older sons, but was rather strict with the two younger. Of her two eldest boys, Sloane was the most pampered, always getting what he wanted from his mother while Millard Franklin favored Ty.

Once when she was walking across campus, Sloane had passed her, put on his brakes, and backed up. "I'll give you a ride. Get in. I'm going home."

"I'm going to see my mom, so I'm not going home."

"I'll take you out to see her and bring you back to get your car."

"It's a long drive."

"It's a gorgeous day and you're a gorgeous woman and I'd be delighted."

"Since you put it that way, I accept," she said, settling back against the seat.

He drove her to the home and waited patiently while Talia talked to the nurse on duty, then motioned to him.

"Mom's out on the lawn. You can wait here or you can come meet her."

"I'll come meet her," he said in the same manner as if she had been inviting him into her home. Together they strode across the lawn where he met Kate, who could converse with them as long as they spoke about light and cheerful subjects such as the weather, the birds, or the flowers. Sometimes Kate forgot the drift of the conversation and the topic would change in midsentence, but if it bothered Sloane, he gave no indication. Talia was grateful that he had come.

Sloane accompanied her often after that day until Kate seemed to know Sloane as well as she used to know some of Talia's old friends. Talia was grateful for his company and for the opportunity to talk to someone about her mother's condition. She rarely spoke with Rebecca these days.

When Talia got home she hurried up the stairs and almost collided with Ty on the landing. Startled, she backed up and he steadied her.

"Who's the big date?" he asked with a teasing smile. He was dressed for a formal occasion, handsome in his black tux. He struggled with links to go in his cuffs.

"There isn't one. I was just hurrying. Here, I'll help you," she said, taking his wrist and completing the job, aware of every inch of flesh touching hers, noticing the gold links that bore his initials as so many of his possessions did.

"Do you have time to come talk to me a minute? I have to be somewhere in ten minutes, but I want your advice."

"Sure," she said, following Ty into his bedroom where he closed the door, and motioned for her to sit down. "I've been offered a job as president of Egland Enterprises. It might be more of a challenge than the bank, yet Dad has counted on me to take over. I'd have to prove myself there whereas at the Franklin banks, they'll be tolerant."

When she laughed, he arched his brows in question. "I don't think you have to concern yourself about people being tolerant. You work hard, and you excel at whatever you do."

His white teeth flashed in a smile. "My word! I'm a paragon!"

"Don't let it go to your head!"

He crossed the room to her and her pulse seemed to speed with each step closer he came. His dark eyes glittered with an emotion she couldn't read as he placed his finger under her jaw and tilted her chin upward.

"I thought you needed advice," she said softly, barely aware of her words. He drew her to her feet, and she could catch the faint scent of his aftershave. His dark eyes seemed to penetrate her very soul. Ty held her, seeing that lethargic, sensual look come to her eyes even though he knew a protest was rising to her lips. Her full, red lips beckoned to him.

"I do. And you're the only person outside of the family whose judgment I trust. But suddenly I'm not that interested in your judgment."

He leaned down, covering her mouth with his, opening hers, touching the wet warmth of her tongue with his. He crushed her to him, bending over her, holding her around the waist with one hand, the other sliding over her curves.

"You're going to be late," she said breathlessly, pushing away. "You said you only had ten minutes."

"Yeah," he said, barely hearing her, realizing she had changed since she first came to work for them. Her hair was longer, more attractive now. She seemed taller, more poised.

Talia collected her thoughts quickly and moved farther away from him. "Have a good time," she said, leaving the room.

"Yeah, sure." Ty watched her go, his desire growing. Her kisses were exciting, and he wanted more.

The next afternoon Ty sat in the weekly loan committee meeting. He ran his finger over the mahogany table that was plain, unlike the ornate hand-carved table in the locked board-room where framed pictures of his great-grandfather, his grandfather, and his father Millard hung. Someday his own picture would accompany them.

Millard spoke to him and Ty sat forward, his pulse racing with excitement as he recounted the loans he had made the past month and the new business for the bank they had generated. As he read the figures, he heard the approval of the committee, and he knew he would never leave the bank to go with Egland. The offer hadn't even been tempting. There was enough opportunity here. He intended to expand the bank's facilities and watch it grow into one of the major banks in the country. He had spent the previous year as the vice president of the special industries department, working on oil and gas lending. In that time the assets of the bank had grown and currently were almost one billion dollars. He wondered when his father would step down and felt a twinge of impatience thinking about it.

He concentrated on his report, finished, listened to the congratulations and discussion and then as they went on to Fred Barthe's report, Ty's mind wandered back to last night, to Talia's kisses. He still intended to discover the secrets behind Talia Wade's sensuality. He would have to wait for the right moment.

Dressed in a filmy red nightgown, her black curls tousled, Rebecca lay sprawled across the bed listening to Greg as he paced up and down the room. "I have a promotion! You can quit singing in that sleazy nightclub. My salary will be two hundred dollars more a month!"

"That's great, Greg," she said, trying to sound enthused, rolling over on the black sheets and stretching.

"We can get married."

Her head jerked up as he crossed the room to catch her by her upper arms and pull her off the bed to her feet. "We'll get married. You can quit working and lead a normal life— no more sleeping all day and working all night. I never see you and when I do, you're too groggy to talk. Oh, baby, we can buy a house now." He kissed her hard, and she wrapped her arms around him, returning his kisses so he would stop talking, trying to fight a sense of panic that was developing in her.

She was tired of Greg, and the thought of being tied down by marriage to a house, a husband, and kids, gave her a chilly fright. She didn't want responsibility, and when faced with it, she always wanted out. Talia had always been the one to take on the responsibility of household chores. Rebecca wouldn't even know where to begin.

She listened to Greg make plans all evening. It all sounded like a trap to her. Finally at nine o'clock it was time for her to go to work. It was winter in Chicago and they had to fight the snow and the wind, but Greg went with her for the first time in months. He sat at a corner table until midnight, listening to her sing. He went home then; she followed later and found him waiting for her.

He pulled her into bed, undressed her, and made love to her before falling into a sound sleep. When the alarm went off the next morning, she stirred, lying with her eyes closed until Greg left for work. She threw back the covers, got her suitcase from the closet and packed, finding the canister she kept hidden away in the back of the closet and taking the four hundred dollars she had secretly saved. In an hour she was on a bus to Los Angeles. It would be warmer than Chicago, and far away from Greg.

The first job she got was as a waitress in a cafe on a major highway. By the end of the month, she had a job singing in a nightclub. The manager who hired her was Sam Gordano, a short, brawny, swarthy man who she knew watched her constantly. During her interview, his dark eyes had raked over her boldly, and Rebecca had gazed back at him just as openly.

The Sunset Club had palm trees in the parking lot; pink flamingos and a peeling golden sunset were painted on the cracked walls. It was always crowded on weekends. After the cold winter in Illinois, she loved the sunshine and spent afternoons lying in the sun whenever she got the chance.

She stood singing with her hand on the mike, letting a breathlessness come to her voice, on her fourth Saturday night at the Sunset. She wore a clinging scarlet silk dress, cut to her waist in front, revealing her curves. There were slits up to her thighs on both sides of the narrow straight skirt.

Sam had a cigar clenched in his teeth, and he always seemed to be in a hurry, except for occasional moments when he sat at a table talking to customers or friends, or when he paused to watch Rebecca perform.

She could see him now in the smoky gloom and she sang to him, not particularly caring about him as a man, but as her boss. He held the purse strings. She knew he was twice-divorced, thirty-eight, and tough. The waitresses said little about him, except to warn her to watch out for him. What she was supposed to watch out for, she didn't know.

When she finished and went down the hall to the tiny cubicle they gave her for a dressing room, Sam was waiting for her. He followed her inside, lounging against the door. His curly black hair was shoulder length, his cream-colored shirt open to the waist, a gold necklace around his thick neck.

"Hey, kid. That was pretty good."

"Thanks, Sam."

"I'll take you home tonight. Go up to my office and stick around."

"Sure," she said, nodding.

"Kid, don't change."

She looked into his black eyes and nodded. The nightclub

was second-rate, and in the dusky gloom it looked okay, but if the lights were turned on, the peeling paint on the pink flamingos showed as well as the threadbare carpet in the entrance. Upstairs was different. Sam's office was deluxe with a plush red carpet, a big desk, deep comfortable chairs and a white sofa that curved around one corner of the room. Doors opened off his office and she explored the area, as curious as a cat. One room revealed a small bar, fully equipped, and the next door opened into a bathroom decorated with tiger-striped wallpaper. The last door opened into a bedroom with mirrors on the walls and ceilings. She opened the closets, looked at his suits, then went back to wait in the office.

"Hi, kid," he said when he came in. "I ordered dinner sent up." He stubbed out the cigar in a crystal ash tray. "You're pretty good."

"Thanks. I think I'm going to like it here," she said in her sultriest voice, wondering how generous he would be. As his gaze raked over her, he crossed the room to her. He was only a few inches taller and he stopped close in front of her. "You're pretty, Rebecca," he said, his voice getting husky.

"Thanks," she said, looking at his broad face, his large eyes, and hooked nose. He wasn't handsome, but he was noticeable. His black eyes held one's attention, accentuating his no-nonsense attitude.

"New Orleans, Chicago, L.A., you've been around."

"Yeah," she answered.

"And you're real pretty," he said, reaching out to stroke her arm. She smiled at him and he slipped his arms around her, pulling her to him for a kiss. Within minutes her red dress fell in a heap on the floor.

She moved in over the Sunset Club two weeks later. Three months after that she asked for and received a raise. In three more months, she asked for another raise and Sam refused.

They argued about it for a month, and then she got a job singing in another club for more than she had asked Sam for. She wasn't going to tell him until she had moved, but he came in when she was packing. She thought he was gone for the day. Instead, he stood inside the doorway with his fists on his hips. His eyes narrowed as he walked over to the bed where she stood.

"What are you doing?"

"I'm moving to an apartment," she said, dropping her dress into the suitcase.

"And when were you going to tell me?"

"I'm telling you now."

"I didn't expect to be here today. You would have been gone when I got back."

"No, I wouldn't have. I'll be here to sing tonight."

He hit her, the slap making a sharp crack in the room, spinning her across the room against the bed. She gasped, shaking her head, rubbing her jaw. She looked up to see him coming after her and she scrambled away from him. The second blow was just as bad, and it knocked her to the floor. She screamed and tried to run. He caught her hair and yanked her back, shoving her down. "Unpack, you ungrateful little bitch. You'll do what I tell you!"

He left her sobbing on the floor. She hurt and she was terrified of him. No man had ever hit her before. Rage and hatred surfaced. She unpacked, put cold washcloths on her face and that night she was able to hide her bruises with makeup.

For the next two weeks she was sweet and docile and he began to relax around her, becoming pleasant again. One of the first things she did after the beating was to go out and buy a black cape, and a huge black cloth purse. She wore the cape and carried the purse whenever she left the club so everyone became accustomed to both items.

Taking her time and using care, when Sam was gone during the day, she went through his desk, through his files, finally finding the combination to his safe. She opened it and discovered two sets of books for the club. Rebecca sat cross-legged on his thick red carpet and spread the books in front of her. She began reading.

An hour later she locked them up again and waited until a Monday when Sam would be gone all morning. Knowing his men had been told to watch her, she put on layers of underwear, four dresses and the cape. She packed as much as she could in her big black bag. Opening Sam's safe, she took his private books and stuffed them into the bag along with her clothing.

When she sauntered into the bar downstairs, she perched on a stool. Harry was drying glasses and putting away bottles. His blue eyes raked over her. "You're going out."

"Yeah. I told Sam. I'm getting a haircut and perm."

"You cut much off and you'll be bald."

"Man, this is long!"

"When will you be back?" he asked casually, and she answered with the same careless tone.

"About six hours. I might shop."

"Make it four hours. Shop tomorrow."

"Sure, watchdog!"

He snapped his jaws and growled at her. She smiled and slid off the stool, swaying her hips as she walked out, her heart pounding in her chest. She sauntered outside into the sunshine.

She went straight to the post office, wrote a letter to Sam, telling him she had taken something that she knew he would want returned. She would tell the IRS to return it to him. She sent the letter to Sam and the books to the IRS. Next, she boarded a plane for Reno, because she didn't think it would be good for her health to remain in Los Angeles.

In August Talia took the twins to the house in Mississippi. She sped along the highway skirting the water that stretched endlessly out of sight, blurring into the blue horizon. While the twins played a game in the back seat, Talia cast continual glances at the water. She loved the beach and the peaceful little hamlet along the Gulf.

The sand was white, glistening in the hot sunshine, bordering the blue water. On the other side of the road were tall palms and two-story houses with screened porches set back from the road, oaks and palms gracing the long, sloping lawns. As they neared the house, the twins sent up a howl. "There's Pete and his mom." They screamed and waved until Talia quieted them.

"Let us out here. Please, please!" Jeff begged. "C'mon,

Tali, just this time," he said, his brown eyes imploring, and
Tali slowed and pulled off to park. Already dressed in suits
and eager to reach the water, the boys flung off their shirts.
The sun felt glorious, and after Talia had talked to Pam
Robertson about watching the boys, she walked across the
road to the house to get her suit. Sloane's car was in the drive
and as the kitchen door slammed shut behind her, she called
to him.

Music blared from the den, and she called out again as she
walked the short distance through the kitchen to the family
room. "Slo—" She stopped.

Sloane and a younger man scrambled to yank clothes in
front of them. A mirror was on the coffee table with two
lines poured on it, a small bag of white powder beside it.

"I'm sorry," Talia gasped, stunned, her face flaming,
wishing she were a hundred miles away. The beat of the
music was the only sound for a moment, then Sloane's mouth
curved into a smile.

"Hi, Tali," he said slyly.

"I'm sorry," she whispered again, turning away to go
through the dining room to the stairs. Shocked, she went to
her room, changing to her swimsuit and pulling on a yellow
terry coverup and sandals. When she went downstairs, the
music was turned off and the house was silent. She entered
the kitchen, getting out a basket and beginning to gather
apples and cookies for the boys.

"Pretty soon you'll know all the family secrets," Sloane
said from the doorway.

She turned to look at him. He had dressed in cotton pants,
but his muscular torso was bare, his biceps bulging.

"I didn't mean to walk in on you," she said, blushing
with embarrassment. "I didn't know—I left the boys on the
beach with Pam Robertson."

"I should have been more careful, but this is the middle
of the week and I thought everyone was busy at home." He
was polite, a faint smile curving his mouth. He lounged in
the doorway, looking handsome and friendly.

"What you do is your business. I didn't mean to intrude.
Where's your friend?"

"Chad left while you were upstairs." Sloane sauntered to the table. "Sit down and talk to me a minute. Pam will watch the boys."

"Sure." Talia pulled out a chair and sat down facing him.

"You know I date Melissa."

"There's no need to discuss this with me, Sloane. What you do is your business. I don't talk about your family to you. I won't talk about you to them," she said with far more calm than she felt.

His white teeth flashed in a grin and he stretched out his long legs. "And you don't condemn me?"

"No. I can't sit in judgment on you."

"So we're still friends?"

"Yes," she said, thinking his eyes were beautiful with his thick lashes. His mouth was full, curved, almost feminine, yet masculine, and she was still in shock over her discovery about him, because she wouldn't have guessed that he was gay. He dated and there was a time when she was sure he was having an affair with a woman. Then Talia realized that Sloane must be bisexual.

He sighed and stroked her cheek. "You're sweet, and young, and innocent, Tali. If it weren't for that, and for wanting to avoid a storm with Pauline, I would have made a pass long ago."

Shocked again, Talia saw amusement surface in his eyes. "I like both. Men and women. And you're growing up into a lovely woman, but I guess now is not the time for me to come on strong with you."

"I'm not much younger than you, Sloane. You sound like you're aged."

"I wonder how many Franklin secrets you know?"

"You won't worm them out of me. You know how many it takes to keep a secret? Only one. When there are more, it's no longer a secret."

"Do you like us after all this time? Mother's a snob, quite a pushover for Ty and me. Millard has his discreet affairs. Oh, oh!" he exclaimed, his brows arching, and she realized her surprise must have shown. "I figured you knew about Millard."

"No," she said, thinking of Pauline, who was so prim and proper.

"Millard has a double standard. He's old-fashioned. If Pauline were ever unfaithful, he would crucify her. So there. Pauline's weakness is giving in to Ty and me. Particularly me."

In spite of everything, Talia smiled. "I didn't think you'd admit it!"

His perfect white teeth flashed in a grin. "Only to you, love. She's my champion, and Lord knows I need one. Ty is Millard's idea of perfection. He's all the things I can't be, and Millard has always thrown them at me. You said you had an older sister."

"Yes. Our situation isn't like yours exactly, except Mom did spoil Rebecca, although I wasn't too aware of it at the time. I guess I knew it and just accepted it."

"What does your sister do?"

"I don't know. After our father died, she got her own apartment."

"She had an apartment and you lived with your mother?"

"Yes. Rebecca wanted to be on her own. Frankly, she's a drifter. She doesn't like responsibility."

"So different from you. You spend more time with the twins than you need to. More than any nanny before you. You're like a mother to them. So you don't hear from Rebecca?"

"No, I don't."

"Tali, I've seen you with Ty. He has a streak like Millard, ruthless and cold and he's a womanizer."

She blushed, surprised that her attraction to Ty had been so obvious. "I know I'm hired help. I never forget that and I don't expect anything of Ty."

"I just don't want to see you get hurt," he said softly.

"Thanks."

"He can be charming, and he can be deadly when he wants something."

"So far all I've seen is the charming side," she said, uneasy when the topic concerned her. "And I expect him to announce his engagement any day to Victoria." Before this afternoon, she would playfully have asked Sloane about Melissa, but not now. She stood up. "I better see about the boys. Want to join us?"

"Sure. Thanks, Tali, for just being you."

She smiled at him, picking up the basket of food and pop. Sloane took it from her, gathering both their towels. In minutes they crossed the road in the hot sunshine.

"Wait a minute," she said, balancing on one foot to remove her sandal. Sloane steadied her, his hand firm on her waist, and then she pulled free the other sandal and stepped into hot, deep sand. As he went striding ahead of her, she glanced at him again. He had shed the cotton pants before they left the house and wore his swim trunks and sandals. His body was bronzed and as fit and muscular as Ty's. He was handsome, and she saw two women watching him, their speculative gazes taking him in. Talia wondered if the family knew about Sloane, and she suspected that they didn't—with the possible exception of Ty. Ty and Sloane were close in age, as close in many ways as the twins. Sloane was sensitive and a good listener, and she suspected he and Ty had few secrets from each other. Her thoughts shifted to Sloane's warning to her about Ty, but she didn't think she was in danger of losing her heart to him, if only because he would never give her the chance.

Two weeks later on the first of September, 1974, shortly after the national furor over Richard Nixon's resignation, the senior Franklins, Talia, and the twins spent the weekend at the Mississippi house. Sunday morning, the Franklins left, taking the twins with them, and Talia stayed behind, planning to drive her own car back later. In the middle of the afternoon while she was stretched on the beach on a towel, she felt sand trickle down her spine.

She rolled over, expecting to find the twins' friends. Instead, she looked up into Ty's laughing black eyes.

9

Fall 1974

As Ty opened his fist to let sand trickle down on her midriff, Talia jumped to her feet.

He grinned, standing inches away, his body lean and bronzed, his black eyes sparkling with laughter. "I couldn't resist. Race you to the water."

"This is one time you're not going to win, Ty Franklin!" she snapped, giving him a push down onto the soft sand and yelling, "Go!" as she turned to dash for the water. "Last one in is a loser!" she called over her shoulder, seeing him already getting to his feet and sprinting after her. She laughed and just before she plunged into the water, his arms caught her from behind, spinning her around. She locked her arms around his waist, pulling him with her, knowing it was useless.

"A tie! It's a tie!"

"Oh, no, it's not! I'm going to beat you into the water." Suddenly he stopped and looked down at her, mischief evident in his eyes. "Maybe it will be a tie," he said, scooping her into his arms, carrying her and marching into the Gulf. She shrieked, knowing he was going to duck her.

"You win! I give in! Ty, put me—"

He fell forward into deep water, taking her down with him, her words ending in a sputter. His body felt warm and hard and marvelous against hers, and she was more aware of him than of the cool water that swirled over her head. She pushed to the top, coming up with him, his hands on her waist.

Ty held her, and their laughter vanished as he felt her soft curves. He looked into her darkening green eyes. She inhaled, and he lowered his gaze, the temperature heating between them in spite of the cool water. He wanted to run his hands over her, to peel away her bathing suit, and he wondered if she had ever slept with anyone.

He had thought of asking Victoria to marry him, but now he knew he would definitely postpone it longer. If Talia could tempt him, he didn't want to get tied down yet. And she tempted him. Ever since she had started working for his family, he had wondered at various times what she would be like in bed, but their timing was out of synch, and so he had followed the safest course and gone back to the current woman in his life. Talia's cheeks were flushed, her skin golden from the sun, her lips red and inviting. He had stopped at the house on an impulse, and now he was glad he had as he looked into eyes that held a smoldering speculation.

His arousal was swift and hard. His hands tightened on her waist while he saw the searing change in her expression. Hungry longing showed in her eyes. Watching her, he pulled her down gently into the water, letting them sink to their chins.

"I wish we were alone," he said, aware of the rasp in his voice, aching to possess her. Beneath the water, he reached up, sliding his hands over her ribs, watching her eyes as his thumbs slipped over the underside of her breasts, then moved up over her nipples, feeling their hard peaks. Gasping, she closed her eyes. He pulled her to him, crushing her in his arms as he kept them both afloat while he kissed her passionately.

When she stopped him, she wriggled out of his grasp. "Ty, don't. I can't take much of that."

"Why not?" he asked, his heart hammering.

Instead of answering, she swam away, coming up out of the water to stride to her towel, her firm buttocks flexing beneath the suit with each step.

He watched her walk away, his eyes raking over her while he tried to calm his body. She picked up her towel and went toward the house. He caught up with her before she crossed the highway.

"I want to show you something. Will you get dressed and

go with me?'' She slanted him a curious, wary look and in return he hoped he gave her his most disarming smile. ''Please, Talia,'' he said coaxingly, and she laughed.

''You and Sloane—both of you could talk the world into turning the opposite direction!''

''How I wish! If I could do that, do you know what I would do first, rather than spin the old world backward?''

''What?''

''I'd talk you into my bed,'' he said, watching her closely.

She blushed, the pink suffusing her cheeks: ''I think you'll have to settle for changing the world.''

He slowed his stride to match hers. ''Back to what I was asking. I want you to see something. Will you come with me?''

She should refuse. There was a recklessness to him, and the moment in the water had shaken her. His kisses had shaken her like a jarring earthquake rearranging her footing in life. She answered yes, laughing with him, wondering what he would show her or if it were merely a ploy to get her into his bed.

''You'll have to change. Wear shorts or slacks or something like that.''

''Okay, Mr. Franklin. I'll go put on something like that while you change.''

He winked at her, pulling her close to walk with him, his arm around her waist, so that her thigh brushed his with each step.

While he changed, he was aware that she was doing the same only a room away. They were home alone, and he would prefer to lock the doors, stay home and try to seduce her, but he held back. He wanted her; he had planned to have her, but Talia could become a complication in his life that he could ill afford. And his mother might lose a damn good employee. That would bring the fury of his younger brothers down on his head because they loved Talia like a sister. He was amazed at how good she was with them. He had seen her help them build their models, patiently teach them to ride their bikes, do the things his mother should have done, but never had. When they were growing up, he and Sloane had been on their own for so many things; their Dad had done more with them than Pauline, urging them on to win, drumming it into Ty's head that he had to win, until Ty suspected he would lose not only his father's love but also his interest if he didn't succeed. And when Sloane rebelled or lost or didn't try hard enough, there was hell to pay. That was when Pauline rose up and made herself heard. She loved them all in her own way, but she protected Sloane like a mother lion with a cub. Sometimes Ty thought his mother needed their care and attention more than they needed hers.

He stepped into white poplin pants, yanked on a green T-shirt, fastened a thin leather belt around his waist, and slipped into top-siders, then raked a comb through his hair, shaking his head so black strands settled above his forehead. He hurried down the hall to Talia's room just as she stepped out to meet him.

She wore pale blue slacks and a matching shirt, her blond hair fastened in a long braid down her back, making her look younger and less sexy until he met her eyes.

He took her hand, pulling her toward the stairs. "Hurry! This is a special surprise!"

His exuberance was contagious, and Talia felt a tingling excitement as they climbed into his Jaguar and roared down the driveway onto the highway. He drove too fast, the wind whipping against her, conversation lost because of the rush of air. The ocean was on her right. They headed east and turned in a slewing curve that made the tires squeal. On the flat land stretching beyond the dirt road was a short landing strip and a line of small planes tied down beside a metal hangar.

In a cloud of dust Ty braked and cut the motor, climbing out and taking her hand when she joined him. He hurried to a plane and stopped to wave his hand at it. "How do you like it?"

"It's lovely," she said, eyeing the red-and-white Piper Arrow while Ty removed the blocks beneath the wheels.

"Climb aboard," he said, hopping up onto the low wing and reaching down to swing her up. He stepped down through the single door and held her hand as she followed, and they both buckled into their seats.

Hoping she liked the plane half as much as he did, Ty's

pulse raced with eagerness. He turned on the battery switch, watching the gauges jump. He knew the fuel was okay. As he hit the fuel boost pump, he said, "I've saved my money for this, and I just got a bonus from Dad for the increase in business in my department at the bank."

"Do you know how to pilot a plane?" she asked with a slight frown.

"Nope. We're going to learn today."

Her head jerked around, and then she met his gaze and visibly relaxed while she laughed. "I should have known! How long have you had a pilot's license?"

"For years," he answered, blithely aware she had grown more poised in the years with his family, remembering how easily he could fluster her that first month she had been at the house. He turned the ignition, and after the propeller swung and caught, he checked all his instruments. He released the brake, revving the engines, and when they taxied forward, he picked up the mike.

"November forty-two Charley taking the runway, going to depart to the west," he said.

Excited and careless, he ignored the take-off checklist at the end of the runway with only a glance toward the direction of arrivals. He pushed forward on the throttle, watching the air-speed needle pick up. At sixty-five knots, the small plane became light on the wheels, lifting. Whenever he became airborne, his exhilaration climbed along with the plane. Ty pulled back on the yoke, reaching over to tug the gear handle, settling into a climb speed of ninety knots as they headed into the sky.

They soared up and out toward the beach. Talia, who hadn't flown in a small plane before, found it fascinating to be so close to earth, to watch everything below: the traffic, the people sunning on the beach, the bright blue water. They skimmed over the water, flying out over the calm Gulf until they lost sight of land and it was a world of blue above and below.

Excitement hummed in Ty like the roar of the motor. He wanted to see more enthusiasm from Talia, to get more thrills from the ride. He always pushed everything and everyone around him to limits, including himself. He turned the nose down, accelerating and sending the power screaming as the plane sliced through the air.

For a split second Talia thought he was going right into the water. She screeched, watching him grin, while a spreading wall of water surged closer. Her heart pounded as she watched the barrier loom up until at the last moment Ty leveled off only feet above the blue surface at one hundred and twenty knots. The propeller kicked a wide wake, water splashing onto the windscreen while everything flashed past to her right and left. She gasped for breath, knowing they were flying as no one was meant to fly, winging it only feet above the water, the feeling of speed as stimulating as a drug.

She gripped his arm. "Ty, get us up!"

"Up, the lady says, so up it is." He turned the nose in a steep climb to gain altitude, the motor straining. Talia screeched again, laughing this time because she felt totally safe with him. Ty dazzled her. Wealthy, extroverted, active, and handsome, in spite of his egregious recklessness, he always seemed in control and sure of himself, and she gave her worries over to his care. She laughed with him, and wondered if anything ever frightened him.

Ty watched her. He had taken Victoria up the second day he'd had the plane. When he went into a stall and the slipstream thudded against the shuddering plane, she had turned deathly pale, screamed, and thrown up on his new plane. When they landed, she had made it clear that as far as she was concerned, a plane was for transportation only. Her black eyes flashed with anger against skin as pale as snow.

He glanced at Talia. Her eyes were narrowed, squinting at the water. Her hands gripped the seat, a faint smile curved her lips, and her eyes sparkled. Her breasts strained against her shirt as she laughed. She looked as if she was having the time of her life, and a mounting elation filled him. He remembered the first afternoon he had met Talia, and thought again about how much she had changed.

Once they were stable with a normal cruise setting, Talia settled and relaxed and watched shrimp boats loom into sight, then fall behind, on the Gulf below. When he thought she was lulled into complacency, he reached out to pull the mixture level back, and the engine stopped.

Wind rushing around the windscreen and air vents was the only noise. The prop kept turning as Ty knew it would because of the wind. Decelerating force pushed them both forward in their seats. He turned the yoke left, banking the plane, starting into a dive. Water rushed up to meet them while Talia gripped his arm again. Laughing, she leaned forward to gaze earthward.

Excited by her fearlessness at the danger he had created, he cut it as close as possible, then waited until he was five hundred feet above the water to throw the mixture lever forward. The engine caught and he leveled out over the Gulf.

She screamed with delight, falling back into the seat, and in that moment he vowed to do whatever he could to seduce her that night. He had planned to accomplish that long before now. He reached over and caught her chin, turning her to face him, leaning across space and levers that separated them to kiss her hard.

After her first moment of surprise, she returned his kiss, her tongue thrusting into his mouth deeply, making him groan, the sound lost in the noise of the plane. He pulled away, looking into her green eyes. The day was special. Talia was special.

They flew almost to the Louisiana line and back to land smoothly on the short strip. As his hands closed about her waist to swing her down to the ground, he held her.

"Want me to teach you to fly?"

"Me?" Her eyes flew wide. "It would be expensive."

He laughed. "Miss Practical! It won't cost you anything. Do you want to learn?"

"Of course!" she said, sliding her hands higher on his forearms, feeling the sinewy muscles. Power seemed to exude from him; his thickly lashed black eyes were magnetic, his body lean and powerful, and she could go on looking at him forever. "You have everything, Ty! I wonder if you know how fortunate you are."

"Not everything," he answered lightly.

"What on earth could you want?"

"You," he said solemnly, and her breath stopped, her heart seemed to thud against her ribs. Before she could answer, he went on. "I want power, Talia. I want to do things that people will remember.'' His gaze came back to her. ''I want to kiss you,'' he said, leaning down to kiss her a long time. Finally she pushed him away.

''We're in public and here comes someone!''

''Yeah,'' he answered, turning away to talk to the line boy long enough to pay him. Then arm in arm, Ty walked with Talia to the car while he answered her questions and told her about his flying lessons at age fourteen and his experience. He took her to a restaurant in the next town. It was on a dock in the water, a luxurious room with linen tablecloths, a deep blue carpet, and a gorgeous view of the Gulf and the sunset, golden rays playing across the blue water and white sand.

He drove too fast going home, but she seemed to love that as much as he did. The wind made conversation impossible. He wondered what *could* frighten her as he pressed the accelerator to the floor, watching the needle of the Jaguar climb while they sped along the highway. Still she showed no fear, and finally he slowed to his usual speed, slightly over the limit. When they stopped at the darkened house, his pulse began a dull, heavy beat in anticipation as he reached down to take her hand while she stepped out of the car.

''Let's get some drinks and go down to the beach for a night swim.''

''I've never been in the Gulf at night, not any of the times we've been down here. Your folks won't let the twins swim at night.''

He stared at her, wanting her to want to do everything he liked to do, disappointment dawning when she tossed her head. ''It's inky black out there and I don't know what's in the water, but if you'll stay with me . . .''

''I'll stay with you,'' he said, satisfied. ''Let's change and I'll meet you in the kitchen. First one down gets some beers.''

They hurried upstairs, and as he pulled on tight black trunks, he wondered at himself. It had never been as important before for women to enjoy what he did. But today in the plane he wanted to keep on sharing what he liked with her, to see the same enthusiasm in her that he felt. He picked up a towel, glanced at the room and yanked up his clothes to toss them into the closet. He turned a light on low near the bed, then left to find her in the kitchen.

They dropped their things on the deserted beach, and he expected she would balk about going into the water. He took her hand and together they walked into the surf, swimming out in long strokes. She kept right with him.

Later they lay on a blanket in the sand and watched the stars gradually shift in the sky. His fingers drifted up and down her arm, over her shoulder while they talked. They gathered up their things and walked back to the house where he turned on the pool lights and opened the beers. They sat on yellow chaises in the shadows at the edge of the patio beneath the spreading limbs of an oak, the bright blue pool yards away in front of them. They talked far into the night. Finally she said she should go and he stood up with her, walking upstairs. At the head of the stairs, he turned her to face him. The only light was from the hall downstairs, and a soft glow from the open door of his room.

Her eyes were opened wide, a dark green in the dim light, her straight brown brows were drawn closer in a frown of concentration, her lips parted.

"In the plane I wanted to do this," he whispered.

Talia's breath caught as he leaned down to kiss her. His arm circled her waist, pulling her against him. They were still in swimsuits, narrow strips of material that barely covered their warm bodies, and the moment she pressed against him, he felt as if he had brushed against a flame. Her body was soft in his arms, and while he held her close with one arm, his other hand traced the sweet curve of her back, feeling her smooth flesh. His hand slipped down over the slope of her buttocks, pressing their firmness, touching her thigh.

She moaned softly and he picked her up, carrying her to his room while he kissed her the whole time. He sat down on the bed, holding her on his lap, touching her, responding to her desire. His hand carressed her full breast, then he untied the string behind her neck. His fingers followed it down, shifting to cup her breast and flick his thumb over the nipple. She gasped and clung to him, returning his kisses wildly, and his senses spun more than they had in the tumbling aircraft earlier.

Talia was lost in his arms, wanting him, knowing he was awakening forces in her that she couldn't—wouldn't—control. Tyler was as unreachable as the handsome god Apollo, a myth to her. He would never be hers more than now; she wanted him to hold her, to kiss her, to take her. He was more exciting than any man she had ever known.

She found Ty watching her through half-closed black eyes that smoldered with desire. He was male perfection with his finely chiseled features, his thick black hair, his strong, virile body. She wanted to look and touch, to let him possess her, to know she was his.

Her sultry gaze was like a hot caress, and his pulse roared in his ears. He snapped the clasp that held the top of her swimsuit, slipping it away and letting it fall unheeded. With a gentle push, he moved her off his lap, standing up to cup her breasts in his hands, to watch her gasp and close her eyes, while her hands caressed his chest, tangling in the crisp, dark mat of hair. Talia's innocence vanished beneath the onslaught of Ty's passion, igniting desire within her, and she was awed by the handsome man who seemed to adore touching her. She was shocked at the power she held over Ty who had always been in absolute control. With the stroke of her fingers across his chest she could make him gasp; her caress on his bare thigh could make him tremble.

He peeled away the bottom of her suit, sliding his hands down the outside of her legs, and he could barely catch his breath as he looked at her flawless body, the strips of pale flesh where her suit had been, the tawny tangle of curls at the juncture of her thighs. He swung her into his arms and knelt on the bed to place her down, to let his hands drift over her while his tongue trailed across her flat stomach, down to her thighs. She gasped, her hands tangled in his thick hair, pulling lightly on him, but he ignored the tug as his fingers plundered the moist softness between her thighs, and she cried softly with pleasure.

Suddenly she pushed against him, her eyes opening to meet his in alarm. "Ty, I'm not protected."

"I'll take care of it," he said brusquely. He straightened up, pulled a cellophane-wrapped package out of his nightstand draw, and shed his constricting trunks that no longer hid his arousal. His penis was thick and blue-veined. As Talia looked him over, she rolled on her side to stroke his thigh, her hand moving upward, her fingers pale against his engorged flesh.

He groaned and lowered himself to the bed beside her, pulling her to him roughly, wanting her as much as he had ever wanted anything. His need escalated and in minutes he moved between her thighs, watching her, drinking in her beauty, thinking she was more beautiful than any woman he had ever known.

He lowered himself and her hands held his bulging biceps, then grabbed his broad shoulders. The tip of his cock pressed against her, then he thrust into her softness. Her cry was muffled by his mouth for an instant. Frowning, he raised his head, and she saw the surprise and accusation in his eyes, realizing then that he hadn't expected her to be a virgin.

She raised her hips to meet him, pressing on his firm buttocks, closing her eyes and biting her lip. His mouth came down hard, opening hers as he thrust into her, taking her cry, moving, because he was unable to hold back any longer. She hurt, yet she wanted him and she moved beneath him, feeling his quick, shuddering release, hearing him groan and gasp her name as his mouth twisted from hers.

His weight came down on her, crushing the breath from her lungs. She held him tightly, stroking his back, knowing it was a night that would be etched in her memory for as long as she lived, wondering if any other man in her life could equal the thrill that was Tyler Franklin.

He turned to kiss her shoulder, his hand stroking her. "That wasn't fun for you."

She gazed into his eyes, biting back the answer that anything that involved him was fun for her; that tonight was magical and unforgettable. "Yes, it was," she said simply. "I wanted you to want me, Tyler."

He groaned and kissed her throat, moving beside her to pull her close to him. She felt wanted and she basked in the knowledge.

"You're beautiful, Talia," he whispered, giving her a ripple of pleasure. His hands drifted lightly over her, exploring her while she discovered the feel and shape of his body. During the next half hour, their lazy conversation changed, his touches were no longer light or aimless, but erotic, stroking her breasts, sliding along her silken inner thighs, and she felt his arousal come swift and strong once again.

"Ty, if I showered—"

His hard kiss stopped her words while his hand slipped between her thighs to stroke her rhythmically until she was lost in need, clinging to him, caressing him. This time was different. Sensations rocked her, and she lost awareness of the world, knowing only his body and the wild rapture that made her cry out his name, hearing his hoarse voice mingle with hers as they soared over a brink of stored emotion and gained release.

To Ty's amazement, he didn't want the night to end. Usually he could be satiated, and think clearly, but not tonight. She abandoned herself to his lovemaking as wildly as she had abandoned herself to his flying, and he adored it.

At dawn as he held her close, their bodies damp with perspiration, she trailed her fingers over his chest. "I should be up and on my way home in a few hours. I have to be there this afternoon when the twins get home from school."

"That's hours away."

"I know, but I have to go."

"You'll be there," he said, kissing her ear, trailing his tongue down her throat and feeling her wriggle closer to him. In minutes she rolled over to lock her hands around his neck.

"You'll teach me to fly, you'll teach me to become decadent. Do you know how long we've been doing this?"

"Not half as long as it's going to be," he said gruffly, surprised at the strength of his desire. "You were meant to be in a man's bed. You're as sensual as hell."

"Am I now?" she asked, stretching and rubbing her bare body against his, relishing his every reaction, enjoying his every touch.

He groaned and crushed her to him, rolling her over to kiss her.

They left in a rush for his plane early in the afternoon and once they were airborne, she laughed and squeezed his thigh. "I'll have to come back and get my car."

"I'll bring you back, but this is the only way you'll make it home in time to meet the twins."

As they climbed, she began to think about reality and the future. "Your mother won't like this at all, Ty."

"She won't know unless you tell her."

"I won't do that, but we'll have to be careful. I don't want
to lose my job. I'm going to graduate a year early, but even
so, I need to work now. I want your mother's good references."

"You'll have them," he said firmly, glancing at her. He
still wanted her. He was amazed at his own reaction and
growing a little alarmed at it. He would take Victoria out
tonight and try to get Talia out of his system.

He kissed her goodbye at the airport, and she took a cab
to the house, climbing out to note with relief that Pauline
wasn't home, only Sloane, who arched his brows.

"Where's the car?"

"I had car trouble," she said uneasily. As she approached
him, she saw that he was watching her.

"Did you stay at the house all alone?" His dark eyes
seemed to bore through her, and she thought of all the times
they had talked, shared confidences, and her cheeks flushed
as guilt came. "Pauline hasn't missed you, because she's too
worried about Ty. He was supposed to fly in here last night,
and he hasn't shown up or called. Millard wants him about
some loan he is supposed to handle. He must have forgotten,
and Millard is about to blow a cork."

Talia stared at Sloane, wondering how much she could
trust him. "What time was the appointment?" she asked,
knowing how punctual Ty usually was, how unlike him to
forget.

"Oh, it isn't time yet, but Ty said he'd be in last night.
The appointment is at five o'clock today."

She sagged with relief, then realized Sloane was studying
her. Mentally debating the situation and realizing Ty might
forget the appointment, she placed her hand on Sloane's arm.
"I know where you can reach Ty if you want to call him."

"I thought you might," he said quietly, surprising her.
"Where is he?"

"He said he was going to get a haircut."

"I'll call him."

In her room she changed clothes and was braiding her hair
when she heard a knock.

When she opened the door Sloane leaned against the jamb.

"I talked to him and he hadn't forgotten. He's already talked to Millard."

"That's good."

"Want to go to dinner tonight?"

Occasionally Sloane had taken her with the twins to eat, usually a spur-of-the-moment invitation when they were all together anyway, but this was different, and she suspected there was a purpose behind his invitation.

"I know the twins are going to the Grossmans' at five," he added, "and they won't be back until the birthday party is over at nine. We can pick them up on our way home."

"I'd like that," she said, smiling at him. "Thanks."

He winked at her. "I'll be downstairs whenever you're ready. Pauline is meeting Millard at the bank, and they won't be home either, so as soon as the boys are ready for the party, we'll leave."

That evening after they had deposited the twins at the Grossmans', Sloane took her to an Italian restaurant where they sat in an alcove with candlelight and he ordered a bottle of Chianti Riserva. Candlelight flickered on his high cheekbones; his thick lashes were dark shadows framing his eyes. She knew that his modeling jobs were more frequent now. She could see the close resemblance to Ty in their black eyes and swarthy complexions and in their strong jaws. Sloane leaned back in the booth after their wine had been poured, smiling at her as he raised his glass. "Here's to a happy future."

"Amen," she whispered, refusing to contemplate the future.

He leaned forward over the table. "I wanted to talk to you about something." Several possibilities came to mind: the afternoon she had surprised him at the house, his knowledge she had been in Mississippi with Ty last night.

"Go ahead."

"I heard Millard talking to Ty. One of Millard's banker friends told him about your father."

Startled, she lowered her wine. Long ago when Sloane had gone with her to visit her mother, she had confided in Sloane about her parents. "I never have told your parents about my father's suicide. Or about the money he embezzled."

"It's amazing someone hasn't said something to him or to Pauline before now."

"Our families didn't move in the same circle."

"No. I understand he found out quite by accident. It won't make any difference, but I wanted you to know. If Mother gives you a difficult time, let me know."

"Thanks, Sloane. I'm trying to finish college as early as possible. Until then, I hope I can keep this job, because it's perfect."

"You'll keep it."

While they ate steaming calzone and fettucini with scampi, their conversation drifted to other topics, their future plans, his business, the twins. Over coffee after dinner, he sat with his elbow on the table his chin in his hand, talking quietly to her.

"Millard is putting pressure on me to marry Melissa."

Talia felt uncomfortable with the change in conversation. "And you don't want to tell him that you don't want to marry her?" He gave an indifferent shrug that she found distasteful.

"I don't mind telling him. I just don't know if I want to get married."

"Sloane!"

"Oh, Melissa knows about my feelings. I'm an androgynous male. Or I have been."

"And Melissa doesn't mind?"

"Melissa accepts me the way I am. I can give her security and comfort, and we have fun together. In turn, she can give me respectability. But I live in both worlds, and I don't want to give either one of them up."

Talia thought about that while she sipped her black coffee. "With your gentle, sensitive nature, she might want you all to herself in time," Talia said carefully. "Then what would you do?"

He arched his brows, dropping his hand over his knife to turn it back and forth, the silver gleaming dully in the candlelight. "I don't know, because I love her. I've lived with her off and on for two years now," he said bluntly. "Millard is threatening me. He wants me to work in the bank, to marry Melissa, to change my ways."

"Does he know—?"

"That I like both sexes?" he asked bluntly. "No, I don't think he could face that fact even if I told him to his face," he said, anger rising in his voice. "But I'm sure he suspects or he wouldn't be taking such drastic measures. He's threatening to cut me off from the money."

Impulsively she reached across the table to squeeze his hand. "I'm sure you'll work it out. I'm sorry you're having trouble. Just remember, marriage can be binding."

"Not in this day and time," he rejoined, covering her hand with his. "You've been good for our family."

"You were good for me," she said in return.

"I hope he doesn't hurt you."

She started to say, "*Who*?" but knew there was no need to. "He won't."

"I hope not. He doesn't deserve you. It's almost time for the twins to be leaving."

"Good grief, is it that late?" she asked, sliding out of the seat and gathering up her purse. "You're good company, Sloane. Thanks for dinner."

"Sure. One thing about it," he said as they walked to the front. "I've been stashing money away for years now. I can afford to do as I please when it gets right down to it." He grinned. "But I'd hate like hell to see Ty get all my inheritance!"

"I'm sure you'll work it out."

"Either that or Millard will finish me off. His threat isn't idle. I guess Ty and I inherited a little streak of violence from Millard. He can be violent when he doesn't get what he wants."

"I've never seen him get violent."

"That's because there are few things in his life now that don't go exactly his way. I'm about the only exception. Occasionally Ty is, but Millard and Ty are close and Ty usually comes around to Millard's way of looking at things. If Millard only knew that Ty is a shark and that a young shark will eat its parent under the right conditions, he would be more careful."

"Sloane!"

"Ty will do what he wants to achieve his goals, and the day will come when Millard's methods are going to be outdated. The time might come when he stands in Ty's way. See how patient Ty is then!" He held open the door of the car, shutting it when she was seated.

When they slowed in the driveway at the Franklins' the twins got out of the car, but Talia barely noticed. Parked only yards away was the dusty green Jaguar. Ty was home.

10

Ty heard the twins running up the stairs. He raked his fingers through his hair, then hurried downstairs. His gaze met Talia's the moment she stepped in sight. He had cancelled his date with Victoria—and every other date for the week—wanting to spend every possible moment with Talia.

He said hello to Sloane, but all his attention was on Talia. As the twins pushed past him and headed for the pool, he turned to Sloane. "Want to watch the boys swim? I'd like to take Talia for a ride."

"Sloane, you don't have to watch them!" Talia protested.

"Sure. I'm not doing anything. I'll swim with them."

Ty winked at her. "Come on, before he changes his mind."

She opened her mouth to protest again, but after one look at his black eyes, she bit back the words. In the car he reached across to squeeze her shoulder.

"No more stick shifts after this. I want you next to me. Have you and Sloane been with the twins all evening?"

"No. They were invited to a party, and I should be home to get them to bed because it's a school night."

"I won't keep you long and they're still excited from the party. They'll settle down and sleep better after they work off their energy swimming. I want you to see my condo."

His words sent a tingle of anticipation through her. She raised her face to the wind, letting it blow her long hair as they sped along. When he closed his condo door behind them and switched on the lights, she walked through the entrance into a spacious living area decorated in forest green and beige with French fruitwood furniture.

"I missed you," he said huskily, the sound of his voice

enveloping her like a warm, woolen cape, his intense gaze drawing her close.

She looked up at him, wanting him, seeing desire smolder in his eyes as his arms encircled her waist and he pulled her to him, kissing her hard.

Feeling as if she were the luckiest woman on earth, Talia saw him every night that week and three nights the next. Then Tyler had out-of-town bankers to entertain and she was studying for an exam.

At first Ty didn't want to recognize just how strong his feelings for Talia were, but during work he would find himself preoccupied by thoughts of her, something that hadn't ever happened before. Women had never interfered with his work. He gazed at the loan portfolio on his desk and anticipation made him eager. He glanced at his watch, saw it was time for the appointment with the bankers from Chicago, and stood up as the buzzer on his desk sounded.

An hour later, he followed the two northern bankers to the door, shaking hands with them. Ty had wined and dined them for the past two nights. Now, he had their business but he held back his grin until they were gone. Then he went straight to Millard's office with the deal papers.

The same size as Ty's, Millard's office also had an oak desk and filing cabinets, comfortable leather furniture and plants. Ty kept his plans for his future office to himself. "Dad?"

"Come in, Tyler."

"I sold the loans. We have an upstream lender now. I upstreamed two commercial real estate loans to Northern Shore Guaranty of Chicago."

"That's good, Tyler," Millard said politely, realizing that Tyler would never be satisfied confining himself to working in one city. They had occasionally found upstream or bigger banks to buy overlines, to participate in loans, but it wasn't often.

"These are one-hundred-percent participation!" Ty said, watching the surprise on his father's face, jubilant, because he could see new possibilities for the bank's growth unfolding swiftly. "All we had was the service fee. I sold them the loans—our origination fee was one percent, so First Bayou just received one hundred thousand dollars on the two loans that have one-hundred-percent participation, and both borrowers have opened accounts with us, so we'll continue to get their business!''

"I'll be damned, Tyler," Millard said with pleasure. "Congratulations. So that's what you've been so busy doing the past two nights."

"Yes, and it was worth it!" He glanced at the thin gold Gucci watch on his wrist. "I have to be in court in twenty minutes so I better run."

"I hope we win this suit and the bank gets something out of the case. Always make good loans, Tyler. A lawsuit is no way to try to get back the bank's money."

"Sure, Dad," Tyler said patiently, barely listening to the same old advice he had heard for years. "I'll let you know as soon as I get out of court."

"Congratulations, again, son," Millard said fondly, watching Tyler, who radiated vitality and enthusiasm. Someday, and probably sooner than he realized, Tyler would want to take charge. Millard smiled. Tyler was executive vice president of lending right now, but soon he would be ready for another promotion. It was time Tyler settled down and asked Victoria to marry him.

The second week in November marked the annual dinner and ball given in celebration of the completion of the Franklin mansion back in 1841. This year the twins were old enough to attend the first two hours and observe the festivities. Talia was invited because the twins were included. Long ago Ty had invited Victoria, and he carefully explained to Talia that he thought he shouldn't break the date. And she, just as carefully, agreed with him. While Talia wondered how she would be able to stand an entire evening of watching Ty with Victoria, she was also excited just to be near him in public.

Two days before the ball, Ty battled with his emotions, coolly weighing the consequences, ultimately breaking his date with Victoria. Talia didn't know it and he didn't intend to tell her until she asked.

That night as the twins stopped at her room to get her, she

opened the door to face them. "My, don't you two look handsome!"

Jeff grinned and blushed, and Travis scowled. "I hate parties!" he said. "My collar is tight."

"Let me see," she said, kneeling down to see if she could make it more comfortable. Both of them moved closer, and Jeff touched her hair.

"You look pretty," he said, studying her.

"You smell good too," Travis said. His blue eyes were as thickly lashed as Tyler's. His black hair was smoothed down while Jeff's curls were tangled in spite of Pauline's efforts to comb them into a semblance of order.

"Thank you both," she answered, thinking all the charm in the family had funneled to the four sons. Millard and Pauline were cold, formidable people while their children had personalities that could cajole warmth from a snowman.

"How's that?" she asked Travis.

"It's better, but I'd rather watch television."

"None of that. It's a special occasion, and someday you would rather go to a party than watch television."

"I don't think so," Travis said dubiously, giving his twin a look of patient tolerance.

"Yeah, when you're grown up and *in love*!" Jeff said, drawing out his words and breaking into giggles.

"Come on, you two. It's party time."

"Are you in love, Tali?"

"No, my friends," she answered, feeling slightly guilty for not being forthright. Just then Travis peered over the banister of the upstairs hall and spotted a tray of hors d'oeuvres below.

"Food!"

"Wait a minute! How can you be hungry? You ate a hamburger before you got dressed. Mind your manners and don t eat everything in sight. Promise?"

"We promise."

"That's fine." She walked between them, feeling tall next to her two short charges, knowing that soon they would be as big as their brothers. They were already wiry and muscular and just as competitive as Sloane and Ty. As they descended the steps, Ty met them at the bottom, his arm casually leaning

on the banister while he watched Talia. As soon as she saw
him, she lost all awareness of everyone and everything else.

Ty's heart thudded as Talia came down the stairs with the
boys. Her raspberry crepe de chine dress clung to her slender
figure, the ankle-length flared skirt swishing against her legs
with each step, the soft fabric clinging to her full breasts.
Her shoulders were bare except for thin straps of material
against her honey-colored skin. He wanted to take her right
back upstairs to bed. He tried to greet his brothers and give
them some attention, but he was grateful when they followed
a waiter with a tray of hors d'oeuvres.

"Where's Victoria?"

"She isn't here," he answered quietly.

Her breath stopped as all the implications of his answer
became clear.

"This is worse than Chinese torture," he continued in a
husky voice.

"What is?"

"Standing here unable to kiss you." He touched her silken
hair, which was caught up high and pinned on either side of
her head behind her ears, a spray of tiny orchids secured
along one side behind her ear while the rest of her hair fell
in a golden cascade down her back. His touch was light, yet
she felt it intensely.

"Ty, someone will hear you!"

"No, they won't. It's warm. Let's walk outside." He fell
into step beside her, slowing his long stride as they strolled
across the porch. He stayed at her side through dinner and
whenever she was with the twins. And when the dancing
commenced, he led her onto the dance floor.

"Your mother isn't happy with us. Particularly with me.
We're drawing her attention."

"Let me worry about Mom."

"Gladly!" she said and smiled, thinking she didn't have
any worries when she was in Ty's arms.

"I don't think I've ever known a woman who trusted me
the way you do," he said solemnly, realizing Talia would
make a beautiful, submissive wife. She was trained in the
social graces by Pauline, and she would fall into the same
mold as Pauline.

"I don't know why they wouldn't trust you implicitly. You always seem so sure of yourself and you always get what you want."

"I hope so, because there's something I'm beginning to want badly."

The look in his eyes intrigued her. They danced in silence, watching each other, while the tension between them built. The music stopped and then started again, this time with a rock beat, and Ty released her. The floor cleared of older couples as Ty and Talia's peers crowded together. Ty danced with a masculine grace, his hips moving slightly, his half-closed eyes drifting over her while he turned in front of her, and her pulse quickened as she moved to the throbbing rhythm.

Later that night he led her to the darkest part of the lawn where he pulled her into his arms and kissed her until she made him stop, finally telling him good night and going up to her room while Millard and Pauline said their last goodbyes to their guests.

"Ty, I want to talk to you," Pauline said, moving to the living room, and he followed. Her eyes were filled with anger, and spots of color showed in her cheeks. "What happened to Victoria tonight?"

"I didn't bring her. I don't see her as often as I used to."

"Why not?"

"I guess I don't want to. I'm a little old for this discussion."

"No, you're not, because I'm afraid you're about to throw away something very important. All I ask, Ty, is that when you marry, you chose someone of your own social standing."

"You ought to ask that I chose someone I love and think I can spend my life with; a woman with intelligence and qualities that count."

"That's exactly what I'm asking. Qualities that count. Not a servant, no matter how much fun or how pretty she may be."

"It was a nice party."

"I'd fire her tomorrow if I thought it would help." Ty started toward the door. "Ty! She'll make you miserable. She's not good enough for you."

"Good night," he said, controlling his temper, knowing that he shouldn't let Pauline goad him into an argument. He left the room, closed the door, and faced his father, who stood staring at him thoughtfully.

"I heard her. You ought to think long and hard about what she said. You need someone who can help you rise in the world. Not someone you have to pull up with you."

"Yes, sir."

"Women are always available, Ty," he said, snapping his mouth shut as the door to the living room opened, and Pauline appeared.

"I think it's time for me to say good night," Ty said lightly, hoping his anger didn't show. "It was a nice party." He strode out of the house without looking back.

As he left, the senior Franklins went upstairs, where Millard closed the door to their adjoining rooms. "You made a mistake, Pauline. You gave the boy a challenge."

"Are you saying I should have kept quiet?"

"It might have been better."

"Will you talk to him?"

"No, I won't. He's a man now, and a damned intelligent one. Hasn't he always come out on top?"

"Yes, but there's always a first time, and this could change his future."

"To hell with that. He's a Franklin. His future is as secure as our vault. If you want to worry about someone's future, talk to Sloane. He needs to work at the bank, settle down, and marry."

"Sloane will do what he should."

"He's always done just as he damn well pleases, and you spoil him rotten!"

"You spoil Ty. This is old ground, Millard. Sloane was here tonight with Melissa. I don't know why you want him to get married and yet you don't care what Tyler does!"

He dropped his shoe and looked up, anger rising in him. "I've heard rumors Sloane is gay!"

"That's absurd! He's handsome and dates and he's athletic. Leave the boy alone. Just because he isn't as tough as Tyler—"

"He's as tough as Ty when he wants to be! That isn't what worries me."

"Sloane is cooperative and wonderful, and those are just ugly rumors that don't have a shred of truth. He's as normal as you are," she said. "And you're not helping matters by arranging a job for Talia next year."

"All I did was tell her whom to see for an interview when the time comes. She'll be an excellent employee, just as she has been for us at home. Her grades are straight A's; she's intelligent—"

"And she's after Ty."

"Then she isn't alone. How many girls have been after him since he was ten years old, and look what good it's done them!"

"I hope she doesn't ruin his life!" she snapped and swept out of the room to her own bedroom.

Downstairs Ty strolled outside to stare across the wide expanse of lawn. He circled the house, going down to the pool area where the lights still shone. He sat on a chaise in the shadows and stared at the sparkling pool, thinking about his father's remark. He knew Millard kept mistresses and had done so for years. And he knew just as well that if he caught Pauline having an affair just once, Millard would divorce her.

Women seemed to accept a double standard, but at the moment, he couldn't imagine exercising that prerogative if Talia were his wife. She wasn't his wife, and she wasn't the type of woman he had expected to marry. She wouldn't be an asset as far as family connections were concerned, but a hell of a lot good family connections mattered when he was in bed!

Talia enflamed his senses; she left him unable to concentrate on work. He thought of how she had trusted him in the plane as well as in the bedroom. A virgin. Each time they made love she was more sensual, more sexually hungry than before. Becoming aroused, he changed his thoughts to Pauline. He had to make some decisions soon. Victoria would be seething with anger at him for canceling tonight, and while he knew he could soothe her and win her back, he wasn't sure that was what he wanted. Would Talia be such a misfit in his life? He couldn't imagine how she would be. She was intelligent, beautiful, and growing more poised as time passed. She had filled in on one occasion as hostess when Pauline was sick, and she had done an excellent job, handling the party and then the guests with ease. He intended to go out with her tomorrow night, and he wanted days alone with her, something that was impossible.

Following the suggestion of one of her accounting professors who did private consulting, and with a recommendation from Millard Franklin, Talia made an appointment in December with Central Southern Bank, a suburban bank, for a job interview with the personnel manager, and then an interview with the head teller. Because of her grades, record, and the recommendation of the Franklins, she was offered a job as a teller in January. The bank would pay for the last part of her education with the agreement that when she had her degree, she would go into management training. She needed only six credit hours, and since she could take them at night during the spring semester, she took the job.

In the third week in December, she had finished her finals, and her job with the Franklins was officially over. She moved to a new apartment in spite of the twins' protests. Her first night alone Ty took her out to dinner at Antoine's and afterwards told her that he had to christen her new apartment. So she wasn't alone after all. On Monday, she started work at Central Southern Bank.

She parked in front of the two-story red-brick colonial with white columns and a white pediment with a bronze eagle mounted in the center. Inside, the wide front lobby curved in a semicircle, the teller's windows along the rounded north wall of the bank opposite an inviting area with soft green carpet stretching in front of a stone fireplace with cherry wood desks on either side. Glass-enclosed offices flanked the tellers' windows.

Wanda Stewart, a tall, auburn-haired, freckled woman who was ten years older then Talia and who had started with the bank right out of college, was the personnel manager. She showed Talia around the bank and introduced her to Larry Prima, the president, who removed his glasses and gave her a firm handshake. At first Talia simply watched another teller,

Janie Hoffholtz. After the customer closing hours, Talia learned how the computer worked, and how to strap the money, watching Janie's short, pale hands move efficiently.

"Put the ten-dollar bills together, ten tens to a strap," Janie said, her glasses slipping forward on her nose. She pushed them up, shook blond hair away from her face, and picked up another stack of money. "The twenties will make a three-hundred-dollar strap, the dollar bills will be twenty-five-dollar straps.

Janie slid open her drawer and pointed to a stack of money under a clip at the back of a drawer. "There's the bait money. If you're robbed, give them that stack. When it's moved, the alarm goes off."

"How often have you been robbed?"

"Once since I've been here. Guy came in with a mask and a stun gun. Thank heavens he didn't come to my window. I would have fainted. Push this camera button if a theft commences. In fact, push it if anyone acts questionably."

Talia learned more about security from Wanda.

"If there is a robbery, there are steps to follow: First the doors will be locked immediately after the thief leaves the bank. The bank is closed. The police will have been notified by our alarm system. Don't talk to others until the FBI arrive, don't touch things, don't touch the door handles. The tellers' drawers will be locked as soon as the robber leaves."

By the end of her first day, Talia was tired from standing, but eager about her job. Briefly she told Ty about it, saw his eyes glaze over, and realized that to an executive vice president of a bank, a teller's first day would be of little interest, so she changed the subject.

Talia liked the first week, and wouldn't admit to herself that banking interested her because it was what Ty did. She intended to move up; she wanted a career with a large enough salary to live comfortably, a challenge great enough to keep her intrigued, and enough security for her future. Most important, she wanted to be independent.

Each morning she got her cash drawer. At the end of the day, she had to balance out, figuring her starting cash, what she had taken in, what she had paid out, and balancing out to the same amount she'd had at the start of the day.

Friday afternoon was the busiest time since people deposited paychecks and withdrew cash for the weekend. In spite of the line of people waiting, she slowed down so she would be accurate and not make a mistake. She completed a deposit and closed her drawer, reaching up as a paper was slipped through her window.

She pulled it over, seeing a message scrawled on it, and her heartbeat accelerated as she read: "Will you go to dinner with me tonight?"

Her head snapped up to see Ty leaning close, smiling at her. "If they see me in here at my competitor's, my reputation will be ruined."

"If I stop to talk to you, my career will be ruined!"

"I can take a hint. Give me an answer," he said, glancing at his note.

"Yes!" she said with eagerness.

He winked. "Pick you up by your car at five minutes after five."

"Fine. Now go!"

That Christmas was a magical season. She was in love with a handsome, exciting man. She and Ty saw each other regularly. They went to the twenty-eighth annual Christmas caroling in Jackson Square. They walked down the neutral zone and looked at the lights on Canal Street; they strolled beneath the oaks in City Park; on Christmas Eve they took a cruise up the Mississippi River to see the bonfires on the levees, Tyler leaning on the rail, the blaze of the fire on the levee highlighting his cheekbones, shadows hiding his dark eyes while he kept his arms around her. The black satin ribbon of the Mississippi slipped past below them with orange streamers from the fires reflecting on its inky surface.

"See—you've lived here and never seen the bonfires. They light the way for Père Noël, the Cajun version of Santa Claus, while he paddles his gift-laden pirogue downriver."

"We should have brought the twins."

"And share you with them? Never!" He framed her face with his hands, and then he leaned forward to kiss her, ignoring the others on the boat. Ty pulled back and looked down at her. "Will you marry me?"

Talia nearly stopped breathing, then she tightened her arms around his neck, standing on tiptoe. "Yes!"

He reached in his topcoat pocket and pulled out a box, taking her hand and slipping a large diamond ring on her finger. It caught the light from the dancing flames along the shore, glittering brightly. The stone was awesome, but not as dazzling as the man. From the first moment Ty had over-whelmed her with his power and charm, and those qualities had been enhanced as she got to know him until she was as blinded by love as if she faced bright sunshine. She met his searching gaze and fought back the impulse to throw herself into his arms.

"Your family will object," she said with a matter-of-fact-ness that belied her racing pulse.

"Then to hell with them," he answered quietly.

"Oh, please don't say that!"

"I can win them over and you can win them over. I know what I want. I've always known. I love you more than I've ever loved any woman. I want you now and I'll want you all my life."

The words fell like golden chains wrapping around her heart, binding her to him, and she lost all caution and doubt. He gazed at her with a frown on his handsome features, his eyes full of concern.

She flung her arms around his neck. After the first split second of surprise, he lowered his head to kiss her, his strong arms crushing her to his chest.

Talia had to face Pauline the next day. Ty invited the family to dinner, and over glasses of champagne, he announced their engagement, saying their wedding was planned for the first Saturday in March. Pauline's only reaction was a thinning of her lips, but her face paled and Talia caught a quick, con-temptuous glance. The twins were jubilant; Sloane grinned and leaned over to kiss her, whispering, "She'll adjust and then she'll love you!"

Millard stood up and came around to take her hand and pull her to her feet. "This calls for a toast. I think my son has very good taste," he said, and for the first time since she had known him his voice sounded warm. His eyes met hers in a level gaze, and she discovered he could be as compelling and probably as charming as Ty when he wanted.

He kissed her cheek, squeezed her hand, and said, "Take care of my son."

She nodded, glancing across the table into Pauline's blue eyes, which looked as cold as an Alaskan glacier. Talia faced her without looking away, yet without rancor, while Millard proposed a toast and they all drank except Pauline.

Ty lowered his glass. "Mother, don't spoil the happiest night of my life."

"It would be better to spoil an evening than to see you ruin your life," she said stiffly, glaring at Talia. "I wish you had given us a warning, Tyler." Talia felt her cheeks grow hot beneath the whiplash gaze of anger. The walls of the room seemed to close in, and she felt just as she had that first day in school after her father's suicide and the embezzlement had become known. Embarrassed and momentarily uncertain, she wanted to fling herself into Ty's arms to avoid Pauline's anger. Instead, Talia sat quietly gazing into Pauline's eyes.

"Mother, for God's sake!" Ty snapped, his face turning red with anger.

"Welcome to the family, Talia," Sloane said dryly. "I'll say it for Mother."

"Pauline." The quiet word was a censure, and Pauline's face flushed as she stared at her husband. Millard reached across the table to take Talia's hand. "Mother is very protective where her sons are concerned. There are five male Franklins who'll adore you."

To her amazement, he winked at her and held her hand until she gave him a faint smile in return.

"Boys, have your first taste of champagne," Sloane said, pouring champagne into two empty coffee cups and pushing it in front of the twins, who had been startled by what was happening around them. They eagerly drank while Ty put his arm around Talia.

From that moment on, all the men at the table acted as if Pauline's insulting words had never been spoken. Millard wanted to know their plans, and dinner proceeded with only Pauline remaining in stony silence. As soon as dinner was finished, Millard stood up. "I'll take you home now, Pauline," he said, his words as cutting as a knife. Her eyes flashed with anger, and Talia knew they would have a fight as soon as they left the restaurant. In minutes they were gone, and she felt limp with relief, yet a cloud had been cast over the rosy glow she experienced.

"Sloane's right and Dad's right. All of the Franklins adore you," Tyler said emphatically, putting his arm around her shoulders. "Mother will come around. You just spoiled her plans temporarily. You wait and see. By the time the wedding takes place, she'll be back trying to run our lives."

He made it sound so simple. Sloane winked at her. "I'm sure Ty is marrying you because you're so neat and efficient. He'd never propose otherwise."

"He would so!" Jeff said, frowning. "She's pretty and she's nice."

"Thank you, Jeff! Sloane, stop teasing!" She smiled at Sloane, knowing he was trying to cheer her. Ty gave her a squeeze.

"Sure. Miss Efficient, who'll keep my life in perfect order."

Sloane laughed. "That's a lifetime job. Ty never throws away a thing."

"Ty has his first football in the attic," Travis said.

"And his first teething ring, *and* his first roller skates!" Sloane said dryly.

"And my baby teeth," Ty added.

"Your teeth!" Talia exclaimed, sincerely laughing for the first time that evening. Ty leaned closer.

But as they all relaxed and the conversation turned to other topics, Talia worried about the scene she could expect from Pauline.

She didn't have to wait long for her future mother-in-law's summons. Monday morning Pauline called and asked Talia to stop by the house during her lunch hour. Even though she didn't want to go, Talia agreed, because she knew she had to get along with Ty's parents if at all possible.

Pauline closed the doors to the living room and turned, gazing with an imperious demeanor and not a vestige of apology in her manner.

"You've won over all the men in the family with your

quiet ways and your beauty. And men don't see that anything more is important. When you become my daughter-in-law, the deed is done, and I'll stand beside you and support you, because it will be to my son's interests, but I'm warning you to make Tyler happy.''

"I intend to try.''

"I'll help plan your wedding so you won't embarrass Tyler, who has standards to maintain. I know you can't afford it, so we will pay all your bills.''

"I have some savings,'' Talia said quietly.

"You can't begin to pay for the kind of wedding Tyler will want. You'll see. I've already contacted the florist and I'll call a caterer this afternoon.''

"Mrs. Franklin—''

"You can hardly address me as Mrs. Franklin once you are part of the family. You may call me Pauline. It won't do you any good to argue about the wedding, because I've already offered and Ty has accepted.'' She shook her head as she stared at Talia. "You're not the woman for him,'' she said with venom. "You're nothing but a little slip of a girl whose father was a thief and whose mother is an alcoholic mental case—''

"Mrs. Franklin, I don't have to listen to this,'' Talia said quietly. "I came because I hoped we could get along. We both love Ty. If we can't have a civil conversation, there's no use in my staying,'' she said, intimidated, yet refusing to take Pauline's abuse quietly. "Excuse me.'' Talia left the house, trying to calm her nerves before she returned to work.

That night she tried to discuss the morning with Ty. "Ty, I want to pay for the wedding. I've saved money.''

They lay in front of the fire on the floor of his condominium, and he idly let her hair slide through his fingers. Her head was on his chest, a blanket thrown over both of them, their bodies still warm and bare from lovemaking.

"Hon, let her pay and keep your savings. Everyone will be happy that way.''

"I don't know about that, Tyler,'' she said, sitting up. He pulled her down and returned to toying with her hair.

"I'd like to do the planning.''

"I'll tell her, but let her have a part, and let them pay.

They want to, they can afford it, and it's absurd for you to worry about it.'' He began to kiss her neck.

"Tyler, are you listening to me?"

"Mmmm, sure, luv."

"Tyler!"

The subject never was definitively resolved between them, but when the time came, Pauline and Millard paid for the wedding.

They planned a two-week honeymoon. Millard made Ty a present of a trip to Rio for their honeymoon, and a week later he casually asked Ty if, while he was in Rio, he would take a few hours one day and check on their sugar plantations to the south of Rio near São Paulo.

Ty agreed, keeping their trip a secret to surprise Talia. He was dreaming and counting the hours until he could have her all to himself for two whole weeks. He was amazed she could take so much of his attention and time. He had never been so interested in a woman before. She seemed to adore him, as other women had, but there was something in Talia's absolute trust and her fearlessness that pleased him more than anything. He lived recklessly sometimes, and he was still delighted that she didn't try to make him stop. In fact she enjoyed whatever he was doing with as much zest as he did. He didn't want to marry a woman who would mother him and scold him if he drove too fast or skied too dangerously. He expected her to be the wife he wanted: a gracious hostess, a wanton in bed.

Only once did the topic of her job come up for any serious discussion. Ty lay behind her toying with her hair while she pulled on her stockings.

"Do I remember your telling me something earlier about your sister?"

She laughed softly. "You definitely had your mind elsewhere!" Her smile faded. "Rebecca called me today at the bank. She can't come for the wedding. She has a new job as a singer in a nightclub."

He rolled over, propping his jaw on his fists, his bare body stretching the length of the bed. "I get the feeling you and your sister are about as much alike as the moon and a cat."

"Which am I, the cat or the moon?" she asked, glancing

down the length of his muscular body, thinking again she
was the luckiest woman in the world.

"Definitely a warm, soft cat. Now you can quit your job."

She glanced over her shoulder at him, amusement showing
in her voice. "I just got started! I want a career, Ty, the same
as you do."

He smiled indulgently and lowered his gaze to look at her
in a sensuous appraisal. "And where do little babies come
into this picture?"

"We'll have them, but I'll probably go back to work
someday."

"That's absurd," he said, confident she wouldn't, his gaze
moving to the thin blue lacy bikini panties that seemed useless
to him. She stood up and pulled on her pantyhose her breast
tumbling forward and straining against her wispy bra, but he
reached out and yanked her back down next to him, the subject
of banks and careers forgotten.

Finally the moment came. On March 1, 1975, Talia started
down the long aisle of the New Orleans Episcopal Church.
Tyler stood waiting, so handsome that her heart stopped as
she gazed at his dark cutaway coat, the wing collar, and white
tie. Her train pulled slightly on the waist of her embroidered
Swiss lace dress covered with appliquéd satin leaves with a
scalloped hemline. Six bridesmaids dressed in rose taffeta
faced her. Melissa was her maid of honor.

Beau and Gloria brought Kate, and Millard gave the bride
away. She took Ty's proffered arm and gazed up adoringly
at him as they said their vows.

Early Sunday morning they flew over Guanabara Bay with
Sugar Loaf Mountain standing like a dark Argus guarding a
sparkling turquoise gem, as it towered over blue water and
white beaches. March was the early part of Rio's balmy fall
and it was seventy-two degrees when they landed at Rio's
International Airport after a twelve-hour flight from Dallas.
They had flown to Dallas in Ty's plane. In the rental car,
Tyler drove with a flourish, challenged and amused by the
"me first" attitude of the native Cariocas.

"Tyler, there's a red light!" she cried as he barreled
through an intersection, horns blaring, the squeal of brakes
to their right. His strong hands gripped the wheel, his eyes

focused on traffic as he concentrated on driving until they were through the intersection. He laughed. "Parted just like the Red Sea! If we stop for a light, we'll get clobbered!"

They roared through a tunnel and emerged on Avenida Atlântica, where they drove along the Copacabana Beach while she relaxed and gazed with joy at the banana trees, the palms, the crescent of white sand laced with tan bodies, the bustling, luxury hotels contrasting with the lazy, coaxing blue water opposite them, the tamarinds and figs and tropical flowers. There were masses of people everywhere, but Talia's attention would return to the handsome man seated beside her every few minutes.

As they sped past the peninsula separating Copacabana Beach from Ipanema Beach, breakers smashed against a rugged outcropping with signs posted on the eastern side. When she asked about them, Ty glanced at the ocean.

"*Perigo. Praia do Diabo.* Devil's Beach. It's a strong tide, consequently the warnings, but it's not impossible. Actually, it's a challenge. I'll show you."

"Challenges are irresistible for you, aren't they?" she asked, and merely received a grin.

The land leveled off into calm again, the water a brilliant cerulean blue as they drove on Avenida Vieira Souto to the elegant Caesar Park Hotel on Ipanema Beach. Their suite overlooked the beach, and for the first three days they never left their rooms. If she had been dazzled before by Tyler Franklin, she was blinded by radiant love for him now. He was a god, virile, strong, and handsome. He had wealth, charm, and looks, and she couldn't get enough of him physically to satisfy her desire.

Tyler was equally taken with his new bride. When he thought about his mother, which was only once during the entire trip, he burned with indignation. He could not believe that she had the audacity to suggest that Talia was less than perfect, that she was the wrong mate for him. To hell with family ties and social standing. He could provide enough of that for both of them. What he wanted was what Talia gave him: adoration, flaming erotic sensuality, fun. She was beautiful, intelligent, charming, and he suspected that she held more promise as a dutiful wife than any other woman he had known.

They went to the beach, to Jardim Botanico, the botanical garden with its six lakes. Talia constantly took pictures of Tyler beside a pool of giant lily pads that were like colorful platters, of Tyler standing beneath delicate orchids and insectivorous plants, of Tyler on the beach, of Tyler on their terrace. They toured the elegant National Museum with its engaged Doric columns and long narrow windows and doors. This building, which had been the royal palace for eighty-one years, was founded by the Portuguese king, Dom João VI. They rode a cable car to the top of Sugar Loaf and watched the myriad lights of the city come twinkling to life. Ty taught her to wind surf when it was calm, and she watched while he went hang gliding. Rio was magical and enchanting to Talia, who was protected more than she realized by Tyler from the crime, insulated somewhat from the poverty, and barely aware of the *favelas*, the shanties on the mountainside.

She had the time of her life until the morning Tyler left her to shop while he went to meet with two agronomists and a plant pathologist who worked with the Franklins' Brazilian sugar cane planters. Wandering from shop to shop, she bought outlandish things for Tyler—tiger-striped bikini shorts, a gold chain necklace, onyx cuff links. She bought herself a new swimsuit, a new evening dress, and with an armload of packages she proceeded back toward the hotel, only to get herself hopelessly lost in the maze of Rio's streets. At first she was annoyed that she was lost, but she thought she could find where she started by walking only a block or two. Somewhere along the way she took the wrong turn and instead of getting back to a familiar place, she discovered she was quickly leaving the fine hotels and chic shops for a poor section of town.

She tried to retrace her steps, coming out on another unfamiliar street. Loaded with packages, she was hot, worried, and lost. In spite of the midday hour and the busy city, she was on a street of closed businesses, empty buildings, and deserted walkways. It was devoid of life with the exception of two bronzed, muscular men dressed in cotton pants, their shirts open to their waists, who stepped out of a doorway and smiled at her.

She panicked. She turned to run, knowing she might be making a bad situation worse because she didn't know in which direction to run, but she had to do something.

11

Clutching her packages, Talia ran. She heard the men calling from behind her. She turned right down the next two streets and suddenly she was back on a main thoroughfare, where an outdoor cafe was only yards away. Wracking her brain for the few phrases in Portuguese she had learned, she approached a waiter. Ty had made fun of her for struggling with the foreign phrases, telling her she wouldn't need them in bed. When the white-jacketed waiter looked up, she blurted, "*Quanto devo? Quero seguro um taxi? Queria um quarto.*"

To her consternation the man stared at her, his dark brows arching, and she feared her Portuguese was indecipherable.

"May I help?" said an amused, deep voice behind her. Talia turned to face a tall, blond man, whose hazel eyes radiated sympathetic mirth. His speech had a familiar soft drawl to it. Never had a phrase from a stranger sounded better to her.

"You speak English!"

"The same kind you do—N'awlins, Louisiana, or I miss my guess."

"Oh, thank heavens!"

He said something in Portuguese to the waiter and took the packages from her hands. "Let's have a drink and discuss your dilemma. I'm Lance Douglas from N'awlins."

"I'm Talia Wade. Talia Franklin! I'm sorry. I'm newly married and a little flustered. I've been shopping and I got lost. I was several blocks back that way." She pointed over her shoulder, and he frowned.

"That's not a good place for a beautiful lady to be."

"So I learned. I got lost so fast, and then two men appeared and started calling to me, so I ran."

"No wonder your phrases were a little mixed! Next time take the new hubby shopping. You could have gotten hurt. This is a big city with almost five million people. The crime rate here is high."

He leaned forward to smile at her. "If I were your newly married husband, you wouldn't have gotten lost alone," he said softly. He was flirting, yet since he had come to her rescue, she could hardly be annoyed with him. She laughed and scooted closer to the table as the waiter set drinks in front of them.

"Have you had a *caipirinha* before?"

"No."

"It's the Brazilian equivalent of Mexican tequila. *Caipirinhas* are made from *pinga*, or cane alcohol. It's potent, but you have to try it."

"I'm so grateful to you. It's wonderful to find someone from home!"

He nodded his head, his eyes twinkling with laughter. "Maybe you should carry a phrase book."

"It's back at the hotel. I tried to memorize a few lines, but I must have mixed them up."

"Everything's fine now," he said smoothly. "Except that we met after the wedding instead of before. Where's Mr. New Husband?"

"Ty had some business," she said and instantly realized that it sounded as if he were neglecting her. "Just a little business for his father. This is our first morning apart. What are you doing in Rio?"

"I'm working. I'm with an oil company and right now I'm mixing business with pleasure. I have a few days to kill, and oh, how I wish we had met sooner!"

She laughed and sipped the strong, sweet drink that made her cough and blink. "You don't stop, do you! I'm very much in love with my husband even though he isn't right here at my side."

He grinned, a boyish, wholesome grin that kept her at ease. "I believe you. And we're both from New Orleans. Is that where you'll live after the honeymoon?"

"Yes, it is. Both my husband and I are in banking, though we work for different companies. Where do you live?"

"I live far from Louisiana now. For the past year I've been in Brazil more than the States."

"Do you always work in Rio?"

"Nope. I've worked out on rigs in the Amazon, but that was a long time ago."

"What's the Amazon like?" she asked, intrigued, relaxing as she drank. She studied him while she listened. He was a handsome man, not as handsome as Ty, but he had a golden, boy-next-door manner. His hazel eyes were quick to notice everything around him; his voice was deep. He had a broad face, a slightly pug nose, thick, wavy hair bleached to a golden white that reminded Talia of wheat ripened by the Brazilian sun.

And he was almost as charming as Ty. The time passed before she realized how long she had sat with him. When she rose and gathered her packages, he took them from her hands. "I'll drive you back to your hotel. You're probably in the vicinity of Caesar Park."

Her eyes widened. "You're right! How did you guess?"

"I'm at the next hotel to the west. I confess that I've noticed you on the beach."

"How can you remem—never mind!" she exclaimed with a laugh. "Then you saw Tyler with me."

"No, I didn't see Tyler," he said, holding open the door of a rental Renault.

"He's always been with me."

"Maybe so, but I didn't see him," Lance said, easing into traffic and accelerating. When he stopped he pulled out a black lizard billfold from the pocket of his blue cotton slacks. "Here's my card in case you ever get lost again."

His hazel eyes held hers as he faced her. Thinking she would never use it, she accepted the card from him, glancing at his name and the Brazilian phone number.

"I probably won't even tell Tyler about this morning," she said, thinking about what a perfectionist Tyler was, how aggravated he could become with mistakes or accidents. He would never have gotten lost.

"That's fine with me," Lance said softly, and her head jerked up as she realized he had misinterpretated her reasons.

"He gets impatient with dumb moves and mistakes, and I made one this morning in getting lost."

"Aw, shucks!" Lance said in mock disappointment.

"With your charming manner, I'm sure you won't miss my presence," she answered in the same light tone. Her voice sobered and she impulsively placed her hand on his. "Thanks. I was terrified."

He squeezed her hand. "Oh, how I wish it had happened before the honeymoon!" He turned to open the car door. "I'll carry your packages."

At the elevator in the hotel, she turned to him. "I can take these now."

He grinned and handed them over. "So I'm not going to be invited up. Can't blame me for trying. Bye, Mrs. Talia Franklin. Maybe we'll meet again in N'awlins."

"Thanks. Maybe so." She stepped into the elevator and faced him while he stood watching her. Just before the doors closed he winked and then he was gone from sight. She sighed, feeling infinitely better to be back at the hotel, anxious to see Tyler. She forgot Lance Douglas immediately.

Tyler was waiting, standing by a window, and she wondered if he had seen her cross the parking lot with Lance, but he immediately turned and held out his arms with no questions in his eyes.

She dropped the packages on a chair and walked into his embrace. He caught her, yanking her blouse out of her skirt, sliding his hands over her warm flesh to flick the catch on her bra while her blood pounded in her veins and she kissed him desperately. In seconds he pulled her down on the soft carpet, and Talia was lost to a burning need.

The next day they drove to São Paulo, winding through its maze of twisted streets in traffic so busy that Talia closed her eyes.

"Thank heavens you're driving and not me!" she gasped.

"Nothing to it. Just lean on the horn and keep a steely nerve." They turned inland to visit one of the Franklin plantations. Tyler sped along a dusty road, sending a spiral of red dust flying behind the car, then slowed in front of a Georgian mansion that made her feel as if she were back on the River Road at home.

"It's so southern!"

"It should be. One of the Franklins fled here after the Civil War. A lot of Confederates moved everything—slaves, families, possessions—and came to Brazil to start again. Some settled around Belém and along the Amazon. Some settled here. Come on, I'll show you around."

For the first time she began to realize the immensity of the Franklin wealth. She had seen their plantation, Devonwick, near Loreauville, with its endless acres of sugar cane, its sprawling house, and modern equipment. The family who managed this plantation lent Tyler their small plane so they could fly over it. The foreman rode with them, commenting and directing their attention. At dinner they were entertained lavishly and stayed in a guest house, leaving the next day to drive back to Rio. Within an hour of arriving at the hotel they were on the beach. Talia came out of the water and stretched on a towel in the sun while Ty continued to swim. Lying on her back, her hat over her face, she soaked up the warmth until a deep voice said, "As I live and breathe! We meet again!"

She pushed away the hat and looked up to see Lance Douglas standing beside her. Dressed in swim trunks, his muscular body looked as fit and tanned as Talia had suspected it was. He held a drink in his hand. He waved it at her. "If I'd known, I'd have brought you one. Care to join me?"

"I hate to ask how you knew it was me with my face covered," she said, sitting up. He dropped down on the sand beside her, sitting cross-legged only inches away, thoroughly appraising her body.

"Honey, I would recognize you even if your face was in a sack. And before you send me packing for saying that, have you been lost again?"

"No. You'll get to meet my husband in a minute."

"To be honest, I was hoping he was still working. You have the greenest eyes I've ever seen."

She wiggled her diamond wedding band at him and he grinned. "Just commenting. The beach is crowded, the water's cold, the legs are fantastic."

"Lance! If you do that in front of Tyler, you may wonder what hit you."

"I'll be very careful. I don't suppose I could talk you into slipping out here for a little moonlight swim?"

"I'm a newlywed. Married. Mrs. Tyler Franklin."

"Well, I had to give it the old college try. So long, beautiful," he said, winking at her and sauntering away. In less than a minute a pretty woman smiled at him and the two became engaged in conversation. A shadow fell across her, and she looked up to see Tyler, dripping wet, as he sat down on his towel beside her.

"Who was the guy?" he asked with a frown. "Was he bothering you?"

"No." Tyler's gaze shifted from Lance to her, angry curiosity surfacing in his eyes.

"I didn't want to tell you. I got lost yesterday while I was shopping and that man came my rescue. His name is Lance Douglas. He's from Louisiana, and he speaks Portuguese."

"Well, damn. Why didn't you want to tell me? How much did he come to your rescue?"

Startled, she realized Tyler was angry. "He saw to it that I got back to the hotel. Tyler, *you're jealous*!"

"Yeah," he said. "Maybe so."

"Don't be ridiculous! He's just some guy." She was amazed, a little flattered, and a little alarmed. "Tyler, stop being angry." She smiled suddenly at the ridiculousness of what was happening. "Maybe it's time to go back to our room and convince you that I'm in love with only one man," she drawled, lowering her voice, letting her fingers trail on his thigh.

Suddenly he grinned, his dark eyes flashing with desire. "We better go now before it becomes glaringly evident to one and all what I have on my mind."

She laughed as they hurried back to the hotel, the incident forgotten.

She saw Lance twice after that and each time she was alone. The last time was in the hotel drugstore where she was purchasing a paper.

"You're sure there's a husband?" a deep voice asked behind her and she turned to smile at him, familiar with his voice now.

"I'm sure, and you either have an uncanny knack for popping up the moment he's gone, or you're spying on us."

"I have the uncanny knack," he said, propping his hand over her head and leaning close, hemming her in between himself and the magazine rack. She was aware that Tyler would appear at any moment and quickly remembering his jealous reaction, she slipped out from beneath Lance's arm and smiled at him.

"You'll get me in trouble."

"Jealous husband, huh? Well, I'll be on the beach this afternoon if you get lost."

"I'll remember," she said, hoping he would go away.

With a grin he left. She paid for the paper, hurrying across the lobby to meet Tyler at the elevators. That was her last encounter with Lance.

When they left to fly home, she glanced down at the Bay, then the steely gray waters of the Atlantic Ocean as Rio faded behind them, and she knew they were leaving an idyll behind. She turned to look at Tyler, thinking again that he was the most handsome man in the world. He met her gaze and smiled.

Their first month of marriage seemed like a dream to Talia. She still visited Kate, who remained the same, contented in the institution. Tyler went with her once, but Talia knew he was uncomfortable and impatient to be gone, so she didn't ask him to go again. Talia heard once from Rebecca, who had moved to Nevada. *Saturday Night Fever* was the rage and discos opened in New Orleans. Ty and Talia had a favorite haunt they frequented with close friends. She was awed by Tyler's energy and his need for constant activity. Their social life was busy. He purchased tickets for the Saints' games next season as well as for the symphony and ballet series. Along with all the Franklins, he always went to the Sugar Bowl; Talia had gone with him to watch Alabama beat Penn State. They joined the country club and usually went there on the weekends. Ty already belonged to the yacht club. While they settled into a routine in his condo, Tyler purchased land, studying plans and contracting to have a house built. Talia had little say about the house decisions, because Tyler

hired a decorator, took charge himself, and consulted Pauline
hours on end. Since she was so busy at the bank, and still
wildly in love with Tyler, Talia didn't complain. Tyler
seemed to have strong ideas about what he wanted, and she
was pleased if he was.

She was now in management training and moved to the
credit department, where Wanda showed her the files on
people's credit histories and taught her how to analyze financial statements. Central Southern's assets numbered thirty
million dollars. Talia was given a desk near the tellers' windows, and Wanda showed her how to use the computer. One
day, on their break, they chatted about personal matters for
the first time.

"How's the new house coming?" Wanda asked.

"Fine, I guess."

"You don't know?"

"Tyler's taken charge."

"Well, be thankful for that. My husband wouldn't show
a flicker of interest, and the whole job would be dumped
on me."

"I don't have that problem."

"Oh?" Wanda's auburn brows arched.

"Everything's okay."

"Sure. The first few months can be kind of rocky. Lots
of adjustments. I like your new hairdo," she said, eyeing
Talia's smooth chignon. "It makes you look older."

"That's what Tyler said. He said I'd look more sophisticated. I think it's more businesslike."

Wanda laughed. "You don't need to be more businesslike! He ought to see you at work. Look, when you need to
run a credit report, just hook the phone up to the machine
like this. You sit down and do it. Here are three names. This
machine connects to the credit bureau." Wanda laid a sheet
of paper on the desk. "Now type in the name, social security
number, the address, the employer—all the information on
the page, then push the button and you'll get a printout with
the credit report from the New Orleans Credit Bureau. Any
questions?"

"No, not yet," Talia said. "Thanks."

One weekend during April, Talia and Tyler danced at the club. He smiled at her while they circled the floor.

"You look happy," she observed.

"I am. I have a surprise."

"What is it?" she asked, suspecting for the past few days that he had made a successful business transaction.

"I'm going to run for governor."

His announcement dropped like a bomb, and she missed a step. He steadied her, watching her closely. "If I get into the runoffs, it looks like the opposition candidate will be Ben Holloway, who's been a representative."

"Why?" she asked, aghast that he had made the decision without even consulting her. "You have more than you can do now."

"I want the challenge of it. Dad can handle the bank for a while. I'm late getting into the campaign, but I've already started lining men up."

"Shouldn't we have discussed this? We'll have to live in Baton Rouge if you win!"

"It isn't forever, just one term," he said, trying to placate her. "I want to try my hand at politics."

"You're too young."

"No, I'm not. The law says twenty-five is the minimum age to be governor of Louisiana. I'm a year over that and think what a feather in my cap it'll be if I win at twenty-six!"

"And my job?"

He frowned. "That's what I'm asking you. Will you give it up for me?"

"I can't even understand why you want to do this."

"I want what the job can give me."

"You should have all you want from the job you have now!"

"It isn't the money. I could retire tomorrow, and we'd get along on investments. I want the challenge."

"You want the power."

"Okay, maybe I do. What's wrong with that?"

"It just seems so unnecessary," she said, stunned by his news as much as by the fact that he had already made his decision. She had never realized that he was interested in politics.

"So does your working."

"Don't try to change the subject. What does Millard think about it?"

"He's all for it. He thinks I can beat Ben Holloway. I'm younger and I can bring some fresh ideas to the job."

"And Sloane?"

"I don't give a damn what Sloane thinks about it. He won't disapprove, though. I can tell you that."

The music ended, another couple joined them, and the subject was dropped until they were in their new Cadillac and driving home. She twisted in the seat to face him. "You've already started your campaign, haven't you?"

His jaw firmed, and he answered flatly, "Yes. I've been wanting to surprise you."

"Well, you succeeded," she said, realizing with a shock that Tyler never would consult her on the major decisions in his life.

He swung the car to the curb and cut the motor, turning to take hold of her arms. His voice dropped. "Tali, I want this," he coaxed. "If I win, we'll come back here after this term. I can't do it without your consent. Please."

It was so unlike Tyler to beg for anything, and he was being his nicest, so she hated to point out to him that he had gone right ahead with his plans without her consent. She nodded her head. "Of course. I'd like to come back to my job afterward, if they'll have me."

"They'll have you! Thanks, honey. Thanks!" he said, pulling her into his arms and kissing her. His passion eased away some of the hurt she felt over having to give up her career.

The next Friday night, at the house they had rented until theirs was completed, they had a dinner for his staff. As Talia gazed at the house filled with people, she realized that her husband had been quietly working on his campaign for some time. But when Tyler turned on the charm, she found it difficult to become angry with him. She met his campaign manager, Albert Santos. Short and compact with a swarthy complexion and looking more like a professional wrestler, Santos was ten years older than Ty. His wife Terri was a petite blonde. Bob McNally, Ty's press liaison, was the same

age as Santos. Thin, tall, and blond, Bob had worked for the
Baton Rouge *Morning Advocate*. One by one she met Ty's
staff and watched him move among them. Millard was min-
gling with them also, getting to know them, charming everyone just as much as his son. She already knew Leon Goudeau,
Ty's accountant, and Janine Sanders, his secretary from the
bank.

After the guests and the family finally departed, Ty turned
to take her in his arms. "You were sensational tonight!
Thanks, luv." He leaned down to kiss her, and Talia tried
to ignore her annoyance with Ty and her reluctance to support
his campaign. He turned his head to whisper in her ear.
"Reach in my pocket, I have another surprise for you."

"I'm glad it's something in your pocket," she said dryly,
"and not news that we're moving to Europe."

"You're angry."

"I'm still in shock," she said, opening the box and finding
a sparkling diamond pendant. "Oh, Tyler, how lovely!"

"Turn around and I'll put it on you," he whispered, kissing
the nape of her neck. "And take this off." He slid down the
zipper of her green dress. As she moved back into his arms,
closing her eyes and relishing his passionate kiss, she realized
that the diamond was his attempt to win back her approval.

Monday at the bank, she told Larry Prima about her husband's plans, and to her relief, he promised that if Tyler won
and she lived in Baton Rouge for a term, she could come
back to work at the bank when she returned.

She graduated from college in May. To her amazement,
the entire Franklin family announced they would attend her
commencement exercises, and they invited her to dinner afterwards to celebrate. Tyler's eyes glowed with a special
sparkle while Millard Franklin presented her with a check for
a thousand dollars as a graduation gift.

That same month Melissa told Sloane goodbye, but if he
was saddened by it, he didn't show it. Ty and Talia had the
twins stay with them occasionally, and they became regular
crewmen for Ty's sailing. Talia and Ty moved into their new
house with its white carpeting, a deck and swimming pool,
and a yard that still needed sod and landscaping. It was two
stories; the living room and family room had sliding glass

doors that opened onto the deck. In her elegant house Talia occasionally felt like a stranger. It was lavish, but so precise. It was like a museum, and the white and mauve and deep purple of the decor were not Talia's colors. Its perfect order was typical of Tyler.

Ty launched his campaign and one of the first things he did was hire a detective.

In his office at the bank, Ty shook hands with J.L. Bonebrake and sized up the short, balding man. Bonebrake looked more like a myopic accountant than a detective.

"Have a seat, Mr. Bonebrake. You come highly recommended."

"That's good to hear. After all, a satisfied client is the purpose of my business."

There was a pause and Ty sat down behind his desk. "I'm going to run in the gubernatorial race."

"I've seen your picture in the paper."

"What I want from you is information on Ben Holloway."

"The representative? His background should be public information since he's held public office. I might be a waste of your money."

"I'm willing to pay to find out. His opponent in the race for the legislature was Sam Everage who wasn't aggressive in his campaign. Ben Holloway beat him by a wide margin. That doesn't mean there isn't something in Ben Holloway's background that I shouldn't know."

"I see what you mean. Here's my fee schedule. I'll report back to you within three days."

"Fine. I want as much information as you can get."

To Tyler's surprise, J.L. Bonebrake grinned, his narrow brown eyes looking as cold and impassive as a shark's. "I'll see what I can do." J.L. Bonebrake closed the door behind him. Within three days he returned with a thick manilla folder.

"I think everything you'll want is there. If you want me to dig deeper, just let me know."

Tyler handed him a check and thanked him, tucking the folder in the bottom drawer of his desk. That night he sat on the deck while Talia swam. Sipping a mint julep, he opened the folder. It contained old newspaper clips, pictures of Ben

Holloway, advertising and flyers from the last campaign, and snapshots that made him wonder how Bonebrake had acquired them. Finally he got down to what he was searching for: pages of personal information. And page two gave him what he wanted. His pulse jumped as he read, "Simone Royale Holloway. Married Ben Holloway in France. Father alcoholic, killed in factory accident. Mother, prostitute. Simone Royale: prostitute. Three arrests, each time fined and released."

Tyler let out a yelp of victory, and Talia swam to the edge of the pool, resting her arms on the concrete. "What's so delightful?"

"I've got it! Victory, Tali! I can beat Ben Holloway."

"Congratulations, Tyler! And how are you assured of that wonderful victory when the campaigning is barely under way?"

"You should see this little detective. He doesn't look as if he could get in out of a rainstorm, but he discovered some damaging information on my opponent."

"Why are you so vindictive towards Ben Holloway?"

"I want to win. And we've been opponents before. He bid and won that land north of here where Dad and I wanted to build town houses. Ben Holloway and his campaign manager, Mike Stanton, are going to get smashed this time. They're nouveau riche, trying to move up. They got past me before, but not this time!"

"Tyler, are you going to be a dirty fighter?"

He grinned and put down the papers, crossing the pool to her and kicking off his shoes. He unfastened his belt and trousers, dropping the suit pants in a heap on the wet concrete.

"Tyler! That's one of your good suits! What are you doing?" she asked, knowing full well, her pulse quickening when she saw the gleam in his eyes. He peeled off his socks and shirt in a hurry, then stripped off his shorts and dropped nude into the water beside her. With a squeal she tried to swim away, but he caught her.

"Still trying to drown me, aren't you! Will you ever stop diving into the pool on top of me?"

"On top of you sounds like the best place to be," he said,

pulling her to him, desire kindling between them as he peeled away her suit.

"Simone Holloway is my ticket to victory!"

"Sit down, Mike, and join us for coffee. Maybe you can settle an argument," Simone said, motioning for Mike to join her at the breakfast table.

"Simone, this is between us. Don't drag Mike into it and put him on the spot," Ben said. His white shirt was unbuttoned, the dark hair of his chest showing at the open neck.

"He's got a head on his shoulders," she argued. "Listen to him. Mike, I don't think Ben should run for governor. It's far more demanding than being in the legislature. We're getting older and I want to travel and enjoy life."

"That sounds like a good argument, Ben," Mike said easily, buttering a piece of toast, careful to keep the sleeves of his navy suit from touching his plate as he reached for the dish of raspberry jam. The cook replaced an empty serving dish with another full of hot biscuits and went back to the other part of the kitchen, working silently.

"I don't think Tyler Franklin will be a good governor," Ben said stubbornly. "I think he'll build up a machine that may get enough power behind it to be unstoppable."

"Ben, you don't have to be an avenging angel and save the city," Simone urged. "You just don't!"

"We can fight them, and I intend to do so, and send Tyler Franklin running back to Papa and his family fortune!"

Mike glanced at Ben over the steaming cup of black chicory coffee, and as Ben and Simone argued, he realized that Ben was hiding something from his wife. During the past few years as Mike had climbed socially and joined the yacht club he had met Tyler Franklin. He didn't like the idea of Ben's running against a man like Tyler, so he wasn't surprised that the going was becoming tough already.

"Look at this!" Simone exclaimed. "We have a wonderful home, a wonderful life," she argued, letting her hand drift over Ben's shoulder. He turned to kiss her wrist and a look passed between them that made Mike envy what they had. He wanted one love, one woman who could share his life with him as Simone had with Ben.

Simone turned her head and her dark eyes flashed. To Mike's surprise, there was fear in her expression. "Tell him, Mike. We don't need this hassle!"

Mike glanced around the beige and brown kitchen with its stainless steel sinks, the beige appliances, the cherrywood cabinets. "You have a happy marriage, a wonderful life, and you don't need any hassles."

"But you understand why I want to run, don't you?"

Mike glanced at Simone. Dressed in a pink satin robe with pink feathers fastened to her chin, she waited patiently. She still looked far younger than her years. Her figure was as good as ever, the fine lines around her eyes and mouth were usually hidden by makeup, her white-blond hair beautifully framed her face. Mike knew how much Ben had liked being a representative. He shrugged. "I think I'll pass on an answer."

I give up!" Simone said, throwing up her hands in exasperation. "I'm going upstairs, so I don't have to listen to you two talk about the campaign."

After she had gone, Ben and Mike sipped coffee, and Mike knew there was something disturbing Ben. Finally Ben set down his cup. "Let's go to my office where we can talk."

"Sure." Mike stood up, his dark suit coat swinging open revealing the smooth front of his white cotton shirt and the cuffs clasped with golden links at his wrists.

As he closed the door on the oak-paneled office with its rows of bookshelves and its stone hearth, he said, "What's the trouble?"

Ben glanced at him. "You always amaze me. You have a bloodhound's nose for trouble."

"I grew up in a jungle. You develop a keen sense of awareness there."

"Simone and I didn't grow up in suburbia and yet we're not as intuitive." He picked up a sheet of paper. "To get to the point, I received a letter yesterday from Tyler Franklin. He's obviously hired a detective and done a thorough job. He's learned about Simone's past and he's going to give the information to the press if I don't withdraw from the race!"

"Jesus! How can he be that dirty!" Mike snapped.

"He wants to win."

"We both knew he'd fight like a tiger. I've known him for several years now. We belong to the same yacht club; I've raced with him. He'll do anything short of getting disqualified to acquire a trophy. He's young, aggressive, and determined," Mike said, half-thinking about Tyler while considering what would happen to Simone and Ben.

"All right. Think about it and give me your opinion."

Mike sat down on a leather sofa, kicked off his eel skin loafers and put his stockinged feet on a coffee table while he thought. "I'd withdraw."

"The dirty sonofabitch! A threatening letter and I throw in the towel. I don't want to run from him!"

"You don't want to hurt Simone."

"Simone is tough. She's backed me in everything I've ever done."

"None of those things ever threw her in the limelight like this will."

"I'll protect her. If I can weather it and win, she should be able to withstand the heat. Matter of fact, I've been giving it thought all night. I'd like to send her to one of those beauty spas."

"You can't hide her away forever."

"No, but it would get her mind off the fight. She's been to one before. There's one in Phoenix, another at Palm Springs. I'll get her away and then slug it out with him. If he comes out with this, I'm willing to fight him to the finish."

"Well, I think you already have your answer," Mike said dryly, slipping on his shoes and standing up straight and tall. "I better head to the office. I have an appraisal this afternoon and an appointment with Jason Corning to look at Windy Square."

"You think he's going to make you an offer?"

"I don't know."

Ben laughed. "You're always scared you'll jinx something if you admit it's going to happen."

"Could be."

Ben's smile faded. "Mike, there's something I want. Will you go talk to Franklin for me? Tell him I won't withdraw, get him to keep that bit out of the press if you can."

"Sure, I'll see what I can do," Mike said.

"You're the only one who can handle it. I don't know what I'd do without you. You take on every tough, dirty job I hand you. And I don't want Simone to know a thing about it. I get so damned angry every time I read his letter. I'd like to go punch him out!"

"That would end matters," Mike said. "I'd tell Simone if I were you. That way she'll be prepared if he does do something."

"No way! And don't you tell her. If I can just get her out of town. She's not in the thick of society. Her whole world revolves around this house—"

"No. It revolves around you," Mike remarked quietly, wondering if Ben knew how much it did.

"Well, what I'm getting at is, she doesn't have a lot of friends to lose when it gets right down to it."

"That's because she's always been afraid to try to make friends, afraid she would let something slip and she would embarrass you."

Ben stared at him. "How the hell do you know that?"

Mike shrugged, keeping his voice casual. "We've talked. She's not on guard with me."

"Get Tyler Franklin off my tail."

Mike thought of Simone. "I don't often advise you, but I'm going to this time. Get out of the race."

Ben's face flushed. "I want to be governor. This upstart kid, this dirty fighter—I won't hand this to him on a silver platter. Simone's always gone along with what I want."

"This time she'll be in the limelight. She'll be out of her element."

"She's had years to become sure of herself, years away from that past."

"Let me shoot a copy of the letter," Mike said. "I'd tell Simone about it."

"I'm betting you can talk him out of it, and then there's no need for her to know."

"Does Farrell know?" Mike asked, thinking about Farrell deBois, Ben's press secretary.

"No. I haven't told him or anyone else on my staff except you."

"I'll talk to Farrell. He should know so he can field any

questions that might crop up. I'd like to hire our own detective. Tyler Franklin might not have a lily-white background either.''

"Of course. I should have thought of that."

Mike went through the house, making a checklist in his mind of things he needed to do before his first appointment. He didn't expect to gain anything from a detective. If Franklin had something to hide, he wouldn't have attacked Ben so blatantly and be ready to sling mud, but it would be remiss not to check and find out. An hour later he called and made an appointment to see Tyler Franklin at his home the following Tuesday.

Monday afternoon Tyler slammed his car door, gravel crunching beneath his feet as he crossed to the sidewalk and headed up the walk to the antebellum home that was the office of his brother's landscape business. The grounds were magnificent, Tyler grudgingly conceded. Sloane was a natural at what he did. Not only had the old property been restored to its former grandeur, but, Tyler suspected, in its heyday it had never looked this good. Beds of flowers, fountains, magnolias and live oaks artfully grew on a lawn that was so perfect it looked artificial.

He stepped inside, told a receptionist that he had an appointment with Sloane, and was ushered into Sloane's office. Across a white-carpeted room, Sloane sat behind an antique oak desk. Again Tyler had to admire his brother's taste and talent, but annoyance tinged his admiration.

" 'Morning, Tyler. Sit down."

"Can we talk undisturbed and without being overheard?" Tyler asked, sinking down on a burgundy-colored leather wing chair.

Sloane's full lips curved in a curious smile. "Of course. Sit down. How's Tali?"

"She's fine. My campaign is getting under way and things look good, but I'm going after Ben Holloway with everything I can muster."

"I knew you would."

"And I don't want my campaign blown to smithereens by

my brother," Tyler said, trying to keep his voice calm, staring at Sloane.

"I've already made a sizable contribution to your campaign," Sloane answered, but the lightness was gone from his tone. Both brothers recognized trouble coming, because they had shared tense moments like this since their childhood. Tyler lifted his chin.

"I want you to get rid of your lover."

12

Sloane threw down the pencil he was holding. He sat back and glared at Tyler, who faced him with stubborn determination. "My life is my own damned business."

"Having a fag brother when I'm running for office is my business!" Tyler snapped, his patience wearing thin.

"Get out, Tyler! Sloane said, coming to his feet and moving around the desk.

They hadn't physically fought since they were teenagers, but Tyler sensed the belligerence in Sloane's stance. He knew his brother worked out with weights and was in excellent shape, but he almost welcomed a chance to smash Sloane with his fists. "You get rid of Chad or I will. I don't care about the females."

"You can't control my life."

"You're not going to ruin my chances."

Suddenly Sloane stepped forward, pivoting and throwing his weight behind his fist. Tyler anticipated the blow and ducked, catching a glancing strike on his jaw, raising his fists to throw a right hook and catch Sloane squarely in the mouth.

Sloane's head snapped back, and he swung at Tyler. Fists still raised, Tyler ducked and stepped away, watching blood trickle down Sloane's chin.

"I'm not going to slug it out with you here and get my picture in the paper and questions raised. You better heed my warning, Sloane!" Tyler turned and left without glancing at the receptionist as he strode across the office. Once in his car his mind raced with possible scenarios involving his brother. He wasn't going to lose this election because of his brother's perverted sexual preferences. And since he was going to drag Ben Holloway's name through the press, he knew Holloway would come after him.

That night at dinner, Talia could tell something bothered Tyler, so she became her most charming. She tried to please him, and finally he dismissed all worries over Sloane and pulled her onto his lap.

He wound his fingers in her hair, cupping her head with his hand to pull her close and kiss her. When he raised his head, his voice was husky. "I want a son, Talia."

Her eyes seemed to darken as she leaned forward, her mouth brushing his. "So do I," she whispered, clinging to him, turning to press against him as he picked her up in his arms to carry her to bed.

Mike was ushered into the Franklins' den by a maid. He halted abruptly when a woman instead of Ty faced him. Standing only a few feet away in the center of the room, she was dressed in a tailored navy dress with a single strand of pearls. Her hair was combed into a smooth chignon and she wore pearl earrings. She was the picture of perfection. A twinge of impatience deepened in Mike.

"I'm Talia Franklin, Mr. Stanton," she announced with a lift of her chin, distaste evident in her voice. "I've taken off from work and have an appointment shortly but I wanted to be here since Ty was unavoidably delayed. So if you'll have a seat, I'll stay with you until he arrives."

Her cool, imperious voice made him feel like a recalcitrant child who had to sit with the teacher and wait for the principal. His anger increased. "You can go on to your appointment, Mrs. Franklin. I can wait here by myself. I won't steal the silver," he said in quiet, clipped tones.

Talia stiffened. His blue eyes raked over her with bold arrogance, and although she knew she was fully dressed, she felt as if he had mentally divested her of every stitch of clothing with his insolent appraisal.

"I didn't realize there was that danger," she said in a haughty voice. She wanted to sit down behind the desk where half of her would be hidden from his piercing gaze, but with a lift of her chin she strode to a wing chair and sat down, crossing her legs with what she hoped was aplomb.

Mike sat down opposite her, feeling an intense dislike for the beautiful woman who seemed so serene and sheltered while her husband was working at that very moment to destroy Ben and Simone. Mike's distaste for politics and Ty Franklin now included Mrs. Franklin.

Facing him, Talia was ensnared in a challenging stare. With a mere look she felt their wills clash. He was simply trying to stare her down, but she wasn't going to allow it. And she couldn't think of anything to say to him. He was rugged, with a tough enough air that made him look capable of stealing the silver and everything else in the house. He had a scar along the length of his face, a slightly crooked nose, a lean body that moved silently. His dark brown curls were a tangle over his wide forehead. He was the most unconventionally handsome man Talia had ever met.

She wasn't going to be the first to look away, but then she realized she had let him goad her into a contest that crossed the barriers of polite society. Any small talk about the weather after three full minutes of trying to outstare the other would be inane. Still, she wouldn't look away. She felt as if she were staring at a hungry leopard.

Finally she heard voices in the hall, and she glanced away automatically.

"Excuse me," she said, standing up. She was fully aware of why Mike Stanton was visiting. She hadn't approved of what Tyler was doing, but after this encounter with Mike Stanton, she almost agreed with her husband's tactics. Clearly this man was out for blood. Tyler had an appointment with newsmen and had worked Mike in beforehand. Now that the press had arrived, she realized it was she who held the power in the room.

In the hall she said, "I'm Talia Franklin," and stepped

forward to shake hands with two reporters. Hoping to catch
Mike Stanton off guard as much as possible, she led them
into the den.

"My husband should be here at any moment. He called
to say he was unavoidably detained. Have you gentlemen
met Mike Stanton? He's with the opposition. Mr. Stanton,
this is Brad Drake, and this is Chip Forrester." A tall, thin
man and a shorter, blond man stepped forward to shake hands
with Mike.

"Mr. Stanton has come to ask my husband not to disclose
some information to the press, so perhaps you gentlemen
would like to talk to him until Tyler gets home."

Mike felt anger surge through him, turning his cheeks
scarlet in color. He hadn't known the press would be here,
or that he would have to confront them unprepared. He forced
a smile, and noticed a grin on Talia Franklin's beautiful, rosy
mouth.

The two newsmen could smell a story in the air. Brad
Drake glanced back and forth between Talia and Mike.

"Would you care to elaborate on that?" Chip Forrester
asked, whipping out a pad and pen.

"Actually, it's a little premature to go into the matter,"
Mike answered easily.

"You're not trying to withhold information that's necessary, are you?" Drake asked politely, his quiet words unable
to conceal the eagerness in his voice.

"No, not at this time," Mike replied. "I have some campaign questions and the possibility of a debate that I wish to
discuss with Mr. Franklin. We have opposing stands on so
many issues—the proposed flood control options for Cross
Reservoir that will cost nearly one hundred million dollars
and necessitate an increase in taxes; the funding of the France
Road Container Terminal on the Industrial Canal at the Port
of New Orleans. . . ." Mike enumerated dry political topics
in a flat, informative tone that killed any avid curiosity in the
reporters' eyes. They each dutifully made a few notes. Beyond them Talia Franklin gave him a smug, frosty smile, and
all he could think of while he talked was that he would get
her next time.

He purposely let his gaze drift down over her in a brazen

glance, knowing that was one thing that unnerved her. She turned away as a voice called from the hall.

"Tali?"

"In here, darling," Talia answered, aware she had called him darling in public for the first time in her life. Her blunt statement to the reporters threw Mike Stanton off balance for a moment, but he had disturbed her just as badly and she was relieved to see Tyler stride through the doorway.

"Ah, Tali, thanks," Ty said, crossing to kiss her cheek. She glanced at Mike who was standing. She introduced the two newsmen to Tyler. "And you know Mike Stanton, Ben Holloway's campaign manager. If you'll excuse me, I'll leave you men alone," she said.

"It was *entertaining*, Mrs. Franklin," Mike said with a trace of sarcasm. Ty cast a curious glance at his wife.

Even with Ty's attention on her, Talia noticed yet another audacious appraisal from Mike Stanton. She drew a sharp breath and left, annoyed that she had allowed him to intimidate her in the slightest, yet glad to escape his presence.

"If you gentlemen will excuse us a moment," Tyler said smoothly, "I have something to discuss with Mr. Stanton and then I'll be ready for our interview." Ty and Mike crossed the hall to the library, where Tyler closed the door.

Mike glanced at the shelves of moroccan leather-bound books, the hunting scenes framed and hung on the walls. Ty Franklin came from old money; his family's banking empire in New Orleans had been in the same family since its founding. Mike knew that Ben had a formidable opponent in Ty, but the younger man's dirty tactics left a sour taste in his mouth.

As soon as Ty closed the door, his jovial manner vanished. Mike felt as much antagonism from Tyler Franklin as he had experienced with Talia. For the first time in years he had an atavistic urge to punch the arrogant man facing him.

"As you can see, I don't have long. What did you want to see me about?" Ty asked coldly.

"About the campaign. This is Ben's second time to run for public office. He's happy for anyone to fight him fairly on his record, on his life. But we've had reports that this is going to sink into mudslinging."

" 'If you don't like the heat, stay out of the kitchen,' "
Ty answered. "Isn't that how the old saying goes?"

"You'll have a fight on your hands either way. Ben Holloway isn't going to pull out of the race. Nor will he stoop
to your level."

"I'm not going to do anything unlawful."

"We're talking ethics. His wife is an innocent party."

"Come on," Ty scoffed. "She's his wife! He wouldn't
run for office over her objection. And if there's something
dark in her past, the voters have a right to know about it.
He's smart enough to know a man needs a clean record to
go into politics."

"Ben's record is clean. That's not what we're talking about
here."

"His family is just as much a part of him, so if there's
something unsatisfactory about Simone Holloway, the voters
will learn about it. We're wasting each other's time, Mr.
Stanton. I have an appointment for an interview."

Mike's temper flared. He knew he wasn't changing Ty's
mind, and that Simone and Ben were both going to get hurt
badly. "And your own family is without blemish? Don't start
something you'll regret." For just an instant something flickered in the depths of Ty's eyes, and Mike mentally pounced
on it like a fighter finding an opening. "Once you start this,
it'll go all the way," he said, unable to keep a bitter note
out of his voice.

"I have nothing to hide, and neither does my wife, which
is more than Ben Holloway can say. The public needs to
know what kind of person they're electing to office."

"Don't hurt Simone or Ben," Mike said as the two men
mentally measured each other, and Mike knew Ty Franklin
would be a tough opponent. The trophies in the glass case
were a mute testament to his ability and determination to win.

"No one is forcing him to run for office. He chose it
and he'll have to pay the consequences of gaining public
attention."

"And you'll have to pay the consequences as well. I swear
to you I'll see to that," Mike said, taking a step closer, his
fists clenching.

"Are you threatening me?" Ty blinked and his jaw came up, and Mike could see he was ready to fight.

"Damned right, I am! It's senseless. You don't need to hurt him or Simone. You try to ruin Ben, and you'll pay," Mike said, his control slipping.

"You touch me, and I'll have the district attorney on your back so fast, you won't know what happened," Ty snarled.

"To hell with that," Mike rejoined, trying to control the urge to hit Tyler.

"Get out, Stanton!"

"You hurt them, and I'll get you!" Mike strode from the house, stepping into the sunshine while his rage was at its peak.

He wished there was some way to protect Simone. One good look into Ty Franklin's adamant black eyes told him that this man would stop at nothing to get elected. He remembered Ty's slight hesitation when he had mentioned the Franklin family. There was some skeleton in Ty's closet, and Mike was determined to find out what it was.

As he slammed into his car, he thought of Talia Franklin and how she had thrown him to the wolves, giving the reporters a lead they might otherwise have been ignorant of. He thought of the staring contest they had shared. She was as stubborn and self-assured as her husband.

As soon as the interview was over, Tyler drove straight to his campaign headquarters uptown on Magazine Street, where he knew he could find Janine Sanders, his appointment secretary. She was also his executive secretary at the bank, and both he and Janine planned to be at campaign headquarters each morning this week. Her black eyes were bright, and she nodded her head slightly as he talked. She had capable hands with blunt fingers and short, clipped nails that looked almost masculine, and she took notes while he talked.

"I don't want to take any calls from Ben Holloway's campaign manager or secretary. If he wants me, he can call me himself. As soon as you can, schedule some time with Bob." Tyler reviewed his concerns as he thought of his tall, thin press liaison. An old college fraternity brother, Bob McNally had quit his job to become Ty's press secretary and speech-writer. Tyler had been pleased with his choice because Bob knew how to write just what Tyler needed to say in just the manner that Tyler would have phrased his speeches had he written them himself.

"I want a staff meeting scheduled. What's the schedule for tomorrow?"

She opened an appointment book in front of her and ran her stubby finger down the page. "Meeting at nine in the morning with C. Clanton, one of your pollsters. At ten you have a meeting with the ad agency man, Marvin Hawthorne. You have a staff meeting scheduled for Friday."

"That's soon enough. I want to see Bob today, and I want to talk to Al as soon as possible," he said, thinking about his campaign manager.

"You have an appointment with him at four today. Do I need to make one sooner?"

"No, that's fine. I haven't looked at my schedule." He relaxed and grinned, realizing how tense he had become. "I'll try to remember to look at my schedule before I interrupt you."

She flashed him a wide smile. "That's what I'm here for." He winked at her and went into his office. His pulse drummed with excitement. He liked a battle, because he knew he was going to win. He was in his element when he was fighting for a goal. Ty figured that if fighting hurt Ben Holloway, he should have had more sense than to step out into the glare of public opinion.

Ty studied the calendar in front of him and he wrote, "Sloane," reminding himself to check and make sure his brother heeded his warning. His anticipation heightened at the thought of his upcoming appointment soon with his pollsters. The last report had been favorable with a growing number of voters giving him support. Ben Holloway shouldn't have run for governor; he wasn't strong enough, and he didn't have the political machine behind him that Tyler was quickly creating.

By the time he faced his staff at the end of the week, Ty's confidence had grown. Shrugging out of his suit coat and dropping it negligently over his chair, he held a report in his hands.

"We want the media to go after the undecided vote. Of course, we need to keep our supporters, but the media needs to step up its efforts to bring in the undecided. We can leak information about Ben Holloway's wife soon."

"I think you can win without doing that," Leon Goudeau, Ty's accountant, said, shifting his thin shoulders.

"We've been over it. I want this brought out."

"He's right," Al said flatly. "Ty dug this tidbit up without our help. Let him use it," he said.

"I've warned the man that it's the public's right to know about his wife's past. And I'm going to do it." Ty turned to face Bob McNally, who was stretched out in a chair, his long legs crossed at the ankles, a notepad on his lap. "Bob's got the information tucked into a speech. It'll come out at my talk to the Rotary, and we won't have to do another thing, because the media will pick it up. Right, Al?"

"That's right," his campaign manager said. "Just say it once, matter-of-factly. Holloway has tried to keep her under wraps—of course, if you see her, you'd know why. A governor's wife, she is not. Broad looks like she just stepped out of a strip joint. The men won't forget her."

"They're not going to forget my wife, either," Ty said dryly, always proud to show off Talia.

"I've heard Simone Holloway hates politics and everything about it," Bob remarked.

"Then she should have tried harder to persuade her husband not to run. His campaign manager, Mike Stanton, threatened me if we use this."

"You may have a tiger by the tail," Leon said in his raspy voice. "Mike Stanton is as tough as they come. And a hell of a lot meaner and harder than Ben Holloway."

"I'm not scared of Mike Stanton," Ty said, facing Leon, his eyes narrowing. "Are you?"

"No. But I never have seen a need to take a stick and stir a nest of rattlesnakes."

"He's not a nest. He's only one snake. And I'll take him on any day."

Ty was entered in the Lake Pontchartrain J/24 Gold Cup
Regatta scheduled for that Saturday. The twins and Talia were
his regular crew. They drove out Roadway to the yacht club
on Friday evening to practice with the fifth man on the crew,
Kent Fleury, a friend of Ty's.

When they arrived, they immediately scrambled aboard the
blue fiberglass *Rio*. Talia helped take the covers off the sails.
The 24-foot sailboat was 8 feet 11 inches in the beam, with
263 square feet of sail, a displacement of 3,100 pounds. Tyler
had the keel polished to mirrored perfection, the trailing edges
meticulously sharp to give it speed.

Talia stowed the covers below while the twins and the men
got the lines untangled and laid out. Tyler wore green shorts
and deck shoes; his body was the color of teak from weekends
in the sun. Coming up from below, Talia paused. In the slip
opposite theirs, she saw a man take an agile step onto the
deck of his J/24, the *Sparrow*. It was obvious that he was
the skipper as he gave commands to his crew. His shirt was
off, his body as bronzed as Ty's and just as muscular. He
was slightly more narrow in his hips. Wind ruffled his curly
brown hair, and as he raised his head and gazed across the
narrow strip of water he saw her. She looked away without
a nod. It was Mike Stanton.

Occasionally Stanton won a J/24 race, but no one won as
often as Ty. Talia knew that the second most likely person
was Chet Weatherly. It was the first time Talia had sailed in
a race with Ty, and eager anticipation had made her look
forward to the afternoon. It was a perfect day for sailing.
The sky was blue with fluffy white clouds like blobs of paint
flung against a blue canvas. A steady breeze blew from the
south, creating thin whitecaps on the waves. She watched as
Travis shoved the boat into the waterway. Talia couldn't
believe how fast the twins were growing. They were seven
now, both wiry and strong, both adept at sailing. Jeff was
tanned to the same deep color as Ty, Travis to a shade lighter.

As skipper and strategist, Ty sat at the tiller. Jeff raised
the jib by pulling on the halyard, his muscles tensing while
he worked. In the waterway, he raised the mainsail while Ty
scanned the area, watching the others get ready to race. He

had a faint smile on his face. Talia knew how badly he wanted the trophy. She stroked his knee and he focused on her, but she wondered if he even saw her.

"Relax, Ty. You have lots of time before the race starts."

He turned his attention to the other J/24s, then to his crew to give them instructions. As they went west down the waterway, they were sailing on a broad reach, the wind on the beam until Ty maneuvered out of the waterway. Ty put the tiller over and the boat turned north while Kent loosened the sheets because the wind was from the stern.

Talia and Jeff would handle the spinnaker during the race. Jeff was the "deck ape" who handled the spinnaker and the pole during jibing maneuvers on the foredeck. Talia would control the spinnaker sheet and the guy from the cockpit. They took wind readings every three minutes, averaging them out to test wind speed.

Talia lifted her face to the breeze. Her hair was braided down her back and she wore yellow linen shorts and a yellow cotton blouse. There was still time before the race, and yachts were jockeying for the best position. The committee boat with the judges and referee was waiting at the imaginary starting line, the markers bobbing out in the water. Ty's smile was gone, and he looked hungry and intent, as if he were climbing into a boxing ring instead of setting sail on the local lake.

She wished he weren't so competitive, and then she wondered if he weren't growing more so as he got older.

She had watched him often enough to know that the minutes between the first signal and the start of the race were crucial. If a yacht wasn't in the best position, precious seconds could be lost, often determining the outcome of the race before the actual start.

They sailed in close to the committee boat where Ty could see the order of the race posted on a blackboard. He wrote them on the fiberglass with a soft marker, *A, D, C,—G*. They were to pass markers *A, D, C*, and back to the finish in a triangle on the lake. Every minute was now as vital as during the race, and Ty maneuvered for clear air toward the starting line.

The cannon was fired and the white flag raised, indicating

ten minutes left before the start. Ty called orders and Talia worked swiftly, seeing the space where he was headed, knowing he would like to hover near the starting line as much as possible. They were luffing the jib. The white flag was lowered and then the blue flag raised as the cannon was fired again in a warning signal. Five minutes to go. She glanced over her shoulder to see a sleek, red J/24 coming up behind them. It was trying to sail into position closest to the committee boat, the position Ty was headed for.

They were down to the last seconds before the red flag signaling the start of the race. By now the boat had the overlap. Chet, the skipper, yelled at Ty, "I'm coming up!"

"Trim in the jib slowly!" Ty snapped the command, and Talia's head jerked around. According to the rules, he was supposed to get out of the way.

"Ty—"

"Four seconds," he snapped. "Hold it."

"Take it up!" someone yelled from the leeward boat.

"Stay clear!" Ty shouted back.

"Ty, you'll be disqualified!" she protested, aghast at what he was doing.

"Stall, dammit!" he ordered the crew. "Three seconds, two seconds—now! Take it up hard!" he shouted while the skipper to leeward bellowed at him.

The cannon boomed, the red flag went up and the race was on, Ty sweeping out ahead over the imaginary starting line.

Talia worked swiftly although the shock of what Ty had just done stunned her. He had cheated, something of which she wouldn't have believed him capable. She glanced at him and saw that his jaw was firmly set and a flinty expression showed his determination. If he cheated at a race, Talia thought, what else would he do to win? Would he cheat on her? She stared at him and his dark eyes met hers.

"Talia!" he snapped, glancing at the halyards, and she went back to work, looking over her shoulder to see Chet's *Anna Marie* off to a slow start but working to make up for lost time.

Their first leg was upwind, so Ty was on port tack as he crossed the starting line, on a close reach to round marker A. As the *Rio* rounded the marker, Jeff put up the spinnaker,

Tyler calling commands to all of them, watching the other boats. At *D* marker they dropped the spinnaker to go on a broad reach on a starboard tack.

As she worked, her anger mounted when she thought about Ty's tactics. He was in the lead with Mike Stanton's yacht, the blue *Sparrow*, the closest behind.

"Ready about," Ty called as they approached *C* marker while the twins got the lines ready for the tacking maneuvers. A fine spray washed over the boat, cooling Talia from the warm sunshine. The moment they passed the last marker, Ty threw the tiller hard to port.

"Rudders a'lee!"

Talia loosened the starboard jib sheet and tailed the port sheet while Jeff cranked it in on the port winch, making a run for the finish line. The *Sparrow* was now close behind, the *Anna Marie* was catching up.

Ty sailed across the finish line with a wide lead, giving a jubilant yell and shaking his fist in the air. The twins and Kent Fleury cheered with him while all Talia felt was anger. She had always known that his ambition was strong, but until now she hadn't seen the ruthlessness in him, the extent to which he would go in order to succeed. She shivered in the bright sun. She looked up and saw the *Sparrow* sail by. Mike Stanton was at the tiller, watching their yacht, and as his gaze met hers he gave a slow, negative shake of his head.

She blushed with embarrassment and fury and turned away, busying herself with lines again. There was another race, and Ty took the lead again and won just as handily. As they secured the boat, the twins were jubilant, exulting with the men before they scampered up on the dock and raced toward the yacht club. To her amazement Ty wasn't called before the protest board. Chet called him a string of foul names while both grinned, and Tyler bought everyone a round of beers.

The awards were presented, another round of drinks was downed in celebration, and then Ty took Talia home, dropping the twins off first. They had plans to change and then go to the country club to meet friends for a dinner celebration.

Inside the house he faced her. "I haven't heard congratulations from you," he said quietly.

"Do you have to win at all costs?"

He flushed beneath the tan and his forehead furrowed in a scowl. "Thanks, Tali, for your support!" he snapped cynically.

She felt her frustration build once again. "Tyler, you probably would have won without going to such extremes, and look at the example you set for the twins."

"Results are what count, and I won the race," he retorted, angry that she was condemning him for something she knew little about, wanting her to congratulate him on winning. In spite of the argument he found her desirable in her yellow shorts. "No one called me down for what I did. I didn't have to go before the protest board."

"That's because you weren't caught. You should have gone before them. Chet Weatherly is too much of a gentleman to report you. Winning isn't as important to him." She ran her hand across her brow. "I don't feel like going out to dinner and a dance to celebrate."

"It wasn't that bad!" he snapped. "But suit yourself. I'll celebrate with or without you."

Talia could hardly believe Ty's attitude. "You let the twins pump the sails during the race, and along with Kent, they were using body kinetics, leaning outside the lifelines to heel the boat—that's cheating."

"That's *winning*! Those things happen in every sport on every playing field all over the world. Men compete to win. Something women can't understand anyway!"

For the second time that day Talia saw a darker, more ruthless side to her husband. His eyes narrowed, and he came toward her. She faced him defiantly, seeing the determination in his jaw, knowing she had goaded him into fury.

"There's one way to end this argument," he growled as he lowered his head to cover her mouth with his, silencing her protest.

Tyler let his anger pour out in a bruising kiss, crushing Talia to him, wanting to possess her as much as he had wanted to win the race. He couldn't understand why she hadn't gotten pregnant yet. He wanted a son.

He bent over her, his arm banding her waist tightly while he shifted away and unbuttoned her linen shorts, pushing them down around her ankles, molding her to his will. For once Talia was not dazzled by Ty's passion. She was too hurt, and she did not want to settle this matter with a kiss.

She struggled in his arms, but her protesting body signaled a challenge that made Tyler throb with desire. He unbuttoned her cotton blouse and pushed it away, shoving aside her bra as his hands stroked her breast.

Before she knew what was happening, Tyler swept her up and carried her to the den where he put her down on the sofa, holding and stroking her until her struggles ceased. Talia lay still, knowing Ty would have his way. She did not want to make love to him, but he was her husband. She couldn't refuse him.

He flung off his shorts, then moved between her thighs, taking her in a hard thrust, watching her while her hips began to move beneath him. Talia felt her body betraying her mind. He drove her to the brink of pleasure and then pulled away. She cried out, tugging at him. He saw the power he had over her and he gloated in it, knowing he could demolish her in bed. Their raspy breathing was the only sound in the room. He fought to keep control while she moved wildly beneath him, until he was lost to his need as badly as she was to hers. He dimly heard her hoarse cries mingle with his.

Afterward as he lay on top of her, he pushed away abruptly. "I'm going to the club now to celebrate my victory," he said coldly.

His words were as harsh as a blow to her. His lovemaking had been a power struggle. Her body ached as she got up and moved into the hall, staring at their closed bedroom door. She went into a downstairs bathroom and locked the door, turning to put her head against the hard wood while she cried. She felt betrayed by Ty, betrayed by her body because it had responded to his desire for complete control over her. Talia knew Ty had not felt love for her earlier, and suddenly she felt more desperately alone than she had since leaving her family home.

Upstairs, Ty showered and changed. He was furious that Talia was giving him a difficult time. He left the house without another word to her. He arrived at the club in record time and found a cluster of sailing friends gathered at the bar. They offered him congratulations, and he began to relax. Heather King scooted close to him, a drink in hand, her blue eyes shining, her thigh rubbing against his.

"Congratulations, Tyler! You were magnificent!"

He smiled down at her, thinking this was the recognition he should have gotten from his wife. Heather's blue eyes gazed back guilelessly. She looked seventeen years old with her crop of blond curls, her slender body, and her high firm breasts. But Ty knew she was twenty-seven.

After drinking two glasses in a row of Scotch on the rocks he was relaxed. Heather King was still right beside him, her adoring gaze seldom leaving his, her hand brushing his on the bar ever so gently.

Ty knew she was flirting with him, and he was flattered. He decided to tease her a bit. "Come here, Heather," he said, taking her arm and leading her to the end of the hall until he found an empty parlor used for receptions and parties. He closed the door behind them.

He had meant only to enjoy a few kisses, but the moment her ripe lips opened wide beneath his and her tongue thrust into his mouth while her narrow little pelvis ground against him, Tyler yielded to the sensations she created.

Before he knew it, her blouse was unbuttoned and her skirt was pushed above her thighs. She tugged at his zipper to release his swollen member. Eagerly she pushed him back into a leather chair and sat down astride his lap, pushing him into her. Ty was amazed and excited by her. For a moment he thought about what he was doing. He didn't love her, and he quickly decided he therefore was not being disloyal to Talia. This was just a physical act. She was begging for this and he intended to oblige her. He held her hips as she moved on top of him faster and faster until he groaned with release, seeming to burst inside her hot body. Stimulated by his climax, Heather reached her own orgasm. She sat next to him afterward as they both silently straightened their clothing.

Before they parted, she dropped a hint that she would be home alone at lunch the next day and she would enjoy company.

That night Tyler showered and climbed into bed beside Talia who lay still. "Tali?" he asked softly.

"Yes," she said with both worry and agony evident in the tone of her voice.

"Let's not fight," he said. Guilt over what he had done was beginning to seep into his consciousness. "I shouldn't have made love to you like that," he whispered. "Did I hurt you?"

"No," she lied, and then he pulled her close. Her arms went around him, and contentment filled him. He had possessed two women this day, his wife had forgiven him for his punishing lovemaking, and he had won the race.

Talia closed her eyes tightly, trying to ignore the hurt that filled her.

For a month Tyler had toyed with possibilities and alternatives while waiting for Sloane to cooperate, but when Sloane didn't change his lifestyle. Tyler had to make a decision. He began to ask questions discreetly in certain places, finding the man he wanted, one he had heard about before.

They arranged to meet at the end of a shell road on a swampy bayou south of New Orleans. Ty arrived first, waiting a full hour for his own protection, driving a rental car, his face covered with a ski mask, thankful the weather had cooperated. The night was foggy as mist swirled around him, obliterating everything beyond a few yards, hanging on the water like sunken clouds. A car roared down the road in contrast to the stillness of the swamp. The lights were cut and someone stepped out.

Tyler's eyes had long ago adjusted, and when the man called in a hushed voice, "Hello," he waited until he saw a dark shape emerge from the mist.

"Over here," Ty said, his palms growing sweaty. He was safe. There was no way he could be traced, no proof, he assured himself as a man loomed into view.

"Here," Tyler said, pitching his voice higher than normal, trying to talk as little as possible. "I want a warning, just a scare. I was told you're the man to see."

"What city?"

"New Orleans. As soon as possible. Just enough to scare someone badly."

"Yeah. Suppose it turns out fatal?"

The question seemed to hang and envelope him like the fog while Tyler considered it. "Whatever is necessary, but I don't require it."

"Name the person."

Tyler gave him Chad's name, address, place of employment, and phone number.

"The price is ten grand."

It was a smaller sum than Tyler had imagined it would be. He thought of Sloane's fist smashing into his face, of his campaign, of his potential loss of political power because of this one family skeleton. "I didn't know it would be that high. I can give you six tonight. That's all I brought," he lied again.

"That'll do. Where do I get the rest?"

"Here's a key to a rental box in a mail company. The tag gives the address. When I know the job is done, the money will be put in the box."

"Make sure it is. I'll find you some way if it isn't."

"It'll be there. I promise. Just deliver. I'll lay the key and the money here. Give a count of ten so I can move away."

He laid them on the shell roadbed and stepped back. He had already explored the area with a flashlight and knew where he could walk, seeking the narrow strip of firm grass to his right, careful to keep as close to the road as possible. He turned, backing away cautiously while the man picked up the money and key and then mist closed in behind him. The crunch of footsteps faded; the click and slam of a car door was jarring in the silence.

The motor roared to life, and Tyler flattened himself behind the thick trunk of a cypress, out of sight of low fog beams as the car turned and the lights made brilliant arcs in the darkness, catching a pair of glowing red eyes on a log in the green water, swinging over thick cypress trunks, and then the car was gone.

Ty hurried to his car, climbed in, and started the engine, flicking on the lights as he roared down the road. He couldn't pick up red taillights ahead, and he didn't know if the man was far ahead, or if he had stopped and cut his lights and engine waiting for Tyler to pass. Tyler had picked this spot after hours of searching the area. There was nowhere to pull off, because the water was only inches off the road that cut through the bayou like a knife. He knew where the first connecting road was. He watched the mileage for the turn. He breathed as hard and as fast as if he had just run a marathon. His jaw was clamped so tightly shut it ached, and for an instant, regret consumed him. He relaxed when he thought about being named the governor of Louisiana. No one would ever know about this indiscretion except Sloane.

He had warned his brother but Sloane and his slimy lover had ignored him. Now they would get what they deserved: a good scare. He wanted them to know he meant what he said. This would be a clear warning.

13

June 1975

Three weeks later as Ty sat at his desk completing the forms for a recent loan to A & L Drilling Company, he heard raised voices in the anteroom and then the door to his office burst open. Sloane strode across the room, and Ty took one look at his contorted features, his murderous black eyes, and jumped to his feet.

"What the hell?"

Flinging up his arms, Ty tried to back up as his brother's right fist slammed into his jaw, sending him sprawling. Pain exploded in his back as he hit the sharp edge of the chair and lost his balance, landing on the floor, looking up to see Sloane coming after him. He was aware of a woman's scream, but anger pumped adrenalin through him and he lashed out with his feet, kicking Sloane in the stomach and sending him staggering backward.

Ty came up with agility, his fists raised. Sloane attacked with a straight left jab, but Ty was fighting in earnest now, and he deflected the blow, keeping up his defense. Sloane telegraphed his right, and it gave Tyler an opening. He jabbed straight and hard, smashing his fist against Sloane's mouth and nose.

Sloane lunged, tackling him, and they both fell on the floor, knocking over a table. A lamp crashed. Both got to their feet, but Tyler's guard was lowered. He saw Sloane's bloody fist aimed at him; he yanked his head to the left. Sloane's punch still caught him on the jaw, jerking back his head, something seeming to burst, red streaming into his eye. It was then that he knew Sloane would kill him if he could.

"Murderer!" Sloane yelled.

"You fag brownie king!"

"You've gone too far—" The words were gasped, bitten off when Tyler's fist connected. He followed with a surging blow to Sloane's ribs and threw a straight right punch that slammed into his brother's face and sent him staggering to the wall. Tyler felt the crack of bones in his knuckles, and pain shot through his hand.

Tyler's eyes were red from blood; rage burned in him as he slammed right and left fists against Sloane. Finally the only thing that held Sloane on his feet was Tyler's battering fists.

Suddenly Tyler was gripped from behind. He gasped for breath and a ringing in his ears drowned out all other noise. Then he slumped and inhaled deeply to catch his breath, wiping his face clean of blood. He became aware of people around him, of someone dabbing at his face, and he realized in the recesses of his mind that he had to get control of the situation before news of it got to the press.

He caught sight of Millard standing only a few feet away, a scowl on his face and an uncustomary pallor to his skin.

"Are you all right?"

"Get everybody out of here," Tyler said, grinding out the words. His ribs hurt, his jaw ached, his hand felt smashed, but right now an urgency to get rid of the crowd before questions were raised—before Sloane could talk—concerned him most. "Get them out!"

Millard Franklin issued quiet commands that brought immediate action, and in less than two minutes only the three Franklins were left in the room. Sloane gingerly lay down on the sofa.

"All right. What's going on?" Millard demanded. "Does this have something to do with your leaving for São Paulo?"

Shocked, a bubble of elation rising, Ty glanced at Sloane. "You're going to South America?"

"I'm getting away from you!"

"What the hell is going on?" Millard demanded again.

"This is between us, Dad," Tyler said. "Let me talk to Sloane." For the first time in his life he had ordered his Dad to do something against his wishes. Tyler met Millard's questioning gaze, and Millard left the room.

Tyler turned around. "You're not going to take the governorship from me."

"Damn you! I'm going to the police."

The threat seemed to snap some tiny thread of control that Tyler was exerting. Rage washed back like an incoming tide, and he advanced on Sloane.

"No, you won't go to the police, Sloane."

Sloane tried to sit up, grasped his side, and groaned. "Damn you!" His control broke and tears filled his eyes. "There wasn't any need to kill Chad!"

"I don't know what you're talking about. And you know I wouldn't murder a man."

Sloane didn't look convinced. "Then you got someone to do it."

"I don't know what you're talking about. I've been in meetings for the past week, and today I've been in this bank all day."

"You wouldn't dirty your hands! I know it was your fault. Even if I can't prove it, I can ruin your campaign."

"You won't do that either!" Tyler caught Sloane's shirt front and lifted him up, ignoring Sloane's gasp of pain. "Damn you, can't you understand what I'm saying to you? You're going to cooperate or else!"

Sloane paled, and Tyler released him, letting him fall back

on the sofa. He moaned and clutched his side. "I think you broke my ribs. You win, Tyler. I loathe you. If I don't leave, I'll kill you myself."

"I'll get someone to take you home."

"You bastard! I've always known you were cold and cruel, Tyler, but in the last few years you've gotten worse. And greedier. You're more power-hungry than ever."

"Don't push your luck! And don't go running to Talia. Don't try to contact her!" He strode to the desk and pushed a button. "Tell my father to step in here, please."

As soon as Millard appeared, he faced Tyler. "What happened here, Tyler?"

"An argument between Sloane and me. I can handle it, Dad."

"Tyler—"

"I'll handle it, I said!" Tyler said forcefully. His father blinked in surprise and frowned, studying him, and finally nodding. In that moment, Tyler realized that his father was beginning to show his age. For the first time in his life, Tyler felt that he was a stronger force than his father. "Will you make arrangements to get Sloane home?"

"What about you?"

"I can drive," Tyler said tersely.

"You ought to see a doctor."

He nodded and waited until Sloane and Millard had gone, then he left, easing into his Cadillac to drive straight home. He used a side entrance to his office. In seconds he heard Talia's voice.

"Ty?" She came through the doorway. "I thought I heard—" Her eyes widened and her hand flew to her mouth. "Tyler, what happened?"

"My charming brother."

"Sloane did that to you? Why on earth? Let me call Dr.—"

"No! I don't need to see a doctor. I just want to wash up. Close the door." He shed his coat and stepped into his bathroom. Talia followed him, taking a washcloth from his hands.

"Why would Sloane do this?"

Tyler's dark eyes met her gaze in the mirror. "I told him to get rid of his little boy lover while I campaign. He's furious."

"So he beat you up for that? That doesn't sound like Sloane."

"You're damned quick to defend him!"

"No, I'm not," she said, startled by the anger in his tone.

"Sorry if I snapped at you. My nerves are shot. I think the guy was injured today—I don't know how—and now Sloane blames me."

"Tyler!" she exclaimed, pausing and staring at him in horror. "He couldn't! You're his *brother*."

"Well, he does. I've been in the bank all day. I didn't even eat lunch, I was so busy. I told Sloane, but that was after the fight."

"Surely he can't think that you would do something like that. What did he say when you told him you hadn't left the bank?"

He shrugged, watching her. Her wide eyes were a clear green. To see the tiny flecks of gold near her pupils, he had to be within inches of her face. "He won't believe anything I say, because I was rather forceful when I told him to get rid of the pansy before the election."

"I think you should see a doctor. Your nose is swelling and that's a bad cut on your temple."

"Call Dan. He'll sew me up if I need it and there won't be any emergency room report on it." He took the wet washcloth from her hands and pressed it to his bleeding temple while she hurried to the phone. She returned in minutes. "He'll be right over."

"Oh, hell, he didn't need to rush over here."

"He lives only a block away. I told him I'd bring you to his house, but he said no." She walked up to slip her arms around his waist. "I'm sorry this happened."

He turned around to hug her, his spirits lifting as he gazed into her eyes. He wouldn't have to worry about Sloane. Talia felt sorry for him, and it was over. It was unfortunate Chad had been killed rather than just scared, but he didn't dwell on it. His problem was solved and that was what mattered. He had put the money in the box five days ago, and now he could forget the whole unpleasant business.

He winced and she looked up.

"My ribs hurt. Sloane's a wicked fighter."

"So are you. How badly was he hurt?"

"About the same as I was. Dad got him home."

She laid her head against his chest, her brow furrowed, while she wondered if being governor was worth the trouble.

Two nights later, Tyler announced, "Sloane is moving away."

"Why? Where's he going?" She gazed across the dinner table at him, her brows arching in question.

"I called to see how he's doing. He's getting a manager for his business here and moving to Brazil to take charge of our plantations for a while. They haven't been doing that well, and he thinks with his landscape knowledge, he can turn things around. Which is fine with me."

"I can't imagine him up and moving to Brazil. How was it between the two of you?" she said, suddenly suspicious that somehow Tyler was causing Sloane's move.

"Better, I'd say."

"Really, Tyler?"

"Yes," he said, his voice rising. "It's better. It won't be good until he stops mourning his lover."

"What happened to his friend?"

"A report in the paper says the guy was mugged, his wallet stolen, afterwards, he got up and staggered out into the path of a car. He was thrown ten feet on impact and it killed him."

"Does Sloane still blame you?"

"Probably. Frankly, I'm glad to see him go while I campaign. His sexual preferences could defeat me."

"When does he leave?"

"Next week."

She stared at him in shock. "Next week Sloane's moving to Brazil?"

"I think there's an echo in the room," Ty said dryly.

"How can he go that soon? It's impossible."

"Not if you're efficient, and you have a good reason for going."

"That makes it easier for you," she said, and suddenly Ty's nerves came alert.

"How's that?" he asked casually.

"He won't be available for rumors and scandal," she said woodenly, again questioning Tyler's part in the move.

"You're right," he said. "By the way, I made the appointment for our picture Thursday noon, your lunch hour. Does that fit in with your schedule?"

"Yes, it does," she said, frowning, wondering why Tyler wanted her with him. Did he want her at his side and helping him because he loved her, or because she would further his position. "I think it should be just your picture, not both of us."

"Nonsense! Behind every successful man is an intelligent woman, and I want this intelligent woman beside me. Your picture right along with mine. That way they won't throw the brochure in the trash and all the men will vote for me."

Even though her worries persisted, she agreed reluctantly. "All right, picture at twelve, but we're getting a full schedule."

He stood up and came around to take her hand and draw her to her feet. "Think I can have an appointment with you upstairs in about two hours?"

"I think I can work that in, yes. Yes, that would be just fine."

Later that week, she called Sloane repeatedly and realized he was refusing to take her calls. The next Monday at noon when he came down the steps from his office, she was waiting for him. When he saw her, he paused, and then he walked toward her. She was shocked. He had lost weight; his eyes were still bruised and there was a new crook in his nose. He moved as if something hurt.

"Sloane, I wanted to see you before you left."

"I'm busy."

"Please, just lunch together," she said, wondering why she had bothered to come. But she wanted to know that he was all right. She thought he was going to refuse, but then his shoulders lifted in a slight shrug and he motioned to his car.

"I'll drive." He drove without speaking to a busy Mexican restaurant where they were seated in a booth. Odors of fried meat and chili peppers filled the air, but Talia's appetite had vanished.

"Sloane, Tyler said you blame him for Chad's accident."

His eyes flashed with fires like a glimpse of a furnace. "Forget it, Talia!" he snapped.

"Sloane, remember me, Talia Wade? We used to be friends."

"Now you're Talia Wade Franklin."

"Do you think I had a hand in Chad's death?"

His features changed; sorrow replaced anger as his lips thinned to a grim line while he raked his fingers through his hair. "No. I know you didn't." The anguish in his voice vanished. "I know that just as well as I know that Tyler did."

"He didn't! For Lord's sake, Sloane, he's your brother!"

"When he wants something, he goes after it one—" He broke off as a waiter came and they both ordered.

When they were alone, she said, "He didn't. He's hurt and he's worried."

"Like hell he is!" Sloane leaned across the table, spots of color appearing in his cheeks, and she was shocked at the rage in his voice. "He's got you snowed, Talia. You're his wife! You love him and he loves you and he does everything he can to keep you happy. Do you think he's going to come home and say, 'I murdered a man today'?"

"Sloane, I can't believe this conversation," she said, worry and frustration filling her entire being because she couldn't shake his convictions. "Tyler didn't harm Chad. He was in the bank all that day—"

"Oh, hell!" he exclaimed, shifting in his seat in exasperation. "Of course he was in the bank. I know Tyler wouldn't dirty his hands with the job."

"You're saying your brother hired a killer?"

"I'm saying exactly that! He never did learn how to lose. Now he's going after big stakes, and I stood in his way. This isn't a tennis trophy, it's a high public office that could lead to a higher one, with even more power. You may not believe me, Talia, but you should believe this: my brother is power-hungry and he doesn't know how to lose." He looked across the restaurant and rubbed his jaw. "Life is a struggle and we all have to cope in our own way. Tyler's way happens to be a little heavy-handed."

"And what's your way, Sloane? Tyler's got some broken

bones in his hand, a cracked rib, and bruises.'' When he flushed, she was sorry she had snapped back at him. "Sloane, I saw how upset and worried he was the day you had the fight. He was worried about what you thought!''

"Look at his withdrawals at the bank, Talia. See if there hasn't been a large one for a payoff—''

The waiter appeared and they became silent again. She watched while a steaming plate of golden cheese enchiladas was placed in front of Sloane and a crisp green salad in a large crystal bowl was set in front of her.

"Why are you leaving?''

"I want to be as far away as possible from my brother! He carries out his threats!''

She paused with her fork halfway to her bowl. "Tyler threatened you?'' she asked, knowing then that one brother was lying. She suspected it was Sloane out of mistaken hurt and anger.

"I think you better talk to your husband and not me. You're getting two versions. Mine's the true one, Talia, but you're married to the guy, so I know what you'll believe. My life is a danger to Tyler's career. All four of the Franklin children have been spoiled and indulged, particularly Ty and me. We like to get our way, to have everything we want.'' He sat back in his chair. "Why don't you tell me how your job at the bank is going?'' he asked, a bland note coming to his voice that didn't quite hide his rage.

"It's going fine,'' she answered, humoring him, because she saw that they were at an impasse. "As a matter of fact, I just got a promotion.''

"Congratulations.''

"I'm going to miss you,'' she said, knowing she had lost a good friend. Because of Tyler's attitude there would always be tension between Sloane and her.

"It wouldn't be the same if I stayed. You're his wife, and what he is will wear off on you. You'll change. You've already changed.''

"How's that?'' she asked, realizing she had grown so tense that muscles in her neck ached. His accusations hurt! She thought it sad that Sloane felt this way about his brother.

"You're more sophisticated than when you came."

"I should hope so! I was so green," she answered, trying to force a lightness into her voice that she didn't feel.

"I liked you that way."

"I haven't changed much, and I mean it when I say I'll miss you."

"Thanks."

They finished the meal in silence. There didn't seem to be much more to say, and she didn't have an appetite. Sloane drove back to his office and she stepped out next to her car. She gazed into his black eyes, and then impulsively hugged him.

"Take care, Talia," he said.

"I'm sorry about Chad."

"Yeah," he said as she stepped away. She climbed into her car and drove off as he disappeared into his office. his accusations swirled in her mind. She couldn't believe that Tyler would hire someone to give a man a beating or to cause an accident—it was unthinkable, yet she couldn't forget how he had manipulated the sailing race. *Look at his withdrawals at the bank. See if there hasn't been a large one for a payoff.* Sloane's words hummed in her mind. She had never checked Tyler's account and he kept track of their joint account.

That night she and Tyler attended a dinner dance, and as they drove along, she told Tyler about seeing Sloane.

"I'm sorry he feels that way," he said, "but I can't convince him otherwise. Maybe time will help."

"I hope so," she said, studying her husband, seeing the lines of worry in his furrowed brow. She squeezed his hand, and in minutes they arrived at their destination. Throughout the crowded party she forgot about Sloane.

During the evening, she danced two dances in a row with Ted Granville, who was recently divorced and dated Nancy Larson, one of Talia's friends. When she returned to the table, Ty took her arm. "Let's leave, Tali," he said.

She agreed, and it wasn't until they were home that she realized something was bothering him. "What is it, Ty? Something's wrong, isn't it?"

"Who were you dancing with?"

"Ted Granville. Why?"

"I don't like to see you in another man's arms for a second."

"Don't be ridiculous, Ty!"

"You're mine, Tali, and you'll never belong to another. I'll never let you go!"

She was amazed at the force in his words. Tyler had never acted like this at other dances. "You won't have to."

"Damned right I won't!" he snarled, pulling her into his arms.

"Sometimes, Tyler," she said, looking into his black eyes, "I think you view me the same way you do the house and the car. I'm a possession of yours, an extension of you. I have to have some independence. Sometimes the only place I feel like a real human being is at work!"

"I don't want to share you." He molded her to him, bending over her, surprising her with a hard kiss that hurt her lips.

In the bedroom his lovemaking was rushed, and Tyler pleased only himself. There was a fierceness in him that was stronger than ever before and it frightened her. When he rolled over and fell asleep, she lay staring into the darkness. This wasn't what she had wanted or expected from her marriage. Tyler had changed too drastically and too fast.

I'll never let you go! His words echoed in her mind. If she ever wanted to leave Tyler, would he really hold her against her will? She knew that he never made idle threats and that he didn't believe in divorce—if only because it would be too much of a blow to his ego. She thought about his angry lovemaking, and then she ran her hand across her brow. She had certain rights and Tyler would have to respect them. Then a cold, horrifying thought came to her. What if someday she *did* want to leave?

14

Rebecca set a plate of scrambled eggs, toast, and bacon in front of a man who smiled at her. She smiled in return.

"I'll refill your coffee," she said and left to get the pot of steaming black coffee, wondering how she had been stuck in a daily eight hour, sometimes longer, job. No one would hire her as a singer; waitressing was all she could find. She had a tiny, dingy furnished apartment above a grocery store and she hadn't met many appealing men since she had arrived in Nevada.

And she wasn't going to in this greasy-spoon cafe on the highway. She poured another cup of coffee for two customers, and went back through the kitchen, stepping outside and pulling a cigarette out of her pocket to have a quick smoke. She blew smoke overhead, and wondered if she should move back to Chicago and try to get her old singing job back. The work hadn't been as grinding or as hard on her feet, and she'd had a chance to meet men.

She ground out the cigarette, went back inside, and figured up two of the tickets. The first she took to a couple, whom she barely noticed except to wonder if they would tip.

The other was the man who had ordered scrambled eggs.

"Anything else I can get for you?" she asked perfunctorily.

"Maybe so, doll," he drawled, and Rebecca looked at him. He wore a gray plaid suit and his straight black hair was feathered away from his face. His eyes studied her. He was good-looking, Rebecca realized. She smiled. "Yeah? What would you like?" she said, trying to sound her sultriest,

198

yet keeping her voice low so others around them wouldn't hear.

"I'd like to get to know you. What time do you get off work?"

"About six o'clock."

"How about dinner at seven?"

She laughed. "I don't even know your name!"

"Marco Daroca. And you're Rebecca—?"

Rebecca was written on the badge she wore on her collar. She answered, "Wade. From New Orleans."

"How about dinner?"

"Sure." As she gave him her address, he jotted it on a slip of paper.

"See you tonight, Rebecca, at seven o'clock," Marco said, and winked.

She nodded and carried the dishes to the kitchen. She went back to finish cleaning the table, watching him through the window. Thin and wiry, he moved with an easy stride, climbing into a shiny red Corvette that whipped out of the parking lot, leaving a cloud of dust behind. She picked up his dirty dishes and found a folded twenty-dollar bill under his plate. She jammed the money in her pocket. Marco Daroca. Maybe things were looking up.

At seven she was dressed in one of her best outfits, a slinky scarlet crepe dress that was cut low in the front and clung to her. When she opened the door to face him, he was in a navy suit, and looked handsome. After the twenty-dollar tip earlier, he looked gorgeous!

He took her to a nightclub with a floor show where they ate and talked, and later they went to a hotel bar for drinks and dancing. Then he took her to his place, a two-story condo with a king-size bed and red satin sheets. When Marco reached for her, she turned to wrap her arms around his neck, fitting her body against his, her hand sliding down his back over his firm buttocks.

Later in bed, he stroked her, murmuring to her. "Baby, you're good. Too good to waste your time slinging hash."

"Don't talk about my miserable job and ruin the evening. I'm having a wonderful time," she said, her hand playing over his flat stomach. Marco was fun, and he was able to

exert more control than any man she had known. His body
was thin and hard-muscled, his torso long, his legs short.

"You want to be a waitress?"

"God, no!"

"Okay, come to work for me."

She laughed, rolling over to prop her face on her hands
and look at him. "Doing what? You said you're in investments. I can't even type."

"No, baby. No typing. You could earn a lot of money."

"Doing what?"

"I said I had investments. I have several things. I own a
club here. I have some girls that work for me. I have a house."

She sat up, staring at him. "You mean be a prostitute?"

"You're a natural," he remarked, and she stared at him,
too shocked to be angry. "This is a high-class joint, not
streetwalkers, but good-looking, particular women who want
money. You'd make the big bucks."

She didn't know whether to get up and walk out in indignation or to listen. "Damn! That's all you wanted with me
tonight."

He grinned, his white teeth flashing. His body was covered
with thick black hair. "That wasn't all I wanted with you,
Rebecca. I'm just making you a good offer. I don't make
this offer to everyone."

"I have a feeling I should slap your face and walk out!"

He shrugged. "It wouldn't be the first time, but think about
it. Money. You're a beautiful, sexy woman. These johns
won't be bums off the street."

"Lots of money?"

He grinned. "I knew you'd like it. I'll take you out there
tomorrow and introduce you to Sally. She runs the place."

"Can I quit if I don't like it?"

"You can quit anytime you want. I don't have trouble
finding girls."

"I'll bet you don't," she said, eyeing his sinewy body.

The next day she was shown around the parlor house on
a gravel road two miles off of the highway. The yard was
surrounded by a high fence and devoid of grass. Cactus grew
there instead. A wide gate opened onto the narrow dirt road

that led to a landing strip in back. There were eleven women working plus Sally, the madam, who was striking, an inch under six feet tall with flaming red hair. Rebecca was shown the girls' rooms, the sauna, the massage salon, the bar with its dark mahogany wood, red vinyl seats, mirrors and rows of bottles and glasses. Souvenir T-shirts, bumper stickers, baseball caps, and decanters were sold behind a narrow counter near the door. She was told what her rent would be, the rules, and then she was given a list of minimum charges.

"You keep sixty percent of what you earn," Sally said. "We're a generous house. Forty percent plus your expenses goes to us. The fee is collected first, and delivered to me immediately and I'll enter it in the books. Your room and board is ten dollars per day. You pay for your clothes. Any questions?"

"I can quit anytime?"

"Anytime. I run a good house."

"Sounds okay," Rebecca said, reassured that at any moment she could quit and walk out, but the money Marco had told her was possible to earn kept her listening to Sally.

"You'll have the room I showed you. First thing, you'll see a doctor for a pelvic to make sure you're free of disease. And you'll have to go to the sheriff's office, register, and pay a two-hundred-and-fifty-dollar permit fee. You'll have a quarterly fee of two hundred dollars. They'll fingerprint you for their records, too. Money doesn't change hands in my parlor. Collect in your room."

Eventually Rebecca was ready for her first night. The parlor looked like the set of a Gay Nineties movie with heavy gold brocade drapes, Victorian furniture, and huricane lamps. A pleasure menu hung above the mantel listing various offerings of sexual delights. The girls wore clinging, strapless satin dresses that were slit in front above the knee, ample to give a glimpse of bare legs and spike heels.

Rebecca's first trick was a tall, lanky, blue-eyed man in jeans and a white shirt who said his name was Brian. As they talked, she noticed his Gucci watch, his hand-tooled boots, and the hat tossed casually aside with a Stetson label. They sat on a brocade loveseat; when Brian leaned forward to caress her leg, her blue satin skirt fell open. He kissed her throat.

In minutes they went to her room. He held her, his hands sliding down over her buttocks as he asked softly, "Honey, what's the cost for a Binaca blast and sex?"

It was forty dollars minimum, but Rebecca was going to make this worth her while or quit, so without hesitation she said, "Four hundred dollars."

"Okay, honey. Here's my part," he said, pulling out a fat wallet and her pulse skipped. He was nice-looking, pleasant, and so much more polite than Sam.

For the first three months Rebecca thought this was better than dollar tips and cleaning tables. But it was confining, as well as boring during the long, empty hours of the day. And she was scared she would get a disease. She learned to size men up quickly, to judge if their bodies looked healthy. But by the fourth month, she told Sally she was quitting.

She packed, took her savings which were substantial, and returned to Chicago, where she got a job singing in a nightclub again under the name Holly Bright. She found a cheap, furnished apartment.

Rebecca was determined to find someone who would provide for her without going back to prostitution or slinging hash. The second month she was there, she noticed a man and his date seated with another couple in the front row. He was handsome and wore a diamond on his pinky. He listened to her attentively, so Rebecca sang to him. She wore a glittering sequin-covered long-sleeved gold dress with décolletage to her waist revealing her curves.

He was back in the same seat the next night along with another man, but no women. She stood in the spotlight and sang in a breathless tone; her sultry voice was deep and haunting. Then she moved to the tables, pausing and singing to particular customers, finally stopping in front of the golden-haired man. His blue eyes watched her steadily while she sang to him, leaning forward to brush his shoulder with her hand, giving him a full view of her breasts, before she drifted on to the next table.

While she was in her tiny dressing room, a waiter brought a note asking her to have a drink with the man at the second table.

It was he. She changed quickly into a simple, knee-length

black silk dress, splashed on cologne, and went out to meet him. He watched her as she approached his table. When he stood, he was over six feet tall, golden, and handsome.

"Miss Bright? I'm Bernard Koffskey. Just call me Bernie. Won't you sit down?"

"Thanks, Bernie," she said, going on instinct. "And you can call me Rebecca. It's really just plain Rebecca Wade."

"Never plain," he said, his white, even teeth showing in a smile.

"What's your line of business?"

He shrugged. "Just oil," he said. "Let's talk about you. Do you work every night or can you go out with me one night this week?"

"I can go out with you," Rebecca said, emphatically, thinking she would go if it cost her the job.

"Good. Any chance I can take you out after work tonight?"

"You surely can." She gave him her best smile, gazing up wide-eyed.

Again he grinned. "Tell me about yourself."

Rebecca talked for a few moments, glossing over most of her life, and then switched the subject to Bernie. He was born and raised in Iowa, went to Oklahoma University, majored in petroleum engineering, went to work for an oil company. When he was thirty-four, his father died and left him a sizable estate. Bernie started his own drilling company and had been lucky, because the business had grown. He leaned forward in his chair, his blue eyes assessing her. "So now I'm thirty-nine, single, one divorce early in my life when I was twenty-one, another bad marriage when I was twenty-five. I'll tell you now, I'm not the marrying kind."

"Neither am I," she said, and meant every word.

He smiled. "Just my type. And you know all about me."

"Not quite all," she drawled, licking her lips and letting the tip of her tongue stop in the corner. His eyes flickered, and his voice dropped a notch.

"Can you leave? Go somewhere where we can dance?"

"Sure, Bernie. Let me get my things," she said, smiling at him, humming as she hurried back to her dressing room.

15

Mike strode from his office to Ben's, closing the door. Ben looked up, his thick brows arching in question. "What's wrong?"

"He's done it. At the Rotary luncheon today, he alluded to Simone's past, that it's questionable, so you're questionable."

Ben swore and slammed back his chair, standing up and striding across the room, his blue eyes blazing. "I know you told me he'd do this, but I didn't believe you. The bastard! The stinking bastard!"

"I've talked to Farrell and he's preparing your answer to the press about how long ago Simone left France, how difficult her childhood was, that sort of thing. He'll make it as sympathetic as possible, but nothing is going to soften the blow. Particularly to Simone."

Ben ran his fingers through his hair. "No. You tried to get me to tell her, but I couldn't. This will devastate her. She's spent all her life in the U.S. trying to hide what she did in France. All for me. That's what I can't get through to her. I don't care what she was in the past." He turned around, anguish turning down the corners of his mouth. "Will she know?"

"Of course, she'll know!"

"She might not."

"Ben, you're hiding your head in the sand! You can be so tough and practical except when Simone is involved."

"I adore her!"

Mike bit back the answer that Ben shouldn't have run against Tyler if he adored Simone so much. He rubbed the bridge of his nose. "Tell her and get her prepared to face the questions and the publicity."

"She doesn't have to do that! We can tell them 'no comment' and let it go at that."

"The public will want more. If you come right out and say it was long ago, if Simone would get involved in some community things—"

"You know that's not her sort of thing. She doesn't have women friends; she never did cultivate others. By the time I went into politics, it was too late for her to start."

"It's not too late, and it might save some agony."

"Damn him to hell, anyway! I want to see the statement Farrell has drafted for me. How'd you find out so quickly? The Rotary luncheon ought to just be getting over now."

"A reporter friend of mine, Nelson Bordeaux, left the luncheon to call me."

"Thank God we have some time before it hits the news."

"Ben, listen to me. When it hits the news there will be a furor. The more you try to ignore it, the louder the clamor will be for you to answer questions. Talk to them," Mike urged, aghast that Ben wasn't facing the problem squarely. "Use Farrell's statement on the subject. Get Simone working on a charity project."

"I'll think about your advice, Mike," Ben said in a quiet, cold voice. Mike's spirits sank because he knew he wasn't getting through to Ben. "Don't tell her. You have to promise me," Ben demanded, facing him in a belligerent stance with his long legs braced, feet apart.

"I promise if that's what you want," Mike replied with resignation, "but I think you're making a mistake. You can't shut her away from the world. She's going to know."

"In two weeks it may be a dead issue."

"In two weeks you may be out of the running if you cover this up!" Mike snapped.

"If my pollsters find I'm slipping, I'll turn it all over to you. Until then, I want to try to protect Simone from the whole thing. But I'm not withdrawing from the race. I'll talk to them about her past, but she doesn't have to."

"That's a step in the right direction. I think Tyler Franklin will do every dirty thing he can."

"He can't do any worse than this," Ben said, and the words sent a prickle of wariness through Mike. He could feel disaster coming. The campaign was starting out with mudslinging by Tyler, and Mike suspected it would get worse. "Ben, there isn't anything you haven't told us, anything he might dredge up about you?"

"No. If it were me, it would be easier to handle," Ben said without hiding his gruffness.

"I'll talk to Farrell," Mike said and left.

On Wednesday at a meeting with the Save Our Wetlands people, Ben gave the answers Farrell de Bois had prepared for him. Mike knew the strategy, knew Ben's reply about Simone would hit the news as swiftly as Tyler's accusations.

Mike had to stop by the Holloways' to pick up some papers Ben had left for him, and while he was standing in the front hall with Dalton, Simone stepped out of the dining room.

"Mike! I didn't know you were here," she said, stopping in the doorway.

"I needed to get these papers and I told Ben I'd come by," he said. "Getting ready for the dinner party tonight?"

"Yes. I don't know whether to put the Brocktons next to the Duvalls or next to General Davis."

"Put the A.G. next to General Davis," he answered absentmindedly, giving a moment's thought to Edward Duvall, the Attorney General. He crossed the hall to glance at the long table ladened with crystal, Gorham sterling, the gold-bordered Royal Doulton china. "It looks beautiful," he said, glancing down at her. She moved away into the dining room, but he had seen her red eyes, the thick makeup that gave her pale cheeks a pink glow. He followed her into the room, and she faced him.

"It'll ruin him, won't it!" she exclaimed, anguish unmistakable in her voice and expression as she knotted her fingers together.

"Let him worry about it, Simone," Mike said, knowing his voice sounded grim. "He doesn't want you to know."

"Mike, I'm going to ruin him!"

"No, you're not!" he replied forcefully, realizing that she was taking it as hard as he had expected she might. He knew how she avoided social contacts, other women, and he knew the reason was her past and her love for Ben. Dropping the papers on a chair, he crossed to her to place his hands on her shoulders.

"Let him worry about it. That's the way he wants it."

"He's never gotten what he wanted because of me! I can't give him children. He wanted a son so badly. He'd be a good father. He thinks of you as a son, but he never had a baby of his own because of me. Now this. My past will hurt his future, it'll ruin his political career!"

Mike wanted to swear. "Simone, please don't worry. Ben will survive this. He's been in tough situations before and survived. The main thing is that he needs your love," he said, thinking the words had a hollow ring, because if that was all Ben needed, he wouldn't have run for office.

She blinked back tears and looked up at him, her face pale and vulnerable, her eyes full of sorrow, her makeup garish against her pale skin. "I haven't been the wife he should have had, but I didn't mean to hurt him."

"You haven't hurt him! Stop saying that."

She moved away. "You're right, Mike. I better see about dinner."

"Simone—" He felt at a loss for words. "Ben loves you. Try to stop worrying."

"Sure." She went toward the kitchen, and he suspected she was crying. He stared at her helplessly for a moment, then picked up the papers and left, his long angry strides taking him to his car. He mentally swore at Tyler Franklin and ached to have a chance to flatten him, to vent the physical frustration that had built inside of him.

He was almost as angry with Ben for not warning Simone what Tyler would do. Mike wasn't a political person; he accepted the job of campaign manager, because Ben wanted him. If he were Ben Holloway, he wouldn't have run for office.

That night half the guests called and declined to attend the dinner. It was stiff and awkward for the first few minutes, then everyone seemed to relax. But Mike could see the strain on Simone who entertained for Ben only when asked.

Friday night Mike had a date with Aimée Toussaint, his latest lady friend, who enjoyed politics and meeting important

people almost as much as Simone disliked it. Mike had met
her at a party and had learned she was with the New Orleans
Ballet. The next performance he had a seat in the front row
and the following night they had their first date. He liked
Aimée, but a lasting commitment never crossed his mind.
Mike peeled off his shirt and tie, dropping them on a chair
while he thought of Aimée and her sultry dark beauty, her
almond-shaped black eyes, her dark skin. He could have
stayed the night with her, but he had to be up early in the
morning and review the latest poll results as well as some
parish reports and the accountant's last statement. He hung
up his dark slacks, showered and climbed into bed. In what
felt like less than ten minutes the ringing of the phone woke
him. He squinted at the clock, saw it was almost four in the
morning as he picked up the receiver.

"Mike? Mike, come over."

It was Ben. His voice was shaky. Mike awoke instantly,
the hairs on the back of his neck prickling in a primordial
premonition of disaster.

16

"I'll be right there," Mike said, stepping out of bed and
yanking open a drawer. He replaced the receiver. Within ten
minutes he arrived at Ben's home.

Police cars lined the drive and a waiting ambulance was
parked beside the front steps. Mike's forebodings mounted
by the second as he entered the house and asked a policeman
where he could find Ben.

He paused one moment at the door to the master bedroom.
His gaze swept the room and paused at a sheet-draped form
on the floor. His heart lurched. Murder was his first thought.
With red eyes Ben stood talking to a policeman, but at the
sight of Mike he came forward to clasp his shoulder.

"Simone killed herself," Ben said, his voice breaking.

"Oh, Jesus, Ben." Mike felt as if a fist had plunged through his chest. Questions swirled in his mind, but he held them back. He put his arm around Ben's shoulders and held him while Ben sobbed uncontrollably for a moment. Mike clamped his teeth together so tightly his jaw ached. He fought for control of his emotions.

Ben went to stand by a window and stare into the darkness. A detective moved beside him, speaking so softly that Mike could barely hear.

Mike turned to another detective and extended his hand. "Mike Stanton. Look, can some of the questions be asked a little later when he's more composed?"

"I'm sorry, but we have to have some information now. We'll try to keep it brief."

"Yeah," Mike said grimly, leaving the room to phone Jerry Stein and tell him to come over, knowing that he might have more influence with the police. Next he called Farrell de Bois. "I need you here at Ben's," he said in an undertone. "Simone's dead. It's suicide."

Sick at heart, Mike stood to one side in the spacious pink bedroom. He had witnessed death time and again in Nam, but this hurt went deeper. In Nam the threat of death had been ever-present, but Simone had always reminded him of what was good and vibrant and possible in this world. She had been special, as Claude had been special, and suddenly a loss greater than any he had ever known enveloped him. His vision blurred as tears filled his eyes.

Just as he felt himself breaking down, Ben showed him the note that Simone had left behind. It was a tear-spattered slip of paper with her rambling thoughts about not being able to give him children, of hurting his career, and of fearing she was a social embarrassment to him. The last sentence trailed off incoherently, and Mike listened while Ben told a detective about the drugs Simone had recently been taking. The list shocked Mike, making him wonder if her depression had been augmented by a dangerous drug interaction. She had clearly taken an overdose of valium, but several other empty pill bottles indicated her determination to end her life.

If she could see Ben now, she wouldn't have done it, Mike

thought, wondering if Ben would survive. Both Ben and
Simone had been tough people who had overcome hard times,
but each had a vulnerable side where the other was concerned.

Ben sat hunched over, his elbows on his knees, his hand
over his face while he cried. He couldn't talk to the detectives.
Finally realizing it, they moved around him and left him alone
with Jerry Stein at his side. They talked instead to Mike and
Farrell and Hannah, the maid, trying to get the information
they needed.

Mike felt dazed. All he could remember was Claude's death
and the day Simone had come to help him. Beneath his shock
was a kindling rage. Tyler Franklin might just as well have
put a gun to Simone's head and pulled the trigger. Anger
welled up inside him as he clenched his fists tightly to his
side. Her death was so unnecessary. Tyler was expected to
win the October primary by a wide margin; he could easily
have done so without killing Simone. Mike knew that in
destroying her, Tyler might have also destroyed Ben.

As days passed Mike's anger grew. When he saw the
enormous spray of red roses from the Franklins, he picked
them up and carried them out the back where he jammed the
flowers into a trash can. The day of the funeral seemed to
last for fifty hours. In the days following the service, instead
of trying to pick up the pieces and go on with life, Ben lost
interest in living. Because of Simone's death, public sympathy had swung to Ben, but he no longer campaigned as the
election approached. In November Tyler Franklin won by a
healthy margin, and Mike gave Ben's conceding speech. Facing the glare of the television cameras, Mike felt numb, dimly
conscious of the somber feeling that enveloped Ben's supporters.

In another hotel the atmosphere was jubilant. Tyler glowed
with success, his exuberance driving away Talia's misgivings
over her job as she reminded herself that Tyler deserved this;
that she could go back to work when his term of office was
over. But the nagging fear remained that once he tasted the
power of politics, he wouldn't want to give it up.

As weeks passed, Ben sank further into despair while Tyler
made headlines. Governor-elect Franklin's transition team,
headed by Al Santos, swung into action with Leon Goudeau

as chief economic advisor and Cullen Hanzo as research director. In addition to his legal staff Tyler hired an office manager, a security chief, and advisory commissions.

Each time Mike read about Tyler in the papers he vowed to carry out his threat against the new governor, even though he hadn't yet figured out any legal way to do so. He lay awake at night, sometimes with Aimée sleeping beside him, and brooded over Tyler and Ben. Mike had learned long ago to be patient. He intended for Tyler to pay for what he had done.

Once Aimée had opened her eyes, gazing at him as he stood by the window. "You're thinking about Tyler Franklin, aren't you?" she had asked in a husky voice, sitting up and pulling the sheet to her chin.

"Yes, dammit!"

"Mike, forget the past. He's out of your life now and you won't be able to help Ben through revenge. You can't do anything to him unless you run against him for office."

"I know," Mike answered, raking his fingers through his hair.

"Mike . . ." Her voice changed as she seductively called his name. He turned around. She let the sheet fall to her waist, and he went back to bed. Later he lay awake, his physical hungers appeased, but a yearning for deeper satisfaction still unassuaged.

Eventually Aimée vanished out of Mike's life and he occupied himself with work, realizing that Ben was slipping in every way. He had become indifferent to his business, and he was drinking heavily. The house was neglected, and the servants quit until only Hannah and Dalton were left.

In all practical ways Southern Market, Inc., became Mike's company. Then one morning Mike received a call from Ben asking him to stop at the house. Mike found him in the room with the white Danish furniture. It was littered with papers and dishes, and the drapes on the glass doors leading to the pool were drawn. Ben announced, "Southern Market is yours. I don't want the company. I have enough money saved to live out the rest of my days. I put the company in your name and I'm selling my house."

"You *what*? Dammit, you can't do that!"

"I've already done it." Ben spoke more forcefully than he had in months. Bearded and twenty pounds lighter, he looked Mike in the eye. "I know what I'm doing. And you won't persuade me to do otherwise. I can't concentrate on my work, nor do I want to." He paused. "I was right about you," he said. "You didn't disappoint me. You're the son I never had and you've been good to us. You've made the company worth more now than ever before and you deserve to run it as you see fit."

"I've been lucky in the business and in my investments. I like the work and I had a good instructor. But, Ben, don't quit," Mike said gruffly, emotion making his voice thicken. "Keep going," he pleaded.

"Sorry, Mike."

Mike's arguments were to no avail, and the simmering rage he had felt toward the Franklins now became a constant fury that burned within him. Ben sold the house, dismissed Hannah and bought a condominium. It seemed that within the year, he had turned into an old man.

Mike was determined to prosper, and the boom years of the late seventies had helped his business enough so that he now was able to pursue other investments and interests, although commercial properties remained his main endeavor. By the summer of 1980 the rate of inflation was eighteen percent. A slight recession hit part of the nation, but land continued to grow in value in Louisiana. Because of the energy crisis, domestic oil became more valuable, reaching thirty-two dollars a barrel. Mike invested in a successful well, and combined with the commercial properties he managed and earned for his clients, he was financially successful. He had bought a condo, then sold it to buy a house. He now moved in the same social circle as the Franklins. He saw them occasionally at parties, and he still harbored anger and resentment toward the ex governor. It seemed that their paths were again destined to cross more frequently in New Orleans.

Tyler ended his term with a surplus in the state treasury and he had successfully backed additional funds for education, promoted a bill for navigation projects for the Mississippi River from Baton Rouge to the Gulf of Mexico, and another for the Mississippi River Ship Channel. He had supported bills for flood control of Bayou Cocodrie and the Teche-Vermilion Basin. Talia Franklin had designed her own "Visit Louisiana" program to help state tourism.

Tyler decided not to run for a second term, a fact that Mike found annoying. It was as if Tyler had wanted the battle more than the prize; anyone who had gotten in his way would have been crushed. Mike had realized long ago that he wasn't dealing with Leech, but someone who was infinitely more clever and subtle. The only way he could wreak revenge would be to know the man well. He had waited for him to return to New Orleans. He would now wait for the right opportunity to beat Tyler Franklin at his own game. When Mike was invited to join a golf foursome on Saturday mornings he eagerly did so because Tyler was part of the foursome. Mike was his friendliest; since becoming governor Franklin's ego had grown so great that he had forgotten the small battles and enemies who had given him little trouble, thinking nothing could harm him any longer. He was open and friendly with Mike, and Mike went out of his way to become involved in the same civic projects as Tyler. He often talked to him at parties and eventually he handled a small condo Tyler wanted to sell. Mike gave it his full attention, it sold quickly, and the closing went smoothly. Mike opened an account at First Bayou Bank.

One afternoon at golf, Tyler and Mark Galliano discussed the possibilities of two different oil investments. One was a well being drilled in the Anadarko Basin.

"They're doing some deep drilling there. Hell, one of those wells was down to fifteen thousand feet. The cost will run four million, maybe more."

"That's a hot spot right now," Mark said. "This well I'm telling you about won't be that deep, maybe eight to twelve thousand feet. It'll be drilled near a Lower Tuscaloosa wildcat in West Feliciana Parish. And this isn't a brand new company."

Mike listened, knowing full well what development they were discussing. The other three men gradually showed interest in investing in the well. Mike did so only because it would involve him in a business deal with Tyler. He watched Tyler step up to tee off. Tyler's body was as coordinated as that of a pro, and he moved with a natural ease that heightened when he became intent on winning.

Months later, near the end of the year, Mike made an appointment to talk to Bob Vicari, the senior vice president of Commercial Lending at First Bayou.

Mike presented a description of his business and his professional training, his credit references, a description of the property he wanted to purchase, the amount of loan he needed, projections of its resale to a developer, and the properties he could use as collateral. Sandy-haired and friendly, Bob Vicari discussed the loan with Mike and gave him the proper forms to fill out. Within the week, Mike had his loan, one that he didn't need. He made the purchase, and to his gratification, he sold the property to a developer much sooner than he had anticipated. He had selected this particular transaction with care, and it was profitable. He repaid the loan. Two Saturdays later on a chilly March morning while he stood beside Tyler, both watching Stan Hebert putt, Tyler said, "I've been told you're one of the bank's customers now. Thanks for the business."

"Thanks to you. Bob Vicari made a loan for me, and I sold the property quickly."

"You handle investments, don't you?"

"Sure. So does your bank."

Tyler shrugged. "See what you can find. This is your specialty. I don't always go through the bank. I'd like to get something, a condo, a strip mall, something where I can see a good return."

"Come by my office this week and let me know what you're interested in," Mike said casually. This was exactly what he had hoped for all these years. He glanced into Tyler's black eyes and smiled. "I'll find something you'll like."

"You're the best in town, they tell me."

Mike gave a self-effacing laugh. "Stan got a birdie. Shall we go?"

Tyler's friendliness increased, but Mike had yet to look into Talia Franklin's green eyes and see anything except a glacial coldness that barely concealed her antagonism when they met at parties. He always noticed her when they attended the same gathering, despite the fact that she somehow grated on his nerves. Often he glanced up across a crowded room to find her watching him, and each time she looked away instantly. But he realized she was as conscious of him as he was of her.

Talia studied the blue-eyed man talking to Tyler. Mike Stanton. He was becoming one of Tyler's best buddies, and it made her uneasy. That night she mentioned it to him as they lay in bed. "For someone who was once an outright enemy, Mike Stanton is becoming a close friend."

"I enjoy Mike. He's good company, and a damned good golfer."

"That was a bitter campaign."

"You don't like Mike?"

"I barely know him, and Al Santos said he's a mean one if he's crossed. I know Al has warned you to be careful about him. Al thinks he's out to get you."

"Bull, Talia! Al's a worrier."

"Maybe so, but I think it's odd Mike Stanton is so friendly."

"I don't," Ty persisted, stroking her hair, winding it through his fingers. "That was long ago, and he's no politician. He managed Holloway's campaign because they were friends and worked together, almost father-son . . ."

"There! You said it," she exclaimed, sitting up, pulling the sheet to her chin. "Father-son. How could he become your bosom buddy after what happened to Ben Holloway?"

"Speaking of bosoms," Tyler said, becoming tumescent again, his voice developing into a rasp. "Quit your job," he said abruptly, his dark eyes blazing into hers in the soft glow of the lamp. "You don't *have* to work, Tali. And it might be easier for you to get pregnant, if you relaxed more. You don't need the money."

"It isn't the money, Ty," Talia said, not wanting to repeat an old argument.

"It's absurd for you to stick to the notion that you have to work. That damned independence of yours!"

"Tyler, don't start. My job isn't keeping me from getting pregnant. I quit working the four years you were governor . . ."

"And I liked it that way. There are contacts you could make that would be valuable for me if you socialized more."

"The Franklins need contacts like an Eskimo needs snow. And on that subject of socializing—you hardly ever see Sloane since he came back from Brazil. We should have him over sometime soon."

"You're trying to change the subject."

"No, I'm not. I'm trying to heal the rift between you and Sloane."

"That may not be possible." He stroked her shoulder. "The doc said some women are too uptight."

"I'm not as uptight as I would be if I didn't work. I've been promoted to a loan officer now. I don't want to give that up."

"For God's sake why not?" he snapped, glaring at her.

Realizing he was angrier over the issue than she had ever seen him, she said, "I'm as entitled to a career as you are! What do you want me to do?"

"I want you home where you belong! Like my mother. She's always kept an active social life and done charity work. I gave up politics."

"Don't imply you did it for me. You did it because you wanted to. You'll want to run for the Senate someday," she said, slipping out of bed and moving restlessly across the room on the pretext of getting a tissue. His caresses bothered her. Their argument was bound to escalate as their rifts so often did lately.

"I *will* run for the Senate. You gave up your job when I was governor. And it was good."

"Yes, but I didn't get pregnant. We can adopt."

"Hell no! I want a Franklin. I want a son with my blood, not a stranger."

"Ty, if we adopt a baby, it won't be a stranger."

"No, dammit, you're changing the subject. Quit your job."

"I don't want to quit. I've thought about it, and every time I come back to the same decision. I like working, it gives me a feeling of security—"

"Security? You have the most secure life in existence. You could lounge around this house every day for the rest of your life if you wanted. I have enough money, Talia. I don't want your money, and you don't use it. It just gathers interest in a savings account. I'll match your salary and you can save that!''

"It's more than money. I can't get rid of that feeling that I need to be independent. I wish you could understand, Tyler."

"I can't. Independent of what? Me?"

"No. But suppose something happened? Life changes. If I get pregnant, I'll quit until our babies are school age."

"That's a promise!" He seemed to pounce on her statement, and she was taken aback momentarily.

"Yes, it's a promise," she said, knowing that her need for independence was clashing with his need to get his way.

"That's a step in the right direction," he said, and she heard the note of steel in his voice.

Tyler glared at her, realizing that for once in his life he was confronting someone he couldn't bully or trick into obeying his wishes. He was annoyed at her stubborn attitude. Ninety-nine percent of the other women he knew would have quit their jobs in an instant if they could afford to live as luxuriously as Talia. His gaze raked over her. The filmy peignoir and dim light enhanced the sexy allure of her beautiful body. She had the most gorgeous legs he had ever seen, and her skin glowed.

Amazed at how she could still excite him after all this time, he wanted her again. And as angry as he became with her at times, he had never once wanted to leave her or divorce her. There had never been a divorce in the Franklin family, and he wouldn't be the first. He didn't want to lose Talia for any reason. There was just one real problem between them: her damnable independence. He knew that after they argued Talia never wanted him to touch her. For a moment he thought about taking her over her protests, then he angrily flung aside the sheet and left the room, silently cursing their misfortune that she hadn't conceived.

Talia watched him go, knowing he was growing angrier each time they quarreled. Lately it took longer to make up. Their relationship had definitely changed.

The tension between them was increasing, and she knew

the real root of it was not her job as much as her inability to get pregnant, yet every doctor had said she was normal. Ty refused to take any tests. She began to wonder if the girl he talked about in college had been pregnant with Ty's child or someone else's but she knew she couldn't ask. And another problem had arisen: she noticed Ty flirting more often with other women. She began to wonder what he did when he was away from her.

In the morning, when he emerged from the shower, she was already on her way to eat breakfast. Abby, their cook, arrived at seven, and at half-past seven breakfast was ready. Talia had protested that she didn't need a daily maid when there were only the two of them, but Ty had insisted that they employ one every weekday. He stood with a towel around his middle, watching Talia.

She stepped into black pumps and smoothed her black woolen skirt and the prim, crisp white blouse. Her golden hair was combed into a chignon. She picked up her purse, rummaging through it. He remembered how she had looked last night, his gaze mentally stripping away her work clothing. His erection was swift, and he crossed the room to her before she realized what he was doing. He scooped her into his arms and carried her to the rumpled bed.

"Tyler! Put me down! I'm dressed for work."

"You need to get pregnant, Talia, and we're going to put our minds to the task. And a few things besides our minds," he added, holding her in spite of her struggles.

Talia was in no mood for sex. She pushed against him. The thrust beneath the towel made clear his body's readiness.

"Ty, really! You'll make me late and I don't want—"

Kissing away her protest, he pushed her down. He had one knee on the bed beside her hip and his hand slipped under her skirt, sliding between her thighs, reaching beneath her panties to touch her.

In spite of her struggles, he peeled away her skirt and panties. He paused, seeing her lying there in her white blouse that was now a mass of wrinkles. Her hair was tangled and her eyes squeezed shut when he mounted her, lost in a frenzy until he gasped with release.

"I love you, Tali," he whispered. "I always will."

But it will always be on your terms, she thought, lying still. He had deliberately made love when he knew she hadn't wanted to, when he knew it would interfere with work, and she realized that lately they made love only when Ty wanted her, and it was always rough and rushed. "I'm late for work."

"So call in. It'll be the first time."

She slid away from him going to the closet to take off her blouse and change into another. He came up behind her, slipping his tanned, muscular arm around her waist and leaned close, looking at her reflection in the full-length mirror. "Angry with me?"

"I'm livid," she said mildly, trying to curb her irritation.

"That's my girl. No matter how much we fight, I love you. I always will and I won't let you go."

She believed him. She had learned long ago that he was a jealous husband who never liked her to dance with his friends, who questioned her if she talked to other men for too long at the club. She seldom did anything to provoke his jealousy, so it lay dormant, but she was aware of his feelings.

"Tyler, you're a damned dirty fighter," she whispered.

"That I am, luv. It pays to be."

By late 1981 the oil boom was in full swing; there were more active Louisiana rigs than ever before. Land values still climbed. Ronald Reagan was president, and earlier in the year fifty-two American hostages in Iran had been released.

One morning in December Tyler's father came to his office and closed the door. He held a piece of paper in his hand and laid it on Tyler's desk. "Do you call that collateral?" he asked.

Tyler glanced at the loan he had approved the day before for Claude Dansereaux for a Livonia field well to be drilled in Pointe Coupee Parish. "Look, Dad. We're making money for the bank in oil and gas lending. Things are different now, and we have to go with the times. The assets of this bank are growing faster than ever. You're the one who drilled it into me that a profit margin of one-half percent on a corporate loan is good. Well, we're doing better than that!"

"The only good loan is a repaid loan, Tyler. In petroleum

lending, we've always followed a policy of making loans to people who can pledge existing oil-and-gas production. You've got an 'evergreen revolver' going here, making new loans on old loans; it's free credit. You're pushing us out on a limb that may break off and leave us stranded. Or worse.''

"I know what I'm doing," Tyler said, annoyed that Millard would question him. And I'm doing what any progressive banker would do under the circumstances. Let it ride!''

"This loan application looks like your handwriting!''

"I filled it out for him. We were in a hurry.''

"A hurry! Tyler we could be closed down for this! This violates all the laws of banking.''

"Dad, it's all right. I know this man. Look at who it is—in the past two years he's been one of the most successful oilmen in the state. This month there are forty-five hundred active Louisiana oil rigs—not rigs producing oil, but rigs exploring for oil, according to the Texas tally. We're riding the crest. Your ideas are old-fashioned—'' Tyler bit off the words when he saw Millard flinch as if he had hit him.

"I did a damned good job running this bank for many years.''

"Of course, you did! I didn't mean you didn't do a good job, but times have changed.''

"We've grown steadily, and it was solid, built on a good foundation. We're approaching one-and-a-half billion in assets.''

"And do you know how much the assets have grown since I became executive vice president?'' Tyler asked.

"We're growing, but you're taking chances that are foolhardy! I've seen tough times, Tyler. You haven't!''

"Oh, come on, Dad! Times are great! We'll be a bigger bank this year than last year. You're just not attuned—'' Once again he broke off and flushed. "Sorry.''

For a moment they glared at each other, and then Tyler looked away. He looked over the elegant office that had just been redone with thick green carpeting, a new hand-carved mahogany desk and brown leather-covered furniture. It was such a contrast to his father's plain office with its scarred old desk and metal file cabinets. His gaze came back to his father, who was rubbing his head.

"Maybe it's time I step down from running the bank," Millard said flatly.

"Maybe it is," Ty replied quickly. He would have more freedom, more power, if his father retired. "Frankly, you'd make Mother happy, because she would like to travel."

"You mean I'd make you happy!" Millard gave him a frosty smile that was more like a grimace of pain while he stared at his oldest son. He had hoped Tyler would urge him to stay, not jump at the chance to take over, but he should have known better. It wasn't Tyler's nature to take orders and be second in command, and his need for control had grown worse over the years. For a moment Millard studied the handsome son of whom he had always been so proud. The loan portfolio frightened him because Tyler was taking incredible risks.

Millard rubbed his head again. Perhaps Tyler was a visionary; there was no question that he was a born leader. With a saddened feeling, Millard realized that maybe he was out of step with the times. Yet conservative banking principles had built First Bayou into a strong bank. He did not see a need to change.

He looked at the fancy office. The physical trappings that were always so necessary for Tyler. He was a state-of-the-art person, always wanting to own the latest fancy equipment, the most expensive trinkets. As he looked into his son's black eyes, he could see that Tyler made no effort to hide his eagerness. For a moment Millard had the urge to tell Tyler he would be moved to another department. Then his shoulders sagged, because he knew he should give Tyler control. The bank's problems were growing, and his willingness to battle them was diminishing. And not only was he back on better terms with Pauline, but there was also a new woman in his life. Laura was beautiful and made him feel young again. He deserved a few relaxed years, and Tyler was ready to hand them to him at this moment.

"You want this."

"I'll have to admit, I'll be glad to take charge."

Millard gave a dry sound akin to a laugh. "Perhaps it serves me right. You want to run it all."

"Yes, I do," Ty said, and he held his breath. "Does this mean—"

"Don't be so damned eager, Tyler!" his father snapped. He ran his hand across his forehead again.

"You've talked about letting me take charge before. You'll still be on the board."

"Yes. I'll step down. I'll announce it at the end of the week. This is the last of the year. In January 1982, First Bayou is all yours." He stood up and faced his son. "Just remember, this bank has now been in our family for four generations. Don't let your ambition ruin a fine institution."

"I won't!" Tyler said, trying to hide his enthusiasm. "I damned well won't! I'm going to make this one of the biggest banks in the South."

"Tyler, sometimes you want things too badly. I never did teach you how to accept defeat."

"No, sir. And consequently, I haven't had to."

The phone on the desk buzzed, and Tyler placed his hand on the receiver, looking questioningly at his Dad.

"Go ahead. Take your call," Millard said and left the room. The moment the door closed behind him, Tyler broke into a grin as he yanked up the receiver.

The following evening Talia and Ty drove home from a dinner party at the Goudeaus' house. Talia stared out the window.

"What's wrong, Tali?"

"That's the most conversation we've had all evening," she said.

"What are you talking about?"

She sighed and settled against the black Connolly leather seat of Ty's new Silver Spirit Rolls Royce. "I guess I don't like watching Belinda flirt with you. Or watch you flirt back with her."

"Don't be ridiculous! There's only you," he said, reaching over to slide his hand beneath her skirt.

"Tyler, not while you're driving!"

As soon as they were in their bedroom, he turned her to face him. "You're beautiful," he whispered, bending down to kiss her, and their argument was forgotten.

After he had gone to sleep she stared into darkness and prayed she would get pregnant. There was an urgency to Ty's lovemaking that made it a purely physical act. It was sometimes painful—he seemed to be trying to impregnate her as if he were trying to make a touchdown. And if he noticed that he no longer satisfied her, he gave no indication of it. He seemed wrapped in his own world, full of his own concerns, and she was just now realizing how everything they both did, with the exception of her job, revolved around what he wanted.

Mike had studied Tyler, gleaning bits of information about him. He knew about Tyler's awards and trophies, the sailing races, Ty's barging—shouting at opponents until they were so shaken they made costly mistakes—the other cheating he did during races. And Mike knew that Tyler was jealous of any male attention to his wife. He was possessive, arrogant, sharp-witted, and strong. And through a private detective, Mike learned about the infidelities that were random discreet scores. He also learned that Talia Franklin was faithful to her husband.

During his spare hours, Mike checked on property until he found what he wanted: some swampland along a bayou south of the city to unload on Tyler. The owner lived in a shanty built on stilts, water standing beneath it, a rickety bridge connecting it to solid ground. A pirogue was tied to the porch, and as Mike approached on the sagging, squeaking bridge, a hound dog raised its head and barked. Mike spoke to it, and the dog's tail thumped. Somewhere close by a bird let out a high, shrill call and a turtle swam past, only its head showing in the fork of the waves that trailed away in a vee behind it.

"'Morning, mister," a man said, stepping out, a shotgun in the crook of his arm, his watery, blue-eyed gaze taking in Mike's muddy boots, khakis, and tan sweat shirt.

"Are you Louis Gilyot?" Mike asked, feeling transported back in time to childhood, his speech taking on the local patois that he hadn't used in years.

"That's right."

"I'm Mike Stanton. Looks like good fishing weather."

"Yep. It is."

"Caught any lately?"

"Sacalait, goggle-eyes. Some bass this morning."

"Nothing tastes better. Unless it's trout," Mike said with an easy grin, letting his hands rest on his narrow hips. "What did you use? Crawfish or worms?"

"Worms. Sometimes crank bait. Used bread for the goggle-eyes."

"I came on business, because you own this swamp."

"How'd you know that?"

"It's on record in town. May I talk to you about it?"

"I reckon you might. Set yourself down and rest your feet. Move over, Rascal."

Thumping its tail, the dog stretched out while both men stepped over him to sit in hand-hewn rockers. For just a moment Mike was tempted to try to make a deal to buy the place for himself as he gazed at the green water, tall, moss-draped cypress, thick bayou orchids, and water hyacinths. It was still and peaceful, and Mike knew that it teemed with crawfish, bream, catfish, and bass.

With his long legs stretched out in front of him, Mike talked about fishing and the weather. He guessed that Gilyot was probably like his grandfather, and a deal would depend more on how much he trusted a man than on anything else. With an effort Rascal unfolded to sniff Mike's boots, then sat closer to let Mike scratch his ears, finally flopping down beside him.

By the time Mike was ready to talk business, he and Louis had finished bowls of red-eye chowder and boiled crawfish and had consumed a few swigs of home brew. Mike followed a hunch and told Louis more than he had intended, explaining a little about the election, Ben, Simone, and Tyler, finally getting down to what he wanted. Louis agreed and Mike reached into his boot to pull out cash, seeing the gleam come to the old man's eyes.

When he had counted out the money, he stood up and held out his hand. "Thanks, Louis. All I need you to do if there are inquiries is to indicate that highway people have asked about the property. And don't get to it right off."

"I understand what you want."

"Thanks again, for the best food I've had in a long time."

"You come back."

"Sure," Mike said. "I may do that sometime early enough to fish with you."

The following Saturday, while his foursome was waiting to tee off, and two of the men were at the cart out of earshot, Mike said casually, "Ty, you said if I hear of any likely land deal to let you know."

"Yeah," Ty said, pulling out a driver. He paused, his eyes narrowing beneath his gray canvas golf cap. A crisp January wind buffeted them as he glanced at Mike and asked, "What is it?"

"Go ahead. You're up. I'll tell you in a minute."

Standing at the eighth hole, they had another chance to talk and Ty brought it up again. "What's this deal you were talking about?"

"Right now it's a swamp, but there is serious discussion about running a new four-lane highway through the area. According to my friends in office, the highway will be approved. I've already had a developer contact me about the land."

"And you haven't bought it yourself?"

"I just poured what I have available into other investments. And I've bought part interest in another well. At the moment I can't swing this big a deal." He shrugged. "Just something I heard about."

That was the last that was said until later when they sat in the glassed-in porch of the clubhouse sipping drinks. Ty stretched out his long legs, the sharp creases in his brown woolen trousers extending right down to his lizard loafers. "That land you were talking about. Tell me about it."

"It's swamp now, but I've seen the plans. The new highway will go right past it, and there will be a major artery from the highway across the land. There's one man who owns a long stretch of swamp. He's the one to talk to."

"A major artery will go there?"

"Yes. It's not public information yet," Mike said, leaning back in the chair, pushing his navy sweater sleeves high because it was warm inside out of the wind. He wore dark Levis that fit tautly on his sinewy thighs. He had exchanged his golf shoes for his western boots.

"I could get a bunch of fill for a little or nothing," Tyler mused. "If the land were reclaimed and a new highway built, what could I ask?"

"Ten dollars a square foot wouldn't be unreasonable."

Ty drew a deep breath, a faint smile playing on his face. "Do you have any idea what I'd have to pay?"

"No, but we can go talk to the owner. Of course, once they know it's a member of *the* banking Franklins, the price may jump considerably. But there are ways around that."

Ty rubbed his chin and gazed at Mike with a frown. "You're right. Would you go talk to him? Keep my name out of it."

"Sure, Ty. That's easy," Mike replied, glad Ty had made the suggestion.

"Let me know what he says."

"I'll do it first thing Monday."

"Thanks, Mike. Here comes my wife."

Mike didn't need to be told that bit of information. He had been watching Talia since she had stepped into view from the tennis courts. He had to admit that she had the best legs he had ever seen. In spite of the cold January weather, she wore shorts and a tennis sweater. Her cheeks were bright pink from the wind, but even after a tennis game, she looked neat and unruffled.

He knew she had noticed him, and he waited to see when she would acknowledge him. He knew he disturbed her, and he wondered if she was aware that she disturbed him. He let his gaze drift over her. He wondered if she responded instantly when she kissed, knowing she must, because her husband had a sexual appetite that wouldn't last long with a cold woman.

Entering the glassed-in porch, she walked down its length toward them. When his gaze met hers, she was watching him, and he gave her a mocking smile. "Hi, Mrs. Franklin."

She nodded and turned to Tyler. "I thought you'd be finished and waiting here an hour ago."

"Sorry," Tyler said, swirling his drink, "we were delayed getting started because of the foursomes ahead of us."

"I'll change and meet you inside," she said while Mike stared at the lawn. Tyler had just lied to his wife. The golf foursome had teed off at their regular time and finished promptly so Tyler had been somewhere besides home before he joined the men for golf.

She turned away abruptly, but not before Mike noticed her frown. He realized that she probably suspected her husband's infidelities. He watched Talia Franklin's legs as she walked away quickly. With an effort Mike tore his gaze away before Ty caught him staring at his wife.

"She'll be ready in ten minutes. Time to finish my drink. It's bitchy windy today. Too windy to sail."

They talked about the weather, and golf, and then Ty left, telling Mike he would call during the week. Mike settled back, knowing he had just thrown out the bait. Now he had to see if Ty took it.

On the way home, he stopped to visit Ben, who now looked years older. Mike had hired a male nurse to live with him.

Saturday morning, while Mike dressed, he unfolded the paper. Inside there was a picture of Tyler and his wife as they led a charity drive for the arts. She was smiling at the camera, Tyler was smiling at her.

Mike picked up the paper, studying her picture, the blond hair combed into a sleek chignon. He knew how possessive Tyler was, how haughty Talia Franklin was. Mike wondered how vulnerable she might be. He held the picture in front of him, sipping hot black coffee as he studied it.

"Mrs. Franklin, I'm going to seduce you," he said softly, a flare of anticipation uncurling in him. He tossed the paper aside, knowing that if he succeeded with the two courses he intended to follow, he would have full revenge on Tyler Franklin.

Two weeks later, on a Monday morning, Mike phoned Ty and was put through to him immediately. "Just wanted to let you know about the property. I thought maybe you'd like to drop by and discuss what I learned."

"How about meeting for lunch? Ralph and Kacoo's at twelve?"

"Fine. See you then," he said, smiling when he replaced the phone.

As he faced Tyler over plates of crab and shrimp, he kept his voice calm. "He knows the highway is going through there. His name is Louis Gilyot if you want to talk to him yourself."

Tyler groaned and swore under his breath. "I hoped you'd find some old swamp rat that didn't know civilization exits!"

"Nope. Highway people have talked to him when they were surveying."

"So it's not a good deal."

"I didn't say that," Mike said casually, feeling as if he were in the middle of a round of poker. Tyler's dark eyes flashed with curiosity and greed.

"How much?"

"A dollar per square foot."

"A dollar! I can reclaim that land for very little. Buy at a dollar, sell at ten or more a square foot. That's a damned good profit!" He ate in silence and Mike remained quiet, knowing Tyler was lost in thought over what he was going to do. And Mike had lost his appetite, hoping now that Tyler played into his hands, that he wouldn't have to suggest a thing. He forced himself to eat and gaze at other people around them.

"Every time a Franklin wants to buy a piece of property in this town, the price instantly jumps," Tyler said.

"I guess that's so. I have a few other clients that have the same problem."

"We might work out a deal. You buy that land for me."

"I'd be glad to, but I told you, Ty, my money's tied up."

"I can make you a loan, put the money in your name at the bank. Weston Murdock is loan officer. He'll do whatever I ask. I'll open an account in your name and put the money in it."

"Sure," Mike answered, realizing the rumors he had heard about Tyler's slipshod banking methods were true.

"I'll look at the land. Let you know. If I talk to that Gilyot,

I'll say I'm asking for you. No need to let him think two people are interested in the property.''

Mike looked at his watch. "I've got an appointment," he said. "I need to run." He picked up both checks just as Ty reached for them. "I'll get the lunches. Let me know if you want to buy."

The wheels were in motion, and Tyler's greed was carrying him forward.

Talia sat at her desk looking at the stack of papers in front of her. She now had glass walls around her desk for greater privacy. Glancing again at the report she would give at the loan committee meeting, she suddenly realized that she truly liked the loan department. The bank's earnings came from investments and small fees from trust and management, but the largest percentage of earnings came from loans. As senior loan officer, she couldn't approve a loan over sixty thousand dollars without getting the committee's approval. She checked her notes on each loan she would discuss.

The bank had grown; its assets now numbered sixty-four million dollars with a loan portfolio of forty million dollars. Talia's phone buzzed, and she lifted the receiver to hear Ginger Grant's voice. "Mrs. Franklin, you have a call from your sister."

Talia was startled. She couldn't remember the last time she had spoken with Rebecca. She picked up the phone and heard her voice as husky as ever. "Talia, how are you?"

"Fine. It's been years, Rebecca!"

"Not really years. We talked last July."

"It was longer ago than that," Talia said dryly. "Where are you?"

"Here in New Orleans. I'd like to see you."

Talia felt as if she was talking to a stranger rather than her sister. She knew Rebecca had not fared well over the years, but she was the only family Talia had, apart from Ty and her mother. Her silence did not keep Rebecca from rambling on.

"I want to live here. I thought maybe I could stay with you until I find a place."

Shocked, Talia blinked and stared into space. "Of course."

"Don't be so enthused," came an amused answer.

"You weren't so pleased at one time when I wanted to live with you," Talia retorted. "We'll be happy to have you," she said, wondering what Tyler would say.

Rebecca clutched the phone and smiled, studying the sparkling diamond on her right hand. It was over a carat, and she would have to hock it if Talia didn't take her in, because she had only five hundred dollars left. She slipped the ring onto her left hand, deciding to be a widow. It might arouse sympathy. Mrs. Bernard Koffskey. She wished Bernie were dead every time she thought of the last fight they had. Better to use another name. She didn't want any ties to her life in Chicago. She glanced at the Bible. She wanted a name that sounded like Wade. Mrs. Gideon Wayne.

As soon as she replaced the receiver, she hurried to bathe and change. An hour later she stepped out of the cab.

The driver's eyes swept over her, then saw she was watching him, and he looked down at the meter.

"Seven-fifty, lady," he said, wanting to go on looking at her. Her tousled black hair framed a face with large eyes and a mouth that was red, pouting, and inviting. He couldn't remember when he'd had a fare like her, and he wondered if she were a visiting movie star. He hopped out of the car. "I'll get your bags, lady."

"Thank you," she said in a careless, offhand manner. He suspected men jumped to do whatever she wanted wherever she went.

He unloaded Rebecca's four suitcases and several hat boxes and then stared at her tight skirt while she tipped him. "Ma'am, may I ask you something?"

Her green eyes sparkled with amusement, and he felt stupid. "Never mind."

"Go ahead." Her voice matched her looks, sultry enough to boil a man's blood.

"Are you in the movies?"

"No. I'm a singer. Nightclubs."

"Ahh. I thought so." They both smiled. "Show business! I ought to get your autograph."

She laughed, a sound that raked over his nerves. "I'm not

that famous yet! Thanks for carrying my bags," Rebecca said, amused.

"Yeah, sure. My pleasure," he murmured and backed away, turning to glance at her again. She waved, forgetting him instantly. The house was magnificent, and she was glad she had decided to come back. With this kind of house, Talia's contacts would be fantastic. Maybe Ty could introduce her to a rich husband.

A uniformed maid opened the door, and Rebecca said, "I'm Mrs. Wayne. Mrs. Franklin's sister."

"Come in. She told me she's expecting you," the maid said, smiling and stepping back as she held the door open. "I'm Abby. I'll get someone to carry your bags to your room."

Rebecca let her, looking around with satisfaction and a tinge of awe. She should have come sooner. She had no idea Talia had married so well. Rebecca had the impression that Tyler Franklin, in her sister's eyes, was a hunk. He had been governor and he was old money, but she hadn't expected this much grandeur. And if he was handsome as well—? That was something Rebecca would decide for herself, but with this kind of home, any man would be the most glamorous creature she could imagine. Rebecca smiled, following the maid up the stairs, barely listening to her chatter, except to hear that Talia would be home soon.

As Rebecca threw off her mink jacket and unpacked in the sunny room given to her, she heard footsteps approach. For an instant she didn't recognize her sister and stared at her until Talia raised her arms. "Rebecca!"

"Talia?" She stood quietly while Talia hugged her, catching a whiff of Chanel. "You've changed," Rebecca said in amazement, taken aback by the cool, beautiful woman who faced her, so unlike her younger sister.

Talia smiled. "I'm the same."

"No, you're not. Definitely not."

"I'm glad you're here."

"I won't stay long."

"You never do!" Talia exclaimed with a smile. "You look gorgeous!" thinking Rebecca had changed too—she no longer was merely pretty, she was striking in a tousled, wind-swept manner. Suddenly Talia felt a surge of warmth for her sister.

"Tali?" Tyler called from downstairs.

"Come meet my husband," Talia said, both women going into the hall.

Rebecca noticed Tyler bounding up the stairs two at a time. He paused at the top and smiled, his brows arching in curiosity while one sweeping glance took in Rebecca from her head to her toes. Instinctively, she licked her lips and drew a deep breath, her breasts thrusting against her tight crepe blouse. She was astounded by Tyler's incredible looks.

Tyler saw the swift appraisal while he made his own, having realized early that the sisters must be as different as two strangers, but he was surprised. Rebecca's sensualness was blatant from her tight skirt and clinging blouse to her full red lips and bold gaze. Her hair was tousled where Tali's was neat. Rebecca's skirt was six inches shorter than Tali's which was fashionably long. Rebecca's dark hair and olive skin gave her an earthy appearance, whereas Tali was as cool and blond as a Nordic beauty. Sexuality radiated from Rebecca, and it made him feel as if he had come home to discover a burning stick of dynamite in the upstairs hall.

The flirtatious look in her eyes was unmistakable to a man as experienced as Tyler, and while his occasional flings were something he could excuse as casually as scratching an itch, his wife's sister was another matter. He knew he would have to be careful with this one, because her gaze right now was all but searing his flesh.

"Ty, this is my sister Rebecca. Rebecca, this is Tyler."

"How do you do," Rebecca said in a raspy voice. She extended her hand, and Ty took it in his, feeling her warm, dry flesh.

Wry amusement surfaced in his voice. "At last we meet," he said, releasing her hand and putting his arm around Talia. He kissed her cheek.

"I'm moving back to New Orleans, and Talia invited me to stay her tonight."

"We're glad to have you," he said, still glancing down at Talia. "Why don't we eat at the club? On the way, we can drive you around and show you how the city has changed.''

"That's nice, but I don't want you to go to any trouble.''

"We won't, Rebecca," Talia said while Ty's hand tightened on her waist. "I'll change and meet you downstairs.''

"Sure. I want to change. How long—''

"Take your time. We can have a drink in an hour and then we'll go," Ty said smoothly.

"Good," Rebecca answered. "I'll be ready." She disappeared into her room while Ty and Talia went into the big master bedroom where Ty closed and locked the door. Ty pulled Talia into his arms and thought how interesting it was going to be having Rebecca in his house.

17

March 1982

Mike attended a party during the first week of March at Stan Hebert's house. The March weather had warmed, and the party had been moved out of doors. The lawn held tables of food in silver serving dishes that gleamed in the slanting rays of late afternoon sunshine. A piano player sat near the open doors to the patio while guests mingled in and out of the house. Mike knew the Franklins were also on the guest list.

He had a drink in his hand and was standing alone on the lawn when he saw Talia. She held Tyler's arm as they stepped through the French doors onto the terrace. Mike had already learned that the brunette in the red dress who was clinging to Tyler's other arm was Rebecca Wayne, Talia's so-called widowed sister. Mike's detective had told him that Rebecca was no widow and Gideon Wayne had never existed. But only one woman interested Mike.

Cool and poised, Talia was clad in white crepe. She was

slender, except for her high, full breasts. She could have been
a model. Besides her physical appearance—her slender neck
and patrician forehead, her symmetrical features and glow of
healthy vitality—she commanded appreciative attention in a
regal manner that didn't fade when she smiled or laughed.
She might have been visiting royalty. Mike studied her with
smoldering determination while people smiled in greeting,
some turning to watch her after she passed. In spite of his
antagonism toward the couple, Talia Franklin stirred his admiration. He had to concede that she was stunning to watch;
seducing her would be an unholy pleasure.

Over an hour later, Rebecca saw Tyler standing alone, and
she hurried to his side before he joined some of the other
guests. "Nice party, Tyler. And it's nice to be living under
the same roof with you," she said in a sultry, flirtatious voice.

Amusement quirked the corners of his mouth as he watched
her. "We'll have to get to know each other better," he said
softly, his gaze lowering to her breast.

"You're right. I didn't know my sister was married to such
a handsome man!"

"And I didn't know what a sexy sister Talia had."

Rebecca glanced beyond him and drew in a deep breath.
"Speaking of Talia—here she comes. I'll see you later, Tyler." She moved from a group, sauntering to the tables of
food where she paused near a cluster of guests, taking a bon
bon from a silver tray. Names swirled in her mind, and she
glanced over the crowd, pausing to put a name with a face,
wondering who was married or single.

"Looking for someone?" a deep voice asked, and she
discovered a sandy-haired man watching her. Perhaps an inch
shorter than Rebecca, he looked as if he should have a wife,
a child, a home in the suburbs, a station wagon, and a dog
—he was not her type at all. Dressed in a plain brown suit,
he stood where there had just been a cluster of people. But
they were all gone, and Rebecca wondered how long he had
been studying her.

"Just trying to remember names and faces."

"How about starting with mine? I'm Ed J. Dessauer."

"And I'm Rebecca Wayne."

"Rebecca. Regretfully Mrs."

"I'm widowed," she said, looking at the crowd for some-one more interesting to meet.

"Sorry."

"It was seven years ago."

"Are you a friend of the Heberts'?"

"I just met them. Actually I wasn't even invited to the party."

"Ah, a beautiful crasher. That's good news, because it won't matter if I take you away from here then."

"Why would I leave with you?" she asked with amuse-ment, her attention returning to him.

"Why not?" he rejoined, a sparkle in his hazel eyes. "I can take you to dinner and get to know you—that sounds more interesting than munching tidbits and talking to people I see all week."

"Thanks. I can't leave with a stranger."

"I'm no stranger. I'm a guest, so I'm reliable."

She could believe that. He looked as substantial as the Franklin mansion. Suddenly he looked startled and gave her a rueful grin. "Ahh, you came to the party with a man."

"Don't look so crestfallen," she said, still amused at the emotions that showed in his features. "Yes, I came with a man. My brother-in-law."

"Great! Now we can go. I'll take you to dinner. What do you like to eat?"

"Thanks, but I should stay. I'm moving back to town and I need to get to know people."

"Then I'll introduce you, we'll spend another tedious hour in idle chatter with the crowd, and then we'll go. How's that?"

"I'll have to give you high marks for persistence and com-ing on strong."

"Only with you, sweetie. I think it'll be worth my while," he said, giving her a speculative look that surprised her. She looked at him more attentively and saw that his ears were large, his nose straight, his hair thick and sandy, streaked with blond. There was nothing distinctive about his features except an alertness in his eyes that made her feel as if he could read her thoughts. Other than his curious hazel eyes, he looked about as interesting as a glass of milk, and she wanted to move on. As she studied him, he asked, "Is there anyone in particular whom you'd like to meet?"

"Wealthy men," she said recklessly, figuring Ed J. Dessauer would say goodbye within the next sixty seconds. "They make life more interesting."

He stopped in his tracks. "Uh, oh! We've hit a bit of a snag."

"How's that?" she said, looking down into his eyes, realizing for the first time that his shoulders were broad.

"I don't fit in the category. I work and I can't shower you with diamonds and furs."

"Then you can introduce me to someone who can."

"There goes my evening! I should have known! A wealthy man, huh? I presume single. Okay. I'll introduce you to some of the wealthiest in town. Do you want a politician or an oilman or an entrepreneur? We have them all. There's a senator," he said, pointing to a slender man whose brown hair was streaked with gray.

Startled, she laughed, amazed that Ed Dessauer hadn't been shocked and annoyed. Instead, to her surprise, after introducing her to guests seated on a corner of the patio, chatting for almost half an hour, Ed led her to another group of people. "Now, that Charley I just introduced you to owns a fleet of shrimp boats, land along the river, and one of the largest mills in the state."

"You're not kidding!"

"Were you?" he asked, still eyeing her with speculation. "What did the late Mr. Wayne do?"

"He owned a nightclub in Chicago. He died at forty of a heart attack. I sold the nightclub and came home. I don't have any ties to Chicago," she said glibly, repeating the story she had fabricated for Talia and Ty.

"On to the next one."

An hour and three wealthy men later, Ed asked, "Think we can go to dinner now? I can mention I know you when I see them again this week."

"Sure. We can go to dinner," she said, studying him a little more closely. "Let's find my sister and tell her I'm leaving. Or my brother-in-law. Do you know Tyler Franklin?"

"Oh, no!" Ed exclaimed, such a look of disaster sweeping over his features, she wondered what Tyler had done to him.

"What's wrong? You don't like Tyler?"

"He's my boss! I'm executive vice president of investments in the Trust Department at First Bayou. I'm flirting with my boss's sister-in-law."

"Is that all! You had me worried!"

"Did I really?" He stood staring at her in such consternation she wondered if the dinner invitation had been withdrawn.

"It was nice to know you Ed J. Nice and interesting. I guess the dinner invitation is off."

"Of course not," he said, taking her arm again. "I might as well live recklessly. Besides, I don't intend to make you angry, and if I don't make you angry, my boss won't get angry with me. Simple."

"That's absurd! Why would Tyler care if you take me out?"

"He won't care this one time, but suppose I want to marry you—that's a different matter." He said it so matter-of-factly, she had to smile.

"Marry you—aren't you rushing things a bit?"

He paused to look at her, his gaze drifting down over her fantastic figure, his hand stroking her arm. "I said suppose, but now's the time to think about it before things get sticky. Of course, if you're searching for a man with a fat wallet, that lets me out anyway, so I guess we'll just settle on being friends. Perhaps I can help you find the guy." He held out his arms. "I can be Cupid."

The thought of the squat, plain-looking, big-eared man standing in front of her calling himself Cupid made her smile and shake her head. He laughed and slipped her arm through his. "There's Tyler now. Shall we break the news that we're going to dinner?"

She pulled back. "Tyler doesn't know I want to meet wealthy men."

"It's our secret, sweetie. May we have many more," he said and winked at her.

They went to dinner at an elegant restaurant atop a hotel on the riverfront. The lights were dim, and there was a dance floor. They sat by a window where Rebecca could see twin-kling lights along the river while they ate whole lobsters flambéed in cognac. He asked her about herself and told her how he had started in credit, analyzing corporate lending, learning to glean the important data from a corporate report, learning personal lending before moving to the Trust Department. After midnight she went back to his apartment with him where she discovered that beneath his business suit, thirty-four-year-old Ed J. had a very powerful body. And a sexual appetite that surprised her when she had thought she would never be surprised by a man again.

At the Hebert party Mike mingled with the crowd, and it was almost an hour later when he saw the opportunity he wanted. Standing with a group of men in the study, he looked at Stan's latest gun purchase. When he grew bored with the hunting conversation he walked into the hall. Talia Franklin was walking ahead of him toward the back and he fell into step behind her, admiring the slight sway of her hips.

Abruptly a man emerged from a bathroom and collided with her. Talia gasped but recovered instantly as the man gave an exclamation of surprise, followed by profuse apologies. She was carrying a glass of red wine and now it was splattered like blood across the front of her white dress.

"I'm sorry!" John Kimmer said. "So sorry! I'll have it cleaned and I'll get you a new dress."

"Don't worry about it. I'm fine. The dress is fine. I'll get Tyler to take me home and I'll change. Don't worry, please."

Mike listened while John prevailed on her to promise to send him the cleaning bill, and then Mike stepped forward. "Mrs. Franklin, I'll give you a lift. Your husband is en-grossed in a conversation poolside. I'll get the lady home and back, John."

"Now you send me the bill. That was a promise."

"I will," she said, dabbing at a spot while John Kimmer seemed to wait. She glanced up at Mike. "You don't—"

"No, I don't have to, but I'll be glad to. My car is right at the curb where I can get away without disturbing others." Caught between his offer of a quick ride home and more apologies from John Kimmer, she turned to go with Mike.

As soon as they stepped through the front door, she paused. "I can get our car, and you don't have to do this," she said, knowing Tyler's jealous nature, but it seemed ridiculous to get Tyler, who would be annoyed at the disturbance. Besides, others would have to move their cars off the drive in order for Ty to get their car out. It was more convenient to go home and change and be back in minutes with Mike Stanton. Had anyone except Mike Stanton made the offer, she wouldn't have hesitated, but even his hand casually touching her arm was jarring.

"To tell the truth, I'm getting tired of the party. I don't mind or I wouldn't have offered. Come on. We'll see if we can ride four miles without slitting each other's throats."

She bestowed a cynical smile on him, but he could see her still hesitate while he looked into her wide, green eyes. "C'mon," he urged again. "You're not afraid to ride with me, are you?"

Her full red lips curved into a smile, revealing even white teeth and a dimple in her cheek, a smile that probably had won her husband more than a few votes from male constituents. "No, Mr. Stanton. I'm not afraid of you."

"My car is at the curb." He led her to a black Ferrari and held the door open.

"Nice car."

"Thank you. I like cars. And beautiful women." He sat down on the tan leather seat and started the engine.

She glanced at him with raised eyebrows. "If that had been said by anyone else, I'd say, thank you, because I'd presume it had been intended as a compliment."

"But you don't think so from me?"

"Leopards don't change their spots. I don't know why you're giving me a ride home," she said, glancing at him, thinking he looked darkly handsome in his navy suit and white shirt.

Mike laughed at her blunt statement, and his gaze moved to her long legs. "Our confrontation was years ago, and I'm far removed from politics. Tonight I acted impulsively; you were a damsel in distress. John Kimmer can worry the socks off someone, and I was bored with the party. Call it momentary madness."

When he laughed, it softened his features, changing the impression he made. His smile was appealing, his eyeteeth slightly crooked.

"I find it difficult to stay angry with a beautiful lady. Is there any reason I should?"

"Of course not! Thank you for the compliment. It was long, long ago." She settled in the seat.

"Mrs. Franklin—"

"If you can bring yourself to say it, my first name is Talia. And you're Mike."

"You remember."

"Of course, I do. How could I forget?"

"That you didn't trust me with the silverware, or that you tossed me to the wolves on the interview?"

"You see. Leopards don't change their spots. You remember and you're probably still angry."

"And yet you're not afraid to ride with me."

"Should I be?"

He gave her a raking glance, and his voice dropped. "How I would like to say yes. But I'm a very ordinary man and you're married to a friend."

"Ordinary?" She gave a soft laugh. "That's probably the last thing you are!"

"And I enjoy golf on Saturdays with your husband. I wouldn't want to jeopardize that foursome," he said, making her smile, catching a whiff of her tantalizing perfume while they were in the close confines of the car. "He should turn pro."

"He likes to win. And he's a good athlete."

"So are you. You like sailing, tennis, jogging—"

"How'd you know that?"

"Your husband talks about what you like: 'Tali's gone sailing. Tali has a tennis game. Won two yesterday—' "

"Oh, my word! It's a wonder the rest of you don't boot him out of the foursome."

"No one minds. The other guys talk about their wives."

"And whom do you talk about, Mr. Stan—"

"Ah, none of that Mr. Stanton stuff. Mike. I'll talk about Zorro, the retriever I used to have."

She laughed again, and he found her easy to be with, but

he was trying his best to please her. Even though they talked about harmless topics, the crackling friction that had always generated between them hung in the air, barely suppressed by their polite words. But Talia felt its effect differently this time. He took a long way to her house. Her contact with Mike caused an excited stirring within her rather than an annoyed response. Maybe they both had changed in the past few years, she thought as she invited him inside.

"Let me get you a drink," she said. "It's nicer now out by the pool. This is perfect weather."

"I agree." He followed her into a large den, moving to the bar as she stepped behind it. He glanced at the costly antiques, the fine oil paintings and thick, white carpet. "You have a beautiful home," he said, thinking it looked as cool and aloof as she did.

"Thanks. Tyler and a decorator and my mother-in-law get the credit."

"You weren't interested?"

"I was at work," she answered too casually, and he suspected it hadn't been her choice to be left out of the decision. "What would you like?"

"If you trust me with the silver, I can make my own," he said lightly, and she laughed. There was a soft glow from the overhead light, and her face was bathed in it. He was only a few feet away and could see her smooth, flawless skin, her thick lashes that were only shades darker than her hair. She was a beautiful woman with high cheekbones, glossy golden hair, and eyes the color of green winter wheat. Her smooth, sophisticated beauty was a barrier and the urge to grab her and shake her, to see her golden hair tumble down, was so strong that he clenched his fists.

"You won't let me forget will you?" she asked without moving, studying him in a manner that made his pulse quicken.

"*Au contraire*! Of course, I'll let you forget! I beg you to forget! I pray you'll forget!"

"It's forgotten!" she said with alacrity, laughing, throwing up her hands. He noticed her long slender fingers. Two large diamonds rings caught the light with her every movement; she had one on each hand.

Her mouth was inviting, and he wondered what it would be like to kiss her. Boring? Fun? He couldn't imagine too many thrills. She looked so cool and reserved. She was probably too self-centered to generate much excitement. As he studied her mouth, a flush crept into her cheeks.

"What kind of drink would you like?" she asked, aware of feeling shut away with a stalking leopard. The scar on the side of his face gave a harshness to his features; his blue eyes were unreadable, but when they fastened in a steady gaze upon her, she couldn't look away. He seemed dangerous even though she couldn't say why.

"I was going to do it, remember?" he said softly, taking her arm and pulling her gently out of the bar while he stepped behind it. She was as conscious of his casual touch as if she had made contact with a red-hot coal. And in spite of her trepidation, her gaze lowered to his mouth.

For a fleeting moment she wondered what it would be like to be kissed by him. His lower lip was full, his mouth masculine, but well-shaped, his upper lip thin. Shocked by her thoughts, she looked away, meeting his eyes and seeing a mocking light in them that made her blush, something she seldom did. Mike Stanton always threw her off balance.

"I'll change and be right back," she said curtly. "Make yourself at home."

"Sure," he said, watching her leave the room. Maybe she wasn't as cold as he had thought. The look she had just given him had been almost invitingly warm.

Upstairs, she moved quickly. The intensity in Mike Stanton's glances disturbed her, and she wanted to change and get back to the party. When he focused his incredibly blue eyes on her, she felt touched by an exposed electric wire. She changed into a Giorgio Armani deep blue silk jacquard, belted at the waist with a flounce at the hemline. Her hair was neat, her makeup still intact, and she was ready.

Mike waited in the dimly lit hallway. The first thing he saw were her long legs. The skirt swirled around her calves with each step and he drew a deep breath as his gaze roved upward, because she was stunning to look at.

As soon as she had descended enough stairs to see him,

she paused with a slight break in stride. "Oh! I thought you'd be relaxing out by the pool."

"I figured you were about ready, so I came in to see," he said, crossing to her.

"Mike," she said, hesitating. His curiosity surfaced while he waited. Whatever was bothering her was difficult for her to say. "This is a long time in coming, but I'm sorry about Simone Holloway."

Stunned, his eyes narrowed. "It has been a long time."

Her gaze slid away, but not before he had seen the guilt in them. Shocked by her condolences, his assessment of her underwent a change. "The Franklins sent flowers," he said.

"I know," she answered so softly he had to lean forward to hear. "But I feel that she might not have done that if . . ."

Her words faded and she glanced at him. "If your husband hadn't humiliated her," Mike finished harshly and instantly regretted it when he saw the flicker of pain in her eyes. Suddenly he didn't want to hurt Talia Franklin. He saw that she was a beautiful, sensitive woman who was married to a ruthless man. "I'm sorry. I shouldn't have said that to you. You can't help what he does."

"No, I can't," she said so bitterly that he was surprised. "You needn't apologize for the truth."

Compulsion to touch her made him stroke her jaw. Something flickered in the depths of her eyes and his slight touch made him intensely aware of her. "I shouldn't have been cruel to you when you were trying to be nice to me."

"How is Ben?"

Mike shrugged, refusing to add to the hurt he had already inflicted. "He's fine."

"I've heard he's retired and become a recluse," she said, sounding sincerely concerned, and Mike realized his judgments of her had been inaccurate.

"He stays shut away," he answered gruffly, looking at her, realizing that he could never go through with his plan to seduce and destroy her. She was lovely, intelligent, and married to a man he despised.

She couldn't seem to let the matter drop. With a deprecatory wave of her hand, she said, "I didn't know that day you visited us how devastating Tyler's announcement would be. There were a lot of things I didn't know then," she added.

"Talia." He said her name, feeling drawn to her, wanting to touch her again. "Thanks for your concern." He smiled and waved his empty glass. "What's the old proverb? 'If wishes were horses, beggars might ride.' I wish we could stay here."

Her eyes widened in a startled look that was gone almost as swiftly as it had come. She shook her head. "There's another old proverb: 'Wishes granted are never appreciated.' "

"That's one I haven't heard." When she smiled, he suspected she had made it up, and he had to smile in return. He was intrigued by her. He wanted to know more about her and he felt frustrated that he had not known her better before.

"I switched off the bar lights," he said.

"You're efficient. Ty can't remember lights. I guess it was instilled in me as a child to remember to turn off the light when I left a room."

"Did you grow up in New Orleans?" he asked, catching a fragrance of inviting perfume that he couldn't identify. He held open the car door and caught another glimpse of her long legs as she stepped into the car and her skirt slipped up to her knees.

Talia's animosity toward him vanished. Mike Stanton was charming, appealing—breathtakingly so—yet she was wary of him because she knew he could be a formidable foe, and few men would forgive what Tyler had done, much less a man as tough as Mike. Since her marriage to Tyler she had had experience in dealing with duplicity, and she was finding it increasingly difficult to trust any man. Yet she was beginning to like Mike and hoped there was no need to be cautious.

When Mike whipped back into the same parking place, she stepped out and thanked him. As they crossed the front lawn, she hurried her stride, knowing that she might face Tyler's wrath for leaving with Mike.

"Once more, thanks," she said.

"I was glad to take you home. It gave us a chance to know each other better," he said warmly. A quality in his tone of voice made her pulse skip a beat.

She left him, her back tingling, because she could imagine

him standing behind her, watching her walk away with that intense, smoldering gaze of his. To her relief, Tyler was still in the same place at the back of a yard talking to a group of men. She sauntered toward him, and if he even noticed that she had changed dresses, he didn't mention it. Nor did she.

Later when she was home with Tyler, he said, "I saw you talking to Mike Stanton. Looks like you two have buried the hatchet."

"I can carry on a civil conversation with him if that's what you mean," she said.

"Glad you can. I'm going in on a business deal with him."

"Do you think that's wise?"

"You just don't like the guy, Tali. Face it."

She shrugged, realizing she didn't want to study too closely her reactions to Mike Stanton. But she was wary of his motives and his friendliness, because he had valid reasons for wanting to retaliate against the Franklins. "He was the opposition, and everyone says he's tough. Suddenly he's your friend."

"It isn't sudden. We play golf. That crosses a hell of a lot of barriers. The campaign was years ago. And he's got a reputation for having a Midas touch in commercial real estate. I'll come out of the deal in great shape. I always do."

The following Saturday Talia received a cruel shock when she picked up a jacket Ty had casually discarded after coming in from work on Friday afternoon. She noticed a smudge on the collar and tried to brush it off. Looking closer she realized it was lipstick. She frowned, staring at it for a long time. She turned the jacket in her hands, noticing a bit of white sticking out of a pocket, and she withdrew one of his handkerchiefs. It was smeared with lipstick, and a faint trace of perfume clung to it. It was such a classic piece of evidence that Talia almost laughed.

But all she could think of was how possessive and jealous Ty was if she spent ten minutes in public talking to another man. He emerged from the bathroom and stopped, his gaze going to the handkerchief in her hands. He wore a white towel around his middle, his skin glowing from the shower, but in her anger she couldn't find anything strongly appealing about him.

"Don't jump to rash conclusions, Tali. Just a secretary who—"

"Don't lie, Tyler. I know better," she said with icy dignity, and his brows arched in surprise.

"So the kitten has claws," he drawled and shrugged. "Honey, it was only a few kisses. Nothing else."

"Don't lie. It only makes it worse."

"I'm sorry," he said, crossing the room to take her in his arms. "It won't happen again."

"Just leave me alone!" she snapped, moving out of his grasp abruptly and leaving the room. Tyler stood watching her go, tempted to yank her back. She would get over her shock, and he could convince her it was a one-time thing. He had been careless in leaving the handkerchief in his pocket even though Talia rarely bothered with his clothes—the maid usually saw to everything.

That night he handed Talia a box tied with pink ribbon. "I promised Al and Terri we'd meet them for dinner, but before we go—open your present."

She untied the package, unfolding a note: "Please forgive me. I love you."

"Oh, Tyler!" she said, in exasperation that he would think he could buy back her affection and trust with an expensive bauble. He misunderstood her exclamation and smiled, nodding eagerly.

"Open your present."

She lifted the lid to see a sparkling diamond bracelet. "Tyler, every time I look at this I'll remember why you bought it!"

"No, you won't," he said, taking her in his arms. "You'll remember that I slipped once, Tali, and that I won't again. I love you. You're mine always. My wife. I was just caught off guard for a moment. You and I haven't been on the best of terms lately, and a man has needs. I don't care a thing about the woman. It was chemistry and meaningless."

"You sound as if you're talking about spilling a cup of coffee, not infidelity."

"It isn't infidelity when you're the only woman I love. *You're* my wife."

"Suppose I did the same?"

"You wouldn't, and I know I was wrong; I deserve your anger." He rubbed her arms, leaning down to kiss her, but she twisted away.

"It isn't easy to forget!"

"Let's go eat. You'll see. I'll make it up to you."

She laid the box with the bracelet on the table. "I'll get my purse."

Tyler watched her leave, her hips moving with a tantalizing sway. She was angrier than he'd ever seen her, but she'd get over it. He wanted her now and if he thought he could get her in bed, he would call and delay dinner, but he knew he would have to wait until her anger cooled.

Mike leaned back in his chair with his feet propped on his desk, while he called Ty at the bank. He could take the first step in his revenge on Tyler if he wanted to, yet Mike felt little satisfaction. He had thought of Talia constantly since the party, and he wanted to see her again. For the first time in his life he had conflicting feelings about revenge, not because of Tyler, but because he didn't want to hurt Talia in any way.

The greeting of the bank's operator broke into his thoughts and he gave his name and asked for Tyler Franklin. While he waited he debated with himself, remembering Talia's quiet apology about Simone, her concern about Ben. Then Tyler came on the line.

"Mike Stanton, Ty. Only take a minute. I have to leave town by three this afternoon." He paused, thought of Talia, and impulsively said, "Tyler, that land is no good. You ought to forget it."

"The hell you say! Since when did the prospects change?"

"You know how these deals blow hot and cold."

There was a long, silent pause. "I still want you to buy the land for me," Tyler said, a belligerent note coming into his voice. "It's still available isn't it?"

"Yes, it is, but it may be worthless."

"I'll take a chance. Go buy it for me the way we discussed."

Mike's eyes narrowed and he could guess the suspicion rising in Tyler's mind over Mike's sudden protestations about the value of the land.

"Okay, Tyler. Whatever you say," Mike said. He had tried.

"I'll put the money in your account now and make out the loan papers. You put the money up, and get a contract. You promised me this."

"I sure did," *before I knew your wife*, Mike added silently.

"I want you to get it for me," Tyler said emphatically. "Keep the Franklin name out of it. You can deed it over to me. I'll take care of the forms. That's simple. I can use some of the information off the loan application you made with us months back. Just tell them you want to purchase the land."

"My collateral won't be enough."

"I'll fix that. You just get me the land."

"That I'll do," Mike said softly. "I'll come by the bank at one."

"I have an appointment. My secretary will have the check. You won't have to do anything else except pick it up."

"I'll call the other broker now and tell him the land is sold. If I hadn't tied up everything you wouldn't have had a chance at this," Mike said.

"Call me when it's done."

"You bet," he said, and replaced the receiver. *You greedy, suspicious sonofabitch*, he thought. He stared into space, thinking about Talia. He'd tried to stop Tyler, but the deal wouldn't really hurt him. The loss would be peanuts to them, but he hadn't wanted to do anything to cause trouble for Talia. He knew the protective reaction he felt toward her was unlike him. Lately Talia filled his thoughts more often than not, and Mike wondered if he was in any position to judge the situation clearly.

That's for you, Ben. And for Simone, he said quietly to himself. Tyler was falsifying loan applications. Ironically, Mike hadn't had to do a thing. Tyler was getting himself in enough trouble all by himself. Mike suspected the examiners would find the First Bayou Bank records fascinating reading, as would the FDIC. Sooner or later they would discover what Tyler was doing.

Mike plopped his feet on the floor and moved restlessly to the windows to stare outside, his hands resting on his narrow hips. Tyler would soon be caught in webs of his own weaving; the thought of Talia being ensnared as well worried Mike. She was married to a self-centered, ambitious man, and she deserved better.

Mike's mouth twisted in a cynical smile. If she were married to a nonpareil, would he be any more able to resist seeing her? His attraction had nothing to do with sympathy.

He tried to stay away from her, to busy himself with other activities, but he couldn't get her out of his thoughts. The lady was married, albeit to a jerk, so he couldn't call her for a date, but he wanted to see her badly. He needed to know if his reactions to her were still real or imagined. Finally he did the same thing he had done at First Bayou. He called Talia to make an appointment to ask for a loan that he didn't need.

Two days later Mike sat down across the desk from Talia. She looked amused and as self-possessed as ever. She wore a double-breasted hemp-colored linen dress with a notched collar. A thin gold chain circled her slender throat and the vee of her dress revealed the slightest hint of curves disappearing beneath the linen. Mike's pulse drummed with anticipation but he forced himself to relax, placing his foot on his knee and holding a folder in his lap.

"I came to see you about a loan for a business venture I want to make."

"I'll have to admit, I'm surprised that you would come here," she said, curious about him. She still didn't trust him completely, but she also liked his style very much.

He grinned. "This is a good, sound bank from what I hear."

"What can I do for you?" she asked.

Talia was amused that Mike had wandered into her office not knowing she was the Senior Loan Officer; she sensed his discomfort. Talia also felt slightly ill at ease. When she looked into Mike's blue eyes she saw arrogance mixed with recklessness. She also saw sincerity, and the combination was enticing.

"For starters," he said with a smile, "I'd like a loan."

"How much are we talking about?"

"Fifty thousand dollars."

She could make this loan without going to the committee. "Why do you need the loan? What's your business?"

"Commercial real estate," he replied, knowing she knew.

Mike opened his briefcase and took out snapshots, leaning forward to place them on her desk in front of her. His hands were big with strong, blunt fingers; a thin white scar ran across the back of his right hand. She wondered where he had gotten the scars. She had heard Tyler say Mike had a tough background, but she hadn't listened beyond that.

"It's just a small shop, twenty feet across, seventy feet deep. Fourteen hundred square feet in all. I can buy this at a good price, resell it, and make a nice profit. I'm asking for a short-term loan, say ninety days to turn this property."

"What makes you think you can sell it and come out ahead?"

"Here's the address," he said, placing another picture on her desk. "This is why I think I can make a profit. The owner died and his widow wants to sell. Since it sits next to a nice strip shopping mall, it's close enough to attract mall business. It can easily be made into a gift shop, a small carry-out restaurant, or any number of possibilities in such a high-exposure location."

"For ninety days? That's a short time to sell a business."

"Every shop is taken except this one."

"If it's so good, why hasn't it already sold?"

"It isn't on the market yet," he said with a smile. He glanced at his Rolex. "We've run into the lunch hour. Come on. I'll take you to lunch and then show it to you."

"Oh, thank you, but—"

"You have to eat lunch," he said, amusement flaring again in his voice and eyes. "We can carry on a civil conversation; we proved that last time we were together. And I can give you my best sales pitch."

"I don't think—"

"—You should be with me. I understand, but give me a chance to convince you of the soundness of the loan." He stood up. "Come on. Let me take you to lunch, Talia."

When he said her name, Talia felt her pulse quicken. She

didn't know if the tension they generated crept into every word, but she was keenly aware of her name rolling off his tongue. She was unaccustomed to lunching with other men, and Tyler was a jealous husband, yet it seemed ridiculous to refuse. "Very well," she answered with more reluctance than she realized.

He gave her a sardonic smile.

"We have some kind of effect on each other," she admitted.

"No harm in lunch. Get your purse."

Once more she was tempted to say no. Instead, she did as he told her, and when they left the office, he held her arm. She stepped out into warm sunshine with him, matching her stride with his as they walked to his shiny black Ferrari parked at the corner of the lot beneath an oak. He tossed his briefcase in the back, slid behind the wheel, and whipped out into traffic. "Do you like jambalaya?"

"On that we agree."

A smile lifted one corner of his mouth while he kept his eyes on the road. "This place has the best crawfish jambalaya I've ever eaten." To her surprise the café wasn't all that inviting, nor was it in a decent neighborhood. On the fringe of downtown, the Cajun Cat restaurant was a ramshackle old house with tables on the porch, but the parking lot was full and the porch was crowded with customers. Mike parked behind the kitchen door and Talia arched her brows in surprise.

"Won't you get towed?"

"I know the cook," he said. He held the door open, and she entered a kitchen bustling with cooks and waiters, enticing smells of frying fish and spicy peppers wafting in the air, while everyone gave quick hellos to Mike as he ushered her through to the dining area.

"Busy today?" he asked a waiter.

"Never too busy, Mike. Follow me."

"You're getting special treatment," she said, when they were seated in a crowded corner table for two.

"I know the cook *and* owner. I used to sell him catfish I caught in the bayou."

Startled she looked up from her menu. His head was bent

over the table as he read the menu, and as she looked at his thick, curly brown hair, she wondered what kind of life he'd led, selling catfish and obviously getting into street fights. He raised his head, catching her studying him, and he lifted one dark brow in question. She shifted her attention to the menu quickly, finding him amazingly appealing.

Over hot jambalaya containing peppers, rice, sausage, tomatoes, spices, and crawdad tails served in thick white bowls, they carried on a civil conversation. Every time they got personal he carefully changed the subject back to neutral ground. Conscious he was exerting an effort to be affable, she assumed it was because he wanted the loan.

All through lunch Mike could feel the tension build between them. And exhilaration gripped him simply from being with her.

He paid, and they left through the kitchen, calling goodbye to the busy workers. He drove swiftly and in minutes he pulled up in front of a small brick building. Talia knew instantly that it would be a good investment. The neighboring shops were as attractive and busy as Mike had claimed. When he unlocked the door to the building, she asked in surprise "You have a key?"

"I told the owner I wanted to bring a banker by to look at it." He stepped back, holding the door for her, and she went ahead, catching the fresh cottony scent of his shirt as she passed him. She entered a room with a dusty floor. There was a back room, and Mike led her to that door and held it open so she could glance inside at the storage space. Empty crates were tumbled about. In the main room, she gazed at support posts, a box, and paper covering the front windows letting very little light into the place. She looked up at Mike.

His riveting blue eyes caught her off guard, mesmerizing her. He stood only inches away, and as Mike gazed down at her, she felt more attracted to him than wary of him. She didn't know precisely when her feelings toward Mike Stanton had changed, but she clearly recognized the tension between them as a physical response. She also knew that the more she learned about him, the more she liked him. Having heard a little about his humble past, Talia found herself wanting to know all about him.

"I don't see how this can fail to sell quickly," he said.

"Possibly," she replied cautiously, frightened by her reaction to him. She felt drawn to him, and she shouldn't be. "It's a tiny, run-down, empty building."

"The answer is no?"

"I'll look at your credit report—"

"And then you'll turn me down in spite of my credit rating," he said, his words making her stiffen. "A little prejudice, Mrs. Franklin?"

"That's my prerogative," she retorted, disturbed by him.

"And you'd refuse the loan, because you don't like me?"

She drew a deep breath, making her breasts strain against the linen and his gaze lowered. He could always make her feel as if he had stripped away every stitch of clothing in his mind. Her cool control shattered. "I'll have to study its investment possibilities," she said. "I should get back to the bank now."

"You're a little liar, Talia Franklin," he drawled. He stepped in front of her, blocking her path.

"Get out of my way." She raised her chin, glaring at him, dumbstruck by the curious blue eyes that seemed to make her heart stop. She was trapped again in another one of his silent contests of wills, caught by something deeper. His brows arched; his gaze lowered to her mouth.

"No!" Her heart thudded violently. "No!" she said again, trying to stop the tingling sensations she felt. But it was no use; it was as if she were fighting an unseen rushing current. With an imperious lift of her chin, she moved past him, brushing his shoulder.

Without thinking, Mike reached out and caught her arm, spinning her around. Her eyes opened wide with surprise, as if this was the first time in her life that a man had upset her usual poise.

His arrogance goaded her beyond reason. She tried to yank free of his grasp, but he pinned her arms at her side instantly, pulling her against his chest. Their faces were inches apart; both gasped for breath. Her lips parted, and the pupils of her eyes dilated.

"Is there anything there except ice?" he growled, lowering his head, unable to resist kissing her.

Talia struggled, and his arms tightened around her. She pursed her lips closed in a wild, silent battle. His tongue touched the corner of her mouth, played over her lips while she resisted him.

Finally Talia could not help responding to such insistent temptation. Her lips parted and Mike kissed her, his tongue probing deeply while both terror and ecstacy engulfed her. Her body responded instantly to him, desire shooting up from her loins.

Her last vestige of control vanished and she ardently returned his kisses, lost to the sensation of the moment. Holding her tightly, he kissed her as if she were the only woman in the world; as if they were removed from the restrictions of time and place and circumstance.

"Put your arms around me," he commanded, turning his head to kiss her mouth again. Trembling, she lifted her arms and did as he said, clinging to him until his hand slipped over her hip and down to her thigh. Suddenly reason came back to her like a cold north wind.

She broke away from him, gasping for breath. They stared at each other in shock, because there was no mistaking the fiery attraction that had just fanned into life between them.

As Mike watched her, he was overwhelmed by emotions; she was all woman, passionate and vulnerable. "Talia," he said softly, stroking her cheek, aware of her quick intake of breath. Recalling the steely control she always showed Mike realized how much she must have fought her impulses moments earlier. "Talia," he repeated, as if he had just made a monumental discovery. His heart threatened to burst through his rib cage, and he knew he would remember this afternoon for the rest of his life.

He gazed at her solemnly. All he wanted to do was make love to her. Yet she was another man's wife. And she was the wife of the man who had turned Ben into a feeble, unhappy old man. Mike had planned revenge for years and now that it was partly within his grasp, he did not want it. The last thing he wanted to do was hurt Talia Franklin.

Talia shivered and rubbed her arms. Stunned at her reaction to Mike's advances, she could only stare at him in wonder. "I'm married," she blurted, the words sounding like an argument to herself. Guilt consumed her even as she knew that should Mike reach for her again, she would probably walk right into his arms and respond as quickly as before. Indeed, at that moment, it was what she wanted more than anything.

"We'd better go," he said in a husky voice. At the door he turned her around to face him. "I guess I know now why we've always sparked each other whenever we met."

She wanted to say that this would never happen again, but she couldn't. "That's the first time since I've been married . . ." she said, her voice trailing away. Her gaze lowered to his mouth, and his heart hammered violently. He reached for her, sliding one hand around her waist, the other across the nape of her neck. In the past few minutes he had learned that this was the woman for him.

Her eyes flickered and seemed to darken, but she shook her head and resisted him. "No," she whispered. "I won't do that again."

She sounded panicky and uncertain. Her cool aplomb was gone, and her green eyes looked surprised as they searched his face for an explanation of what had just occurred between them. He brushed her lips, wanting more, so much more.

On the drive back to the bank and in her office, Talia was reserved and quiet, looking pale and shaken. She gave him papers, and he left. That night at home when he filled out the forms, he made false financial statements, listing his income, his net worth, and his investments as far less than they actually were. He had no intention of allowing the Franklins to know how wealthy he was. He had used the loan only as a ploy to get to see Talia again.

The incident caused a deeper rift in Talia's feelings for Tyler. Their relationship was already on rocky ground because of their battles over her job, over having a baby, and her independence. Long ago she had realized that she had been wearing blinders where Ty was concerned. She now saw him as an ordinary man with weaknesses and strengths instead of as a god. She realized more than ever before that she had been dazzled by Tyler because she had been young and inexperienced. Trying to blank out the moments with Mike, she refused to remember her yearning reaction, yet she couldn't keep him out of her thoughts. She had tried to hold her marriage together for several years now, but she couldn't help thinking it was becoming a long, futile struggle. For the first time she began to consider other alternatives, because Tyler would never change. And she feared she *was* changing. She could no longer accept his infidelities or his rigid attitudes. She craved love and acceptance and a nurturing partner. But she knew that Tyler would never agreeably let go something that was his.

Rebecca lounged on the patio, then went upstairs and showered. She had a date with Ed tonight. He wanted her to move in with him, and it suited her more than living with Talia, which she found tedious. When he could, Ty flirted with her, but he treated her in a condescending manner, as if he knew about her past, and that bothered Rebecca. She heard a door bang downstairs, and she knew the maid was in the kitchen. Rebecca stared at her reflection in the mirror, thinking of Tyler. He was so patronizing, so high and mighty, yet she would bet every diamond she owned that he wasn't faithful to Talia. She had heard rumors and Ed had given her the names of several mistresses but he had no proof.

Wondering what to wear, she remembered Talia's closet full of designer clothes. She could borrow a dress and return it without Talia ever knowing the difference. Her sister probably wouldn't care, anyway. Rebecca looked down at her nude body. Her skin was pink from the shower. Raking her fingers through her thick, black curls, she wrapped a blue terry towel around herself and started down the hall when she heard Ty's voice. Feeling devilish, she smiled to herself. Flirting with Tyler and confusing him would relieve her boredom. She sauntered down the hall as he came up the stairs, taking them two at a time until he reached the top and saw her. He paused, his gaze sweeping over her and she smiled at him.

He *was* a handsome man—she would never cease to be amazed at his attraction to Talia. His suit coat was negligently slung over his shoulder. His tie was unfastened and he had pulled his shirt out of his trousers. He looked as if he had started undressing as he climbed the stairs.

"In a hurry, Tyler?" she drawled, giving him a smile that she hoped was sultry.

He stood staring at her, a sardonic gleam in his eyes. He glanced once in the direction of the kitchen, then jerked his head toward the open door of his bedroom.

"I'm going to play golf. What do you want, Rebecca?" he asked as he walked into the bedroom.

"I need to get dressed, Tyler," she said playfully. "Talia said I could wear one of her outfits."

"You might as well come in and look."

Feeling reckless, she moved ahead of him. She heard the soft catch of the door behind her. She turned to look quizzically at him.

His gaze raked over her while he tossed his coat and tie on a chair. He pulled off his shirt and dropped it. He was a snob, but his body was well muscled, virile, and deeply tanned even though it was only March.

He looked her over, desire flaring in his expression. She let the towel slip lower and the bottom corner flipped open over her bare hip. She wanted to tease him.

Her gaze drifted down over his hairy chest, down to the bulge in his slacks, and she gave him an inviting, knowing smile. "I'll come back and look for a dress later."

She laughed, knowing he wanted her. As she walked toward the door, he caught her by her upper arms.

She gazed up at him and her amusement vanished at the harshness in his expression. There was a wildness in Tyler's gaze that scared her. "I was teasing. Let me go now."

"You've been begging for this!" He yanked away the towel. His breath caught as he looked down at her incredible breasts that were high, thrusting up at him in a manner that made it impossible for him to turn away. She had a beautiful body, and he burned with desire and curiosity. He wanted the conquest. Rebecca's nude body was tempting him beyond belief.

"Let go!" Rebecca snapped, struggling in earnest now.

He overpowered her easily, pulling her to him, his mouth coming down hard on hers, his hands roaming over her freely, feeling her hips against his.

He unbuckled his belt, pushing away his clothes.

Rebecca resisted him, anger washing over her like cold water. "You bastard. Forget it, Tyler. I'm leaving." She snapped, twisting to get away from him.

Catching her, he shoved her down on the bed, fell on top of her and fit himself between her smooth thighs. Rebecca's struggles and name-calling ceased. There was no stopping Tyler. He thrust into her and she moved beneath him, hating him for arousing her, hating herself for responding. This time she knew she had gone too far. Gasping for breath, he shuddered with release and then quickly moved away from her.

Satisfied, his interest vanishing now that he had possessed her, he stood up, looking down at her as she stared up at him. "You bastard," she whispered again.

"You're a cheap slut. Get out of this house by the end of the week." He crossed to his billfold, opening it and pulling out two one-hundred-dollar bills. He threw them down and they fluttered to rest on her bare stomach. "Get out." He reached down, yanking her up in a grip that bit into her flesh, pulling her close as he leaned over to look into her eyes. "Don't tell your sister."

Rebecca drew a deep breath and nodded, suddenly frightened of him. She had suffered beatings; she had seen men who were enraged, but they paled in comparison to the look in Tyler's eyes. In his wildest rage, Sam had never looked as mean as Tyler. "Do you understand?"

"Yes," she gasped.

He released her suddenly, and she fell. She threw the money at him. He hit her so swiftly that she barely saw the blow coming. It caught her on the side of her face. "Don't ever cross me," he said.

Snatching up the towel she stalked past him, forgetting about the maid, Abby, until she was in the hall, but no one was below. With shaking hands, Rebecca closed the door to her room behind her, leaned against it, and vowed she would get back at him. She went into her private bathroom and placed a cold cloth against her face. She looked at herself in the mirror. "I'll get even, Tyler Franklin!"

Rebecca moved in with Ed that night.

One Friday morning just before noon Talia answered her intercom and learned that Mike Stanton wanted to see her. Seconds later when he was ushered into her office, she sat with hands folded behind her desk, trying to erect a physical barrier between them.

"Good morning," he said, taking in her tailored navy suit and crisp white blouse. Color rose in her cheeks, but otherwise there was no indication that his presence affected her.

"I came in to repay my loan and thought I might take you to lunch and celebrate the quick sale of my property."

"Thanks, but I'm sorry, I shouldn't," she said swiftly.

The corner of his mouth lifted in sardonic amusement. "I just asked you to lunch—is it that dangerous?"

"You're not dangerous!"

"Good. Then let's go to lunch. I want to celebrate."

Suddenly she laughed, and her eyes sparkled. "Maybe I should put on a suit of armor instead of my jacket," she said lightly, catching him off guard. He was amazed at her ability to laugh at herself. And he couldn't help smiling in return. He liked her sense of humor.

"I'd say there's no need for armor between us! Besides, I'll be on my best behavior," he said, enjoying her glowing smile. As he took her jacket and held it for her, his hands brushed her shoulders, but if she noticed, she gave no indication.

"Ready for more jambalaya, or would you like a change?" he asked when they were in the Ferrari.

"The jambalaya was great," she said, noticing his large hands on the steering wheel, remembering clearly how strongly they had held her.

Suddenly she realized that he must have asked her something. "I'm sorry. My thoughts drifted," she said, burning with embarrassment, amazed how he always threw her off balance.

He gave her another quick, searching glance. "I asked how the sailing has been."

"Great. I was out early Saturday morning and the lake was perfect."

They went to the same restaurant and were seated at the same corner table. Mike was his most charming. He listened to her and he asked her about her career and what she liked about the bank. Talia talked, unaware of time passing, while he seemed to give her his undivided attention. When she glanced at her watch and saw it was half-past one, she was horrified.

"I didn't know it was so late."

"No, neither did I," he said with a grin, watching her. "I was enjoying the company."

Pleased, she stood up, and he helped her on with her suit jacket. She should have ignored his light touches but she couldn't. Outside he opened the car door, then moved so he blocked her way. Startled, she looked up to meet his direct stare.

Her lashes fluttered, and his gaze lowered to her mouth while he momentarily enjoyed the memory of her kisses. Talia's lips parted; she touched the tip of her tongue to her lower lip, realized what she had done, and closed her mouth quickly. His suit coat was negligently open while wind ruffled his curls. He was handsome in a rugged, commanding way. He was so tall that she had to look up at him. With a mocking smile, he stepped aside and she climbed into the car.

On the drive back to the bank as they approached an intersection, the green arrow for their lane flashed on. The brown car ahead of them was going over forty, speeding toward the broad intersection where two four-lane highways crossed. As it turned into the intersection and Mike followed, he saw an approaching green car coming up fast, still trying to get through before the light changed, heading straight for the brown car.

"Oh, sweet Jesus!" Mike muttered. Talia gasped as he jammed his foot on the brake.

18

The green car barreled through the intersection straight toward the brown car. Mike applied the brakes, the tires squealed, and the car swerved while he gripped the wheel, fighting to avoid the two in front of him. Talia gasped, hearing Mike swear as they skidded to a stop. The two cars hit in the center of the broad intersection.

Bits of glass and metal flew through the air while the fronts of the cars crumpled like toys. A car door flew open and a man tumbled out from the passenger side. Steam and smoke spewed into the air.

For the first few seconds after the crash, no one moved. Then Mike leaped from his car and ran to the brown car. A man was slumped over the steering wheel; another man was stretched out on the pavment.

Stunned, Talia stepped out as Mike leaned into the car, applying his handkerchief to the driver's bleeding scalp.

"I'm here to help. You'll be all right," Mike said quietly in a reassuring voice. Talia hurried to the gas station at the corner and told the attendant to call the police and an ambulance.

When she returned to the intersection, people still sat in their cars, lines of traffic forming as those nearest the accident seemed to be in shock. Mike had moved the driver of the green car to the pavement. He lay with his feet elevated and with Mike's suit coat and another man's coat covering him. Mike knelt over him pumping his chest, applying cardiopulmonary resuscitation.

Talia stepped into the intersection and motioned to a lane of cars to move, and in seconds, she was directing traffic.

About five minutes after an ambulance arrived, a bystander offered to take over her post. She turned to hear Mike talking to the paramedic about the injured people. Police had arrived, and Mike gave them his name and phone number as a witness. He climbed into his Ferrari beside Talia, and he maneuvered the car through the traffic.

Mike drove in silence, turning onto a side street of quiet two-story houses and tall oaks. He cut the motor and turned to her. "Are you all right?"

She was pale and a lock of her hair tumbled down on her shoulder. She gave a positive shake of her head. "Yes, I'm fine."

"Liar," he said gently. It seemed natural to reach for her, leaning over the gear lever and space between their seats. They were both shaken, and she clung to him. She was soft and smelled sweet and he closed his eyes, his arms tightening around her.

"The person who was thrown from the car was killed, wasn't he?" she asked.

"Yes," Mike answered gruffly, holding her tightly, remembering how she had risen to the occasion. She had been a great help. After a moment she pulled away, running her hand across her forehead.

"Sorry. That was unnerving," she said.

"You never let your hair down, do you?" he asked in a husky voice, playing with the fallen curl.

"Ty likes it this way," she said perfunctorily, her mind on the wreck, aware that Mike had been capable of more kindness and consideration than she had previously attributed to him. Her gaze met his while she wondered if his words held a double meaning. She was conscious of his nearness, of his fingers touching her hair. "He says it makes me look more sophisticated."

Mike pulled out one of her hair pins and let another lock fall. "You did a bang-up job back there. You should have been a traffic cop."

"I didn't even know what I was doing. I just did it. You're the one who should get the credit. The man you worked on regained consciousness. Where did you get medical training?"

"In the Air Force; I was a Pararescue medic in Vietnam. Everyone should learn C.P.R. Our motto was, 'That Others May Live.' "

She stared at him, seeing another side to him. He had always appeared so hard and tough, yet he had been competent and compassionate in handling the accident. "You did a good job driving, or we would have been in the crash, too."

He barely heard her. With her hair falling over her shoulders, she looked younger, more beautiful. He was close enough now to see tiny flecks of gold in her eyes near the dark pupils. He let his hand slide behind her neck. She had been looking beyond him, but now her gaze met his and she inhaled deeply, waiting.

Desire ignited in Mike like a flame, and he lowered his mouth to hers. He brushed her lips lightly, winding his fingers in her thick, soft hair, tasting her sweet, scalding kisses. His arousal was swift and hard.

As soon as his lips touched hers, Talia's heart seemed to thud against her ribs. Mike's kisses made her tremble even though she didn't want them to affect her. He left her breathless. What she felt went beyond Mike's sweet kisses. This was a man who had grudgingly won her admiration. He wasn't part of a fantasy as Tyler had been. Nor did she see him as naively as she had seen Ty. Mike attracted her in spite of their past conflicts because he was sensitive to others, sincere in his own feelings, and most of all, understanding of others' shortcomings.

Finally she pushed away gently, and he released her. "I shouldn't have done that," she whispered, turning away. "I need to get back."

"Yeah," he answered gruffly, looking at her. He swore quietly and turned to start the engine. He drove more slowly and more carefully than usual.

"Mike. Take me home please. I can't go to work like this."

He glanced at her. Her mouth was red from his kisses, her hair falling in a golden cloud over her shoulders. "You look gorgeous," he said, his voice holding a rough note. The pink in her cheeks heightened. "I'll wait while you change and take you back to the bank."

"You don't have to do that."

"I'll wait."

At the house, she told him to fix himself a drink while she changed. "You know where everything is."

She seemed tense, and he suspected she was nervous about having him in the house.

"Go change. I'll wait outside on the patio," he said, walking through the house. He sank down in a chaise, his nerves rattled, though he didn't know whether that was due to the accident or Talia's kiss.

"I'm ready," she said from the doorway, and it took all his control to keep from walking straight to her and taking her in his arms. She had changed to a navy sailor dress with stylish brass buttons and a wide white bow at the neckline. One look at her green eyes and Mike knew that if he tried to kiss her, she would let him. But he hesitated. When she turned away abruptly, he followed. Both remained silent on the drive to the bank.

Knowing that she entered the Crescent City Classic each year, Mike signed up for the ten-thousand-meter road race sponsored primarily by *The Times-Picayune* and Coca-Cola. The race was on Saturday during the second week in April, 1982. Ty usually entered, but at golf last Saturday Mike learned that Ty had to fly with some oilmen to meet with some Michigan bankers.

Mike parked, glancing at the old buildings in the Quarter, thinking how far he had come. He now owned several apartments, which were sound investments because they were still appreciating in value; some drew the highest rent in town. The ambience of the Vieux Carré was the heart of New Orleans. The timeless charm of the old buildings, the mixture of food and music and people, would always be here, providing an excellent investment as far as he was concerned. He hummed as he headed for Jackson Square, his nerves tingling in anticipation. Overhead the sky was blue and clear and camellias were still in bloom. Across Decatur Street beyond the levee a barge was headed down the Mississippi. Around him, people were gathering for the race.

It was easy to spot Talia in the crowd. Her hair was in a long braid down her back, a sweatband around her forehead. She wore red shorts and a red knit shirt and flashed a smile at him when he approached. His heartbeat quickened as his gaze swept over her, lingering on her long, bare legs.

"Hi," he said, his voice dropping. Her gaze flickered, and she smiled up at him.

"Hi," Talia repeated, excitement coursing in her. She had spotted him half a block away, his head and brown curls showing above the crowd.

"Ready to run?"

"As ready as I'll ever be. How're the vacant lots doing?"

"I'll be in the bank next week. I sold them."

"Maybe we should turn some bank repossessions over to you."

"I'll be glad to take them on."

"I did give your number to one of our clients who's looking for an apartment complex," she said, trying to ignore the rapid beating of her heart. Mike looked incredibly fit in his white tank top and green shorts; his body was lean, muscular, and tan.

"Thanks. What's his name?"

"Walter Riera. I just gave it to him Friday," she said, her gaze returning to linger on his chest, which was partially bare because of the skimpy tank top.

"How's the banking business?"

"Pretty good. I just got a promotion."

"Congratulations! What's your title?"

"Executive vice president," she said, unable to keep a note of satisfaction out of her voice.

He smiled at her. "That's great! That ought to charge you up enough to win the race."

"Thanks," she said, pleased at Mike's praise. She hadn't told Tyler yet, because it would only annoy him.

"When did you get the promotion?"

"Yesterday. You're the first to know." She spoke before she thought, and quickly realized that he could misinterpret her comment.

"We'll celebrate. After the race I'll buy you a drink."

"Okay. You're on," she said. Tyler was out of town, and a drink with Mike should be harmless. She refused to analyse her motives further.

"They're lining up," Mike said, looking at the mass of people in the street. The air was warm; a trumpeter played, the music adding to the festive air.

"Pretty good music," she said,

"You like jazz?" When she nodded, he said, "Then sometime you'll have to hear some friends of mine from the Quarter. They're the best."

"You grew up in the Quarter, didn't you?"

"On the fringe." He looked around. "That was long ago. The good part I'll always remember. This is a unique town, and I love it—the Creole food, the jazz, Mardi Gras, the people, the Saints, the Mississippi, the history."

"Mr. Chamber of Commerce!" she exclaimed, smiling. "I like it here too." She moved toward the crowd gathering at the starting line. "You'll have to wait for me at the finish."

"That's what you think," he said with a crooked grin. The gun fired for the start and everyone began to jog, run and walk, streaming down the street in bright sunshine. Mike fell into step beside her and she had to laugh. "You won't come in first at this rate!"

"I don't give a damn if I don't come in first."

Startled, she looked up at him, and realized how refreshing his words sounded, and how accustomed she had become to Tyler always trying to get in the lead in every competition. "If you stick with me, you may bring up the rear."

"It wouldn't be the first time in my life. You jog every day?"

"Just about."

"Do you ever run on a track?"

"Three days a week, usually Monday, Wednesday, and Friday, I run at the high-school track close to our house."

"Cleveland School?"

"Yes."

"What time do you jog?"

"About seven, when Ty leaves. I jog until half-past and then rush home, shower, change, and get to work. That's the advantage of living close to the bank."

"It's also the advantage of being your own boss." He winked at her. "What else do you do?"

"Tyler and I usually go out every night on the weekend. We eat at the club on Sunday nights. What do you do, Mike? Who's the lady in your life?" she asked casually, but her attention to his answer wasn't casual.

"No specific one. I usually go out every night on the weekend," he said, making her smile, something he found he enjoyed. They talked about politics, the race, and movies. She ran easily and wasn't winded, and it was easy for him to keep pace with her. Talking all the time, they followed the course through the historic Garden District where the senior Franklins lived, along Prytania Street to Audubon Park.

They finished in a respectable time and walked to a nearby restaurant, where they sat on a balcony beneath an awning. Mike ordered lunch and drinks. She felt more relaxed than she had in a long time, grateful for this one day of celebrating her promotion, enjoying Mike, and refusing to think about tomorrow. When he asked her to go sailing, she accepted. The breeze was sufficient, a cloudbank building to the southwest, golden rays of sun shimmering across the water like streamers of fire. She watched him obliquely as he sat at the tiller. He was fun, relaxed and easygoing. His shoulders were broad, his arms muscular. Her pulse skipped as she studied him until he turned to meet her gaze.

They returned to the dock and Mike drove her to another plain café on the lakeshore. The crossed the cypress plank floor to a table at the window with a view of the lake. The tables were covered in white paper, and ceiling fans turned slowly. While they talked, Mike drank a cold beer. She found it difficult to keep her gaze from roaming over him constantly. His muscular forearms were covered with short, curly brown hairs, and his only jewelry was a thin gold watch on one wrist.

The blackened redfish was cooked to perfection, the skillet corn bread hot and golden, and the coffee thick and black.

"How'd you get to know Tyler?"

"I worked for his family. He has two younger brothers, and I was hired as a nanny."

"I've seen the kids on the boat and wondered. I knew they weren't sons."

"No," she said, looking away.

His brows arched. "Sorry. I said the wrong thing."

Startled, she stared at him, wondering how he had guessed her thoughts. "Don't apologize. We've wanted a baby for a long time," she said, thinking how easy it was to talk to Mike.

"If you really want a child, there's such a thing as adoption, Talia," he said gently.

"I'd adopt. Ty won't. It won't have the Franklin blood."

They were quiet a moment, and then he asked, "Go ahead, tell me about when you went to work for the Franklins. What did you do before that?"

He lounged in the corner of their booth while she talked, and he seemed to listen to every word she said with keen interest.

"I had an ordinary life until I was eighteen. I was going to graduate, go to college. I didn't realize how sheltered my life had been. I came home one day and my father had committed suicide and I had to go to work."

"Sorry. That's tough. Where's your mother?"

"She had a nervous breakdown afterward. She was in the state hospital. After I married Tyler we moved her to a private sanitarium."

"What happened to your house?" he asked, constantly fighting the urge to touch her.

"My father had mortgaged everything. We lost it all. I guess that's why I want to work. All three of us, Rebecca, Mom, and I depended on Daddy totally and that was disastrous. I feel compelled to be independent. When I think of quitting work and depending on Tyler for everything, it worries me."

"Kind of a panicky feeling deep inside," he said gently, and she was astounded that he understood what Tyler couldn't see at all.

"Yes, it is, even though I know it's unreasonable."

"So are a lot of things some of us do," he said. "We always carry with us some of the child we once were."

"I suppose. I don't even use the income I earn most of

the time. Tyler told me to put it into a savings account or investments." She told Mike about her past, her job, finding him the easiest person to talk to she had ever known. "What about your life?"

"I practically grew up on the street until I met Ben Holloway. Except when I was a little kid. I lived with my grandfolks back on a bayou."

"Did you really?" she asked, surprised at his rustic beginnings.

"Like to fish?"

"I've never tried."

"I'll take you sometime. We'll go in a pirogue back where there are gators and crawfish."

Her eyes sparkled, and for a moment both of them seemed to forget that he couldn't take her fishing. In the next room a man played a banjo, a woman sat at the piano, and the crowd in the bar joined them. After dinner Mike and Talia moved to the bar to have brandy and join in the singing. The room was aglow with lanterns. The wooden bar and tables were scarred with initials carved on their tops and from drink rings. It was dusky, smoky, and relaxed, and as Talia sang, she glanced across the table to see Mike watching her.

With a jerk of his head, he stood up and took her hand and they moved to the crowd by the piano. Mike helped her onto a barstool and stood beside her while they sang along with the others. His hand rested lightly on her waist, and her arm was draped casually across his bare shoulders.

She was as conscious of his hand on her waist as she would have been if they had been alone and there wasn't clothing beneath his palm. She was aware of every inch of her flesh that touched him, of the hard muscle and warm flesh beneath her fingers. His voice was deep and full, and she realized she had enjoyed the day more than she could remember anytime for years. Mike was relaxed, confident, and he seemed to be truly interested in everything around him, but mostly in her. And she knew she was on dangerous ground.

When she glanced at her watch and saw it was after eleven o'clock, she felt a little jolt of surprise. "I'd better go home," she said, leaning over to speak in his ear.

"What's that?" Mike asked, his hand tightening on her

waist. He had heard exactly what she said, but he liked her being close; he wanted the excuse to hold her even closer.

She moved closer to tell him again and he nodded, lifting her off the bar stool. As they approached her house, she became quiet, realizing she shouldn't have spent the day with him. He pulled up to the back door and stopped.

"That's a big dark house. Let me come in with you."

"You don't need to," she said, politely, and the only indication that they were more than casual friends was a husky note in his voice and a breathlessness in hers that she was trying to control.

"None of that nonsense," he ordered, and stepped out. He took the key from her hands, and she turned off the burglar alarm.

"I forgot to turn on the timer. Usually the lights switch on automatically if I remember to do my part," she said without really thinking about timers or lights or anything except that she was alone with him.

"I'll look through quickly and make sure you're safe."

"I'm fine, Mike," she said, switching on a kitchen light. "It would take all night to look around."

"I don't mind," he said in his husky voice.

"I do." She shook her head. "I shouldn't have stayed with you all day. . . ." Her voice faded; all she could think of was that she wanted him to kiss her and it wasn't right to want or allow it. "Thanks for the dinner and the celebration." As if trying to memorize the moment, she gazed intently at the crisp dark curls showing above the scoop neck of his tank top, his bronzed, muscled shoulders, and his narrow hips. In spite of his toughness, he had an easygoing manner that enabled him to let others win, to enjoy life and people.

The desire in his blue eyes took her breath away. "It was grand," he whispered, waging an inner battle and losing. He reached for her.

"Mike, don't," she said, but her protest was feeble. His arms tightened, crushing her hard against his chest, his mouth covering hers.

For a moment she yielded to her feelings, wrapping her arms around his neck, taking his kisses and returning them, trying to block out everything else. She was amazed once again at her reaction to him. There was no question that what she felt was more than physical desire. Mike was special to her, *so very special*. She felt his swift, hard arousal and she pushed away. "I'm married," she said as if reminding herself. "No."

She stared at him wide-eyed, her breathing ragged, and he suspected it would be so easy to overcome her protests; it would take only the slightest force for the first few minutes and he could possess her. And he wanted her more than he had ever wanted any other woman. The realization shocked him; his eyes narrowed as he watched her, seconds passing in the taut silence. In that moment he knew that he loved her. He had spent empty years looking for a woman who satisfied a yearning deep within him, and now that he had found her, she was absolutely inaccessible.

He refused to think about the possibilities. His eyes blazed with anger at himself, at the circumstances, at the incredible need he felt. He yanked her back into his arms and kissed her deeply, bending over her so she had to cling to him. Her soft, *marvelous* body molded against his.

Releasing her abruptly, he stepped away. "Good night, Talia. It was fun," he said, his voice gruff because what he felt for her was true and strong and as clear as a noonday sun.

Her heart pounded violently. She closed the door behind him, listening to the Ferrari motor surge to life and then fade away. Tears stung her eyes because she felt trapped.

Mike took the drive too fast. The woman he wanted more than anything was *Mrs. Tyler Franklin*. He swore bitterly, thinking that if he searched for the rest of his lifetime, he would never find another woman who would interest him as much as Talia. What was even worse in Mike's mind was that Tyler was ruthless, ambitious, jealous, and self-centered. He didn't deserve Talia. Mike eased his foot off the gas pedal, realizing he was miles over the speed limit. He couldn't believe that the only woman he had ever felt magically attracted to—the only woman he could consider spending the rest of his life with—belonged to another man. He swore again, gripping the wheel so tightly it hurt his knuckles.

Monday when Talia was jogging, there were two men running, one at a slower pace than she, the other at a faster rate. It was bright and quiet and clear outside in the hush of early morning before traffic and before the high school stirred with activity.

"What a gorgeous view!" came an appreciative male voice that sent a tingle racing in her.

She turned to see Mike grinning at her, and he caught up easily.

"I didn't know you jogged here," she said.

"Sure."

"How often in the past?"

"Never." They both smiled, and Mike quickly noticed her blue shirt and blue shorts. "But I'll be here every Monday, Wednesday, and Friday after this."

"That's ridiculous!"

He was barechested, his stomach a washboard of sinewy muscles, the dark curls on his chest tapering to a thin line across his stomach. He turned around to run backward, facing her, his gaze going down over her in a manner that made her flesh tingle.

"To think I've been jogging where all I have to look at are dogs and kids and cars!"

"If you don't look where you're going, you're going to fall flat."

"I've already fallen," he said solemnly, and her heart skipped beats as she gazed into his eyes.

Suddenly she realized that he was about to run backward off the track. A long, low wooden bench was on the sidelines right behind him. "Mike!"

He twisted, and sprang up as he hit it, vaulting over it and landing on the other side. He grinned and shrugged, stepping over and coming back as she laughed and shook her head. "Look where you're going now."

"But I'm having more fun my way," he said.

"You're attracting attention."

"Those two men? They aren't watching *me*."

"They're watching to see what you'll run into next." She reached out and caught his arm, pulling him around so he could run beside her. "You're going to kill a jogger if you don't watch it."

"Watch what?"

"Where you're going."

"I'd rather watch where you're going."

They ran easily together as they talked about the work they each had for the day. She learned he was showing an out-of-town investor some condominiums in Metairie, that he was calling on some potential investors in the afternoon. She told him that the bank examiners were coming tomorrow and would undoubtedly turn their records into a mess. "We have to take them whatever files they want the instant they ask for them. They study the classified loans."

"What are those?" he asked, turning to run facing her again.

"Each bank has its own system for rating loans as to how good they are. The examiners look to see if the bank has classified them correctly for the way the loans are performing. They verify the real value of the collateral if payments are slow or missed."

"They just come once every couple of years, don't they?"

She laughed. "Here I've been telling you all about them, and you sound as if you already know."

"Just a little. I call on bankers about investments sometimes."

"I'm going to be late. I've got to go," she said reluctantly.

"I'll go too," he said, falling into step beside her, stopping at her car. He put his arms out, bracing himself against her car, hemming her in between the car and his body. "I wish we could keep on running or talking or something," he said, looking at her mouth. When she didn't answer, he said gruffly, "See you at the track Wednesday morning."

He held the door and winked as he closed it.

She drove home and later to work, remembering every word he had said, and the few casual touches they shared. Each moment was etched in her mind with absolute clarity, particularly a vision of Mike, running barechested in front of her, his body virile and healthy, his blue eyes always sparking an electric current.

Wednesday morning he was already on the track when she

arrived. She watched him run in a long, easy stride, the muscles in his legs flexing. She went out to wait until he came around the track again, falling into step beside him as he slowed down to her pace.

"Don't slow on my account."

"I can't think of a better reason to slow down. It's seems like years since I saw you last."

She looked ahead, trying to keep her voice level. "You shouldn't say things like that to me. I'm married."

"I know what you are," he said sharply. "Are you crewing in the regatta that's coming up?"

"No. I won't do it again. I didn't like it."

"I guess you wouldn't," he said gently. "Sometime I'd like to meet your mother."

"Fine," she said with a slight twist of pain, because she was constantly reminded of how limited their friendship could be. She barely knew Ben Holloway and she would never get to know him better, yet he was so important to Mike.

It was a beautiful April morning, Mike was beside her, and she didn't want to think or talk about Tyler. Mike's brown curls were in disarray—soft, temptingly dishevelled—and she imagined how they would feel tangled in her fingers. "Why's your boat named the *Sparrow*?" she asked in an attempt to focus on a less personal subject.

"I thought the little bird ought to get some equal attention. Boats are named the *Eagle* and the *Hawk* a lot. Give the little fellow some acknowledgment," he said, turning to run backward again.

"You're the type who always cheers for the underdog, right?"

"Probably. Why's yours named the *Rio*?"

"Tyler bought it after we got back from our honeymoon in Rio," she said quietly and saw what she thought was a flicker of pain in his eyes. He turned to run beside her again. She glanced at the slight crook in his nose. She was on his left now and noticed the scar down his face. She knew it was done by Leech, the guy Mike had told her about and she wondered once again just how bad things had been for Mike growing up.

"I meant it about your mother. When do you go see her next?"

"Probably Friday after work."

"I'd like to meet you there."

"That would be nice. It'll take until six for me to get there."

"Can you tell Tyler you'll be gone for dinner?"

"Sorry. We have plans to meet friends that evening."

When they walked to the parking lot, he casually draped his arm across her shoulder, then seemed to realize what he was doing and moved away. They both looked at each other, and they realized how comfortable they had become with one another and how volatile such comfort could become.

Mike had parked beneath an oak and he took her arm. "Come sit down with me a minute where we can talk."

Her pulse beat faster. She nodded, knowing they could talk perfectly well on the grassy expanse between the track and the graveled lot where they stood.

As he slid into the car, he turned to face her. "There isn't anyone in the parking lot now because the other joggers have gone home. There's a dumpster between us and the street and no one can see us," he said huskily.

"Mike, I can't—"

As if he hadn't heard, he leaned over, his mouth brushing hers lightly, yet his kiss was scalding and made her tremble. He slipped his arms around her. The gears between them were in his way and Mike swore, releasing her.

"I should go," she said breathlessly, climbing out of the car. She waved and hurried away from him, fighting the longing to get back in his car and cling to him.

During May they saw each other constantly at parties, at the yacht club, at the country club, and once at the Superdome. The moment Talia entered a room, Mike felt more alive, and he would turn to meet her wide-eyed green gaze that no longer was glacial, but smoldering and inviting. They jogged together and often ate lunch together. The ties that neither would openly acknowledge grew steadily stronger.

The more Talia was drawn to Mike, the more intolerable

life became with Tyler. The sparkle in her relationship with Tyler had long ago been extinguished as they each became busier and as their fighting occurred more often. She frequently fell asleep on a couch or in the guest bedroom, using first one excuse and then another to Tyler in order to escape physical intimacy. She had no illusions that Ty was living a celibate life; she had known for years that there were other women, but she no longer cared.

Mike met Kate, and visited her again the next week with Talia. As they left Kate on the lawn by the pond, Mike took Talia's arm and led her around the building to the parking lot.

On the deserted east side beneath a spreading live oak with gnarled branches and moss trailing in streamers, he tugged on her arm and turned her to face him. He wore a gray glen-plaid lightweight wool suit and a maroon tie. Brown lashes framed his eyes, and she ached to feel his arms around her.

"We're alone." He waved his hands helplessly. "I feel like a kid sneaking around trying to avoid a chaperon, only it really isn't that simple."

"No, it's not. And we're sort of in a public place," she protested, but was lost to a hungry need that had built like a tidal wave. She hadn't wanted to stop and assess what she felt for Mike, but she knew. He was becoming vital to her. Even though they did ordinary things, the moments with him were the most precious in her life.

His eyes were compelling and a deep longing tugged at her. Her gaze shifted to his mouth.

"Oh, hell," he said softly, stepping close and taking her in his arms to kiss her.

Her heart thudded violently. She wrapped her arms tightly around him, wanting him more than she had ever wanted anything in her life. "Mike," she whispered, gazing up into eyes darkened with emotion as he lowered his head to kiss her again.

When he released her, she looked at him solemnly. "I never thought I'd do something like this," she said, her voice throaty and breathless, her heart pounding, because she wanted to pull him close and never let go.

"Well, I sure as hell didn't plan it this way!" he snapped, his gaze burning with anger and desire. He wanted her. She was beautiful; she was *necessary* if he were to keep his sanity. He felt complete with her.

He crushed her to him, bending over her, holding her tightly, knowing someone could come along at any moment, knowing she had to go home to another man. He released her abruptly, his look crazed, a frown creasing his brow. She turned and walked away swiftly, and in moments he followed her to tell her goodbye in the parking lot.

"I wish you could go eat dinner with me. You could tell Tyler you're eating here."

"No, I couldn't," she said, meaning it. This situation was getting out of hand. She had to stop it from going further.

He saw she was fighting to control her emotions, and he wanted to crush her in his arms and take her home with him. She lifted her chin.

"I'm all right."

"Yeah. You have the busiest social life of anyone in New Orleans."

"Tyler just has to keep on the go, to get out and meet people, to do things. Besides we're not that compatible when it's just the two of us," she said, stating something she had realized long ago.

Mike rubbed his knuckles lightly on her cheek. She tried to resist the compulsion to turn and kiss his hand.

"Goodbye, Mike," she whispered.

"Until next time," he said, watching her go.

Rebecca moved around the room brushing her hair in quick strokes while Ed stood in front of a mirror knotting his tie. She tossed the brush on the bed and pulled on her stockings. Clad in a black bra and bikinis, Rebecca was dressing to go to dinner with Ed. "How much do you know about Tyler?" she asked casually.

"Enough."

She paused. "What's that mean?"

His hazel eyes gazed at her reflection in the mirror, and he turned around to look at her. "What do you want to know?"

She shrugged. "Does he ever do anything he shouldn't?"

"How long a list do you want?"

Startled, she asked, "Tyler? I don't mean being unfaithful to Talia. I know he does that."

"I'll bet you do," he said, eyeing her.

"Don't get that gleam in your eye again!" she snapped, knowing Ed had an uncanny knack for guessing things. "You promised to feed me."

"I will. I didn't say when."

"You said tonight. What else has he done?"

"He cheats when he sails in races; I imagine he cheats in everything he does. He cheats at the bank."

"How?" she asked fastening her hose to her garter belt.

"I'll tell you the answer to that one after midnight."

"Why?" she asked, straightening up to face him.

His gaze raked over her again. "To see what kind of bargain I can strike with you for the information. What you'll do for me if I tell you what you want to know."

She smiled, knowing what he wanted. "I think you have a double supply of hormones."

"Maybe so, sweetie. Let's get back early and see what my hormones can do."

She laughed, watching him, wondering what Tyler had done at the bank.

It was one in the morning before she found out, and she couldn't keep a grin of malice off her face. "Ed, honey," she drawled, letting her fingers run along his bare thigh while she sat nude on his waterbed beside him.

"What do you want, Rebecca?"

"Bring me copies of some of the loan applications Tyler has falsified."

His hazel eyes bore into hers. "What will you do with them?"

"I'm going to show them to my sister. Tyler Franklin has this coming."

"You're not thinking. You cause my bank to fail, I go down with it."

"How long can he keep up before he's caught?"

"You have a point. We have the regional supervisor for southern Louisiana, plus five more bank examiners from the Office of the Comptroller of the Currency of the U. S. Treasury coming again in two weeks."

She studied him, shifting her thoughts to Ed. "What will you do if there's trouble?"

"I'm clear."

"I'll bet you are," she said, bringing a grin to his face. She had learned not to underestimate Ed. He wasn't what he appeared. She found him devious, sly, and clever, with a voracious sexual appetite. "You look like Mr. Average American."

"I am."

"Like hell you are!"

"What have I done?"

"Well, if we start with sex—"

"Skip that. What else?"

"Your body. When you're dressed all your muscles don't show."

"Muscles don't show beneath a suit."

"You can tell on some men, but not on you."

"It's my plain face, sweetie. Tyler Franklin has difficulty remembering my name even though he's promoted me to vice president of the Trust Department for the work I've done."

"Ed," she said, her thoughts going back to Ty, "he's going to get caught anyway. Why don't you move on now?"

"I'm making plans."

Excitement gripped her. "Then bring me copies of the applications. Sooner or later Tyler will get caught, and if you have another job, I want them."

"You sure you won't show them to the Feds?"

"Oh, no!" she said with a smile. "I'll just show them to Talia. He thinks Talia is so holy. In spite of his affairs, he keeps her on a pedestal."

"Isn't that a little incongruous?"

"Yes, but that's Tyler. He isn't unfaithful to her emotionally, only physically. He thinks she's perfect, too good for anyone else to disturb. I know my sister. Her conscience will make her turn him in."

"You are a little witch. But I think you're wrong. She wouldn't bring her own world crashing down around her. And if it's ever discovered she knew what he was doing, *her* career in banking would be over. And when it comes out about Tyler, her superiors will ask her if she knew about it —any bank will ask wherever or whenever she wants work."

"Talia will survive easily. With their money she doesn't need to work anyway."

"Of course, there's Talia and Mike Stanton. The looks he gives her would melt ice. And vice versa."

"My sister and another man? Never!"

"Watch them, sweetie. And if you want to see someone doing a slow burn, look at Tyler watching them."

Rebecca laughed. "It would serve him right!" Her smile faded, and she shook her head. "Talia is too proper, and Mike Stanton is all man—he doesn't look the type to settle for friendly conversation at chance meetings. Talia will never have an affair. You're wrong. And you'll see I'm right about the loans. She'll turn Tyler in to the authorities." Rebecca wriggled beside him, her hip pressing against his thigh. "Please, Ed. Bring me copies." She bent down to run the tip of her tongue over him.

"How many do you want?" he asked gruffly, his fingers winding in her hair.

Ed kept Rebecca continually off guard. He was impulsive, so when he came home the next day and said he wanted to take her to Dallas the next Friday after work, she was surprised and pleased. He told her to pack a good dress and he would buy her something at Neiman's and take her to dinner. They drove to Dallas, and Saturday morning they went to Neiman-Marcus, where Ed bought her an Albert Nipon black silk dress. Entranced with her gift, because it had been a long time since a man had bought her such a lavish one, she hummed as they turned into a jewelry store.

"Go along with me," Ed said, and winked.

He was dressed in a conservative navy suit, and as he talked to the blond woman who wanted to help them, he was pleasant and friendly, placing the Neiman's box on a high chair where it was plainly visible. His diamond ring flashed in the bright lights of the store as he said, "I want to buy my wife another diamond ring. We'll celebrate our tenth wedding anniversary this month and we're going to take our three kids and fly to Acapulco to celebrate."

His accent switched from Louisianan to Texan, and he patted Rebecca's hand. She smiled, curious about what he was leading up to. "Nothing's too good for my sugar. I want at least two carats."

"How nice, Mr.—?"

"Jackson. Philip Jackson. And this is my wife, Mary."

"I'm Ruth Browder. So glad to meet you. You live in Dallas?"

"Yep. I'm in the brokerage business."

"Let me show you some diamonds," Ruth Browder said, disappearing behind a door, returning with a small bag. She placed a velvet tray in front of them and dropped out loose stones that glittered and caught the light.

They studied stones while Rebecca wondered if Ed would buy a ring for her, yet she couldn't imagine his doing so in addition to the dress.

"What kind of mountings can you show me?" Ed asked, and Ruth Browder leaned down to pull out a tray. "Wait a minute, he said, pointing to a tray of mountings farther down the counter. "I see one there I like."

She leaned down with her back momentarily to them. Ed reached out to pick up a stone, his hands moving over them, then he dropped it back in place. They looked at diamonds for another quarter of an hour, narrowing it down to two that pleased him.

"Mary and I'll talk about it, and we'll come back. If you'll give me your card, I'll call and let you know. Then I'll be back downtown Monday when I come to work and I'll stop in and get the one she wants."

They made arrangements, thanked her, and left. Outside the store Ed took Rebecca's arm. "Move it, sweetie. We're hot."

She looked up at him. "What?"

He pulled a stone out of his pocket, the light sparkling in its depth. She stopped in her tracks, her jaw dropping open. He caught her arm and pulled her along. "Come on, baby, or we may be behind bars." They turned a corner and she took little running steps to keep up with him.

"Here's the car," he said, unlocking the door and tossing the Neiman's box inside, hurrying to climb in. In seconds they pulled away from the curb and were in traffic, and he grinned at her triumphantly.

"How'd you do that?" she asked. "She would have noticed if a stone was missing."

"One wasn't missing."

"What did you do?"

"I switched stones. There's an inexpensive yellow diamond with a flaw back there in the tray. I dropped it in and picked up this one."

"I'll be damned!" she said in awe. "She didn't even watch you either."

"Don't I look trustworthy?"

"Yeah, you do. Dogs and kids love you. A stranger would probably trust you with her kids."

"I'll get your ring made at home. You can get rid of that garish rock you wear. This is a better stone."

"I'll have Bar—Gideon's ring made into a necklace."

"Drop the phony husband bit, too, Rebecca."

She stared at him, feeling a shiver run across her shoulders, too shocked to deny his accusation. "How'd you know?"

"You've slipped on the name before. You never talk about him. A hunch." She stared at him. She had never known anyone like him. He told her he had grown up in New Orleans, gone to LSU, started in Management Training at the bank, and lived a very ordinary life. But Ed Dessauer was anything but an ordinary man. She had met his parents and *they* were ordinary people, friendly, pleasant, and proud of their son.

"We're wanted," she said in awe.

He grinned. "Yeah, but it was fun."

"Have you ever done that before?"

"Nothing like that, but I've thought about it before."

She was shocked by him, aware that it wasn't the first time he had surprised her and suspecting it wouldn't be the last. They drove home to New Orleans where they ate dinner late. For days she listened to the television and read every newspaper, but she never saw anything about a robbery in a Dallas jewelry store.

The last Friday in May Rebecca called Talia and asked her to go to lunch. They met in a seafood restaurant on

West Esplanade. Rebecca was waiting, her purse and a large manila envelope on the seat beside her, a martini in her hand. Her gaze ran over Tali's black and white dress, knowing from looking in her closet that it was an Oscar de la Renta. She still marveled at how sophisticated and poised Talia had become. She wondered how Talia would take the news about Ty. Remembering her scene with Tyler in his bedroom, she wanted to tell Talia about that too, but she was afraid of Tyler. If she did not mention the incident, he would never know how Talia got the information. Rebecca had no doubt the news would raise hell at the bank. She also knew Tyler would eventually weather the storm, because men like Tyler always survived. But he wasn't going to like getting caught. And he'd have trouble at home with Talia, whose principles would create an even greater rift in their marriage. Rebecca couldn't help thinking that it was time Talia saw her husband for what he was. She had been fooled for long enough.

"You're early," Talia said, sliding into the seat.

"A little. I ordered a martini for you."

"Oh? Thanks."

Rebecca laughed, reaching across the table to take the drink from Talia. "How smoothly you handled that! It's mine. I know you won't drink at noon when you're working."

Talia smiled, noticing Rebecca's blue cotton dress. "You look marvelous as always. Working yet?"

Rebecca nodded. "I'm selling perfume at Maison Blanche. This is my lunch hour."

"That's why you smell so good!"

"It's Opium, by Yves Saint Laurent," Rebecca said, holding out her wrist.

They paused to order, Talia getting a shrimp cocktail, Rebecca ordering gumbo. "Have you seen Mom lately?" Talia asked.

"No. I'll go see her sometime, but she doesn't remember your visit ten minutes after you've gone."

"You don't know for sure. Go see her, Rebecca. Promise me you will."

"Okay, I will."

They talked about dresses and shops and inconsequential

things until Talia was finished eating. Rebecca seemed more relaxed and contented than Talia had ever seen her.

After coffee, Rebecca held the manila envelope out to Talia. "This is why I wanted to see you." Puzzled, Talia saw it was sealed. "Don't open it until you're alone," Rebecca said. "I hate to be the bearer of bad tidings."

"What is this? And how bad is the news?" Talia asked lightly. She couldn't imagine what Rebecca was talking about since their lives followed such divergent paths.

"I thought you'd want to know what's going on."

Suddenly Talia realized it might be pictures of Tyler with a woman. "Maybe I don't want to see what's in here," she said quietly.

"Yes, you will, because it's going to affect your life, probably in the near future. It has to do with the banking business."

Surprised again, Talia laughed. "Why don't I just open this now?"

"No! Wait until you're in your office. You'll have a moment to yourself, won't you?"

"Sure," Talia answered, her curiosity piqued because it dawned on her that Rebecca had probably gotten from Ed whatever was in the envelope. "I'm going right back." She picked up the checks. "I'll get the lunches. Let's do this again, Rebecca."

"Don't be angry with me. It's something you were going to learn about sooner or later anyway. And it'll be better for you to know first."

"Sure."

Talia drove back to the bank, closed her door and sat down at her desk. With a letter opener she slit open the envelope and pulled out forms that were loan applications from First Bayou. For a moment she stared at them, wondering why Rebecca had given them to her. She riffled through the pages, and then she stiffened, because she recognized the familiar bold handwriting that was on each page, the same scrawl that had signed the different names of the loan applicants.

Astonished, she began to read and her heart seemed to lurch against her ribs as she reached the second from the top. The signature read Michael Stanton.

19

She skimmed the form, inhaling deeply when she read the amount of money, thinking of the relatively small loan Mike had made and repaid quickly with her. Opening her drawer, she withdrew the copy of Mike's loan application, which she kept separate from his file, and read the listing of his assets. He didn't own what Tyler had written. According to the application, Tyler had made Mike the loan to buy property for development purposes. Clearly Tyler had falsified the loan application.

Shock and anger at Tyler's poor banking procedures were her first reactions. The revelation diminished Tyler once again in her estimation. How could she possibly continue to respect him? She faced the fact squarely: *she wanted a divorce*.

Tyler had lost all scruples as he had grown older. He was unfaithful, demanding, and autocratic. To cheat in a race was one thing—to break the law was another. His ruthlessness and dishonesty were appalling to her. Divorce was her only choice. She looked down at the applications again.

All the implications of Tyler's actions began to dawn on her. It was only a matter of time before Tyler was caught by the bank examiners. Talia read straight through the stack of applications, making notes, figuring the totals, and was staggered by the amounts.

The oil business was cutting back, the real estate market was softening. Yet if she kept quiet about what she knew, she would be considered as guilty as Tyler by Larry Prima and by future employers. And as Tyler's wife, everyone would expect her to know. Fleetingly, she wondered why Rebecca had given her the information, and knowing her

sister as she did, she suspected Rebecca wanted to hurt Tyler.
It was too easy to guess why.

Talia ran her hand across her brow. Mike would be hurt.
If they called in his loan, he couldn't possibly cover it. Tyler
would be hurt. How could he expect to avoid getting caught?
She thought of Millard and what this would do to him, even
though he was the one who had raised Tyler always to try to
succeed, to win, no matter what the methods, because the
end justified the means. If she knowingly kept quiet, she
would jeopardize her own career and all she had worked to
accomplish. Everyone would think she had condoned what
Tyler had done.

She locked away the loan applications, knowing that she
would rather risk her own career than hurt Mike. And she
wouldn't deliberately cause Tyler's downfall. All she wanted
was a divorce, not his financial ruin. For a moment her spirits
plummeted in the realization that he might end her career in
banking after all her hard work and accomplishments. It was
only a matter of time until the truth would come out, but it
wouldn't come from her. She hoped it didn't come from
Rebecca. And when the truth became known, she hoped all
would survive.

That night there was a Busch exhibition baseball game at
the Superdome. Talia and Tyler were going with Al and Terri
Santos, and it was difficult for Talia to keep her mind on the
conversation during dinner and as they crossed the huge parking lot to enter the fifty-two-acre dome. She knew Mike was
going, too, and when they were seated, he was already only
two sections away on their right. He was sitting with friends.
He glanced at her, and she knew he saw her, but neither of
them acknowledged it. She wanted to tell him she was going
to leave Tyler, but she felt she owed it to Tyler to tell him
first.

Tyler and Al were caught up in the game, and at half-time
they went to get cold drinks. She went to the ladies' room,
and when she emerged, she saw Mike standing across the
hall, waiting for her. Threading her way through the crowd,
she stopped a few feet from him, then moved closer to get
out of people's way. He was dressed in a blue shirt and dark

slacks, and his eyes seemed bluer than ever. He leaned his right shoulder against the wall and faced her, partially blocking her from the view of people behind him.

"Hi," he said quietly, wanting to touch her and knowing he couldn't, looking at her navy short-sleeved sweater and plaid navy-and-red skirt. Her hair was fastened up primly, making him want to run his fingers through it and pull it down the way he liked it.

"Hi, Mike. I saw you when I came in."

"How are things going?"

"Fine," she answered, thinking their conversation was innocuous to an onlooker, inconsequential, yet Mike watched her with a steamy gaze that she suspected she returned.

While they talked, Mike wanted to reach for her. She was as tantalizing as candy at Christmas to a kid. He slipped his hand into his pocket in an effort to resist temptation.

"Mike," she said, struggling to find the right words. "You've made a loan with Tyler."

One eyebrow arched in a manner he had. "Oh? Did Tyler tell you?"

"No. I found out another way," she said in a low voice. "If the bank has difficulty, your loan might have to be repaid immediately. If that happens, and you can't cover it, I have some money saved."

His features were impassive except the flicker of something she couldn't read in his eyes. "Thanks, Talia," he said in a rough voice. "Don't worry about it."

"Tyler shouldn't have made out the application," she said, her voice so low Mike leaned closer to hear her. "I don't want you to get hurt."

Mike felt as if he had received a blow. He wasn't in any danger from the loan application, but Talia didn't know that, and to have her warn him and offer to help made him love her more than ever. As he gazed into her luminous green eyes, he ached to kiss her and to hold her. Unable to resist any longer, he ran his finger along her cheek. "I won't get hurt. Thanks, Talia."

She drew a quick breath when he touched her, and he looked into her eyes, saw a flare of apprehension. "I'd better get back," she said quickly, her voice breathless as she brushed past him, touching him lightly on the arm. He turned to watch her go.

Tyler was as tall as Mike and he stood in the middle of the hallway, head and shoulders above most of the crowd. His eyes blazed with anger, and she suspected he had seen Mike touch her cheek.

"You and Mike looked engrossed in conversation," he said.

"We were just talking."

"Seems as if to me, you're just talking to him a lot lately."

"No more than anyone else."

"I think it is more than anyone else," Tyler said coldly.

She stopped and faced him. "Are you accusing me of something?"

"I don't like to see you with other men," he said.

"Tyler, stop smothering me!" She headed toward their seats, and he caught up quickly, turning her to face him.

"Just stay away from Stanton!"

"I thought this conversation usually went the other way with me asking you to stay away from him!"

"It used to, but lately I've seen him looking at you. Stay away from him."

"Yes, sir!"

His face flushed a deep red, and his lips thinned. "Al and Terri are waiting for us. I told them we'd go home with them and play bridge."

"That is the last thing I want to do."

"I've already accepted," he said, holding her arm as they walked back to their seats.

Every time Talia thought about discussing a divorce with Tyler, something nagged at her, and she couldn't decide what it was. She dreaded the confrontation because she knew it would be bad. To a man who couldn't let five-year-old kids win a harmless swimming race in the backyard pool, his wife's request for a divorce would be devastating. Yet she didn't feel sympathy for him, because she knew it wasn't love or pain from losing her that would hurt him—it was his enormous ego and his inability to admit failure. Dread and reluctance and a worry she couldn't fathom were offset by her desire to be free. Once when bases were loaded and

Tyler's attention was elsewhere, she glanced at Mike, wondering why she had ever thought he looked so tough. His head was covered in brown curls, his blue eyes could heat to blazing fires, and his mouth was enticing. He turned and looked across the crowd at her, and she wanted to be with him more than anything else.

It was one in the morning when they arrived home. Talia turned on the lights in the bedroom, momentarily looking at the white carpet and white satin spread on the big bed—the mauve walls and contemporary glass-and-wood furniture that seemed austere—all selected by Tyler, Pauline, and the decorator. She faced Tyler's dark eyes as he peeled off his coat.

"Tyler, I want to talk to you."

"What is it?"

There was only one way to say it. "I want a divorce."

He blanched, his eyes becoming stormy. "God! Why? There's another man—Stanton!"

"No! It's us. We're not compatible; you're not faithful—"

Instantly the stiffness left his shoulders. "Is that all! I told you it won't—"

"Don't lie, Tyler," she interrupted him. "It's more than that. Our values are entirely different. You won't hold the line at cheating or breaking the law."

"What the hell are you talking about?" he said, his face flushing, anger returning to his eyes.

"Your banking procedures, for one thing. You've falsified loan applications. That's fraud."

"Mike told you I wrote one for him."

"No, it isn't Mike. I don't want to say who."

"It has to be Mike."

"No, it doesn't," she said, running her hand across her brow. She didn't want Mike drawn into the argument. "It was Malcolm Gervais," she said, giving him a name that was on another application.

"How the hell did you know?" Tyler snapped. "Look," his voice rose, "you don't run my business. I know what I'm doing! I've built that bank up until it's more than double what it was when I started. That's none of your damn business—" Suddenly he checked himself. "Sorry, Talia.

I'm upset.'' He raked his fingers through his hair again, studying her, and then he went to her. "You're my wife. We said vows, and this is a shock. I won't be unfaithful again. We can talk about the problems.''

"Tyler—''

"Please, give me a chance. You can't just walk out like this without warning.''

"You've known things have been going badly between us for a long time now. When we married, I was so inexperienced, Tyler. I was awed by you; I don't think I saw you as you really are.''

"And now you see a monster?''

"No, but we're not compatible.''

"Honey, don't say that! We were very compatible,'' he said, suddenly frightened of losing her and the disgrace it would bring to him. She was his, and he didn't intend to let her go. His mind raced. Two months would give him time to figure out what to do. "I guess I underestimated how much you wanted to be your own person. Maybe I've tried too hard to mold you to what Mother was, what I thought you'd want to be as my wife, but for God's sake, Talia, give me a chance!''

"Oh, Tyler,'' she said, knowing his tricks, knowing his ego wouldn't let her go, that it had nothing to do with love.

"You've always been fair,'' he said. "Give us a chance —give me a chance. You can't just drop a bombshell like that after all our years together.'' He rubbed her arms, and she looked into his black eyes, knowing that he wouldn't change. He would still cheat and lie, still be unfaithful, because the rules didn't apply to him. All of the promises were to try to coax her into doing what he wanted.

"Give us a trial time.''

"We've had years together.''

"I'll change. I swear to you, I will. You have to give me that chance!'' Suddenly he pulled on her arms. "Come here.''

He led her to the closet where he flung open the door. For an instant she was startled, and then she saw what he was after as he reached for their book of wedding pictures. He dropped it on the chair beside her and flipped it open. With their arms wrapped around each other, they stood on the beach in Rio, smiling into the camera.

"Look, remember? We can get that back," he said, stroking her shoulders.

She moved away impatiently and faced him. "That was an idyll with two people who saw what they wanted to see in each other, not what was really there."

"It was there. Please, give me one chance."

She rubbed her head and gave a negative shake. "I don't see how it will help or change a thing."

"Give me two months. Please. You owe me that, Talia."

June and July. Forever. She stared at him, knowing that if she gave him two years, it wouldn't change what she felt, because she saw Tyler now as he really was, and she suspected he still wouldn't see what she really was.

"If there isn't a man," he said watching her closely, "give me that much time."

"There isn't a man," she said, because if she hadn't known Mike, she would have reached the same conclusion about her future with Tyler. Mike had reinforced her inclinations, but the final straw had been the loan applications Rebecca had given her.

"Please let me try. Oh, honey, please," he said, his voice cracking as he put his hands over his eyes.

"Tyler, don't pretend!"

He rubbed his eyes and faced her. "After all I've given you, I don't see how you can refuse me two months."

"All right, but I think it's useless," she said with reluctance. "And we'll have separate bedrooms."

"How can we reconcile——" he started to say, saw her expression, and bit off his words. "Thanks. Thanks, honey. You'll see." He crossed the few feet between them, reaching for her, and she turned her face so his kiss landed on her cheek. She saw the flash of anger in his eyes. It was gone as swiftly as it had come, replaced by a smile.

"I'll try my damnedest."

"Our differences cover our lifetimes. Two months won't help," she said quietly and gathered up her things. "I'll move to a guest bedroom."

"You keep this room," he said.

"No. I don't want it. It's your room."

"I have one request," he said. "Can we keep this to ourselves? Give us a chance to work things out in private, Talia, please."

"That's fine, Tyler. No one needs to know," she said, thinking of Mike. Two months. The time would pass soon enough. She left, knowing they hadn't accomplished a thing, knowing Tyler would try charm for a while, and when that didn't work, she would be in for a fight.

Tyler stared at the open door after she left, then looked at his empty bed. His anger churned. A divorce! He couldn't believe it. Mike Stanton—of all the men he knew! He had thought she hated Mike. Tyler gave a bitter laugh. He should have guessed. If the hatred ever existed, it had probably only caused them to notice each other more. Afraid he was losing her, Tyler clenched his fists in frustration and anger because he refused to lose her, to see her in the same places he went, going to the club with another man, causing scandal in his life when he wanted to run for the Senate someday. He slammed his fist against a chair.

He'd be damned if he'd let her walk out on him! He wouldn't watch her become someone else's wife. Bitterness and rage buffeted him. Moving quietly, he went downstairs to a phone in the library. He knew Talia would be shut in her room and wouldn't come out until morning, trying to avoid further confrontations with him. He didn't want her to hear him leave after all his promises, but his emotions were too disturbed to sit alone all night. He punched a number and spoke softly, glancing at the closed door in the darkened room.

"Désirée? Tyler. Are you busy, honey?"

When she gave him a negative answer, he said, "I'm coming over."

Hurrying quietly outside, he climbed behind the wheel, letting the car roll down the drive without turning on the lights. He wouldn't let Talia embarrass him and make him a laughingstock. He had at least until the end of July, and he would either change her mind, or talk her into giving him more time. He wasn't going to let her go.

* * *

"What did she do when she read the loan applications?" Ed asked.

"I don't know. She took them back to the bank. I know my sister. Her conscience will make her turn him in even if he's her husband. Her sense of right and wrong is unyielding."

"He'll get caught even if she doesn't do a thing. It's only a matter of time."

They sat on the floor in front of his television and ate pizza, drinking cold Mexican beer. The weights he had been lifting earlier were in the corner of the room, and he was bare to the waist, dressed in shorts and sneakers. As he lowered the beer, he asked, "Want to do something fun?"

"Sure."

"Remember old Mr. Materne I introduced you to back at Al's party?"

"The one with the beard?"

"Yeah, that's him. He's asked about you."

"No kidding?"

"Yeah. He likes young, beautiful women." Ed caught her hand, turning it so that the fiery new diamond glittered. "Want more baubles like this? Another lark?"

"Doing what?" she asked suspiciously.

"I happen to have the combination to his safe."

"You're kidding! How did you get that?"

"He left some valuable papers in my office. I took them to him, and he asked me in for a drink. He opened the safe while I was there and put them inside."

"Jeez, people trust you!"

"Of course he trusts me. I handle his estate. I make money for him and manage his investments."

"How do you know there's anything except papers in the safe?"

"He showed me. He's proud of what's there."

"If I steal something while I'm his guest, won't he know I did it?"

"I've talked to him about you. He doesn't know about us but he knows you're Tyler's sister-in-law. He wants to ask you to an open house a friend is giving Sunday afternoon.

Sunday night he's going out of town. His plane leaves at six o'clock in the evening. It seems to me that if you do things right, you can go home with him, find a way to keep him occupied while you slip away and open the safe. He might be so busy with you, he won't have time to look in the safe before he goes. We don't have to have the money," Ed said casually, stroking her throat. "If things don't go right, you can quit at any time. If they go okay, everything you bring home is yours, sweetie. He's a self-centered, tough old man, rich as Croesus, and it would be a lark."

"It will be for you! You'll be out of it, sitting safely at home."

"I can't figure a way to keep him occupied as easily as you can," Ed said lightly.

"You don't have any scruples! You don't care what I do with my body!" she exclaimed. "Ed, I can't believe you're that casual about me. You're suggesting I seduce him! I'm a respectable woman!" she said with indignation.

He shrugged, rubbing his finger over her diamond.

"Dammit—"

"Look at this diamond, Rebecca."

"Damn you, Ed. Some poor old man—"

"He's made his money through investments and apartments in a poorer part of town. If his tenants don't pay—out they go, no matter what bad luck they've had. He hasn't made a repair in years. I wouldn't hit a nice old man, but this one has built a fortune on other people's misery. It'll be easy. Walk out if it isn't. Unlock a window so it looks as if there was a forcible entry while he's out of town. C'mon. It'll be a hoot."

"Yeah, for you!"

He held her finger up so the sparkling diamond was in front of her face. "I promise you—it'll be as easy as slipping on ice."

Intrigued as well as annoyed, she began to consider it while Ed unbuttoned her blouse. "Burglar alarm?"

"He doesn't have one. He's old-fashioned, set in his ways, no family, never been married. He dates some very attractive younger women," Ed answered, nuzzling Rebecca's neck.

He flicked open the catch to her bra, pushing away black lace to cup her breasts.

"I don't know, Ed," she said, her voice changing. Ed could really excite her as few men had. He concentrated on her to an extent that made her feel faint with pleasure, quite a switch from other men she had known.

"The safe has two diamond necklaces, cash, gold coins, and other than that, I don't know."

She thought about it, finding the prospect exciting, beginning to lose awareness of anything except Ed's caresses. He stood up, peeling away his shorts, and her gaze raked over him.

"Jeez, Ed, you've got the biggest one known to mankind!" she said, coming to her feet.

"I won't ask how you came to that conclusion," he said dryly while she leaned down to kiss him as she pushed away the rest of her clothes.

He groaned, suddenly catching her up easily. "Put your legs around me," he said while she clung to his powerful shoulders, and he eased her down on him, filling her, watching her eyes close and the tip of her pink tongue touch the corner of her mouth. She moved, setting him on fire, and he thrust his hips, wanting to possess and keep her.

Wearing her black Neiman-Marcus dress, Rebecca went on the date. All the time she was at the open house, she felt as if she were two people, one talking to the other guests, the other trembling over what she would do later.

Norman Materne was a tall, handsome, blue-eyed man with thinning gray-brown hair and a thick gray beard. He was self-confident, a little bored with everything around him except the women, and very attentive to her. From the party they went to his one-hundred-and-twenty-year-old house in the Garden District, where he gave her a tour of the downstairs, showing her his fine silver and Waterford crystal and his collection of antique clocks.

In thirty minutes they were in his bed, and when Rebecca rolled off him, she scooted close to his long frame to hold him, talking steadily in a monotone. Within fifteen minutes he was asleep. She dressed swiftly because if she was caught, she wanted the excuse she was leaving. She closed the door, hanging her bracelet on the knob, a golden bauble that had bells and charms and would clink and make enough noise that she could hear him if he disturbed it.

Downstairs she unlocked and raised a window. Taking a pocketknife from her purse, she slashed the screen and pushed it slightly ajar. Next she located the safe behind a hunting picture just as Ed had described it. Her heart pounded with terror and excitement while she yanked on the cotton gloves and took down the picture, turning the knob to the three numbers she had memorized. Perspiration beaded her brow. In seconds she had the jewels, the coins, and the cash. After stuffing them into her purse, she replaced the painting.

One lesson Rebecca had learned from her father's misfortune was: don't get caught. Without discussing it with Ed, she had already thought about what she wanted to do, and she had seen exactly what she needed when Norman had shown her through his house earlier. She carried a flat, plastic trash bag in her purse. From a server in the hall, she took two sterling candelabra, and put them into the sack.

In a drawer in the dining room she found silver pieces, pushing them in with the candelabra, her hands shaking badly now. Her terror over getting caught with the goods was stifling. Iron bars seemed to dance in front of her eyes. She twisted the tie around the neck of the sack and carried it out the back door. She dropped the sack inside a trash can, moving a bag of garbage over it. Hurrying inside, she locked the door and ran back upstairs, slipping her bracelet off the knob and dropping it into her bag along with the contents of his safe.

Norman lay sprawled in bed, naked, one skinny, hairy leg hanging over the edge of the bed. Carefully she undressed and slipped back into bed beside him, leaving her clothes strewn where they had been earlier, and sighing with exhaustion that was far more intense than what had been generated by his lovemaking.

When he stirred, she turned into his arms, kissing his bony shoulder, her hands drifting over him, pushing him back to the bed. Finally he told her he would have to hurry to get to the airport.

She stood in front of Ed's apartment and waved goodbye to Norman as he drove away toward New Orleans International Airport, and then she went inside to find Ed waiting. Her knees were shaking as she handed him the purse.

"Never again. Not ever, ever again in my life!" she snapped.

"You'll have to go out with him two or three more times when he gets back so it looks legitimate."

"I know. Don't ever talk me into anything like this again, Ed J. Dessauer! I want a drink." For a moment she burned with rage, because she had a horror of being caged up in prison and that was the closest she had ever come to it.

Ed held out a glass of whiskey and soda. "Here, sweetie. Drink up. An hour from now, you'll be laughing about it."

"No, I won't!" she snapped.

"Hey, baby," he said, putting his arms around her and rubbing her back. "You really are upset. It's over. You won't get caught. He's out of town, and he'll think it was done while he was away. Relax, Rebecca."

"Damn you, Ed! I don't want to run a risk like that ever! Don't take me with you to jewelry stores, don't suggest anything!"

He laughed softly. "Okay, never again. I'll take you out and buy you a sumptuous dinner and tomorrow I'll get you a new dress. How's that?"

"Right now, you're a rotten son of a bitch, and it doesn't interest me."

He grinned. "It will."

The theft wasn't discovered until Norman Materne returned from his trip three weeks later. It was briefly described in the paper. The thief had gotten away with jewels, cash, and coins from the safe and some silver, including sterling candelabra. Ed looked up from the account in the paper.

"Silver candlesticks?"

"I figured that if big pieces of silver were missing, he wouldn't think of me, because he took me home," Rebecca replied, studying her new nail polish. "He'd know I didn't carry away any silver."

"So where the hell is it?"

"I put it in a trash bag and stuck it in the trash. It's probably in the dump, and I hope to God someone doesn't find it and take it to the police."

"I'll be damned!" Ed threw back his head and laughed, his hazel eyes sparkling. "Don't worry. People who scavenge through the dump aren't the type to take their findings to the police." He laughed again, and she was pleased that she had surprised and delighted him. She ran her fingers on his arm, thinking she liked Ed better than any other man she had known. Something flickered in the depths of his eyes, and he dropped the paper, leaning forward to kiss her.

She had three more dates with Norman, and then told him she had decided to date Ed on a permanent basis. She used the cash to buy a fur coat.

Talia's promise to give Tyler two months complicated her life more than ever, because now he showered attention on her. It was a frenzied increase in social activities, not any serious effort to bridge the impossible gap between them.

The second Friday in June Lois and Bob Letellier held a large cocktail party to celebrate their tenth wedding anniversary. Talia knew Mike would be going, and Tyler had flown to Canada for the week to fish with several men from the bank. He would be home Saturday afternoon, and Saturday night they were to go to the ballet with the Letelliers.

Friday evening, Talia couldn't keep from dressing with Mike in mind. She finally decided on a lime rayon georgette gown with a narrow skirt, a square, low-cut neckline, thin spaghetti straps, and matching green pumps. The dress was fully lined with a layer of silk that was cool against her skin. She drove the Jaguar, parking at the curb and walking up the long, curving drive to the front door. Anticipation made the sunset brighter, the air cooler, and the party more exciting. The house was filled with people; guests filled the porch. Eagerness made her tingle, and the moment she entered the house, her gaze swept the crowd for Mike. But he wasn't present.

Sipping a glass of dry Mouton Cadet wine, she stood in a

cluster of people, listening to the men talk about the Saints. When she glanced up, she saw Mike appear in the doorway. He was darkly handsome in his navy suit. His blue eyes met her gaze, and for an instant she felt alone with him. His eyes lowered, looking her over, and then the corner of his mouth turned up in a crooked grin of approval.

Moving around the room greeting people, Mike appeared to wander aimlessly, but soon he joined Talia's group, standing next to Don Whitcomb and facing Talia. In a few more minutes she turned to saunter away, and in seconds he was at her side.

"You look beautiful."

"Thank you," she said, aware of his height, his nearness, and happy she could relax and talk to him.

"I don't see Ty."

"He had to go out of town."

Mike turned to study her, and she kept her eyes straight ahead, afraid what he would see if she looked at him.

"How's your job as executive vice president?"

"It's growing more complicated with the economy slowing. Thank heavens we've been conservative on loans, because times are getting tough. How's the deal you were working on with the Texas people?"

"They'll give me a decision Monday." They talked, walking across the green lawn with beds of pink roses in bloom. They sat down at a table beneath a bright pink umbrella. The lawn held tables and chairs, and the patio had a table laden with food, but she didn't go near it, preferring to sit talking to Mike while he nursed a glass of bourbon and water. The sun sank lower and long shadows covered the yard.

"The guests are beginning to leave," she said reluctantly.

"The evening is early. Have you had dinner?"

She shook her head.

"Then let's go eat. I'll follow you home, and you can leave your car there."

"I shouldn't," she said solemnly.

"You have to eat dinner, and you might as well not eat alone."

"That wasn't why I said I shouldn't."

"Just this once," he said, his blue eyes intense, the words
making her breath catch. Once. They had been alone far more
often than that. She nodded in agreement.

"I'll say goodbye to our host and hostess."

"I'll be along," he said, and she knew he would see to it
that they didn't leave together.

She drove home, refusing to think beyond the next few
hours. Wanting to be with Mike was as natural as breathing.
And she wondered if she had known what love really was
when she had married Tyler.

When she came out of the garage, Mike pulled up and
stopped, holding the car door open for her. She expected him
to drive to another one of his Cajun cafés and was lost in
conversation until he turned into a driveway that was surrounded by pines and oaks, a sprawling glass-and-wood house
nestled back in the trees.

"Mike?"

"I want you to see where I live. I can throw steaks on the
grill."

Protests died when he looked at her, and together they went
inside. Fishing poles, boots, and tools cluttered the utility-
room entrance at the back. They stepped into a kitchen that
was rustic and inviting with a wide brick hearth, cherry-wood
cabinets, and yellow wallpaper.

Appealing and warm, the house was special because it was
Mike's. He draped his arm casually across her shoulders.
"Let me give you the ten-cent tour," he said, and together
they walked to the wide glassed-in living room that looked
livable with a blue carpet and furniture upholstered in beige
and dark blue. Adding bright splashes of color were oil paintings of western and Indian art by Jerome Tiger, Pena, and
Stephen Lyman. They went down the hall past an office to
his spacious bedroom that opened onto the patio. The wide
bed had a dark blue spread. There was a desk in one corner,
a fireplace, a wide-screen television, and bookshelves.

Discovering new aspects of Mike Stanton's life, Talia wandered around the room. His reading tastes were eclectic: Tol-
stoy, Dickens, Robert Duncan, and Wilbur Smith, as well as
history and real estate books, lined his shelves. She knelt

down to look at several records—he had everything from opera, to jazz, to rock. He waited while she explored. The closet door was open; she saw muddy boots alongside his good loafers. A fishing pole was propped in the corner of the room; a gun rack hung on the wall. When she glanced at the jeans tossed on a chair and the sneakers on the thick blue carpet, he grinned. "I didn't know I'd have company."

She thought of the cold perfection of her house where Tyler's clothes were lined up in the closet with military precision. Mike's clutter was refreshing.

"It's nice," she said, looking at the big bed, wondering what he looked like sleeping in it, for an instant yielding to her imagination and seeing his darkly tanned body stretched out.

"Talia?"

A flush crept up her cheeks, and his brows arched quizzically. He drew a sharp breath as if he realized exactly what had been in her thoughts. She stepped away, looking at a trophy for winning a Bayou Liberty pirogue race, realizing where he had developed some of his powerful muscles. "Where are the trophies you've won for sailing?"

"I don't know," he said distractedly. "One's on the bookshelf. Some are in the garage."

She smiled at him. "They're not all on display for the world to admire. How different you are." She didn't add, "from Tyler." She didn't want to bring even his name into their conversation.

"Not in one way," he said solemnly.

Feeling a suffocating need to get out of Mike's bedroom, she turned and walked into the hall. He followed. While she sat on the deck in the last dusky light of day, he pulled off his suit coat, loosened his tie, poured two glasses of white wine, and put steaks on to cook. He looked more appealing than ever. She was conscious of their seclusion. The yard, boarded by a high stockade fence, was filled with magnolias, oaks, and pine. The deck held pots of red geraniums and lime green lawn furniture. Most of all she was constantly aware of Mike, and of wanting to yield to the compelling urge to reach for him, to tell him that she had asked Tyler for a

divorce. Yet Mike hadn't asked her to leave Tyler, and she
had promised Tyler she wouldn't tell anyone during the two-
month waiting period.

"Let me make the salad," she offered.

"Nope. You sit still. My suit can take a spill easier than
your dress." He worked and talked, laughing with her, his
white teeth flashing, but all the while the tension between
them was growing. He would forget words in midsentence.
He burned the steaks slightly. She forgot to drink her wine.
Finally they sat down at a wooden table on his deck with
plates of hot, buttered steaks, crisp green salad, and potatoes
he had baked in the microwave. Talia barely noticed the food;
her appetite was gone. She was lost gazing into his blue eyes,
wanting to listen to him talk. His voice was a deep rumble
in the quiet evening that was dusky now. Mike asked her
about her plans for the future.

"I don't know. I used to think I wanted this and that,"
she said, barely aware of her answer. "But now I don't know
at all." She thought she could look into his eyes forever. She
wanted to touch him, and she wanted him to touch her. He
was watching her with a smoldering gaze that warmed like
a flame, and for once they were all alone with total privacy.

"I don't know anymore either. Everything has always been
clear. What I wanted, what I intended to do . . ." he said,
his voice lowering, his words taking on a double meaning
that sent a shiver of longing through her. "For the first time
in my life, choices aren't clear. The circumstances in my life
have been jumbled before, but never my feelings and my
emotions."

Their untouched dinners were growing cold. He felt as if
there was a constriction around his chest. She was beautiful,
a wonder to him. Everything they did together seemed natural
and easy: jogging, sailing, talking.

"My life has changed," he said in a quiet voice.

Silence stretched and lengthened between them. Words
seemed inadequate. She wanted him desperately. His blue
eyes held her, captivating her senses as well as her heart.
Knowing she was losing the biggest battle of her life, she
shook her head slightly. "I'm leaving Tyler."

Something flickered in his eyes. "Oh, Lordy," he whis-

pered, standing up, his white linen napkin dropping unnoticed
on the deck.

He reached down to pull her to her feet, and she came
willingly without a protest, as honest in her response as she
was in talking to him. He framed her face with his hands.
Her eyes seemed enormous, her face pale.

"When?"

"I promised him two months, but we haven't lived as man
and wife for a long time now," she said.

"I want your hair down," he said in a husky voice that
touched her like a lingering caress. He reached out with his
strong fingers, removing a pin from her hair, and a silken
lock fell. She felt the slight tugs, felt her hair fall, her reluctance having vanished long before her hair came down.

With his pulse roaring in his ears, Mike held her lightly.
Her hair was a golden cascade; she was pale, her eyes enormous, and she looked vulnerable, but there was no mistaking the longing in her gaze.

"God help us," he whispered and enveloped her in his
arms while she wrapped her arms around him, lifting her
mouth to his, feeling as if she would faint from his touch.

While he kissed her deeply, his hands slipped down her
sides, exploring the indentation of her tiny waist, the slight
flair over her hips, and her slender thighs. His hands retraced
their course, roaming up over the full thrust of her breasts.
He pushed the thin straps of her dress off her shoulders,
reaching behind her to tug down the zipper so that the material
slid to her waist.

She was bare from the waist up as she wore no bra beneath
the lined dress. The temperature seemed to jump to a jungle
steaminess as he cupped her perfect breasts, his thumbs flicking over the soft, rosy peaks. His erection throbbed so hard
it was almost painful, and he knew it would be difficult to
exercise control, but he wanted to take forever with her,
because their future was so uncertain. She was leaving Tyler
at the end of July. That was eons away.

Now she stood before him, giving herself to him totally.
His eyes had darkened like storm clouds as he bent his head
to kiss her, to take her nipple in his mouth, teasing her with
his tongue, gently biting.

She gasped with a pleasure that went beyond physical sensation, her hands winding in his hair, then reaching down to tug at his buttons. He stepped back, his chest expanding when he inhaled deeply. He unbuttoned his shirt and dropped it on the chaise along with his tie. While he unbuckled his belt and kicked off his shoes, he watched her. Eagerness, desire, and love, all made his hands shake.

Talia stood in her pumps, her white lacy garterbelt fastened to dark hose, her lacy bikini panties covering only a wispy triangle. With feathery caresses, Mike peeled them all away. He didn't want the flimsiest barrier between them. He had dreamed of her, ached for her, and now she was standing before him, letting him look at all he desired.

He unfastened his slacks, throwing them aside with a jangle when his car keys fell unheeded from a pocket. He was tall, his muscular body lithe.

His breathing was rapid, and suddenly time ceased to exist. There hadn't been a before; there might not be an after, because he knew the uncertainties of the future. "Talia," he whispered, brushing his lips across her bare shoulder, feeling her tremble slightly, letting his hands slide over the satiny smoothness of her honey-colored skin. "Talia," he repeated, the word a deep-throated growl filled with longing. He cupped her breasts again, their softness filling his hands as his thumbs moved over her nipples. He bent his head to take first one and then the other in his mouth, to tantalize, hearing her soft moan while her hands played over him.

Gasping, she slipped her hands across his chest, tangling her fingers in the mat of curls. Her hands drifted down, light as a breeze, yet scalding with each touch. She hooked her fingers in his shorts, freeing him from their constriction, pushing them away. As badly as she wanted to caress and kiss him, she knew her need went far beyond that.

"I love you," she said, the words coming clear and without hesitation, from her heart. It was the first time she had admitted it to herself as well as saying it to him, but she did love him and she always would.

He groaned and embraced her. Her body was a flame in his arms, her softness tantalizing. He scooped her into his arms effortlessly, shoving open the sliding glass doors to his bedroom, moving to the wide bed. His muscles flexed as he lowered her onto the soft sheets, then knelt beside her.

She was consumed with need and love, and if it was only this one time, she intended to give herself to him with all her body and heart.

She discovered that a man could be infinitely sexy when he made love, taking time to learn what pleasured her, giving to her completely. Mike's body with its muscles, his hard hipbones and scars, was fascinating. Her hand trailed down touching him, and he groaned.

He kissed her, his tongue creating a fiery trail. Then he stood up and watched her, her green eyes wide, constantly studying him as he leaned down to kiss the inside of her knee, trailing kisses higher, and she discovered he seemed to get the most pleasure out of giving of himself to her, loving her with a deliberate, tantalizing thoroughness.

When he entered her, her slender legs held him close while Mike tried to make it last, wanting to love her forever, yearning to hear her cry his name, to have her softness enveloping him, to never have it end. Perspiration beaded his body as he moved slowly, her hips driving him to frenzy, yet he fought for control, trying to prolong the pleasure for her.

"Talia," he said her name roughly, covering her mouth, kissing her deeply, his control gone. His body shuddered with release. She clung to him, moving with him, lost in waves of rapture, knowing it was Mike who held her, Mike who loved her.

His weight came down and he kissed her throat, her shoulder, tasting her slightly salty warm flesh, catching the scent of roses in her perfume. "Ah, Talia, my love," he whispered, stroking her. He rolled over, holding her close, their legs entwined, their bodies joined while his palm rested against her cheek, his right arm around her. He gazed at her tenderly, stroking her face, his hand sliding down her smooth back.

"What are we going to do?" he asked gruffly.

She placed her hands over his lips to silence him. "I'll leave Tyler, and then we'll plan."

She said it so simply and so positively that it was as if she had merely told him her name. His heart thudded, and he crushed her to him. When he released her, he said, "I love you. I didn't mean for this to happen this way."

"I know. Maybe that's why we were so antagonistic at first. Sparks or something."

"Or something," he said dryly.

She wanted him to smile, to see him laugh. She felt as if she glowed from his lovemaking. She ran her finger over a crease bracketing his mouth, feeling the stubble of his whiskers. Then her finger traced the scar on his face.

"Does that bother you?" he asked quietly.

Her green eyes gave him an answer before she spoke. "I just wish you'd had an easier time."

"I survived. That was long ago." She let her hands drift lower, still wanting to touch him, letting her fingers tangle in the crisp curls on his chest while he stroked her back.

"I didn't know it could be like that," she said against his throat.

"I didn't either," he answered flatly, crushing her to him and burying his face against her throat. "Lord, how I love you, Talia!"

She felt as if she might melt in his arms, and she clung to him, holding him tightly, momentarily refusing to face the problems ahead of them. Moonlight spilled through the open doors and splashed over them, giving a silvery sheen to their bodies. Her golden hair cascaded down her back, and Mike's blood heated with desire again.

His hands played over the smooth curve of her buttocks while she stroked him as eagerly, and finally she pushed him on his back, looking at his face in the darkness. Aroused again, wanting her as desperately as before, he pulled her on top of him to gaze into her wide, green eyes, a faint smile making creases around his mouth.

"Why the smile?"

"Now comes the lagniappe," he started to say lightly. Instead, his smile vanished, his voice developed a husky rasp, and his gaze smoldered with longing. He was aroused, eager with desire as he pulled her head down to kiss her, his tongue thrusting deeply into her mouth.

Later, as he held her close, her head on his chest, her

leg thrown over him, he asked, "Not until the end of July?"

She raised up to run her index finger along Mike's jaw, feeling the rough stubble of his whiskers. "I promised I would give him two months," she said automatically, her thoughts on Mike, not Tyler.

Ignoring Mike's groan, she said, "I told you, we have separate bedrooms and two months won't change anything, but I promised."

"If that's the way you want it."

"No, it's not," she murmured, turning his face to kiss him slowly and deliberately, feeling the softness of his mouth while his arms tightened around her. "It won't be forever." Suddenly her throat felt tight, her voice thickening. "Mike, I made such a mistake!"

He held her close, stroking her lightly. "I love you," he whispered again, trying to reassure her. He turned her face so he could look into her eyes. "This won't be a mistake. I'll promise you that."

She believed him. Mike was real and warm and sensitive. It would be different this time.

They talked quietly, stroking each other, Talia trying to memorize everything about him she could. Joy was boundless and she gazed at his marvelous, virile body until he groaned and came up to swing her down on the bed and roll over on top of her. "Wanton!" he teased.

"Completely!"

"Don't ever change," he whispered.

After a long time he said, "I don't want to take you home."

"I have to go," she said gently.

Mike cursed and then rolled away. "Let's dress. Before I deliver you home, I want you to meet some friends." He pulled her to her feet. "Come on. I'll rub your back while we shower," he said with a grin.

She laughed, "Now that is really lagniappe!"

"Darlin', you ain't seen nothin' yet," he drawled, leering at her, and as she laughed with him, she realized how much fun Mike would be if the dilemma of her marriage didn't exist.

As he zipped up her dress later, Mike put his hands on her bare shoulders. "There's something I need to tell you."

"This sounds serious."

"It is," he said quietly and her amusement vanished. "The loan application I made to you, the copy of the one you have from Tyler—they're false."

Astounded, she stared at him. "Why?"

Mike ran a lock of her hair through his fingers. "Ben and Simone. Tyler ruined Ben and it was unnecessary. I set Tyler up."

She drew a sharp breath, shock coursing in her like a blow. "So what do you intend to do?"

"Nothing," he replied mildly. "The one to you is meaningless. The one to Tyler has been destroyed—or at least I told him to destroy it. He gave that money to me and made out a dummy loan so I could buy property for him. I talked him into the property. It's worthless, but knowing Tyler, the swampland will turn to gold."

"Why are you telling me this?" she asked in a whisper, shocked and sorting out what he had done.

"Because I love you," he answered quietly. "I've always had my revenge, and that's what I had intended to do, but along the way"—his voice changed and a gruff note of tenderness came—"I fell in love. When I did, I couldn't hurt Tyler. As a matter of fact, I tried to talk him out of buying that land, but by that time, he probably thought I'd decided I wanted it for myself and he insisted I get it for him."

"You were as deceptive as Tyler," she said, and he blanched.

"I guess I deserve that, but Ben and Simone were the most important people in the world to me," he said gruffly. "Ben was like a father, and Tyler cold-bloodedly went after Simone, who had never done a thing to harm anyone."

Talia bit her lip, knowing what he was saying was the truth, weighing what he had done, her shock diminishing, because Tyler had ruthlessly hurt the Holloways in a far more lethal way than trying to sell some swampland.

She moved away to stare out the window while she thought about what Mike had done. It was grim, but it was Mike's nature. He had told her about Leech and his past. Even so, to hear him admit what he had intended was shocking.

She turned to face him, and he asked quietly. "Is this going to make a difference between us?"

"I don't know," she replied solemnly. "Tyler has lied and deceived me so much I never—" She broke off her words at the pained expression that came to Mike's features. He clamped his jaw shut and waited while she sorted out her thoughts.

"Why the loan at my bank?"

"I'm worth a lot more than I put down on those pieces of paper and in the future, it might be important that you know."

"Then why on earth would you put down you make less than you do? No one does that!" To her amazement his face flushed.

"Talia, Simone died a very needless, cruel death. Ben was ruined because of it, and I'll admit, I was angry and hurt. I wanted to hurt Tyler and you in return. If you'll remember, our first meeting wasn't sweetness and roses. Then at the party last March when I took you home, I discovered a warm, wonderful woman who was intelligent and sensitive. You apologized for what had happened—and what I felt went far deeper than emotions stirred by an apology. I lost my drive for revenge after that night. And I wanted to be with you again. You were married, and the only way I could think to get to see you again since I couldn't ask you out was to get a loan."

He thought he glimpsed a flicker of a smile, a slight relenting in her stance. The deception he had committed had been before they had fallen in love—and she believed he was telling her the truth. As stunned and slightly hurt as she was, she realized that Mike had freely admitted everything to her—something Tyler would never have done. And Mike had set his trap *before* he had fallen in love with her.

"It won't happen again, Talia," he said solemnly. "In our future, you can always trust me. Can you forgive me?"

"Yes," she said, quietly. "I forgive, and I give you my trust, and I pray I'm not being naive and blind again."

Finally he crossed to her, slipping his arms around her waist, gazing steadfastly into her eyes. "You're not. I meant it. I'll be as honest with you as I am with myself. I just wanted revenge because I was hurt, and then I fell in love and tried to stop the wheels I'd set it motion."

She slipped her arms around his waist slowly, nodding as she listened. "It's the past now. And Tyler probably will make a fortune from the swampland. He has a knack for finding gold everywhere he turns."

They held each other tightly as if they had just passed through a storm. A shudder raked through him and she started to lean back to look up at him, but his arms tightened crushing her to him. His voice was muffled against her throat. "I need you. You'll never know how much I need you!"

She turned her head, slipping her arms up around his neck, standing on tiptoe to receive his kiss.

In a few minutes, he turned his head, holding her tightly while he kissed her throat. "I've waited so long," he said huskily, knowing she had no idea what he meant.

In another hour they dressed and left. Mike drove on the deserted freeway, speeding down to the old part of town, exiting off a ramp and driving down Canal to the Vieux Carré to park on a deserted street. It was dawn with clear morning air and the first pink rays of sunshine spilling between buildings. Papers and cans and cigarette butts littered the streets, mementos of the festivities of the night before. A boy hosed down the street in front of a hotel, sweeping the bricks clean. Mike held her arm as they walked along a narrow banquette past open doors on dark, cavernous bars, doors of private residences locked with shutters closed on windows. The sound of jazz carried clearly, and she looked up at Mike.

"You said you like jazz. I want you to hear this."

The music became louder as they approached an open door. For a moment when they entered, Talia couldn't see until her eyes adjusted to the inky interior. The bar was almost empty. The floor was dusty and littered, a chair was knocked over, and empty bottles were on the tables. Two men sat listening to music, another couple was in the bar, and a customer was sleeping with his head on a table. At the far end of the room were four men, one playing the drums, a piano player, a coronet player, the other a trombone. The music was pure Dixieland, making Talia's skin prickle as she listened to the wail of the horn and the steady beat of the drums. She sat close to Mike, his arm around her while they listened for half an hour. For a moment as the slow, sensuous music enveloped them, time stopped. Mike's arm was around her, his hand stroking her shoulder while they sat in the darkened bar insulated from the world. She laced her fingers in Mike's, and he turned to look at her. She leaned across the short distance between them, kissing him. His arm tightened across her shoulders briefly, while his heart ached with his need and love for her.

The musicians stopped and Mike introduced her, talking easily to the men until they settled back to play. In another half hour, Mike tossed some bills in an overturned hat already full of money. He waved to them and called thanks as they left.

"That was wonderful."

"I wanted you to hear them," he said. "Let's go down to the Café du Monde and eat beignets and have café au lait before I take you home."

"I'd love to," she said, relishing the clear, sunny morning with Mike at her side.

When they reached her empty house, he went inside with her, closing the kitchen door, following her into the den. Mike kissed her hard, and then held her away. "You'll never know how glad I am you have separate bedrooms," he said solemnly, and she reached up to push soft brown curls off his forehead.

She nodded her head, standing on tiptoe to wrap her arms around him again, wanting to prolong the last seconds with him.

He held her so tightly she couldn't breathe, but for a moment she didn't care, kissing him until he released her.

"You call me," he said solemnly. "I better go. Another kiss and I might not be able to." He turned and left swiftly, the car fading and silence wrapping around her like prison walls. She gazed at the house. It was Tyler's house, his cars, his colors, his choices in everything—even his wife.

Living under the same roof with Tyler almost two more months was unthinkable. She didn't love Tyler; she loved Mike.

Tyler came home an hour before they were supposed to be at the club for dinner, and then they had to go to the ballet. It was Saturday night, and she planned to tell him tonight or

early Sunday morning and leave. It was the first time she
could recall breaking a promise, but it was an empty, pur-
poseless promise to appease Tyler. They had separate rooms,
so she didn't see him until she came downstairs. He stood
in the darkened den; only the light from the bar was on.
Dressed in a simple, sleeveless black dress with a straight
skirt, she paused in the doorway, and he studied her. "I want
to talk to you," he said, and she could hear the burning anger
in his voice. "We don't have time now. We'll talk when we
get back."

"Fine, Tyler." She shrugged. He was angry, but she no
longer cared what Tyler felt.

He drove too fast without speaking a word, but when they
were with others it was as if nothing had ever happened.
Tyler could turn on his charm as automatically as a light.
Talia tried, too, forcing herself to eat when her appetite was
gone, an undercurrent of excitement building within her
whenever she thought of Mike. Soon she would be free of
Tyler, yet every time the thought came, a feeling of disquiet
still accompanied it. She attributed her concern to the fact
that she knew Tyler would fight. All through dinner, feeling
an aching void, she wondered what Mike was doing.

The Letelliers drove to the theater with them and Talia
hoped to relax, to sit in the darkness and watch the dancers
and think of Mike and the night before.

As they walked down the aisle, she saw Sloane's dark
head, and a man seated beside him. Sloane glanced around
and nodded at them, and she realized how far apart the brothers had grown over the years.

Along with the Letelliers, Talia and Ty settled in their
seats, and the houselights dimmed. The music began and
carried her back in time. She glanced once again at Sloane's
dark, handsome profile, and at the shorter blond man with
him. And then she remembered something she had wanted
to forget for years.

20

Sloane and Chad. *There is a ruthless streak in Tyler that you've never really seen.* Sloane's conviction that Tyler had caused the death of his lover had been strong. His fury had been intense enough at the time to cause him to move to South America. She watched the ballerinas swirling on stage like thistles drifting in the wind, lovely, ethereal, while a chill shook her. If she tried to divorce Tyler against his wishes, she would put Mike in danger.

As if she had fallen into Arctic waters, a numbness gripped her. She felt Tyler move, and glanced up to see him watching her. He frowned and leaned close. "Are you all right?"

"Yes." She bit off the word, raising her chin, feigning anger when all she felt was terror as she had never experienced it before—not for herself, but for Mike. If Tyler was as ruthless as Sloane had said, Mike's life could be in danger if Tyler discovered she loved Mike.

There was a roaring in her ears that drowned out the music from the orchestra, and she locked her fingers together, trying to think. She would have to warn Mike—and as swiftly as that thought came, she knew she couldn't. Mike was as tough as Tyler. He came from a hard background, was accustomed to trouble, and wouldn't run from a fight. He had told her about Claude and Leech, about his early years. He would try to protect her, but he couldn't begin to understand the extent of Tyler's drive. And he couldn't fight Tyler's wealth. Tyler could manage so many ways to eliminate someone. She saw now how easily he could have accomplished what Sloane had accused him of doing.

She glanced up at Tyler, and he turned. The footlights

313

highlighted his cheekbones and forehead and jaw; his eyes
were in shadow. As never before she felt trapped, because
there was only one way to protect Mike. She would have to
convince Tyler there wasn't anyone else. *For Mike's sake,
she would have to stay with Tyler.*

She looked away in pain, knowing she would have to find
a way out of the dilemma. If she went home tonight and told
Tyler she was leaving him for Mike, she would be signing
Mike's death warrant.

The brief time spent jogging with Mike, the casual talks
at parties, the possibility of a future together would cease.
She had to tell Mike goodbye and convince him she meant
it for his own safety. Later—when she was safely away from
Tyler—she could tell Mike, but not now.

She felt as if an invisible fist had locked around her heart
and was squeezing it while the full strains of *Swan Lake*
played and dancers pirouetted across the stage. Now she had
to know exactly what had happened that year Sloane had gone
to South America. She stared at him, thinking both brothers
were so handsome, yet indulged themselves until their lives
had become warped. Sloane shifted in his seat and glanced
around, looking into her eyes in the darkness and she stared
back. He turned back to the stage.

Memories swirled in her thoughts. Sloane had told her to
look for a large unexplained cash withdrawal. At the time,
she hadn't done it, and she realized that maybe she hadn't
wanted to face the truth. Tyler documented everything, keeping copious notes, exacting records, so it might be possible
to find a withdrawal. She stared at the dancers while the
music soared in crescendo, her stormy thoughts and emotions
keeping pace. She needed proof of Sloane's lover's murder
so that she could go to the authorities. Only then would Ty
give her a divorce.

She wanted to get up and leave the theater and go home
to look at the records. Instead, she sat quietly, leaving when
the ballet was over, trying to carry on polite conversation.
With the Letelliers they drove to the Blue Room of the Fair-
mont Hotel where the Ink Spots were performing. Several
times she caught Ty studying her. She tried to be her usual

self, to relax, to hide the worry and hurt and dismay she felt. Ty drank more than usual, but he was sober when they drove home and were finally alone together.

In the car she asked, "What's wrong, Tyler?"

"Wait until we get home or I might wreck the car!" he snapped. His shoulders were stiff, and he gripped the steering wheel tightly, driving recklessly, making the tires squeal at each turn.

He frightened her and worried her, but she couldn't let him know it and when they were in their den, she faced him again. "Now what's the matter?"

"Last night I called you," he said, peeling off his coat and throwing it down angrily. "Where were you?"

Her heart pounded with fear. "What's the matter with you! I was right here."

Her gaze met his steadfastly, and suddenly he didn't want to know. He crossed the room to her to pull her to him, his dark eyes searching her face, his fingers biting into her flesh.

"Tyler, you have no right to be so possessive!" she snapped, surprising him, making him realize how much she had changed and become more sure of herself over the years. "You've had affairs . . ."

His face flushed, and his eyes burned with anger. "I didn't love any of them. It was meaningless. You're mine and I won't let you go!"

"It isn't because you love me that much! It's your pride, your ego!"

"Dammit, I've given you everything you could want!" He looked down into her implacable green eyes, frustration and anger burning in him. She was the one person he had never been able to control. His mind raced. She had promised him time, but he knew all the time in the world wasn't going to change her. He could see the cool way she looked at him. "You promised me two months."

"I'll keep my promise," she said calmly. He realized he had misjudged her when he was dating her. She had told him about her need for independence, and he hadn't listened, because he hadn't believed it. He had underestimated her drive and intelligence, and now he was paying for his mistake.

She would never be the docile, submissive wife he wanted, but she wasn't going to ruin him with scandal or embarrass him. "Where was Stanton last night?"

The question made her blood chill. Tyler's black eyes burned with rage. He shook her lightly. She drew herself up, pushing on him, raising her chin to look him in the eye. "Let go of me, Tyler."

She twisted away from him, but he yanked her around. She spun against his chest, throwing her hands up to push against him, but he held her in an iron grip. He looked as if he were going to strike her and she braced herself for a blow.

"Where were you last night?"

"I was at home," she said coldly, hoping he couldn't tell she was lying. Her heart pounded with fear that she tried to hide, because she had never seen him this angry. "Did it ever occur to you, Tyler, that I might sleep through your phone calls? It's your own guilty conscience, your own way of living that makes you suspect me!"

Both were breathing as hard as if they had been running. She defied him, staring back without wavering. "Are you going to let me go now?" she asked.

"You were here at home?"

"Yes, after leaving the Letelliers' party." She had to make an effort for Mike's protection. "Tyler, if you want us to work things out, this is a poor way to do it. You'll have to trust me."

Surprise flickered in his eyes. She turned away as his hands dropped from her arms. She walked out of the room, her back tingling, her knees shaky. He had frightened her with his rage, but she didn't intend to let him know it. She locked the bathroom door, sagging against it, pressing her hands to her mouth. Tyler terrified her.

She undressed, turned down the bed sheets, and walked to the window, standing in her darkened bedroom, feeling more alone than ever before in her life. She waited, watching the glowing orange hands of the clock tick over the numbers. At three, she pulled on her robe and went downstairs to Tyler's office. She looked through his desk and files.

Tyler was meticulous about notes, keeping track of what each check was for and where and when it was spent. Even so, it took almost an hour to locate the right checkbook record. She knew the approximate date because she remembered that Sloane had waited to go until after his mother's birthday. The 1975 records were in the bottom drawer of Ty's oak file cabinet.

Her finger ran down the ledger. She turned pages, skimming the numbers and Tyler's careful notations of where the money was spent. *Twenty thousand dollars.* The numbers seemed to leap up at her, Sloane's accusations pounding in her head. There it was: a withdrawal of twenty thousand dollars. On the space beneath was written, ''Sloane,'' because Tyler's habit was obviously too strong to leave off the notation even when it tied him to murder.

The withdrawal was made almost a month before Chad's death. Twenty thousand dollars. She drew a deep agonized breath, thinking of Mike.

Talia sat back on her legs, shivering. Now for the first time she began to see the full extent of Ty's obsession to win and to succeed. He wouldn't stop at murder. Ty was far too clever to get himself involved. She knew he had been telling her the truth when he had said he was at the bank. Looking down again at the figures, she felt staggered by the knowledge, bound in chains to a man who had dazzled her until she saw only what she wanted to see, not what he really was. Ty had caused another man's death so he could become governor. Mike might be in danger already.

''Tali?'' Tyler called sharply.

She started and dropped a bundle of bank statements. Hastily she scooped them up, her hands shaking, because she could hear his footsteps approaching. ''I'm down here,'' she said, cramming everything in the drawer, hoping she could straighten it out tomorrow before he noticed. She yanked a book off the shelf and stepped into the hall.

''What's wrong?'' he asked with a frown.

''I couldn't sleep, so I came down to get a book.''

He glanced at the book in her hands. ''That ought to do the trick,'' he said dryly, and she saw she had picked up a book on figuring income taxes.

''Someone at the bank had some questions about taxes.''

They stared at each other, the tension between them growing taut. She thought of Mike and knew what she had to do.

''Tyler, if you'll try, I'll try.''

His face changed, his brows arching, a puzzled expression coming to his features. He crossed the room to put his arms around her. "Of course, Tali—"

She slipped free. "Not the physical part. The other has to come first," she said, hoping to gain time for Mike without having to submit physically to Tyler ever again. "Let's just get back on a better relationship if possible."

"Of course," he said, his eyes narrowing as he studied her. Together they went upstairs. At the top he pulled her into his arms to kiss her and she clung to him, hating every second, yet terrified for Mike's safety if she didn't.

When his hand slipped to her breast, she pushed away. "Give us both time, Tyler. There are a lot of fences to mend."

"All right, Talia." She walked away, knowing he was watching her. Tyler was sly and intelligent. It would take a lot of convincing to change his mind about Mike. But his enormous ego would help. He would never understand how she could leave him for someone else.

Tyler stood watching her walk down the hall. He never stopped wanting her. She was sensuous and beautiful and he was aroused now, but his ardor cooled as he went into their big bedroom and closed the door. What had she been doing downstairs in his office at three in the morning? He didn't believe for one second that someone at the bank had needed a book about taxes. He frowned and stared at the closed door. He moved around the room restlessly, laid out his suit and shirt for Sunday, thought about the things he had to do tomorrow and Monday. The damned bank examiners were worrying him at a time when his wife was causing trouble. He wanted to know if she had been home last night; he had already found out from Bob Letellier that she and Mike had talked a long time at the party, although they hadn't left together. Both of them were too smart for that.

Tyler opened his door and stared at Talia's door. He went downstairs to his office where he stood in the darkened room with just enough moonlight to see. Nothing was out of order or disturbed. His gaze roamed over the bookshelves, the immaculate room, the desk, the tables and chairs, and his file cabinets. The books were catalogued and in order and he knew exactly which shelf had held the book on taxes. He stared at the empty space and the books around it. He turned and looked around. He was close to a file cabinet. He moved to it and opened each drawer until he reached the bottom where papers and checkbook ledgers were tumbled in disorder. His brows drew together and he frowned, taking a ledger out and closing the door. He switched on the light and looked at the ledger, for a moment puzzled as he looked at the year and realized how old it was. And then he knew what she had been doing downstairs.

At midmorning the next day Talia called Sloane at work, and she didn't make any pretense about the purpose of her call. "Sloane, can you meet me for lunch today?" There was a long pause. "It's important," she added, gripping the phone until her knuckles were white.

"Okay. How about the Glass Garden?"

"Twelve noon," she said. "Thanks, Sloane."

She was there before he arrived, and in minutes they were seated in the airy, glass-enclosed restaurant that was a garden filled with greenery whose beauty was lost to her. Sloane slid into the seat across from her and both ordered. As soon as they were alone, he leaned back, waiting.

"How are you?" he asked.

"I'm all right," she said, thinking he looked thinner, more brittle, but he was still a handsome man. She leaned forward, pausing to glance around. "Sloane, I didn't believe you at the time, but now I need to know about Chad."

His mouth curved crookedly, and a cynical expression came to his features. "So that's what this is about, isn't it? You finally believe what I said about Tyler."

"Yes," she admitted.

"You know the answer without talking to me."

"What do you think he'd do if I asked him for a divorce?"

Sloane gave her a pitying look. "He won't give you one, will he?"

"Not so far. And I know there's not enough solid evidence to go to the police. They can't use assumptions in a courtroom."

"Lord, no! Your word and mine—only hunches. We know the truth, but how flimsy it would sound if you didn't know Tyler. And he's a pillar of the community."

"I know," she said, frowning as she stared beyond him. "Even the withdrawal at the time—nothing could be proved and Tyler can be so clever."

"You can forget the police." Sloane studied her, leaning back as the waiter brought a shrimp salad to Talia. "To my brother, you're his property. If you ask for a divorce, his ego can't stand it. He won't let you go. Don't underestimate him, Talia."

She looked away, staring at green leaves in a hanging pot of ivy. "And if there's another man?" she whispered.

"Oh, God! That's why you wanted to see me!" Sloane put down his fork and his dark brows arched in a sardonic smile. "So now you're in my shoes. Well, I can tell you, if you love the guy, don't ever let Tyler know about him!"

Tears stung her eyes. She had known what Sloane would say, but she had to hear him say it. She felt trapped and she was terrified for Mike's sake. "He may already know."

"Then the man better leave town if he values his life. I'm sorry, Talia."

"This man wouldn't leave town if he knew," she said bitterly. Hurting, she drew a deep breath as she faced Sloane. "At first I didn't see how ruthless Tyler could be."

"He's probably gotten worse. He's been spoiled. I have, too, but I've never had that crushing drive that Tyler has, the greed and ambition and staggering ego. You're his property. You always have been. I'd guess his first affair came within six months after you married him."

"You know?"

"I've heard rumors. Tyler and I are alike in some ways. Fidelity isn't in our nature. We have a model in our father, but to Tyler, in his own eyes, the unfaithfulness is nothing, because he hasn't been flagrant, he hasn't brought embarrassment to you, and he doesn't love the women. He has a double standard. But if you ever hint you're interested in another man, you'll bring down the wrath of Hades on you and on the man. The man will pay, Talia, don't think he won't. If my brother runs for public office again, I'll get out of his way. And my lovers will too."

Startled, for a moment she forgot her problems to stare at Sloane. "*Lovers*?"

"I'm still part of two worlds," he admitted. "I have a male lover and a female lover."

"And that works?" she asked, unable to comprehend his lifestyle.

"Yes, so far."

"I hope you're happy," she said, thinking he had changed; he was cynical, far more reserved with her.

"I'm sorry that things haven't worked out," he said, his voice softening. He reached across the table to touch her hand. "How's Kate?"

"She stays the same. She seems content, and physically she's in good health."

"You have my sympathy," he said, shifting back to Tyler.

"I'm safe, because I'm his wife and he wants me. It's—" She stopped, realizing she had almost said Mike's name to Sloane.

"That's right. It isn't you, because you belong to him. It's the man in your life. I hope you heed my warnings, because I know my brother. The guy is a walking dead man if you keep on seeing him."

They finished, and she drove back to work, trying to concentrate on driving. Tyler would kill Mike if he knew about their love. And when she told Mike goodbye, she couldn't tell him why, because she didn't want Mike to fight Tyler. In due time, she would find a way to leave her husband, and eventually she could tell Mike, but not yet. Right now, she had to convince Tyler that Mike was no part of her life.

Hurting, hating what she had to do, but terrified for Mike's safety, she stopped jogging at the school and refused Mike's calls at the bank. Quick, total severance was the safest way, because it would put Mike at a distance immediately. And it seemed the only way she could handle it. She didn't know how she could look into Mike's blue eyes and lie to him.

For the first time since the Letelliers' party, Mike and Talia were together at the country club at a dance, and it was inevitable that they would end up in the same cluster of people. She tried to avoid him, to avoid looking into his eyes. All evening she stayed by Tyler until nearly midnight when she went to the ladies room. As she emerged, Mike was leaning against the wall waiting.

21

He took her arm, opened the door to the fire exit and led her down the back stairs to a landing.

"What happened?" he asked, his blue eyes searching her face, and for an instant she wanted to throw herself into his strong arms and pour out all her fears. His hair was tangled, brown locks curling on his forehead, and he looked wonderful, his broad shoulders as substantial as the Rock of Gibraltar. She tried to keep her voice calm.

"I belong with Tyler and we shouldn't be here talking."

"I don't believe you," Mike said quietly. He tilted his head to study her. "Has he hurt you?"

Everything inside her screamed yes. Not physically, but in a far worse way, yet there was only one choice open to her. She shook her head. "I'm fine. I want to go back. My husband's waiting."

Mike looked as if she had hit him, and she hated what she had to do, but there wasn't a choice. All of Sloane's warnings and accusations were clear, the damning entry in the checkbook ledger was proof. Mike's life was already in danger. As she tried to pass him, he caught her arms lightly and Talia stiffened. Mike watched her, seeing the quick flash of fear in her eyes. He frowned. "I won't hurt you," he whispered roughly. "Talia. What happened?"

"I came to my senses," she said, and he didn't think he had ever been hurt as badly in his life. She brushed past him and he let her go, standing numbly staring after her, the words hanging in the air. How long he stood on the silent, empty landing, he didn't know. His hands shook and he jammed them into his pockets, leaning back against the wall to take a long, deep breath, fighting to control his emotions. He ran his hand swiftly across his eyes and swore, reluctantly going back inside.

He sat at a table with friends, across the room from where Talia and Ty were seated. It was dark in the room, with a few soft lights, and he sat back in the corner, watching her. She smiled and laughed, danced with Tyler as usual, yet Mike couldn't believe she had such a sudden change of heart. Not after what had happened between them.

He called her Monday to make an appointment for Wednesday to see her, telling her secretary it was about a loan. The appointment, however, was with the senior loan officer. Instead of following the secretary to the correct office, Mike stepped aside and went into Talia's.

She looked up from her desk as Mike closed the door behind him.

"Your appointment—"

"I came to find out why you're afraid to see me."

"I told you, Mike," she said, trying to keep her voice calm, to control the urge to tell him everything, trying to keep from letting her gaze wander over him because she was starved to see him and touch him and be with him, just to *look* at him.

He walked around the desk and her heart began to drum, her breathing stopped as he reached down to haul her to her feet.

"Mike! No—"

Ignoring her protest, his arms banded her and he kissed her. Talia stood stiffly, fighting for control over her emotions, trying to resist his tongue that was probing, his body that was hard and virile, his strong arms that were a haven, the pounding echo in her mind that it was Mike who held her, *Mike who loved her*. His mouth opened hers, his tongue thrust inside her mouth.

She couldn't fight him or resist. Her body softened, melting against his, trembling in his arms, She yielded, kissing him back, struggling to keep from bursting into tears.

Abruptly he released her, his chest heaving, his eyes stormy. "That's half my answer. Now you tell me the other half," he commanded.

She looked away, knowing there was no choice. "I'm staying with Tyler."

"Dammit, look at me and tell me that!" he snapped, knowing something was wrong, but not knowing what it was. "What's he done to you?"

She faced him, her cheeks bright with color. "I swear to you, he hasn't done a thing. I know what I want. He can give me more than you can, Michael Stanton. He's promised to make me the president of First Bayou if I'll stay with him," she exclaimed desperately, saying the one thing she thought Mike might believe. "Leave me alone!"

The intercom buzzed and Talia pressed the switch. "Yes?"

"Your husband is here."

"Tell him to come in."

Mike saw the brief stricken look that passed over her features before she composed herself. "At least move around to the other side of the desk," she said, sitting down as the door opened and Tyler walked in, his gaze snapping back and forth between them.

"Hi, Tyler," Mike said easily, inwardly raging. He had to control an urge to strike Tyler, and he clenched his fists. "I just came to leave some papers with your wife about a loan."

"I didn't know I was interrupting anything."

"You're not," Talia stated. "Mike was leaving."

Mike pulled a form out of his briefcase, a copy of the loan application she already had on file. "Thanks, Talia. See you, Ty."

He closed the door behind him, moving automatically, his thoughts on Talia. For the first time in his life he felt at a loss, unable to battle for what he wanted. The only satisfaction was the knowledge she still loved him. Her kiss made that much clear. President of First Bayou. She was ambitious, and she had told him about her need for independence that Tyler had never understood. Mike wondered if he was being as obtuse as Tyler now. Did she want the promotion enough to stay with her husband?

There appeared to be only one answer, and he clenched his fists and swore again, feeling helpless and more lonesome than ever because only Talia made his life complete. He had wanted her as his wife. But now she didn't want him.

For a moment he toyed with the possibility that Tyler was threatening her, but Mike knew Talia well enough now to know that wouldn't stop her. He drove to the gym to work out, because he couldn't concentrate on real estate. He fully understood how much Ben had suffered when he lost Simone.

"Talia . . ." Mike said her name aloud to empty air.

Ty walked up to face her across the desk, his black eyes blazing with fury. "It's Stanton, isn't it, who's caused our trouble?"

"You'll probably ask me that about any man I have a conversation with during the next two years. *You're* with *me* constantly."

"It's hardly constant!" He reached out and caught her chin, tilting her face upward while he studied her. Talia prayed her mouth wasn't red from Mike's kiss.

"He kissed you, didn't he?"

"Tyler," she said in her most scathing tones, jerking her chin out of his hand, "have you lost your mind? This is a workday! Here's a copy of a loan application I needed from him! Is this why you came?"

"Dammit, Tali—" The phone rang, interrupting him. She accepted the call, making an appointment for lunch the next day with a client. When she replaced the receiver, she looked up. "That was a client, Matt O'Hare. I'm having lunch with him tomorrow. Do you want to join us to make sure I'm faithful to you?"

Tyler's face flushed. "I came to take you to lunch."

"All right, as soon as I take these papers to Larry. I'll be right back," she said.

Tyler watched her go, anger burning like banked fires. She was stiff, ungrateful, unyielding. And it was Mike Stanton. A stranger could look at them and guess that. Talia had always been too open to be good at deceit. Tyler fumed at the thought of a divorce scandal that would ruin his standing in the community. She had made her decision, and he had made his.

At the annual Bastille Day dinner dance celebration Talia wore a green silk dress that clung to her figure and was slashed up to the knee in front. And all she could think about was

Mike, how she both dreaded and wanted to see him, and how difficult it would be with Tyler at her side all evening.

Trying to please Tyler in every way but one, she fastened an ornate diamond and emerald necklace he had given her. He gazed at her with desire showing as they went to the car.

At the club, the big ballroom was decorated in red, white, and blue tablecloths with bouquets of fern with red, white, and blue flowers. The musicians were already playing when they arrived and found their table. It was at the edge of the dance floor and held places set for twelve. The men stood when they approached, and Talia said her greetings automatically, because at the end of her table sat Mike, and she had glanced into his eyes, seeing his quick assessment, the impassiveness of his features that faded when she met his gaze. The noise was too great to talk to anyone at the other end of the table, so she smiled and nodded.

All through dinner she was aware of him, feeling a pull on her senses, fighting the urge to glance his way, sometimes succumbing to it and catching him studying her. After dinner Tyler asked her to dance, and once when they finished a dance and returned to their table, her heart seemed to stop beating because Mike and another man were waiting by her chair.

As she and Tyler reached the table, Mike spoke. "Talia, Tyler, I'd like you to meet a client of mine. As a matter of fact, he's one of First Bayou's customers, so he wanted to meet you. This is Lance Douglas. Lance, meet Talia Franklin and her husband, Tyler."

She gazed into a handsome, boyish blond face that stirred her memory. His hazel eyes were warm, his handshake firm before he turned to shake hands with Tyler.

They sat down with others at the table. While the men talked about golf, Talia was aware of Mike sitting a couple of seats away from her now. She listened to his deep voice that stirred longing and memories. And when she glanced at Lance Douglas, who was talking, she tried to recall where she had seen him. He caught her looking at him, smiled, and stood up.

"May I ask your wife to dance?" he asked Ty, reaching for her hand, and Ty nodded, absorbed in golf talk with Stan, Mike, and Jake. He gave Lance one sharp glance before Stan drew his attention back to their conversation. Without looking directly at him, Talia knew Mike was watching her. She kept her attention on Lance. And then Talia recalled where she had known him, and a smile broadened her lips as she moved ahead to the dance floor, because it was obvious that Lance Douglas didn't remember her.

Lance took her in his arms, holding her a discreet distance. "Talia—it's not an Irish name?"

"Not that I know of."

"Have I got jelly on my tie or something?"

"No! I was just smiling because we've met before. It's a very small world, as they say."

"Oh?" Hazel eyes gazed at her with quick interest. "Where'd we meet and how in sweet hell could I have forgotten?"

"*Bom dia. Nao compreendo português.* Or something like that!"

"Holy saints of Toledo," he exclaimed, surprise and recognition showing in his gaze. "*Rio!* It was Rio! The newlywed!"

"Don't look so shocked," she said, surprised at the amazement in his voice. He missed a step dancing, recovered at once, and then she was aware of his quick, searching appraisal. "You look as if you just discovered a ghost."

"Just surprised I wouldn't have remembered on my own. And that's your husband," he said, turning to give Tyler a long glance. Tyler, Stan, and Mike were talking; Tyler was drawing something on a piece of paper.

"Well, well. It's a small world. I have to ask and I'll hold my breath and cross my fingers—are you happily married?"

"Yes," she answered smoothly, and she wondered if something showed, because she saw the curiosity in his eyes.

"Shucks and gee whiz. There go my hopes again. Children?"

"No. No children. A very ordinary life."

"Except that your husband was governor for a term. That isn't quite ordinary."

"So you know about Tyler."

"Tyler Franklin is a household word. I've been out of state most of the time. I live in Dallas, actually, but I'm stationed here temporarily because I'm a landman and I'm working on some leases. So much for me. Catch me up on you.''

''You didn't know that much about me to begin with,'' she said, smiling, aware he was a very smooth dancer, which made his surprise and misstep moments ago all the more curious. ''Are you married?''

''No. Unfortunately all the beautiful, adorable women seem to be taken, so I'll just have to wait. What have you done since I last saw you?''

She laughed. ''How could I begin to tell you! I still work at the bank and I still like my job. I jog. I sail. That's about all there is.''

''You've changed. You're more beautiful.''

''Thank you. You haven't changed. You look the same and you act the same.''

He gave her his boyish grin, his eyes twinkling, yet she had the feeling he was watching her closely, and she couldn't understand why he would be. The music ended. ''Would Tyler care if we stood right here and danced the next number?'' Lance asked.

''He might,'' she replied. ''Usually I don't dance with anyone except Tyler.''

''So he's still the jealous husband?''

It was her turn to be startled. ''How did you—''

''The drugstore. Remember the last time I saw you and you said I would get you in trouble with your husband? I know about jealous husbands.''

''I remember,'' she said, relaxing.

He took her elbow to walk back to the table. ''And he's watching us. Think he'll agree to another dance with you later if I ask?''

''I don't know. I can't answer for Tyler,'' she said and received another searching glance.

''Where do you work?''

''Central Southern Bank.'' She sat back down between Mike and Ty who were still engaged in talk about land, Mike leaning forward, his finger moving along a dark line drawn on the green paper, and she gazed at his hand, remembering it stroking her flesh, knowing the texture of his skin, how adept he could be, what his hands could do to her to bring ecstasy.

She glanced at him and received a level gaze as he continued talking in the same tone. He was so close, so tantalizing, and she ached to touch him, to have him touch her.

For an instant she allowed herself the luxury of studying him, his jaw, with the tiny bristles showing, his slightly crooked nose, the thick lashes and curls that tumbled on his forehead. With an effort she looked away, her gaze meeting Lance's impassive stare. She turned her head to watch the dancers, wondering if anything she felt for Mike had shown in her expression, because Lance had been watching her. And then Tyler took her hand and led her onto the dance floor, where she listened to him tell her about his plans for this Saturday's golf game and an approaching amateur tournament.

For just a moment once in the evening, Tyler went to the men's room, their friends were dancing, Lance was dancing and Mike was left at the table with her. He moved down to sit beside her. "I wish you'd tell me what the hell is going on. Talia, I want to be alone with you," he said gruffly. "I need to talk to you."

"I told you, I don't want to see you," she said, watching the dancers.

"Look at me and say that."

Her heart drummed. "There's Tyler," she said, and got up, leaving Mike, hurrying over to her husband.

Later that night at home when Tyler reached for her, she stiffened.

"Talia, this is absurd. We can't live this way in separate bedrooms," he said, kissing her throat.

She loathed his touch. "We're getting along better, Tyler, but give me a little more time."

"That's absurd! I love you. I want you, and if we get back what we had, our love will be as strong as ever. You can't expect a reconciliation if you won't let me touch you. Either you want to try and make our marriage work or you don't. Which is it?"

An angry note came to his voice, but she couldn't yield to him. "Tyler, I'll try, but not tonight!" she said so forcefully he blinked, and his face flushed. She knew she had made him angry, but she didn't want to have sex with him.

She paced around the room. "Give me time. I'm trying to change."

"It seems a damned weird way to change," he snapped. Suddenly he caught her and pulled her to him, kissing her in a bruising, demanding way. She held him, trying to cooperate, hating every moment until he released her and gazed down into her eyes and she saw his rage. She twisted out of his arms and glared at him.

"I'm sorry, Tyler. I'm trying!" She walked to the door and turned around. "I'm having difficulty at work. It makes me nervous. Maybe if we could go away, Tyler—go to Rio or somewhere, I could relax," she said, just trying to gain time. She knew Tyler was too involved in too many projects, and that the bank examiners were giving him too difficult a time at First Bayou for him to get away soon. He seemed to relax, the stiffness going out of his shoulders, and his scowl vanished.

"Okay. If that's what you'd like, we'll do that. We'll go back to Rio," he said, sounding surprised and wary. "You should have told me you're having trouble at work. Maybe I can help."

"I'll work it out. I don't want to come running for help with my problems."

"You're too damned independent for your own good. I'll call a travel agent first thing Monday."

"Thanks."

His brows arched. "You're sure about tonight?"

She nodded. "Maybe it's just nerves, but I'm exhausted. Let's take a trip and see how things go."

"Sure, Talia."

In her room, she stared at a calendar. It was July. She was certain Tyler wouldn't be able to plan a trip until September or October. By that time it might be safe for her to ask him for a divorce.

Wednesday morning at a quarter past eleven, her secretary stepped in to hand her a business card. "Mr. Lance Douglas said to give you this."

Talia smiled. "Tell him to come in."

She leaned back in her chair as Lance came in and closed

the door, looking around the room like a cat in new surroundings.

"Very nice! executive vice president. I didn't know you
had brains as well as beauty."

"I guess not! I wasn't using any the day we met. Have a
seat."

"Actually I came to see if I can take you to lunch."

Startled, she blinked, then waved her hand at him. "Mrs.
Franklin. You never have understood that!"

"I understand. It'll be business," he said, walking around
her tiny office. "We can discuss putting my savings in your
bank." She laughed and he turned to face her. "C'mon. Just
this time. Lunch is harmless."

"Sure, why not?" she consented impulsively, wishing it
were Mike.

"See? Persistence does the job." He rubbed his hands
together. "My apartment?"

"No! We go to a restaurant. I'll drive."

"Whatever the lady wants—" he said, holding the door
for her.

They drove to a nearby restaurant specializing in barbecue.
Talia had her usual luncheon salad while he ordered ribs and
beans. "So tell me about yourself since I last saw you."

"I told you everything the other night. There isn't anything
else."

"Oh, sure there is. What hobbies do you have? Have you
been to Rio again? Are you going to work forever? Are you
leaving your husband? And if you do, I want your phone
number."

For an instant his question startled her, but she dropped
her gaze to her lap and hoped nothing had shown in her
features.

"I told you my hobbies. Jogging. I ran in the Crescent
City Classic."

"What about children? Do you want any?"

"Yes, I do, but we haven't had any so far."

He listened to her answers carefully. He was pleasant and
friendly, and when lunch was over, he took the check. "I
should pay you. I've talked the whole lunchtime and you've
hardly said a word about yourself," she said.

"I'm dull."

"Oh, sure. You worked in Rio, in the Amazon, you're single, you travel—very dull stuff."

He gave her a lazy smile. "I sleep, I eat, I play, and I dream of taking out a beautiful señorita who lost her way long ago in Rio."

She laughed. "You haven't dreamed of taking me out! You didn't even recognize me. I was the one who remembered, not you."

"Do you know you've really changed?" When she shook her head at him, he added, "You're more beautiful."

"Thank you."

"What do you want out of life?"

"Now you're getting philosophical—what a switch!"

He grinned and shrugged. "Tell me."

"I want to be me. To know I can be independent," she said, thinking about what she had wanted for so many years, refusing to think about Mike. "I don't like looking ahead."

He smiled. "No, I don't either."

"Enough about me. Where are you working?"

"I'm an independent landman, but the business is changing. It's dwindling fast. Tomorrow I may be back in Rio. How'd you get to know Mike Stanton?"

The question caught her by surprise. "He was campaign manager for Ty's opponent in the gubernatorial race." She realized while she was answering that her voice had lowered and changed, in tone.

"Oh? You're pretty good friends for him to have been in the opposition."

"We're just friends. Do you own a home here?" she asked, trying to change the subject. She felt her cheeks warm when she talked about Mike, and she was aware Lance Douglas was scrutinizing her, but he had always done that constantly. While his questions were sometimes too direct, there wasn't any reason, to suspect his motives were any different than they had been in Rio. She tried to relax.

Back at the bank, she smiled at him. "Thanks for lunch. We never did talk about your savings."

"We'll do it next time."

"Sure."

The Bastille Day celebration was the last time she saw Mike. He moved his yacht—changing yacht clubs or selling the yacht, she didn't know which—and now in the slip across from Tyler's there was a yellow yacht owned by a large family. Mike was no longer a member of the country club, and she wondered where he had gone. She felt a sense of panic at the thought of losing contact with him.

Part of her time was spent planning what she would do when she left Tyler. She intended to find Mike and explain. If he had found someone else, Talia knew she would have to go on with her life, but she loved him and didn't think she would ever stop.

She would have to quit her job and move elsewhere. As vindictive as Tyler could be, there would be a battle, and he would cause her as much difficulty as possible, so the farther away from him, the better off she would be.

In spite of all the heartaches, the important thing at the moment was that Mike was safe from Tyler's wrath.

If Mike was interested in someone else, Talia decided she might move to Dallas. Kate didn't seem to need her or care whether she saw Talia or not, but Talia would move her to Dallas too. She told Sloane and Rebecca her plans. To her surprise Rebecca said she was moving soon too.

They were eating lunch, something they did more often now growing closer after all the years of separation. Surprised at Rebecca's announcement, Talia asked, "Have you and Ed parted?"

"Not yet. It isn't Ed. I just don't like to be tied down. I never have wanted to get married and settle in a suburb."

"Why not?"

She shrugged. "I guess I don't want the responsibility of a permanent relationship. It's easier to drift, except sometimes now, I'm tempted to stay because I think I'm beginning to really love Ed. He makes life interesting."

"You might find you'd like it if you'd settle."

"I don't think so," Rebecca said, knowing how different they were. "I gotta get back. Let me get the check once."

"You can next time," Talia said.

They said goodbye, and Rebecca went back to work at the

perfume counter. At the end of the day Rebecca gave notice
that she was quitting.

Ed was impulsive and unpredictable and she decided to
just leave as she had done so often in the past. A week later
after he went to work on Monday, she got down her suitcase
and packed, feeling a pang of regret, because Ed had been
the most exciting man she had ever known. But if she stayed
much longer, she might become dependent on him, and then
she would be caught in a trap of ordinary, middle-class life.

She would move to Dallas; later maybe Florida would be
exciting. As she gathered her belongings, she was amazed to
discover how much she had accumulated while staying with
Ed, and she had to put away her suitcases, unpack some things
Ed might notice and go out the next day and buy a trunk. If she
didn't get rid of some stuff, she wouldn't be able to stay on the
move. Every few hours, doubts plagued her. She was really
going to miss Ed, and the realization shocked her.

On Wednesday, she packed the trunk, bought a plane ticket
to Dallas, and called a cab and drove to the airport. She
stepped out at the curb, paid the cabby, and looked for someone to take her suitcases and the trunk. She turned around and
glanced up to see Ed leaning against the wall.

22

Dressed in a tan business suit, his sandy-hair ruffled by the
wind, Ed straightened up and sauntered toward her while her
heart thudded violently. "The car is down here," he said,
pointing to the parking lot. He turned around, pulled out some
bills and motioned to a uniformed man to watch the luggage
until they came back to pick it up.

She was so stunned at first that she hadn't been able to
think or talk, but now reason was returning, and anger flared

that he had somehow discovered what she was doing.
"How'd you know I'd be here?"

He shrugged and held her elbow in a firm grip. She had
to take short running steps to keep up with him as they crossed
a lane of traffic and headed to the parking lot. At the car she
rebelled. "I'm leaving. I didn't want to tell you, but I'm
going to Dallas."

"No, you're not," he said with a firm note in his voice.

"I'm going to Texas," she said stubbornly.

He shook his head. "No. I have plans for us. I should
have told you sooner."

"What are you talking about?" They stopped beside his
car and stood in the hot sunshine, wind blowing her tangled
curls. The airport was busy; a car drove through the parking
lot, yet in spite of the ordinary surroundings, she had a sense
of unreality.

"I want you to stay. I want to marry you."

"That's wonderful. But I don't. I'm leaving." She had
told other men the same answer before, but the words sounded
hollow as she said them to Ed. "I never have liked to be tied
down," she added perfunctorily, wishing Ed hadn't complicated her plans.

"Why?"

"I don't know." She shrugged. "I get a trapped feeling
when I think I have to be responsible to other people."

"I'll try and help you get over that," he said calmly. His
tan suit and gold-and-brown-striped tie brought out the gold
flecks in his hazel eyes. Ed was not a bad-looking man, she
realized, glancing again at her watch.

"We'll travel. I'm going into business for myself. I'm
opening a restaurant."

"Where are you getting money for the restaurant business?" she asked, momentarily curious.

"Some grateful clients I had at the bank are putting up
part of the money and buying part interest in my new venture.
We have five more bank examiners from the FDIC at First
Bayou. It won't be long until the bank comes crashing down
on Tyler. I have four clients who had large deposits over the
insured limit. I told them they should move their funds be-

cause their money wasn't so safe. They're grateful to me. And they think I have good business sense," he said.

Rebecca couldn't imagine an uninsured deposit, but that wasn't a primary concern now. "That's nice Ed. I appreciate it and I've loved you more than any other man I've ever known, but it's time to move on."

He unlocked the car door and opened it, holding her arm. He smiled at her as if he hadn't heard a word she just said. "Get in and we'll pick up the trunk."

"Don't you understand!" she exclaimed, wondering if they were going to have a scene. She had thirty-five minutes left until the plane's departure. "This is goodbye, Ed. I'm leaving."

Still smiling he shook his head. "No, you aren't. You either stay with me and lead a normal life, Rebecca, or you go to prison and get shut in a tiny cell, locked in there for years behind iron bars."

"What are you talking about?" she asked, thinking he sounded crazy.

"I'll turn you in to the police for stealing Norman Materne's valuables."

Her jaw dropped. She stared at him in amazement while he smiled in return. Wind ruffled his hair while white-hot rage buffeted her.

"You bastard! You filthy son of a bitch! You put me up to that! I'd tell the police you did."

"Look at me, Rebecca," Ed said gently. "I'm an upstanding banker. I've never done a thing I shouldn't have—on record. I have a good college background, an excellent job history. I'm stable, honest. People trust me and believe me. Whereas, you—whom the police would view as a jilted, angry woman—you have a past as a prostitute, a drifter—"

"How did you know?" she whispered, turning cold, her anger vanishing in shock.

"I know. I've known for a long time."

She felt as if she were trying to grapple with smoke. "You stole that diamond in Texas! I'll tell the police what you did. I didn't have a thing to do with that." To her horror his smile remained in place, and it seemed as if her feet were sinking into quicksand.

"I didn't steal a thing. I just told you I did."

First, she yanked up her hand to stare at the ring, wondering if it were glass. Secondly, she wondered why he had led her to believe he had stolen the diamond.

As if he knew her exact thoughts, he said, "It's real. I pulled that stunt so you'd see how easy it is. That way, when I suggested you steal Norman's jewels, you felt like you could succeed. Just a little self-assurance for you. I could have stolen one of those diamonds, but there wasn't any need to. I've made good investments and I'm well-fixed. We can go anywhere you'd like on a honeymoon."

"No!" she exclaimed, staring at him, feeling as if he could see into her soul.

"You'd rather go to jail?"

"You wouldn't," she said, but her voice faltered, because she knew he would without hesitation.

He pushed her gently toward the car seat. "Get in, and we'll go home now. We can plan our wedding."

"You bastard! You filthy, stinking bastard!"

He laughed and leaned down to kiss her. "We'll have fun. I'll take you anywhere in the world for our honeymoon. You won't have to work when you come back. You can do what you want, except you'll be faithful to me from now on."

"Damn you, Ed J. Dessauer!" She tilted her head and studied him, realizing he was unique, that she had never known a man like him. She had met her match and more. Maybe life with Ed would be as much fun in the future as it had been in the past.

"Our mother never could handle responsibility, and I never have learned how to either," she said softly.

"You won't have to do it alone. You'll be fine and we'll be happier than ever," he said and winked at her.

"You may regret this!" she said, awed by him, the force gone from her voice.

"I don't think I will," he replied. "Get in the car, sweetie."

She stared at him, relishing the twinkle and certainty in his hazel eyes. "It'll be good, Rebecca. I promise."

Suddenly she laughed and threw up her hands. "I guess you're better than the state prison!"

He caught her in his arms and she hugged him, laughing until he bent his head to kiss her.

Mike tried to build a new life for himself, putting as much distance as possible between himself and the Franklins. He tried to tell himself that if Talia wanted a promotion more than love, she wasn't the woman he had thought she was. But his heart couldn't follow the logic of his mind.

Finally he decided to move to Atlanta, Georgia, even though it would mean starting over and building up a clientele again. If he had to work hard, maybe he could forget Talia. And he would be away from New Orleans and painful memories that plagued him everywhere he went: the café, City Park where they had gone during a lunch hour, sailing on Lake Pontchartrain, listening to jazz in the Quarter. He asked Ben if he would move to Atlanta, and Ben didn't seem to care what he did, so Mike relocated them both. Ben needed more attention and care than Vangie, who had married and was happily settled in Kenner and working at her receptionist job.

When Mike moved in September he ordered a subscription to The New Orleans *Times-Picayune*, so he could read such vital statistics as the divorce announcements, because if Talia ever left Ty, Mike wanted to know. He hurt, wondering if there was just one woman in the whole world that he could deeply love. He prayed time would help. The thought always nagged at him that she stayed with her husband only to try to protect him. He swore and threw down the paper, glaring at it. If she had done it for his sake he would be furious. He wasn't afraid of Tyler Franklin. He clenched his fists, wanting her so badly he hurt all over.

23

September 1982

New Orleans at the end of September was muggy as usual. Flowers were in bloom and at least there was relief from the sultry nights of summer. On a rooftop of the vacant house overlooking the Franklin house, Lance Douglas shifted his weight, staring at the empty patio next door, the glistening aqua pool, knowing Talia Franklin would come out for an afternoon swim. It was Saturday and she still followed the same routine she had during July. She would be home alone; Tyler would be playing golf. Lance picked up the Garand and checked for the dozenth time, sighting through the telescopic lens on the yellow chaise longue. The .30/06 rifle was loaded, ready.

Ambivalent feelings still battled in him. He had met her in Rio on her honeymoon, renewed his acquaintance in the past two months, and now her life was in his hands. He thought of the money he would be paid, half of which was already his. The contract had come at a good time because the oil business was in a nosedive. Landmen were going to be as much in demand as day-old garbage. The roof he was standing on was a testament to the times. The house had been for sale for months now and Lance suspected it would be for sale for months ahead as well, because real estate had taken a plunge along with petroleum. Easy money. Eliminate Talia Franklin.

On the other hand, he now knew why a contract was out on her. It wasn't difficult to guess who put up the money. Her obsessive jealous husband was the one he should be waiting for. But there would be no money in that.

Lance's eyes flickered, noticing the movement of the gate.

It opened, and Talia entered the pool area, crossing to the chaise and dropping a book on it. She shed a terry cover-up and walked to the diving board in long, leggy strides. He watched her dive into the pool.

Tyler would rather see his wife dead than married to another man, living in the same town, going to the same places. Lance watched her climb out of the pool with graceful movements, picking up the towel to dry her face, her profile to him. Beneath the skintight black swimsuit, her body was perfectly slender and full-breasted. As he watched her, he felt a stir of desire, recalling how she looked when she laughed. Tyler Franklin was a fool. He should have spent more time making her happy.

Instead Mike Stanton had succeeded in that endeavor. Lance knew Mike slightly. But he had learned enough to see why Talia Franklin was so drawn to him. The guy was likable, successful, intelligent, and he had a sensitivity that would always win women's affection. And he was tough, the kind of man Lance wouldn't cross.

Lance picked up the rifle sighting through the telescopic lens, startled because when he focused on her green eyes, she seemed to be looking right back at him. He lowered the gun, peering through oak leaves that should give him sufficient cover from the distance. To his relief, she was smoothing lotion on her arms. She was one of the most beautiful women he had ever seen. He liked Talia. She hadn't done anything except marry the wrong guy. Whatever had been between Talia and Mike had happened before Lance had been given the contract. He had followed her, and she never saw Mike alone. To outward appearances she was happily married to Tyler, although any intelligent observer would see that it was a front. It was Mike Stanton she watched as he moved through a crowd, not Tyler Franklin. It was Mike who gazed at her with unconcealed longing in his eyes. Tyler followed her with the watchfulness of a detective, checking to see what she was doing or where she was. She deserved more than a cold, self-centered man.

Lance rubbed his forehead. He had to make a decision and he had battled with it for weeks now. She didn't deserve to die, but he needed the money.

He raised the rifle. She seemed restless, standing up to go to the pool, diving in and swimming laps, finally climbing out. He wondered if she had any idea of the extent of Tyler's warped possessiveness. He had pondered why she would stay Tyler's wife when she loved Mike, because unexplained quirks of behavior were important. The only one reason he could come up with was that she thought she was protecting Mike from Tyler. He wondered what she would do if she knew that she needed protection, not Mike. Would she walk out then?

The questions had tormented him for nights. If he killed her, could he live with his conscience that had become active for the first time in his life? Could he live comfortably without the money?

He raised the rifle, looking through the lens as she climbed out and stood at the edge of the pool, water sparkling on her honeyed skin, the bits of black swimsuit barely covering her sleek body. He lowered the sight to her breast and felt a stir of desire. Mike Stanton was a lucky fellow.

He raised the rifle and had a perfect shot. She was sitting immobile in the chaise, facing him, her eyes closed. He felt for his car keys, glanced again around the rooftop. There wouldn't be any evidence left behind. His car was waiting on the driveway below, his ticket to Rio in his pocket. Fifty grand. Talia.

"Goodbye, Talia Franklin," he said softly with a reluctant sigh, and raised the rifle to his shoulder, tilting his head, lining up the cross hairs for the precise shot he wanted, his pulse drumming. His powerful muscles were tense, his hands steady. He held his breath and squeezed the trigger. The shot, exactly on target, was a blast that shattered the quiet neighborhood.

24

The gunshot echoed in the silence. The bang was deafening, and the sudden burning sensation was slight. Nearby, birds flapped noisily skyward. Talia looked down at blood running over her breast and arm and swimsuit, bright red drops splashing on the concrete. Stunned, she stared at the wound in her shoulder, for a moment not feeling a thing, frozen with shock.

Moving automatically, she picked up the white terrycloth jacket and pressed it against the wound, gazing beyond the fence at the surrounding areas in the direction from where the shot had to have come. The likely place was the roof of the vacant neighboring house.

Reaction and feeling began to set in. She staggered to the phone in the kitchen. She called the police and reported that she had been shot, giving her address and the facts, her mind beginning to function. A wave of dizziness struck her as she clutched the phone.

"I feel faint. Call my husband and tell him. He's Tyler Franklin at First Bayou Bank."

Closing her eyes, she sat down in a chair, leaning back, hearing the brisk voice of the dispatcher. And then Talia dropped the receiver back in place.

"Who?" Talia said aloud in the empty kitchen. "Who would shoot me?" And then she knew. *Tyler*. It was Tyler. She sat up, the dizziness gone, her eyes wide as shock buffeted her again. All along she had thought Mike was in danger. But she was in danger. Tyler had hired someone to kill her. But whoever had done it, had missed deliberately or was a poor shot.

Puzzled, she looked down at the bloodsoaked terrycloth. She was free. Tyler wouldn't dare try again. She would be careful, but it would be too obvious and too risky for him to make another attempt to murder her. Murder. She would move out tonight. The wail of sirens came, and suddenly she felt weak. All she could do was sit and wait.

Tyler was bent over books, going over them with a vice-president when the phone rang. He picked it up when his secretary buzzed him on the intercom. He heard a deep voice say, "This is Detective Gideaux. New Orleans Police. I'm sorry to tell you, Mr. Franklin, but your wife has been shot."

Tyler gripped the phone, his knuckles turning white.

"What?" he asked, aware that his vice president was watching him.

"She called us—"

"She called you?"

"Yes, sir. We have a car and an ambulance on the way to the hospital now."

"Oh, God!" Tyler exclaimed, standing up and turning his back. She had lived! Tyler wanted to smash his fist into the wall and swear. The bastard had botched the job. "I'll be right there. How badly is she hurt?"

"We don't know yet, sir."

"I'm on my way."

He slammed down the receiver. "Someone shot my wife. She's alive, but that's all the police know." He left in swift strides, storming out to his car, wondering how badly Talia had been hit.

Talia was taken to the St. Jude emergency room, treated, given a room for the night, and released the following afternoon, because the wound was merely a graze. Dressed in the slacks Tyler had brought to her earlier in the morning, she walked through the wide double doors at the entrance. She felt weak, but strength came back as she thought about the past twenty-four hours, and all that had happened to her. The bulky bandage beneath her shirt made one shoulder appear higher than the other.

Tyler had called to say he would be down to pick her up and she had agreed, because she wanted to talk to him in person. He stepped out of the Rolls and came across the walk to her, wind ruffling his hair. She was thankful there was no one around so they could have a moment of privacy. Out of the corner of her eye, she watched a taxi pull to the curb and stop, the driver waiting as he had been instructed by her phone call.

As Tyler approached her his expression was somber, his eyes swiftly appraising her.

"You don't look as if anything happened."

"We need to talk now."

"Can it wait until we're home?" His gaze slid away from hers. "I have the FDIC men waiting to talk to me first thing in the morning.'' He ran his fingers through his hair. "The damned FDIC is trying to ruin me!"

"Are you in trouble?"

"No! Our bank is too big to be in trouble. I'll pull through this. I can tell you on the way home. Are you ready to go?"

"I'm leaving you, Tyler," she said quietly. "I won't go home with you now. You can't hold me any longer."

"Leaving me?" His face flushed and his eyes burned with anger.

Her heart lurched with fear, but she stood her ground, raising her face to defy him, because if he knew he could bully her, he would win.

"I won't let you go!" The words were clipped, filled with determination.

"You can't stop me," she said calmly, perspiration beading her palms. She braced for a blow, because he looked as if he would strike her at any moment.

"I can stop you! It's Stanton, isn't it?"

"No. I don't know where he is. We haven't seen each other for months."

"Then *why*?" he asked, for once looking at a loss.

"It's been over between you and me for a long time, Tyler. If love ever truly existed. I was so bedazzled by you, I couldn't see you as human. I don't love you. You had someone shoot me, and I know you intended it to be fatal."

Emotions played over his features, anger, shock, his brows arched and his face flushed, guilt showing in his eyes. "That's ridiculous. I'm not going to let you go!"

"Finally Tyler, you're going to learn you can't bully your way through life forever. You're going to have to answer to the FDIC for your fraudulent practices to get what you wanted. And you're going to have to let me go, because"—she raised her chin a notch higher and spoke firmly—"if anything happens to me now, the police will come after you. As twisted as you can be to get what you want and as destructive as you are when you don't, I know you're too self-centered to want to go to prison or the electric chair. I'm filing for divorce immediately. I don't want anything from you except my freedom."

"You can't! I won't let you!"

"There's no way you can stop me."

"You'll be back!"

"I have a cab waiting. Goodbye, Tyler. I'm sure we'll see each other in court."

"Talia! You can't go!" His face was contorted with rage, a vein standing out in his temple, his fists knotted, and she knew that if he thought he could get away with it, he would murder her himself.

She moved past him, expecting his hands to clamp on her arms any second. She climbed into the taxi and gave the name of a hotel, settling in the seat without looking back as they drove away.

She checked into the hotel, consulted a lawyer and turned in her resignation at the bank. And she tried to find Mike. His phone number was no longer a working number; she didn't know his friends, except Ben, who had gone, so she drew a blank there. She called a few people, but no one knew where he was. One person said he had moved to Houston, another said he had talked about Mobile. She decided he must have left New Orleans, and all she could do was keep trying to locate him.

Determined to keep searching for him, she knew she had to go on with her life, so the following week she rented an apartment in Dallas and opened an account in a bank there. When she finished, she drove back to New Orleans to get her things and made arrangements to move Kate later.

The next week First Bayou Bank was closed by the FDIC, and Talia couldn't feel anything except a twinge of sympathy for Pauline and Millard. She went to see them, to tell them goodbye. She told Sloane, but not Kate, because she would be back for Kate. The notice about the divorce appeared in the paper.

On a Thursday afternoon, she stopped at the bank to get her last paycheck. Her car was packed with her belongings. She said goodbye to everyone, feeling her spirits lift because she would be free now. Her hair fell to her shoulders, turning under in a slight curl, bangs feathered away from her face, the hairstyle she wore most of the time. She wore a denim skirt and a short-sleeved red sweater and tennis shoes—comfortable clothes for driving.

The morning's headlines had a long article about First

Bayou and the bad loans, telling how the bank's strength was tied to real estate and oil with collateral that had never existed used for loans. The indications were that Tyler would be charged with fraud. She dropped the paper on Larry's desk, said her goodbyes, and stepped out into the sunshine.

Her black car was parked beneath an oak at the corner of the lot, and as she crossed towards it, her gaze swept over the bank where she had started her career with such high hopes.

A car pulled into the lot, tires squealing as it rounded the corner behind the bank, then braked and stopped. Her heart beat faster when she saw Mike get out and walk toward her. Dressed in jeans and a T-shirt, he had never looked so wonderful.

He stopped, hesitating, and she realized he was uncertain about her. Her heart and lungs seemed to cease functioning. She walked toward him and saw the change in his expression as his questioning look vanished. Stepping forward, he caught her up in his arms, crushing her to him.

"Talia!" His voice was a rasp before he kissed her. After a moment he raised his head. "I saw the divorce notice. What made you change?"

"I stayed with him because I was afraid he would try to kill you."

"Oh, God, why didn't you tell me?"

"Because I knew you'd take the risk," she said simply. Expressions played across his face, but the burning hunger and love in his blue eyes was clear.

"I've tried to find you. I have so much to tell you," she said. He leaned down to kiss her again.

"Will you marry me? Or am I going to have to battle your need to be alone right now?"

"The need has suddenly vanished," she said, standing on tiptoe to kiss him, wanting to hold him forever.